The Onic

A Paninaro Imprint

www.paninaropublishing.co.uk
info@paninaropublishing.co.uk

www.paninaropublishing.co.uk

Contact - info@paninaropublishing.co.uk

A catalogue record for this book is available from the British Library.

ISBN - 13: 978 - 1916088559

Socials;

Twitter @johnnyroc73

Instagram @johnnyproctor90

Chapter 1

Drummond

'Take that Innocent Ngoke for example? The Senegalese boy that Chelsea signed from Stuttgart a couple of seasons back. Couldn't hit a fucking cow's arse with a heat seeking missile yet you should see what he gets in return for his abject performances week in week out. The Everton fans were singing 'what a waste of money' at him last week at Goodison on Match of the Day after missing that sitter. The Scousers don't know the fucking half of it, mate. I was looking at his account the other day. On an average month he gets - after tax - around six hundred large and that's not even including his bonus payments which seem to come into the account at random times. Like the month after they won the FA cup? A nice wee payment of a hundred and fifty k drops in. I mean, that's just the tip of the iceberg, mate. That other player that plays for …'

We all seemed to hear the chat coming over from the bar at once, while it coincided with a brief moment of silence at our table across by the pool table and jukebox. It was a business meeting, after all, and we couldn't be disturbed by all of the jakeballs and undesirables that you would generally find inside The Trap Door at half eleven on a Monday morning.

'Fuck's sake, man. Does that Leckie cunt ever give it a fucking rest with that shite?' Hammy - in response to the enforced eavesdropping that we'd been subjected to - said, looking at Hummel and me. Suitably unimpressed by the fact that the loudmouth over at the bar knew the ins and outs of a football player that even Chelsea fans will have forgotten about in another couple of years time.

'Honestly, man. The cunt needs to bore right off with that patter.' He followed up with before picking up his pint of Moretti and taking a big swig out of it.

'He's not wrong, though.' Hummel backed Hammy up on the topic. 'He's been insufferable since he got that promotion at his work. I'm not even remotely close to what you could class as his "mate" yet I feel like I've been through the whole promotion with the cunt the way he goes on about it when he's drinking in here. Maybe just honeymoon period stuff though, like.'

'Well he needs to go directly to the fucking divorce period then. No way that people are as impressed with his "inside information" as he thinks they are. It's hardly breaking news to find out that an English Premier League player is paid well, for fuck's sake.' Hammy continued on his wee rant before receiving a WhatsApp which stopped him in his tracks as he picked up his phone to read it.

'Aye and about fucking time too.' He said as he tapped out a short reply before putting the phone back down on the table.

'Was that ZX?' I asked him, knowing that he was one of the last of the dealers that we were waiting on squaring things up for the month and someone who Hammy had been trying to chase up. Something that's never the wisest of things to engineer for yourself.

'Aye, I'm still very much unimpressed at the fact he said he'd be in last night for me to collect only for me to be completely rubbered at his front door. You could hear the telly on inside and the lights were on. Definitely having words with the cunt when I see him but aye, that's him saying he's got our dough waiting. I'll head over after we're done here,' he affirmed.

In a lot of ways we were exactly like any other business approaching month end. Trying to have all the i's dotted and t's crossed, receiving payments on all outstanding bills and making our own payments to the people *we* had credit accounts with.

Just because *our* business involved the purchase, flow and supply of illegal drugs across Edinburgh and the Kingdom of Fife didn't mean that we did not follow the basic rules and principles of business. Neglect them and you may as well hang the 'out of business' sign up before you even begin.

Oh aye, a well oiled machine, so we were and I think that was the reason that we were so successful and - just as importantly - managed to stay out of the eye of any Lothian and Borders anti drug task force operations. The partnership between the three of us was just that, a partnership. Each of us - despite already being mates - had something to bring to the table and never a case of someone being allowed to tag along for the ride on account of being a mate.

Nah, we made a go of things *because* of what we all provided and wouldn't have been able to achieve what we did with any single one of us missing.

With Hummel we had ourselves a whiz kid computer geek and someone that - without his knowledge and skills with a laptop in front of him - we wouldn't have even managed past go. In fact, without him we wouldn't have even *known* where go - and the starting point - even was.

Hammy? Well he could have only ever have been considered as the one out of the trio who 'got things done' which is a euphemism for just about anything you'd care to attach it to, when it involves being intimidated into doing something that you were otherwise not going to do previously. Generally based around money. Most definitely a collections man that you do not shake off as easily as you do with the Provie Loans officer who comes to your door.

And myself? I guess - and would say without boasting too much - my position with the org was one of utilising my strategic planning and organisational skills. The type of staff member that *every* company needs on the payroll. A blue sky thinker who doesn't see problems, only challenges and tests. While Hummel was the one to present the idea of the business opportunity to the other two of us it was *me* who devised a way for us to make it a *reality*. Because, as any successful drug dealer will tell you, getting the product in your hands ready for market really is really only a quarter of the battle.

It was all a bit unintentional. The way that we kind of fell into it. We weren't drug dealers. Drug *takers?* Aye, without question, and at an elite level, too. Your classic case of a snowball being pushed down a hill and before any cunt knows it, it then cannot be stopped.

We started off at first just sorting out ourselves, mates and acquaintances but the prospect of buying heavily discounted - but high quality - drugs from mainland Europe to sell at an eye watering mark up proved, quite frankly, impossible to resist in the end.

As long as I live I'll never forget that night sitting in Hummel's living room when he showed me and Hammy what was on his laptop screen. Some site called 'Dr Feelgood' which had just about any drug you could think of - and most definitely some you didn't even know existed - available to buy.

'If I ever win the lottery I will literally need to have my broadband connection cut to my house or I'll be dead within a couple of weeks, tops.' Hammy said, trying to process what I was scrolling and clicking through as I navigated my way through the site. Cocaine, MDMA, Heroin, Crystal Meth, Weed, Uppers Downers and Frowners. You name it, it was there.

It was well confusing to me. Proper baffled, like. How could someone sell stuff like that on a website and not be pinched by the police? I got a ban from Ebay when I tried to sell a chipped PS2, to provide some context.

Hummel explained it all to us as if it was the most natural thing in the world, which it definitely wasn't.

The reason the website could sell such "wares" was down to the fact that it was on 'another' internet, different to the one that we'd always used and - up until that night - had only ever thought was the *only* internet.

This internet - referred to by Hummel as *The Dark Web* - was to quote our geeky pal "The Wild West" where all of the stuff you couldn't get away with on the normal internet, you *could,* there. Including buying and selling gear. He explained that there had to be some form of anonymity when it came to paying for any illegal goods or services on there and that was where crypto currency came in. Specifically something that he called Bitcoin. For the next couple of hours we did nothing but fire questions at him with nothing he didn't have an answer for.

My mind was completely and utterly blown. It felt like we were sat in the future rather than living under the - at times - draconian laws that surrounded drugs in the U.K.

'So you're saying that I can just order any gear from around the world, safely and anonymously, and the fucking Royal Mail will literally walk up to my front door and put it through my letterbox?'

I asked, still thinking that it was some online scam.

'Well, aye. That's *exactly* what I'm saying.' Hummel replied, appearing to be getting some amusement out of our reaction to this bombshell he'd just dropped on us.

'And so how do I buy Bitcoin then? It's Bitcoin you said, eh?' Hammy asked with a face that suggested that the cogs inside of him were also doing some serious turning.

'It's not the easiest thing to do, mate. Not like you can just go into the TSB and ask them to convert some of your money into a currency that - in cyber crime police units - is commonly known as used for paying for illicit goods and services like drugs and hitmen. Don't you worry about it, Hamster. You literally just found out that there's an *other* internet, amigo. I can deal with that side of things.' Hummel replied, having evidently done his research on the subject and the one person out of the three of us who you would trust with your money getting from A to B.

'Aye, let Ben the Boffin, deal with that.' I backed Hummel up on things.

Before we left the house we had collectively purchased some Grass from inside the U.K, a sample pack of ten pingers from the Netherlands and a gram of Ching from Germany.

Still unsure if this really all was on the level we'd sat and agreed that we would all chip in for one single item, just to see if it arrived or not. A scientific purposes test run, of sorts. Obviously we didn't stick to that. We ordered Ching to see how stealthy the "vendors" were at sending it through international mail as that was always going to be the product that we were going to end up coming back for. Pingers *specifically* from Netherlands on account of their pills being legendary and finished up with a quarter of Bubblegum on account of while obtaining some cheeba in Edinburgh was not what you would term a challenge, the prospect of being able to purchase some Amsterdam coffee shop grade weed at the mere touch of a button was simply too good to pass up.

He who dares, Wodders.

It took just over a week for the three separate orders to arrive but fucking hell, they *actually* arrived. As in a complete stranger somewhere in Europe received our money and - as easily as they could have - *didn't* rip us off by bumping us and not sending out the drugs.

This was incredibly fucked up in the most beautiful of ways. A complete game-changer and once those first orders arrived - and in doing so provided us with the peace of mind that anyone was always going to need in a highly novel situation like that - we kind of took the gloves off after that.

Which is probably a bit of an understatement, to be fair to us.

Even at smaller purchases it was working out that you were paying around a third of the price for chemicals that you were in Britain. So to then increase the size of the orders? It was literally a license to print money. Every order, the quantities only increasing from the one that had gone before.

This eventually bringing us to the attention of a new vendor, *Arman88*, who it had been rumoured had bribed one of the admin on Feelgood to gain the stats on buyers and sellers of all of the main drugs on the site. This vendor, Hummel had explained to us, was new on the site and making an aggressive pitch to steal other vendors' customers in some kind of power grab. Offering free samples to potential customers and interest free credit plans to certain large quantity buyers. A category that we apparently had fallen into. Prompting 'Arman88' to reach out to Hummel via private message on the Dr Feelgood forum seeking his future business.

Considering how it started, it definitely all got out of hand - making sure you have the thousands of pounds worth of crypto currency ready for month end to clear your debts with a stranger in another country to then unlock the next shipment for you to go and do it all over again for another month - but when you're making thousands a month and never have to put your hand in your pocket to pay for your *own* drugs, it's kind of difficult to say no to that kind of stuff. Maybe it's just me and I'm just weak but something tells me that it's not.

'Right, with ZX ready with what he's due that's pretty much all we've got to bring in, give or take some smaller ones that isn't going to stop us from paying ze Germans up for the month. You sorting the transfer out next couple of days, aye?' I asked the man who puts the I.T into tit, bringing business back to the table, despite the fact that we could now hear Leckie over at the bar now talking about 'that annoying Cockney cunt who won Big Brother a couple of years ago' and the contents of *his* bank account.

'NO. CUNT. FUCKING. CARES,' Hammy - with his back to the bar - shouted out, frustration obviously getting the better of him.

Hummel nodded back at me with a smile on his face as he reacted to Hammy's explosion.

'Just as well I'm heading to see ZX otherwise I'm going to end up opening that cunt up like one of his bank accounts.' Hammy continued, unaware, and really not giving much fucks either, of what Leckie the banker's reaction had been to his outburst the moment before.

'You needing a Snickers or something, mate?' I dug him over his whole overcast mood that he'd been sat at the table with from the moment we sat down.

'Nah, man, I'm good.' He replied, completely missing my attempt at having a laugh at him. 'You know how heavy stressful this part of the month is, eh? Cunts that you can't walk down the street for seeing the first three weeks of the month suddenly turn into fucking Osama bin Laden. You two don't know the half of trying to hunt some of them down. Been at it all morning catching cunts still in their beds, like. Hoped that I could have a wee quiet lunch time pint and can't even get that because of this monotonous prick behind me.'

'I know, lad. Proper first world problems, that.' Hummel agreed in the most sarcastic of ways before changing the subject by asking what our complete order for next month was going to be as he'd also be arranging that with the connect in Germany.

'A kilo of white and five thousand pills.' I replied with a much more hushed tone to myself, having already looked around to check before answering. Cocaine was the bread and the butter for us and a drug where you didn't need to look far to find someone willing to take it off your hands. I'd made the decision to include some additional Eckies in the order as - having had a look at what events were coming up - with there still being a wee bit of festival season left those wee pingers were guaranteed to be an in demand commodity and were judged, by me, as an opportunity missed if we didn't make our services available in that area, at least for those summer months.

'Thank fuck for that.' Hammy responded to the news of the pills being included on the order. 'Wee Aitchy from Pilton has been nipping my head for weeks about them. A bus - from Edinburgh that he's running - is going down to a weekender in

England and he was asking if we were able to sort out the bus for all their requirements.'

'And *that's* exactly why I get the big bucks paid to me, for my unique skill set of being one step ahead of the customer, eh?' I said with a wee bit pride behind it in the knowledge that I'd decided to get some pills in precisely *because* of multi day events like Creamfields over the summer.

Hammy actually telling me such intel *after* I'd already decided upon ordering some pingers, however, was the stuff that would generally deserve a verbal warning from the gaffer but we got there regardless.

'Right, better get on with things. Need to collect that message from ZX and get it paid into the bank and over to our tech guru here in time for all the Haydock meets going on. Money to be made, lads.' Hammy stood up, necked the rest of his pint and walked over to the bar to put his empty down. He was too far away from us to hear but had made a point of saying something to Leckie which, judging by the man from the bank's nervous - but friendly - reaction could only have been something from the big Hamster's passive aggressive playbook.

'In a bit, motherfuckers.' He said as he passed us on the way out.

'What about yourself? What you up to this afternoon?' I asked Hummel. the pair of us were only one step behind Hammy with our drinks and would be heading soon ourselves.

'Fucking Ikea, mate. Told Debz I would take her one day this week. Didn't think she'd be cashing in that chip at the very start of the week, mind. Need to go and get a shot of my brother's van off him first.' He responded with the look of a man who had just received confirmation that he was scheduled to walk the green mile later on in their day.

'Ouch, sore one, pal.' I winced back at him over the mere thought of walking around that place for an afternoon activity.

'Just keep your head down and think of the meatballs in the canteen at the end of it.' I added, putting some kind of silver lining to things for him as that - from the few times I'd ever visited the store just off the city bypass - was the only real high point of my visits. Them and those wee Swedish biscuits they do as well.

'And you?' Hummel asked while he shaped himself up to get moving by standing up and getting his coat from behind his chair and sticking it on.

'Not too sure yet.' All I could muster. I'd had thoughts to take a bus into the town centre to get a few new pieces for the wardrobe but fuck, that could wait until later on in the week. Maybe play a wee bit C.O.D or take a few hours out to sit, read and recharge from the weekend's excesses. As much as the world being my oyster in my own personal example of living the dream and being self employed - so to speak - the start of the week had been dictated by the end of the month and I hadn't really been able to see past *any* of that until it had been taken care of.

'Cool cool, I'll give you a shout later on then. I'll either get the German sorted out tonight or tomorrow.' Hummel said as - unlike Hammy - he left his empty glass lying on the table when leaving the boozer. Not that Hammy was fooling any cunt with that whole taking the glass over to the bar, anyway. His motivation being so he could say a few words to Leckie than it was to save old Davie from coming out from behind the bar to collect it from the table.

'You know what's really interesting though, about the celebs and the way that they work their finances. It's the funny wee things but …'

Leckie was *still* going at it up at the bar and was now easier to hear with me being sat there on my own.

While I didn't quite know what I was going to be doing for the rest of the day the one thing that I knew as an absolute certainty it was that I couldn't spend a minute longer inside The Trap Door otherwise I was going to be in danger of carrying Hammy's work out for him on the man from the bank.

Intolerable prick.

Chapter 2

Hummel

It almost sounds like someone making up an excuse by me saying that I was literally in the process of logging myself into the T.O.R network to get onto the dark web and discuss business with our associate - Arman88 - in Germany when - while my T.O.R connection was in the process of confirming, her Twitter DM notification popped up in the corner of the Macbook screen. Distracting me just enough to pull me off in a completely different direction to where I'd intended when flipping the screen up and going online. Once I saw that notification pop up well, it was all a case of dark web drug deals being something that could wait.

I'd got talking to her - Irma from Berlin - on Twitter around six months before when she had slid into my DMs following a tweet of mines that had went viral. Wasn't even any kind of a special tweet or anything as well. Just me being a wideo and giving Donald Trump some grief on Twitter. As usual, the cunt was banging on about "fake news" in relation to something that was most definitely *true* news and I'd innocuously tweeted a reply that said something along the lines of 'The only fake news is you cutting about telling people that's your real hair, pal.'

Only took around five minutes before my phone started to blow up in a big way. I was someone with only a hundred and seventy seven followers and not exactly an 'active user' on a day to day basis so wasn't exactly used to much notifications from the app coming up on my phone. Once that tweet was given a retweet by a prominent Democrat Twitter account things just went mental for a good twenty four hours. Had to just dingey my phone in the end until it passed as it all ended up a major pain in the arse as well as a one way ticket towards a flat phone battery. The constant notifications telling me that someone had retweeted or liked it, some Hollywood film stars like Don Cheadle and Patricia Arquette. All of the comments from "friendlies" saying things like how I spoke for all of them and how I had won the internet for the day, whatever the fuck that actually means? And anyway, factually speaking. The day I discovered the "other internet?" Believe me, I won the internet *that* day!

Obviously I winded up with all of those crazy cult MAGA motherfuckers seeing the tweet as well - because of just how viral it had went - who were then jumping in and showering me with abuse in defence of their dear leader. I managed a couple of sarcastic replies to the first few before losing interest again. Gained a lot of followers over those couple of days as well following that tweet although I'm certain that after a few more days of those new followers seeing me occasionally tweet things like asking if Marciano was going to be fit for the weekend or retweeting videos of monkeys throwing their own shit in a pensioners face they probably found that they hadn't actually followed someone part of their blue 'resistance' and, in fact, had been nothing other than someone making a snide comment about what is generally - as well as universally - considered to be the worst haircut in the world. Way, way worse than Gerry Francis.

Out of those new followers however came Irma from Berlin because that was the thing. With over fifty thousand retweets and fuck knows how many likes, it wasn't just America that the tweet was showing up on people's timelines. And that was why it showed up on one belonging to a girl in Berlin. After following me she then took things a step further with a DM just to tell me how much she'd laughed at my tweet. I checked out her account and she seemed like a good laugh and with me having such an insular Twitter experience with me only following locals and fellow Hibees and them following me back I thought fuck it, I'll broaden my horizons and give her a follow.

As you can imagine, though. If a basic throwaway off the cuff comment - the kind that you'll make about someone at any point of the day - like that tweet had made her laugh so much. Then getting a chance to see me just displaying a bit of standard day to day Scottish patter had her in hysterics.

Not that I was looking for some kind of 'online relationship' with her, or anyone else for that matter. Things kind of just escalated though, crept up on me without me seeing any of the signs. Because that's the thing. Me and Debz were brand new together as a couple. Wasn't like I was some feeling sorry for them self poor sapp who was lonely and wanted to talk to someone, even if they were just words on the other end of a phone or computer screen. That wasn't the case for me. Irma was just funny though and having a bit of back and forth between each other eventually reached the point where it was a daily occurrence and when I say 'daily' I mean morning, noon and night at certain points.

When I found myself doing things like messaging her at night when Debz would be out on her back or night shift, I knew it was a little on the shady side. The fact that I would never be in communication with her *full stop* if I was sitting in the house along with Debz kind of said it all. Told myself though it was all good because it wasn't like me and this girl in Berlin were talking in any kind of sexual way or fuck all. None of this sending pictures or sexting stuff. Just sending funny DMs back and forth with links that were more *in jokes* between us both and, as such, better placed for a DM.

Of course though, the sexual stuff naturally ended up following. She was obviously at it, knew exactly what she was doing but that obviously doesn't excuse my own actions in any way, like.

We moved into that whole area the night she "accidentally' sent me that picture in a DM. Proper mortified so she was over the fact that when we were talking back and forward one night on the subject of the Berlin Love Parade, an event I'd said to her that I'd always wanted to go to but had never managed to, while being a local, Irma had.

Oh hang on, I have a really nice picture from there dancing on a float. Give me a second and I'll send you it.

She typed out before going dark for a minute or so. Then the picture popped up on my side of our thread.

But it wasn't no picture from Berlin filled with floats going down the street packed with ravers. Instead, I was sitting looking at a picture of Irma in what looked like her bedroom naked - apart from a pair of high heels and a thong - on all fours looking around at the camera while more than suggestively pulling her thong to the side. Her eyes, the ultimate in 'come to bed eyes' even if, and I have to admit, it was hard to just keep everything fixed *on* her eyes.

I knew she was hot, you could tell that from her profile picture - subject to her being a catfish or not being a catfish - but with her and mines casual social media friendship I hadn't even come close to thinking of her as "hot" in any more of an advanced way. Now though? It was near on impossible *not* to think of her in that way. It was literally being waved in my face for fuck's sake.

NOOOOOOOOOOOOOOOOO FUCK FUCK FUCKKKKKKKK

Her immediate follow up reply to what she had just sent me.

I SENT WRONG PICTURE PLEASE DELETE!!!!

Aye like fuck I'm deleting that, I thought to myself before attempting a reply and when I say 'attempting' it really was a time for choosing one's words carefully. So carefully, in fact, that she had already typed out another one to me.

I AM SOOOOOOOO EMBARRASSED!!!

I had an open canvas left for me to work with. I could've typed anything I wanted back to her in return. I wasn't in any way 'thirsty.' Fuck, if I'd been of that persuasion then she'd have known about it long before that night.

Looking at the picture I've just been looking at, trust me when I say that you have NOTHING to be embarrassed about.

If I hadn't been emphatic enough with my reply I added a couple of fire emojis for good measure.

Irma responding to this with a blushing face emoji. Me combining reading her replies while continuing to glimpse at the photo. I was transfixed by it, by her. The thought of being in that room with her while she looked around with 'those' eyes. I imagined what she would be saying in a scenario like that as she looked behind her. I had never thought about her in such a way before but looking at the picture - and the feelings it was provoking - it all had a feeling of a reset button being pressed on our friendship.

I cannot believe I just did that! My face is so red right now!

Not as red as that arse would be if you shoved it up in the air like that if I was there in person!

I responded. The aim was to come across as a cheeky jokey way but probably was just seen as straight up cringe and pervy, regardless of the 'safety' laughing emoji at the end.

Oh really now? Is that so?

Her flirtatious reply back my way. The initial seconds of embarrassment - if it even *was* that - from her apparently now having passed.

This setting the tone for the rest of our chat that night, and our relationship from then on in. Aye, we just kept on trucking with the general day to day silliness that we would engage in but there was now a sexual dynamic to it. I knew it was wrong, in terms of me and Debz, like. Had told myself that I wasn't cheating on her but deep down I knew that I was working my ticket.

Wasn't like I was going to be fucking off to Berlin and meeting up with Irma, though. Or her coming in this direction. That was the thing that I held on to as some kind of magic wand that I could just wave and clear my conscience any time it got the better of me. Complete bollocks obviously but you tell yourself what you do sometimes to get you over things, even if they make no sense.

It was by no means an everyday - or week - thing but following her "accident" in sending me that photo of her that then led to photos being sent back and forward, sexting and - when schedules would allow and we found ourselves in the mood - face times. I knew she was real anyway - from her photos that she would send, some referencing what we'd been just talking about etc - but I remember that first face time and our devices connecting and me thinking that at least now I absolutely positively knew that I hadn't been speaking to some seventy five year old man who had been sending me pictures pinched from a website.

Due to her sheer sexual appeal I really could never say no to her. Whatever I was doing online, if I saw her name pop up in a notification, I'd generally drop what I was doing just to see what she was saying, or showing.

Exactly why I was sidetracked that night when in the process of sorting things out with our suppliers over on Feelgood.

Hey you! I'm bored, and very, very horny!! FaceTime???

This invitation was followed up a few minutes later with a picture of her lying on her bed in just her underwear with a selection of toys placed in front of her and a mischievous smile on her face.

Well Debz isn't going to be back from work for another hour and technically the Germans don't need paying until tomorrow so … I trailed off in my thoughts as I instantaneously started typing a reply to her.

We were connected within minutes where it was soon apparent that the picture she'd sent had only been taken moments before because there she was, in the same underwear with the toys sitting beside her. Telling me just what kind of a dirty mood she was in and how she was going to *show me* while asking what kind of a mood *I* was in on my side.

Too fucking mad, though. There's cunts who are paying top dollar online to watch women do that kind of thing and I've got one in Berlin just doing it for Scottish Fitba Association, because she wants to and gets gratification out of it.

Was an epic face time though, like. Got so much into it that we were still talking when I heard Debz coming through the front door. Leading to a hasty goodbye between me and Irma before quickly flipping the laptop screen down seconds before my other half walked into the living room.

Close call though, like.

'You been at the porn again, babe, aye?' Debz smiled as she stood over me - sat on the sofa - while pointing at the used Kleenex sitting on the floor and closed laptop sitting in front of me.

'Fucking need to the amount of times I can get you to put out over a week, eh?' I laughed back at her.

'Oh you cheeky bastard.' She said screwing her face up but with eyes that couldn't hide the smile. 'Maybe if you kept up with your personal hygiene more you'd *get* more.' She jibbed back before telling me that it had been a shit day and asked if I would I make her a joint while she got herself into her PJs.

A cup of tea and rolled joint waiting on her coming down the stairs where - for the rest of the night - we sat having a spraff and watching TV until the end of the night.

It was only when we were lying in bed and I was just about to drift off to sleep and found myself going through the thing that your mind does where it seems to go through a hundred different subjects at breakneck speed in what is your very final moments of your day. During this it popped into my head about the fact that through the spontaneous call with Irma and that then running into Debz coming home and me almost being caught on the face time I had completely forgotten about going back onto Dr Feelgood to receive this month's Bitcoin address from Arman88 and place our next order with him and taking care of my part in our business.

I'll message him tomorrow and get the ball rolling with things, I reassured myself as the feeling of sleep descending on me started to become so dominant that there was now no point in resisting it.

Chapter 3

Hummel

You know those times when you know that you've fucked up, royally? When someone doesn't even have to open their mouth to tell you how much you messed up things are. Just the look on their face enough to do the trick. I knew when I saw Debbie's coupon when I walked in the door that I was in a world of shit, most probably to be followed with a world of pain. In fact, in all of our time together I hadn't ever even *seen* her with a look like *that*. And that alone should've - and did - worried me.

Oh just how quickly your world can all change in a single moment. I'd only ducked my head out long enough to get rolls for our breakfast and pop into see Wullie Clark about business. Wasn't even gone an hour but in the time I'd been away it had been enough for the gods to conspire against me and have my girlfriend innocently opening up the MacBook to go and check her Facebook, and be confronted with my Twitter page. Still open from the night before, with Irma and mines thread there for anyone to look at, which if they wanted to could have read all the way from the very first day she sent me that initial DM.

It wasn't even a fucking schoolboy error as a schoolboy would've been too smart to even do that. The combination of reading a DM saying she was bored and horny and asking if I wanted to face time and the picture she followed that up with had been enough to have me scrambling to get ready to have a face time with her. Small and minor details like logging back *out* of my Twitter account - which I admit contained some highly sensitive content - were, at the time, a mere inconvenience and not to be worried about. Of course, though. I doubled down on this by *not* closing things down afterwards. Debz coming home and leaving me scrambling to be left with the appearance - when she walked in the living room - that I had been doing something *other* than sitting having a wank looking at a German girl who was doing what I told her to with her toys. This meaning that the laptop screen had been quickly slammed shut, and all programs that had been in operation at that point still left open.

'Hey you, I'm bored and horny. Face time?'

She said in response to me asking her what was wrong. You couldn't *not* ask her what was wrong with the face she had on her.

Fuck, just oh fuck, I thought to myself as my heart sank and I began to feel an extreme warmth rushing over me as the room started to spin. From the moment I heard the 'I'm bored and horny' I knew things were bad. Debz and I had never experienced anything close to infidelity before though so as bad as I knew it was, I didn't know *how* bad or its potential for the levels of what I was about to be hit with.

'Aye, Paul. I know.' She said with a disgusted look on her face as she paced around the living room floor puffing away on an L and B.

'Look, sit down for a moment and let me explain things.' I replied but I honestly didn't know what I should've been saying in that moment as this was all new to me. Aye, I'd been no stranger to having to dig my way out of holes I'd been in with girlfriends before but that was always through not coming home when I should've done due to drink, drugs and mates. This was a different ball game, though.

'Explain? What the fuck *is there* to explain? All the explanation I need is sitting there in your DMs. Man develops a 'relationship' online with someone. Then one day she accidentally sends you a nude - and by the fucking way if you believe that she sent you that picture by accident that night then I've got a planet to sell you - and how does the man react upon this accident? By telling her that she's going to be the cause of him drawing blood from biting on his bottom fucking lip looking at her?! Over the past couple of months it appears that she's seen more of your cock than I have, and I share a fucking bed with you every night!'

'Look, Debz ..' I attempted to try and diffuse things but I was working my ticket to have believed that I was capable of stopping what was now happening.

'And as for last night? I'm working in that roasting hot factory so that I can bring some money back to us every week and what are you up to when I'm there? Sitting watching women in Germany playing with themselves with fucking sex toys.'

'Awww come on, darling. It's not much different than watching porn though, eh?' I attempted to mount a defence of what was clearly something that the Arrigo Sacchi Milan back four, ten goalkeepers and Johnny Cochrane could not have successfully defended.

'HOW MANY FUCKING PORNSTARS DO YOU KNOW WISH PEOPLE A HAPPY BIRTHDAY IN A DM WITH AROUND THIRTY KISSES?'

She screamed out at me, confirming that she really *had* went through the thread of our conversation while I'd been away, and that scared me. Terrified me, actually, because it left me with nowhere to go to when it came to trying to gloss my way out of it. I couldn't if she knew everything. She already knew any lie I would potentially try to spin to get my way out of things.

'I can't believe you would do such a thing to me. I thought I was enough for you and clearly I'm not. I thought you were *happy.*'

After her outburst on me getting back home she was now in tears. Fuck, it was painful to see. Knowing all of the things said in the DMs, sexual or not. The realisation that some of the non sexual exchanges possibly being *as* painful to read because of it giving an example of some kind of an emotional connection between the two people speaking together.

'B b b b but I *am* happy, *we're* happy.' I tried to convince her but there really was no point, right there. I felt that whatever I came out with - sincere or not - was only ever going to come across as me dishing out platitudes.

'Please.' She sneered at me. 'Someone who is happy with their partner doesn't go around doing things like that behind their back. I actually feel physically sick to think about it. You and her talking back and forward. That she can just send a DM and within minutes you're there on a face time with her, jeans at your ankles.'

'Babe, it's totally not what you think' I appealed to her even though it was *exactly* what she fucking thought.

'Just stop it, Paul. There's no lie that can get you out of what I've just sat and read through for the past half an hour. It's not exactly like I can be accused of getting wires crossed, judging by what is inside your DMs. That first night she sent you a nude - and by the way, the week leading up to her sending it I don't think I've ever seen a thirst on a girl as far as flirting with someone - you had two doors you could have chosen to go through. Door number one being where you displayed whatever loyalty you had towards me, and what respect you had for yourself, or number two which would show what a selfish piece of shit you are who thinks with his dick before anything else. Obviously, from your DMs, I know which door you went through.'

I could do nothing other than sit with my head in my hands and take the humiliating lecture that I'd brought upon myself.

'And she was hardly subtle with that picture either, was she? Anyone with a bit of class might've just left things at the underwear for a first picture but wow, she just really went for it, didn't she?'

'That was a mistake, though. You'd have seen that she was talking about a rave in Berlin. We've all sent the wrong picture at one time or another that's been sitting beside the one we wanted to send in our camera roll.' I tried not so much to defend Irma but just offer some form of counterpoint to what had taken place and how it hadn't actually been intended.

'Aye, Paul. That's why a picture of her in that pose would be sitting beside pictures from a rave years ago … when there's a pair of those same Adidas that just came out not that long ago - and that you were talking about - sitting on the floor in the picture. If I noticed them then *you* definitely noticed them.'

It's true. I had and by clocking them I had known that the picture couldn't have been the old one that Irma had said it was. That was *after* I'd seen the picture though, and what our night had led to. And by then I didn't really care if she was lying about *when* it had been taken.

'Well I hope you enjoyed 'playtime' last night on the big screen because you won't be seeing her in such clarity for a while.' She said this as I had got to my feet and started to make my way through to the kitchen to grab a beer from the fridge. I'm not normally a big drinker in the house, or specifically on a Tuesday morning but with the verbal assault I was being subjected to it had left me feeling like having one, for medicinal purposes, like.

'What's that meant to mean, like?' I stopped to ask before leaving the living room but was just met with a dirty look before she looked downwards to stub out her cigarette.

Her comment became a lot more clearer when I walked through and into the kitchen and was met with the chilling sight of my laptop sitting floating on top of all of last night's dishes in the sink. Soapy water filled up as far as it could go.

I could see what she'd done, apart from destroy over a grand's worth of a laptop. This was a symbolic gesture. What device had it been that Irma and me had been chatting over last night? The MacBook. As pissed off as I was over her destroying such a major part of my every day life. A literal necessity. I *understood* what she had done, and why. And the absolute *worst* fucking part about it all? I couldn't say a single thing. She was in the realms of being able to do anything she liked short of assaulting me and would have still been seen as 'in the right.'

I walked back through - reluctantly - to the living room with my beer to join her, unable to hide the unimpressed look on my face over the MacBook swimming in the kitchen sink.

'You not think that was a wee bit excessive, no?' I couldn't resist asking. I mean, I knew I didn't really have much of a leg to stand on but equally, couldn't help myself either.

'Excessive? Excessive is what I would call someone sending a girl hundreds of miles away, that they've never met, a picture of their dick alongside a Sky TV controller but each to their own. We all may have a different interpretation to the word.'

'I really don't see where you and me go from here Paul, if anywhere other than separate ways. In the mean time do you seriously think that I'm going to go off for my back shift and leave you to sit there on that laptop pulling the head off it with her?'

And there it was, her justification for destroying a one year old Apple laptop. Fair enough I suppose. She could've just as easily taken it to work with her in her bag, like, but I suppose at that exact moment destruction rather than logic may have been the running order of the state of her mind.

With the money Hammy, Drummond and me were making, replacing the MacBook wasn't going to be difficult, more a hassle than anything else. The real irony being that having now been caught by Debz the very fucking *last* thing I was likely to be doing with my laptop would've been to chat back and forward with Irma or go on face time. Debz really would have been safe as houses on that score. Still, better to be safe than sorry and just throw an expensive device into the kitchen sink and erase any potential doubts whatsoever though, eh?

'And to show I mean business you'll find your desktop lying in the bath upstairs as well. I know you hardly use it anyway but I know what you're like so you'll find that is now out of action too.'

Oh, no, fucking hell no. I refuse to believe that she has just said what I heard her say, I convinced myself but already feared the worst. It was the way that she said it, too. With such smugness, as if she was proud that she had thought of everything and been smart enough to fuck with any plan b I might've had to deploy. In reality, her smugness revealed that she hadn't *known* what she had done. Aye, she was angry and wanted to retaliate and this was primarily through motivation of stopping me from communicating with a girl in Germany which, from Debz's viewpoint it was a case of job done. But in doing so, she really had had no idea of what she had done in the process. Whilst I had been pretty pissed off at the realisation that she had wrecked the laptop I was still relatively chilled about it, figuring it could always be replaced. The desktop, and peripherals? That old HP thing that I only popped on to use once or twice a month and otherwise sat there gathering dust in the spare room? That was a different proposition.

'What did you just say?' I asked in that self denial way where you really pray that you're going to hear something completely different to what the person said to you moments before.

'Aye, that, and all the other shite that was lying around it. You don't know how lucky you were that you weren't here when I flipped open the laptop and saw what was on the screen, the rage that came down on me.'

Debz said and put across in a way that - I guess - was meant to leave me thankful that there was a computer lying upstairs in the bath other than me in an ambulance on the way to the Western General with multiple stab wounds. In reality, I'd have much rather chosen the latter to have happened to me inside a day.

'You really have no idea what you've just fucking done. You've fucked me, babe.' For the first time since coming back to the house I let my anger show while standing there in disbelief as my mind ran at the speed of sound with what scenarios were now going to be part of the not so distant future.

'How come?' She asked casually but by this time I had taken the pro active thought to run upstairs and do an inventory check to see what was in the spare room, and what was soaking in the bath.

I - trying to cling on to some shred of hope - headed for the spare room first to check for it but it wasn't sitting at the foot of the computer table where the desktop had sat. Turning around I took the few short steps to the bathroom and right beside the monitor and desktop there it was, sitting floating on top of my keyboard. An innocuous looking slim black box of an external hard drive.

The external drive that I used for our 'e-commerce' business. *The* hard drive where I kept our proceeds and Bitcoin wallet. The very *same fucking hard drive* that contained the twenty two and a half thousand pounds worth of crypto currency that we were due our German vendors that same day.

'I'M HEADING OUT TO WORK. YOU AND ME WILL TALK WHEN I GET BACK.'

I heard Debz - still oblivious to what she had just done - shouting ominously from the hall. Standing there looking at the destroyed hard drive and wondering just how I was going to break this to the other two, or Arman88, I couldn't even muster a reply to her before hearing the front door slamming shut behind her.

Being confronted by my girlfriend over cheating on her had brought on some dizziness and raised my temperature. Looking at that Seagate hard drive there in the bath was ten times worse. Absolute levels above, like. With my hair literally wet from the sweats that had come on I stood there still rooted to the spot trying to decide what the next move would be.

I really much would've rather I had to do neither but I was going to have to tell both my mates *and* a supplier that our money was gone. In which order I done so it really didn't matter. They were *all* going to go completely fucking radge when they learned of this unfortunate episode.

Friends *and* mysterious dark web supplier of large quantities of Class A drugs.

Chapter 4

Hammy

'Ok, Hummel. I've sat and listened to what you've had to say and would just like to ask if you have ANY LAST WORDS, YOU STUPID FUCKING CUNT?'

It's fair to say that I didn't take Hummel's news too kindly.

Neither did Drummond but - as always - he was a bit more methodical in his reaction. Unlike the set to default one of resorting to violence, like myself.

'Slow down, Speedy fucking Gonzalez.' He jumped in while - without actually making any kind of a serious attempt to prevent me - reaching over and putting his hand softly on my shoulder to try and get me back down in my seat again.

'There will be a time for to be angry at this fucking moron sat here beside us, and make no mistake that time will come' he paused to look at Hummel before continuing.

'But now *isn't* the time for it. We've got a supplier who is going to have our name flashing in neon lights for their attention if they don't get paid by the end of today, and no money to pay them with.'

With Hummel having literally just broken the news to us we were still trying to process matters, which is probably never the ideal time to start looking for solutions. Not that it stopped us from doing so. At that point I really didn't have a clue just *how* serious it all was. The only thing I knew for a cert was that if we didn't square up our bill then that would've equalled us not getting our next shipment which would've meant the closed for business signs going up on our operation, virtually overnight. That was the basics of it all and something that had to be avoided at all costs. Everything else - at that point - was all up in the air.

'Well aye, technically our money that we'd had set aside for the German is gone but what about all of our profits from the last six months? Surely that would have us close to what we're due?' I asked Hummel. Drummond - who would've got around to thinking that himself eventually - sat up expectantly in his chair agreeing with me.

Hummel's face just dropped even further than it was already sitting at, words not really required.

'It's all gone, *everything.*'

All that risk we'd gone to. All the scenarios that we'd wound up in due to ending up in that game. All of that hard and dangerous work for high profits all gone, and for what? Just so someone could sit and have a wank over a video call? There has to be an army of people who would be in agreement with me over my desire to inflict serious pain on Hummel, friend of mines or not.

It had also been him who had told the two of us that it would be advisable to keep our profits in Bitcoin, instead of withdrawing each month. Telling us that what we'd made that month could end up being worth ten times as much if we left it to sit, which we did. That was his area of expertise, after all, and with it also involving a portion of his own money we were happy to let him crack on, and he wasn't wrong about the price of Bitcoin increasing, either. This whole purpose is completely defeated, however, when your Bitcoin is sitting inside a wallet that has been destroyed by an angry spouse or girlfriend, leaving you with no possible fucking way of recovering your funds.

'And there's no way that you can log in remotely from ..' Drummond asked a question that from Hummel's reaction appeared like this had been all covered before, which it possibly had. With Hummel being the techie twat out of the three of us we were happy to let him take charge with it and we were possibly a little guilty of switching off when he was banging on about all of the dark web and Bitcoin stuff. Drummond and me weren't really bothered about the labour pains, just the baby.

But aye, *now* we were listening and hearing loud and clear that - unlike your regular bank account - we couldn't just 'log in' anywhere and access our money. No cunt that you could just call and explain your predicament to. Due to the security involved in our operation - and how Hummel had set it up for us - you needed the actual device that your crypto wallet had been stored on.

Due to the price of Bitcoin always fluctuating I honestly couldn't have told you how much I personally lost as part of Debz's rage but it was well over ten thousand, which would've meant the same for the other two. Even if the cunt had stored our profits in a *different* wallet we'd have been able to suck it up, pay the German for the gear out of that pot and began working on building it back up again.

But no, the domestic situation between Hummel and Debbie had well and truly fucked us all up.

'I'm so sorry, lads. Who could've predicted something like this, eh?' Hummel said, sitting there looking like a skinny Tony Soprano in a cosy red white and blue velour Fila tracksuit only with anything *but* a comfy expression on his face. Literally looked like he had the world's problems on his shoulders.

'Well obviously, no cunt, such is the random nature of it all in what you did, as well as the response it got out of your other half.' Drummond said, irritated for the first time.

'And anyway, what the fuck are you doing leaving a hard drive that's - technically - worth over tens of thousands of pounds sitting about? You wouldn't leave that in notes lying around.' He now started to take out some of his frustration on Hummel. A line of questioning that would solve absolutely ride all but make Drummond feel better about himself at the same time.

'It wasn't always holding such high amounts and only seems like yesterday that we were using it for orders of around a couple of hundred pounds. Just sat there through habit like it had always, I suppose?'

'Right then, how are we going to sort this?' Drummond asked, staring into space as if he had already started the process of looking towards a way out of it.

Hummel went to say something before thinking better of it.

'No, on you go, mate. Speak up if you've got any ideas.' I said across the pub table, letting him know I'd clocked it.

'Any ideas? Spit them out.' Drummond - who was treading a fine line between being peacemaker and antagonist - prompted Hummel.

'Well, look. I know this is going to sound like a bit of a piss take from me, considering it was myself who has put us all in this position but - away from the crypto that we had - does anyone have any money stored away? You know we're going to make it back again soon enough, like.'

'Oh, aye. Just take your pick, mate. Take it all out of my Cayman Islands or my Swiss account, I'm not fussed which one, like.' I said sarcastically and slid my phone across the table at Hummel for theatrical purposes. With such force, in fact, that it landed up *off* the table and on his lap.

'Apart from the pocket money that we've been taking out for ourselves each month we *have no* money as we've been watching it grow, on paper.' Drummond adding further realism to matters.

Only one of us even owned a car - Drummond - but was nowhere near worth twenty grand and even if it *was* the chances of selling it before the end of the day were a bit on the no fucking chance side of things. Same with any other possessions. While I'm sure Drummond's Adidas and casual gear collection would run into the thousands it would have also taken him weeks if not months to shift it all. And even then I doubt it would have even *still* been worth as much as what we were due Germany.

Short of robbing a bank or bookies there really was no way that we were going to be paying our supplier. Eventually talk turned to exactly that, the subject of - who Hummel always referred to as - Arman88.

'I thought I'd be better to sit down and talk to you two before I contacted him. As of right now he doesn't know of our problem and will be waiting on me contacting him to receive this months address to transfer the coin to.'

'And now that you're, *we're* out of options. What are you going to do?' Drummond asked Hummel rather than advised. This was Hummel's area after all.

'I guess all I can do is tell the truth to the boy. Maybe I'll get lucky and he'll take pity and only send the one death squad to come looking for me, eh?' He said self depreciatingly.

Due to being on completely different wavelengths about things - in addition to me not knowing what I didn't know - I just laughed at how important he was ranking himself in the international drug game. Talking about death squads looking for him.

'Just bump the cunt. What are they going to do, anyway? They live in Germany. It's probably only a couple of entrepreneurial teenagers that's behind it anyway. Dealing with a debt over a box - with someone in a different country - when you're moving so much weight seems like a hassle not worth taking on. Just fucking bump him, them or whoever it is.'

For what it was worth, my counsel to Hummel. Did I want our business relationship to end with the German connect? Of course I didn't want that to happen but I *also* know that you can only pish with the cock that you've got so if you don't have twenty two grand for someone, then you don't fucking have it. The fact that they can't come around knocking on your front door looking for it only assists matters.

'Look at how companies tackle their debt management.' I carried on despite the fact that both of them were against the suggestion of non payment of funds due to our supplier. 'If someone is due x amount to them and they work out that it's going to cost them x *plus* y to recover the money, what do you think they're going to do? If they're a business that knows a thing or two about making and losing money then, obviously, they're going to just write off the debt. We're due them over twenty thousand, but we're all the way in Scotland so logistically this already gives us a bit of breathing space. If we were due that to someone from Muirhouse or Pilton we'd have had our windows put in, followed by a few molotov cocktails. Luckily we don't have that issue here. Now you mentioned a fucking death squad coming looking for you?' Hummel nodded back as serious as they come.

'Do you have any fucking idea what it costs to hire a hit *man* never mind an actual *squad?* You're probably talking around twenty g's just to hire someone who has a track record and will get the job done. Honestly, man. Just fucking dingey ze Germans and we'll try and scrap a bit of money together, create a new profile on that Feelgood and get be back on the merry go round again before we know it.'

My idea for to simply - and in terms that Hummel would understand - press *Ctrl Alt Del* on the whole gig was met with firm and strong protests from Hummel and Drummond. Only, not for the same reasons.

'Nobody is bumping anybody, here. There's nothing that can't be worked out. The fact that we're even in a fucking position of being in serious debt to a dealer here is *because* we were so good *at it* that we ended up being put on credit terms to poach our business. None of us can disagree that this venture has worked *very* well for us and it's only because of Lesley fucking Grantham here that we've encountered a problem. Self inflicted, like.' Drummond went first.

'Fucking wish we'd stayed on pay as you go now though, like.' Hummel interrupted and was met with a burning laser look from Drummond that had him withdrawing again.

'If we bump the supplier then that's the whole ball burst. Even if they were to give us a bit of added time to scrape together the money, it would be enough to keep us in the game and ensure our regular flow of product and be something we'd all look back and laugh at it after the event.'

'I'm not sure Hummel's going to look back too fondly on it all when he's sitting in his bedsit that he's had to move into because Debz has kicked him out.' I joked but - with Hummel still, after all that had happened so far, to have a 'proper' sit down with his girlfriend - it was possibly too soon. Fuck him and his feelings, though. When you lose all of your mates' money and 'working capital' you *also* lose the right towards receiving any fucking sympathy from those same associates.

'You *do* realise that we've got more to worry about here than simply doing what we can to keep the product moving and the org in business, don't you? And as for bumping our suppliers, Hammy? You really have no idea what we're into here, mate. If you did, you wouldn't have even thought about bumping them never mind put it out there as a viable option.'

Don't get it twisted, either. I appreciate that Hummel had experienced one of the worst days of his life up to that point and how that kind of shit can get on top of you but as he spoke he looked a nervous wreck. His hands shaking while his voice began to waver when talking on the subject of 'Arman88.'

'Well for what it's worth. I think my idea makes sense and is well easier to achieve than raising over twenty two grand with fuck all in the way of gear to sell to raise it.' I, once again, let my feelings on the subject be known.

'With the greatest of respect, Hamster, please shut your fucking mouth.' Hummel said, stressed out to the max.

'Is there something that you're not telling us?' Drummond asked, studying Hummel's face as if it was under a microscope. I was ganting on another pint but things were on such a cliffhanger there at the table I couldn't risk missing something when stood at the bar.

'Well, remember back when Arman88 sent me a DM to get hold of our business? Obviously the very first thing to assume was that this account was set up by the feds and that they were pulling honey traps on everyone. Only, after a few weeks you then started to see reviews for Arman88 being put on the Feelgood forum, most from long term users of the site, proving that the vendor was on the level and safe to deal with. Even so, I'm still not radge enough to just jump into an arrangement with complete strangers so done some more digging. And come up with the strangest thing. Despite the forum being a tight knit community that all looks after each other under the same groove of buying and selling quality drugs online without anyone being ripped off or arrested. No one appeared to have a consistent story to match the other when it came to Arman88.'

He pulled his chair closer to the table and then him, himself, further in towards us and lowered his voice for the next part.

'Due to their ultra aggressive - and until then unheard of - marketing tactics that had seen them rumoured to have bribed one of the Feelgood admin for the site's account holders' details and purchasing history, and how they went about getting everyone's business, they were on everyone's radar from the first couple of days of them being listed as a vendor. But with all that attention, inevitably, brought a bit of scrutiny their way, mainly on the subject of who the fuck he or they were because only a seriously big player would have possessed the ability to supply the amounts that Arman88 could, without receiving the money up front. Some of the theories I've read have included the Sinaloa Cartel having set up a European operation, basing themselves in Germany and have branched out into E-Commerce on the dark web, Russian Mafia, Turks - who have a big presence in Germany - Albanians. I even read a theory from some poster that isn't exactly a million miles away from what Hammy said about it being kids only the theory being that a couple of kids came across someone's stash spot out in the woods or something and are smart enough to get something going online to shift it all and are just going to be around for as long as they have gear to sell and then once it's gone so will they be. Mainly, though. Most rumours link the account to some kind of European based organised crime organisation but the bottom line was that no one really seemed to know who Arman88 was but that *everyone* knew how dangerous he was.'

'Oh fucking great, so we're due money to Keyser Soze, basically.' I said, my choice of words a little more careful after having been sobered by Hummel's.

'Aye, pretty much, like.' Hummel shrugged his shoulders at my assessment of the situation.

'That's not all, though. Like, with the bumping them off and that. Was maybe around six months after we'd started to get our gear from Arman88 and I saw this post on the main page of the forum marked in capital letters

** EVERY ARMAN88 CUSTOMER PLEASE READ **

Inside was a long winded post that was so long - and with very little in the way of space breaks - that it kind of put you off reading before even starting. It was from someone claiming to be the fiancé of the user of whose Feelgood profile name was posting the topic. She seemed to be all over the place, kind of appearing as a paranoid wreck shouting about how people had been sent to her house to kill her and her fiancé after he'd failed to pay for the gear that he'd got on tick. She said that she had managed to stay undetected in a hide space they had under the floor but that she had to stay down there and listen to her fiancé's screams as the men dismembered him. Once they left and she surfaced she found her (ex) husband cut up into pieces lying on their living room floor.'

Drummond and me shot a concerned glance at each other before looking back at Hummel who hadn't stopped to draw breath.

'With how Arman88 is obviously getting help from the inside on Dr Feelgood the original post from the girl was taken down within a couple of hours. The moderator stating that it had broken the terms and conditions of the site to accuse someone of a criminal act of which there is no evidence or charges having been brought against the individual or individuals. Thing is, though. Once she did that initial post on the subject it seemed to be the marker for *others* to hit the forum and share their horror stories regarding business dealings that go south with Arman88. The majority of the stories told second hand with the general consensus being that if you run into difficulties with this vendor then you're probably not going to be around to tell the tale of it. It got to the point - on the forum - where if you posted anything on the subject then you were being kicked off the site with a permanent ban which closed down any more talk of anyone falling foul of the "German" supplier during business dealings.'

'All sounds pretty heavy stuff, like, although I bet half of it is nothing other than boogie man scare stories that once they find their way onto the internet they grow arms and legs.' I said to the two of them.

'You wanting to take the chance that it is, aye?' Hummel replied, a wee bit irritated that after his big speech I hadn't just simply fallen into line and got behind things.

'You're fucking lucky that Drummond and me don't just let you dig your own way out of the hole that you've put yourself and, by proxy, us two into.

Aye, that shut his fucking mouth and no mistake.

'Right then, Humms, here's what you're going to do. You're going to get in touch with this Arman88 and kiss his arse in a way that you've never kissed an arse before. Spell out just how profusely sorry that you are, maybe remind them just how regular and reliable you have always been at paying and how much money you and them will have made over the piece and no matter how much they rip into you and what names they call you or your mum, you sit there and you fucking take it. Proper yes sir no sir three bags full sir behaviour. Whatever they say, you agree with, well, *within reason,* and maybe, just maybe we can stop this thing from escalating to a level that none of us are going to want to experience?'

Drummond sounded like he was more giving a pep talk to a fitba side that is a goal down at half time and needs to turn things around instead of his mate who is about to go and talk to a stranger on the other side of a computer.

'And let me wish you the very best of luck. Your performance very well may hold all three of our futures in the palm of its hand.'

Chapter 5

Hummel

PGP Public Key (paste the public key of recipient you are about to send a message)

-----BEGIN PGP MESSAGE-----

Comment: ARM88 revocation certificate

hQEOA1e+1x6YuUMCEAQAh46BxXHGUuq4pteZRp1rIRm7mqBp
eaZMSdHm9Fy+fyXx
VdrFVOd5BwTplx4E2rkDgXzok6UBg9cQIBNlsfEJi/riI9gh8/wS+Q/
K8ZTXbZ7q
OZ7YsAkzGi9LZCJ8/3WQavyVKWCgH0BWfdRwJ5/
GYPy7Ehuzh9RILEQeQh4cA8cD
/
2M29GOejAC42YrFPzAlxCz0e1B7HsWZ+1lY99CmxuL5ZAa+ww
Azh3gz/GNCsLKu
KXNV0plzKlCRDbYEvl0KfjHM5kFJt2IWgKE71o1bGE24li55lKSq
Qtwy3bwT1UWW
0RNDcjSKQXFwBtL716C9i9EsTgYw+O5pAMxJgwD63KHi0rkB4
xvgE7tA+/SmIcGz
O9P+4VAbmPafDo5Kh+Sqx7fZua2kS2DpYjg8dWZXmPRBWo4pR
uayye0AlV50eGq9
JNygbPZ/g1c0jQatJt4MamhBhyP5C/
2klkkwdH75dqc79K0YeYYJQTBbJUDKzYHB
uvISYPVwPZIdrvMyCMA3k/
Qg2n6Sgp33XAOLQwgNp7+THWbv1cgfx6wwGrkocbP+
Qn7QtBJJmMzA4LbNAVrQZgG17Ovla6vDOqu3yw==
=f7i1

-----END PGP MESSAGE-----

Message to Encrypt (enter the message that you wish to encrypt)

Look, mate. There's no easy way to say this but things are beyond fucked up on this side and I'm sat with a Bitcoin wallet - with your money in it - that I now can't get *into*.

I know this message *should* be me asking for this month's address but there's no point giving me it if I can't send it to you!

We've been doing business for a long time now without a problem on either of our sides so due to that I wanted to ask if there was any way that you could extend our payment window to give us a chance to get your money together? I'm also experiencing a bit of technical difficulties at present and having to send this from my phone but this app is buggy as fuck so can you please contact me on my reekie_cartel@hushmail.com address to make sure I can reply sooner to you.

While the blame for the damage to the wallet lies directly at my door, myself and my colleagues would like to apologise once again to you for this unforeseen circumstance and would like you to know that we will be doing all we can to put together your funds.

Please let me know your thoughts on this and I will get back to you as soon as possible. After doing so much successful business together it is my sincere hope that our future business will not be affected in any capacity by this temporary problem.

Encrypted Message (Paste and send to intended recipient)

-----BEGIN PGP MESSAGE-----

Comment: ARM88 Revocation Certificate

h Q E O A 1 e + 1 x 6 Y u U M C E A P / X w A /
myLceoEAFaooXiZMGOAzeA6czSNpLxcsyxeOPKAn
s7Dr8a0C4WodSIRwjNHwmnubgcb+QEXiFErO7UkvZC69wBJX1r
x/lYUrJ/KuZVXc
g3Csc0O7i8Yw23pmFYu5uhRO3lwp4mhcpYQhOqK+5jITvDLj0k/
9+AuiAhuJD+ID0UujG43g3qItlGkF8lnlMctVbcSfrHZLQCvsezpVfs
mOlkVD55NoAhB4YHLa7Zf
bUYeB4mkDU/czumWnsv1XxUpigqwBxli7GJSQu+UbonV4095j5a/
ygWcrl8TdU1V
g a + J T v a 9 9 m s f W 8 o 6 s g S W Z 6 Z 4 s R /
F5P5A+WwAYcwUR2dF0mUBeC6m0NxRqJ3Be6WH
e / i e y m o Z 2 M y o r H U   8 t p C J 5 /
w0Uf0Juxmg1GuyPaZn6vuBPiBfjhLRxHDPXOuJTTB
w3xFJLS3Gq5ZWTHw8ZSFzaAKsFOgixu7Zc8y2Y1A9UmcncnJqz
2wyA==
=xFGB

-----END PGP MESSAGE-----

And now we wait, I nervously thought to myself having copied my encrypted message for our supplier and sent it off to him via a private message on Dr Feelgood. Feeling like someone who has informed their work that they're having to take the day off but committed the cardinal sin of not calling in and - instead - has elected to send a text message and is now sitting at home, anxiously waiting to see what this chosen form of communication is going to bring about in response.

Don't get me wrong, like. If you're going to have to break the news to someone that you don't have the twenty k plus for them that they were imminently expecting then the medium of an encrypted PGP message on a shadowy online drug marketplace is definitely the way to do it. Seriously reduces the chances of receiving a smack in the mouth, massively.

Not that the distance was going to be solving any problems, long term. All I really could do was let the boy know that payment wasn't coming and look for what kind of reaction this would be met with. I did exactly what Drummond told me to - and I'm not daft, I was going to take that attitude anyway - and apologised as much as I could, used words in the message that I *never* fucking use in day to day life. Tried to come across as professional and serious and not as just some radge who was trying it on with them. Respect goes a long, long way with these types of people which was sound because respect was all that I had to offer.

Definitely didn't have any fucking cash for him anyway.

Through Debz having destroyed anything in the house that had the capability of internet she had near on cut my legs off as far as getting myself onto the dark web. Something that isn't too cool when you're due a big time drug dealer thousands and your only way of reliably contacting them is *away* from the surface web.

After a bit of fucking around in the App Store I managed to find an application that claimed that it could allow your iphone to gain access to the T.O.R network. The scores of one star reviews that claimed it could *not* get you onto the dark web couldn't be ignored but - left with no real other choice - I installed it anyway and hoped for the best.

While the reviewers hadn't exactly been lying about the problems they'd experienced they - most likely - had not possessed the intense *need* and desire to get onto the dark web as I did that early Tuesday afternoon. Something that should have taken five minutes to carry out took nearer to an hour and a half but - from what I could see - I eventually managed to both encrypt a message for Arman88 and get the 'Easy T.O.R' app to remain in communication with my phone - and without dropping which it had done time and time again - long enough for me to log in to Feelgood and fire off a private message. The connection dropping moments after I'd seen the confirmation that my message had been sent.

From then it really was out of my hands and a case of playing the waiting game. Obviously I'd have much rather preferred to *not* have to be waiting on a reply to a message of the nature of what I'd just had to type and send but at the same time I prayed that I would get a reply sooner rather than later to save me from the torture of what my mind was going through.

Debz, as things stood, was already going to put me through *enough* torture when she got back from work.

I was only kept waiting for around half an hour - although it felt like triple that, at least - before my phone pinged with an email notification.

I didn't recognise the name of the sender from first glimpse on navigating my way into my inbox but also, it was not an address that I shared with many people and certainly not the kind of email account that would be showered with any form of junk mail - not with the kind of secure set up I'd had for it - so opened the message without any hesitation.

'Brooooo? What the fuck???

Tell me ur telegram and I will contact you.

They hadn't signed off the email with who they were and the email address. Evidently though, it was from Arman88.

Well, at least the first response on hearing the news of our 'payment issues' hadn't been one of extreme threats of violence, I thought to myself as I tapped out a reply back. Whether that actually stood for anything, however, was anyone's guess.

Doing as requested I replied back with my Telegram name. It was no means ordinary behaviour for a Tuesday afternoon but following pressing send on the email I went and grabbed my stash box and chopped out a large line for myself. You know things are bad when you find yourself hoovering up a Friday night line, on a Tuesday afternoon. I was heavy stressed over the atomic bomb that Debz detonated earlier on in the morning plus knew that I'd need to have myself together if I was going to have even a remote chance of being able to try and talk my way out of things with Arman88 once they reached out to me.

They didn't seem like they were in too much of a mood to let things hang because I had no more made the long white line disappear up my right nostril - and was beginning to feel that instant slap in the face that you would generally enjoy from the stuff that our German connect provided us with - when the Telegram notification popped up on my screen. A message from an 'AM88'

Bro, you're killing me here! Tell me again why you don't have my money!! : 2.17pm

I won't lie. It's my fault. My GF got mad at me and threw my crypto wallet into the fucking bath and now I cannot access my funds. : 2.17pm

That bitch needs smacked. : 2.18pm

Yeah, you can do it then if you like! : 2.18pm

I think I prefer to keep focussed on you. You're in a lot of trouble now, bro. : 2.18pm

Reading that one line - from the person / group that I was in for a lot of money with - made me, and not for the first time that day, want to be physically sick. I'm not a moron, I *knew* I was in trouble. Seeing it confirmed in writing, though, in a rubber stamped way, and from *who* you're in trouble with. It kind of added another level of realism to it all.

Listen, mate. We've done a lot of business with each other and me and my team are VERY resourceful, we'll come up with the money via alternative means. We just need a bit of time to do so. It hasn't exactly helped us for this problem to occur on the very same day that we were going to transfer your money. Worst possible timing you can get. It's our hope that you would be able to give us a little period of grace and goodwill while we figure it out. : 2.19pm

If you're talking hit and hopes then there was my attempt. I sat on the sofa puffing hard on a joint in the way that suggested that I was never going to see one again for the rest of my life. Staring at the phone screen and praying for something, anything, that I could have taken as a positive reply.

I told you, back when we began doing business that everything would be cool with us as long as you paid me what I was owed when I needed it. Today you have broken this agreement, bro. NOT cool. : 2.20pm

I will make this up to you ASAP! : 2.20pm

I pleaded to him while having absolutely zero in the way of an actual *plan* as to how this debt would be paid, *at all,* never mind as soon as possible. Time can make a difference, though. And with nothing to offer him in return, that's all I needed from him.

He had other ideas, though.

Ok, here's what we're going to do, bro. You want my help, yes? : 2.21pm

YES, OF COURSE! : 2.21pm

When the one that you're due over twenty grand - and don't have it - offers you help, you snap their hand, and arm also, right off.

Good good. Now while at this point I should already be putting plans into place and giving the green light on you and your little team to someone in your part of the world, I'm going to give you a break today. : 2.22pm

The wave of relief that washed over me as I read his words was immeasurable. I hadn't even been told what *kind* of a break I was being given yet but it did not involve green lights so aye, I was fully on board with it.

What you're going to do is that I'm going to send you another shipment, like always at this time of the month. Only, I'm going to send you three times as much. You sell all of that? You make enough profit to pay for your shipment AND your outstanding debt with me. After that? We're back to normal, yes? : 2.23pm

It wasn't something that I had been able to offer an immediate response to. Pausing long enough to re-light my joint while trying to play out the implications of taking such a large shipment of Ching. One that I wasn't sure we'd have had a chance of shifting in such a short space of time. Actually, I *knew* we wouldn't shift inside such a short timeframe. We'd never came close to needing three boxes before, one being as much as was ever required inside a calendar month. And he wanted us to shift *three?*

His plan - to ensure that we made the money that would then be handed straight over to him - was solid in a crunching the numbers sense, *if* you had a large enough customer base, which we never.

But what real alternative option was I left with?

He who pays the piper calls the tune, as they say, and nothing was more clearer than the fact that I was going to have to dance to whatever fucking tune this man desired.

I thought of Drummond and Hammy's probable reaction when I told them that I had solved our major problem, by swapping it for a *different* major problem.

Will you be able to move that amount, bro? : 2.24pm

He followed up with, without me having mustered a response yet.

Oh no probs at all : 2.24pm

I straight up lied to him.

Cool cool, bro. Everyone fucks up now and again but I always feel that it is how someone behaves when they fuck up that counts and this is why I am giving you a second chance but PLEASE believe that there will be no more chances. Most do not even get one. God walked with you today, brother. Know that. : 2.26pm

I blew out such a long gasp of relief that by the tail end of it I was choking for air. I didn't even get a chance to type him a thank you reply before he sent his next message which, I admit, had adopted its own individual *tone*, completely at odds with every message he'd sent my way since this little back and forth began.

Now some terms for you to know and follow. : 2.27pm

There was obviously going to be some kind of a kicker to this, and here it came. The realisation that you were going to be faced with the task of selling three times as much Cocaine inside a month *should've* been the worst part of things but - in the situation that I'd found myself in - here was the problem. *That* was the good part!

I waited - almost wanting to cover my eyes - on the t's and c's that he was going to set as part of this special arrangement and fuck me, they were a right boot in the fucking balls when I sat and read through them.

Ok, bro. You are in debt for a lot of money so forget the old arrangement. This is the new one until I SAY we go back to old one. I will arrange a shipment of three for you and you will receive in three to four days. From the day it is received you will have two weeks to pay me in full the €66k for three boxes AND your outstanding funds from this month which comes to a figure of €88.5k but you are going to round this up to €90k as a small thank you for me giving you a second chance. : 2.31pm

I know that in that moment I should've - and up until that point I *had* - been following Drummond's advice and been all yes sir no sir three bags full sir but all I was seeing was the figure of ninety thousand euros and the timescale of fourteen days to earn it in. I didn't think it could be done and without even thinking had replied back.

Two weeks? Not four? : 2.32pm

Yes two weeks, is that a problem? Do you think it would be a good idea to owe me €90k for any more time, further than two weeks? I would advise you to answer no, bro. If you are not happy we can deal with things how non payment is normally arranged if you like? : 2.34pm

No we're good, mate. Just send it and we'll move it and we'll soon be able to put this whole thing behind us. : 2.35pm

My cousin Shona - years back - had called me 'Mr Mañana' as I habitually put everything and everything to the back of my mind by saying that I'd "deal with it tomorrow" and here was Mr Mañana in some real time action. Signing up to a shipment of Cocaine that - without stepping on the wrong toes inside the city of Edinburgh - I had no fucking idea how I'd be able to move it but aye, I'd worry about that "tomorrow" AKA the day that three keys of Ching arrived at my door via my Royal Mail employed local postman.

That would be an outcome that would suit both of us, bro. One last thing before I sign out and you need to pay close attention. You caught me in a merciful mood today, you got lucky but I'm am telling you once. Do NOT fuck this up, brother. Being in debt to me is bad. Being in debt to me to €90k is VERY fucking bad so remember this, bro. If I can send three boxes of product directly to your front door then that is not the only thing that I can arrange to be sent in your direction. You understand what I'm saying? Are we clear, yes? : 2.35pm

Crystal, mate. : 2.35pm

I replied while acknowledging - to myself - the very real prospect that, obviously, he had my home address from the many shipments that had been sent since we were introduced to each other.

And that goes for your associates, Barry Drummond and James Hamilton. Ok, Paul? : 2.36pm

This I have to admit unnerved me, big time. Due to the whole anonymity deal of using Feelgood and Bitcoin there was no way that he could ever have known any of our identities, especially Drummond and Hammy whose dark web experience had amounted to seeing the Dr Feelgood site on my MacBook screen from time to time. And I *know* that I hadn't used any personal details on the dark web. Yet there he was, rattling out all three of our names and delivering it in the deliberate fashion - that he did - and for the maximum impact that he had obviously intended. Which it definitely achieved.

There was just something all a bit sinister about how he knew what our identities were. Without saying anything it said an awful fucking *lot* about the type of person that we were dealing with. That they could be based hundreds of miles away in a different country - or at least that was what the front was saying - and still able to find out our names. For all I know he maybe knew them all along and before deciding to offer us credit back at the start?

I didn't bother to reply to this. Him knowing that I had read it was more than enough for both of us.

You will be messaged your tracking details in a few days or so and be given the address for your Bitcoin payment nearer to the expiry of the two weeks. Do not let me down. : 2.39pm

He sent me one final message before signing out and leaving the chat.

What a fucking day though, like. It was still only around mid afternoon and I was feeling like I'd been to hell and back, and I *still* had the relationship saving talk with Debbie when she came home from work to come.

But sandwiched between this I now had to inform my two best friends and business partners that we were now faced with having to sell three times as much gear in *half* the time or else we'd most likely end up like that poor cunt in the bathroom scene in Scarface.

Fuck my life, honestly.

I even had the IKEA wardrobe still to build although wasn't going anywhere fucking near that until Debz and me had discussed our future as a couple. Fuck building it until I knew if I was going to be staying there or not. I'm not that fucking daft, like.

Chapter 6

Drummond

'See earlier on this morning when I stopped you from ripping Hummel's head off?' I looked towards Hammy, thinking about his explosive reaction hours before upon being informed that thousands of pounds belonging to him had now been 'lost.' 'I'd now like to retract those actions, which I now realise were a touch knee jerk, and now allow you carte blanch to do with what you fucking well want with this rocket sat here. I can no longer - given how much he has went out of his way the past twenty four hours to completely fuck our shit up - protect him now.'

'Don't, mate.' Hammy said. 'It's already a struggle for me *not to*. I don't need any fucking thing in the way of encouragement.'

'Oh, oh. Mon, lads. Gies a break. I fucking saved our skin. Cunt was talking about green lights and that.' Hummel pleaded.

'SAVED OUR FUCKING SKIN?' Hammy's infamous temper - which had been sat at the table from the moment we'd received our update from Hummel - was simply waiting on its chance to be seen and heard, and now it was time.

Obviously, I was in Hammy's camp even if I wasn't serious about having my mate do physical harm to my *other* mate, even if they deserved it, which he definitely did.

Saved our skin? I'd just sat there and watched one of my closest and best friends tell me that in the coming days we were going to be receiving three times as much gear as we'd ever had shipped to us, and that we were going to have to sell it all inside *two fucking weeks*. The consequences of us failing to do so not yet discussed but already assumed to be tortuous, be that figuratively and or literally.

"Saved our skin" equalling the equivalent of a cow being ready to be slaughtered at the abattoir right as the electric goes off through non payment of the bill. But once the bill *is* paid? Well the music starts again, doesn't it?

I fucking told him to go back to our supplier and apologise as if his life depended on it, which it might well *have*. What does he do, though? Stupidly agrees on a deal that - until we start to punt some of the product - would then see us in hock for over *ninety* grand. To who the fuck knows who but the folklore that seemed to be on the dark web about them wasn't exactly encouraging. And I wasn't that bogged down by "where" in the world our suppliers were from, either. Mexicans, Russians, Dutch, Albanians or fucking Scousers. I'm quite aware that any of that list would be perfectly capable of making your life hell and the kind that you didn't know even existed until they got their hands on you.

Hummel was meant to go and find a solution to the problem and, instead, went and sucked us into things even *further*.

Aye, I know, I know. In 'theory' it all made sense. We needed a way out and by selling three boxes of Ching that would've provided it but Hummel fucking knew that when he accepted their terms that it was a pipe dream to think that we could've ever sold that much, but still accepted the deal anyway.

The only way that we had even been *allowed* to operate our wee conglomerate out of our part of the city was by not stepping on the toes of the Davey McKenna's of this world and only selling

- and supplying - to a select customer base. Everyone deserves to eat, everyone. It's only when cunts start clocking that they don't have as much food on their plate that it can become a problem. The only way we were ever going to have a chance of selling the gear would've meant looking outside of our circle and *that* was not an option. Problems locally with others would make issues with our German vendor seem like a drop in the oceans, and quickly.

While 'Arman88' was undoubtedly a threat - even if an unknown one - that was there hanging over us. Someone much more closer to home and a lot more *known* like a gangster of McKenna's reputation was something that I was a lot more concerned about than a username behind a computer screen.

'Well I'll tell you one fucking thing for a kick off, lad. You're the one taking delivery this time. It's stressful enough receiving the one key on the occasions I have to take my turn, so *three?* Fuck that.'

Hammy said. You could tell that he had a lot to say but was struggling to process it all through him also still trying to stem his violent tendencies that he was undoubtedly feeling towards Hummel. A proper battle of wills, like. We'd generally shared the risk when it came to taking delivery of our shipments and would rotate it amongst the three of us using the obligatory fake names. With this being Hummel's fuck up, Hammy wanted to make a point, one that I was quick to latch onto and team up with him on.

'Aye, you can count me out on this one too,' I joined in, letting Humms know he was going to be mopping up his own shite.

'Aye, alright then. Fair enough, eh? Anyway, I've *already* organised it to come to mines under the usual alternative name so you can both keep your fucking wigs on. What's the difference between one box and three anyway?' He said defensively but with a touch of the persecuted about him which, of course, was ridiculous since *he'd* caused all of this in the first place.

'And, of course, who receives it when and where is all rather academic when we're going to be sat with the fucking stuff piling up around us like Hummel's uncle Wattie with those Scotland World Cup winners t shirts back in nineteen eighty two.' I said pragmatically to the two of them. Hummel - from fuck knows where - managing a wee smile at the thought of that summer. Not even five years old all in t shirts - three sizes too big for us - celebrating a World Cup win that, obviously, never happened. One that was *never* going to fucking happen.

'There's got to be a way we can shift it in the timeframe we've got available to us, on the down low, like?' Hammy spoke up but without any actual suggestions.

Over a couple of pints we sat and brainstormed things. You know? One of those meetings where - supposedly - no idea will be judged as too moronic or left field. Even so, though. It had been a stressful day for all concerned so I couldn't help myself in reacting to Hummel's suggestion of offering to sell the gear *to* Edinburgh's largest supplier.

'Look, I know you've had a hard day Hummel but if you're only going to come out with the thoughts of a fucking mentalist who has some kind of a death wish fantasy then maybe you should just sit the next wee while out.'

'Fuck's sake, Drummond. I'm just throwing stuff out there. I'm not saying we have to *do* any of it, like.' Hummel replied hurt, clearly fragile over his day up until then.

'Humms, with absolutely ride all of respect and don't take it personally here but the last twenty four hours you can hardly be celebrated as having made the best - and consistent - of choices. Can you please let the adults talk?' Hammy added.

It's fair to say that the pair of us had had just about enough of our mate and were no longer even trying to hide it, not that Hammy had even started to, earlier in the morning.

'Kind of leaves me not wanting to tell you any of my other ideas I've been having since speaking to Arman88, like.' Hummel said getting up from the table as he picked up our empties to go and get some replenishments.

'Well if they're all as idiotic as the idea of selling Ching to a man who does not know that - up until now - we've been selling it right under his nose and eating into his profits maybe you should just keep them to yourself to avoid further embarrassment, eh?' Hammy shouted after him as he walked away from us to the bar.

Whilst Hummel was gone Hammy brought up a much more realistic - but ultimately non viable - idea of me using what contacts I still had at through Uni from my cameo appearance that I once made as a student studying sports journalism. A period of my life that did not even get past the six month mark. Hammy was correct, though. If there's one thing students like, it's to party and they're no strangers to pills and thrills. In truth, though we were already *using* some of my old contacts to shift what gear we were receiving each shipment.

While my old friends from over those six months - before dropping out - were always good and reliable for taking a little bit each month that's all it was, a little bit. Much like Hummel, Hammy and me, what the fuck was a University student going to do with fucking *kilos* of product?

At least he was thinking straight, unlike Hummel. Not that *he* was done with ideas, though. Returning to the table with our top ups with another suggestion even though he must've known that whatever he came out with he was going to risk being berated further from the pair of us.

'How's about this, then.' He sat down with a self assured and confident look about him.

'We take the majority of the gear - that we're never going to shift here inside Edinburgh or over the bridge - and we turn it around and *sell it* on Dr Feelgood and get the money back that way?' He looked at us back and forth as if he was sitting inside Centre Court, Wimbers.

'Humms? While I admire your spirited never say die attitude that is clearly not going to be extinguished, regardless of what me or Hammy say to you. If you're going to come up with a suggestion can you *please* fucking make it make sense?' I pleaded with him, patience wafer thin.

'That not a good idea, no? It's the *only* way we're going to sell quantities like that and remain completely anonymous.' He pitched with complete confidence in what he was saying.

'Actually he's right, Drummond. We need to sell a large amount of gear without anyone knowing about it. Where better than the dark web?' Hammy said, in agreement with Hummel for the first time that day.

This - out of everything - seemed to irritate me the most.

'For fuck's sake, Hummel. *You're* the computer expert out of us all, right? You're Mr Dark fucking Web here while me and him provide our areas of expertise elsewhere.'

I left it hanging and was met with silence from him.

'So why the fuck is it taking *me* to be the one to remember *you* about the whole fucking Escrow system with Feelgood and how once the buyer receives their gear they have up to fourteen days to hit that confirmation button to tell the site that they *received it*. We won't *have* fourteen days for them to sort their lives out and log in and hit the confirmation button to release our funds from Escrow.'

I spat out at Hummel, really pissed off at him that I was the one who had to point out the major flaw in his - otherwise logical - idea. Had I *not* been paying attention and hadn't taken in the whole Escrow stuff - when originally explained to me - we might well have been sat there agreeing with his idea which would have potentially led us into an even worse position.

'Aye, but most hit the confirm button as soon as they get their gear in the mail, though.' Hummel replied and while true or not did we *really* want to be left sitting in a position of having up to two boxes separated and sent all over the U.K. and Europe and be waiting at the mercy of all of these strangers unfreezing our payments in time?

All of the ideas that had been pitched were of no use, and that was a worry to me because in a matter of days we were going to be taking delivery of three kilos of Ching and from the exact moment that it was in our hands we were going to have to hit the ground running with the clock as much of an enemy to us as 'Arman88' was potentially going to be, depending on what we *did* with our fourteen days.

Chapter 7

Hummel

According to the tracking number, the gear was due to arrive sometime that morning. From the moment my eyes opened I'd had a bad feeling about everything. In saying that, though. Is anyone *ever* meant to have a good feeling when they're imminently about to receive three keys of drugs worth over sixty grand - and to us over *ninety* - delivered to their front door by the Royal Mail?

All those midnight meetings in the middle of nowhere where drugs and money are exchanged - like you see on the telly - a thing of the past. This was 2019 and things had changed. Still, though. It's one thing to trust your friendly postman - or woman - to hand deliver your copy of Roy of the Rovers and your bills and invoices but a complete fucking different kettle of fish when it's something of *that* kind of value. Should've been fucking G4S bringing it although the cunts would probably lose it, like they do with their prisoners.

Things between Debz and me were frosty at best but hey, she hadn't kicked me out over all the shite at the start of the week so I guess that was one thing. Was still sleeping on the couch though, mind. She'd had to change a shift day to fill in for a colleague so had been handed the unenviable task of doing one day back shift, come home to eat and sleep and then up at the back of five in the morning to then do a day shift.

She wasn't there in the house with me nipping my head so *that* was all that was really of importance to me. It was going to be a busy and testing enough day as it was - from the moment I took delivery of the gear - and any added hassles from her definitely weren't required.

I'd already woken to a WhatsApp from Drummond saying - and not for the first time over the previous couple of days - for me to let him know the moment that the postie had been. It was going to be a hectic time of things and he already had some plans that had been thrown together at the last minute in an attempt at making sure we had at least a sniff of getting rid of all of the gear.

You think I want three kilos of Ching sitting in my house for a minute longer than I have to??? Message you ASAP.

The reply he got back from a barely awake me but still put out by what I took as him trying to manage me. There wasn't a manager, just partners. Drummond, though, seemed to always try to act like he *was* our gaffer though.

I quickly checked the tracking while waiting on the kettle boiling for a cup of tea. The confirmation of 'We've got it' on the website stating that my local depot had my parcel and that it was out for delivery that day.

Sitting down with my cup and sparking up a stubbed out joint from the night before I stuck the TV on. The preset channel being ITV from the last time the telly had been on so within seconds I was confronted by that absolute weapons grade cunt, Piers Morgan. Sitting there, red face like a heart attack on the way - faking outrage over whatever flavour it was of the day that he'd chosen in an attempt to get himself some attention and relevance. Clear as day what the boy's hustle is but until the nation susses him out I guess he'll keep getting away with it. Barely lasted a minute of him sitting there at that desk - face like one of those cunts from the Ribena adverts when I was wee - being as loud, obnoxious and shouty as he could before literally telling him to go and throw shite at the moon and changing the channel. Not that he'd have heard me or fuck all, obviously. Pretty mad though that the TV execs at ITV would think that *any* cunt would want to sit and listen to that roaster at any time of the day, never mind first thing in the morning when you're trying to get your head together. Gies a chance, for fuck's sake?

Timing is everything though as they say and whoever 'they' are they fucking nailed it with that. Had I not decided to pop upstairs and get myself that sweater - having felt a wee bit chilly sitting around - and while up there happen to glance out of the bedroom window I guess I'll never know how it all would've played out, but I can't imagine any of it would've went my way, that's for sure.

Before pulling the sweatshirt on I stood with it in my hands as I looked out across the street. At the far end down the road I could make out the usual red mini Royal Mail van parked up. This in itself giving me an instant shot of adrenaline while wondering if my gear was literally sitting inside the back of it right there or if someone was already on route - and foot - with it. With the size of what three kilos would've came to it was already assumed that it wasn't going to be my normal postie who did the rounds each morning. Can't expect those cunts to be carrying boxes of drugs around with them on their rounds. Put their backs right out, that caper, if you combine it with all of the bills, letters and junk mail they've already got to contend with, eh?

As I looked over at the van a navy blue Vauxhall Corsa pulled up right behind it and two men in suits got out and walked over to the driver's side front door of the van and stood talking to the Royal Mail worker sitting inside.

Obviously, you can never be too paranoid in the game that we were in so you can bet my suspicions were kind of aroused over why two men in suits would have the need to have a conversation like they were doing with the Royal Mail boy. Of course, it didn't exactly help that the car they were driving was the exact kind of style of car that Lothian and Borders used away from their actual police branded vehicles.

Aye, I didn't need to be seeing irregular stuff like that on the day where I had all the gear I had coming to me. So I *definitely* didn't need to see the boy in the van getting out of it and leading the two suits around to the back doors of the van and opening them up to show them something that was inside.

With the doors being open and all three being positioned in between I couldn't see what it was that they were all standing looking at. When the doors were closed again and one of the men in suits brought something up to his mouth and spoke into it *that's* when I knew what was going on. And oh the panic that it immediately caused.

I tried to call Drummond. No answer. Same with Hammy although - unlike Drummond - Hammy was a cert to be still sleeping only to surface around dinner time to hit the bookies. I'm not sure what I thought either of them could really have done to help me but I just wanted advice. Obviously, it could've just been the paranoia ripping through me but when you see what appears to be plain clothed police corresponding with postmen in the middle of the street, on the same day that you are expecting three kilos of Cocaine. Wouldn't *you* be fucking bricking it?

Launching myself into survival mode - over something I wasn't sure was an overreaction on my part or not - I grabbed my stash box and gathered up what Ching I had left in it, which wasn't much. Two 'generously' heaped lines that I quickly shoved up a nostril each. Did I want to have two consecutive bumps at that time of the morning? Of course I didn't but neither did I want any undercovers being dicks and pinning a Class A charge on me. The weed? I was much more chill about that figuring that they'd very clearly be struggling for work if they were worried about a quarter of Cheese Kush sitting in someone's house.

After doing both lines I ran back upstairs to check the state of play. The Corsa was gone but the Royal Mail van was still sat there, minus the driver who had been sitting in it before the suits had arrived.

The Ching didn't help in any way - other than now no longer being sat in my house - and only served to fill me full of all kinds of nervous energy.

What the fuck do I do, here? I thought to myself knowing that a knock was going to come at the door sooner or later and what I chose to do - following it - could shape the rest of my life.

I answer it - as I'd done for all the other shipments via the dark web - sign for the package and, it all goes to plan and we then throw ourselves fully into trying to achieve the impossible of actually *selling it.*

Don't answer it and we've then got three boxes of Coke that we are not in possession of, and in a situation where every single minute, hour and day counted.

I answer it *but* the fact I saw an undercover police car parked up beside the Royal Mail van turns out not to be just some coincidence and I get myself busted while actually having already given myself prior notice of it happening when looking out my window earlier?

Fucking hell, what a position to be sat in, like.

By the time the knock *did* eventually come I was still no further forward over deciding what I should do. The one overriding factor, however, being what if I didn't answer the door and accept it, and it all had turned out to be just my paranoia and nothing more. It was already through me that we were in the hole for over twenty k. What was it going to be like though if I was then responsible for turning it into a *ninety* thousand debt And all because I was too scared to open a fucking door?

With no plan of action what - so - ever, I opened the door to find Wullie Stephenson standing staring back at me, large reinforced brown card board box in his hand. Wull had worked as a postie for as long as I could remember. Always used to give me a sweetie any time that he delivered any post to our house and would stand having a wee blether with dad before getting on with his rounds. In fairness, I could've had a *lot* worse a person being in possession of the gear than old Wullie, that day.

'Package for Mr Barry Green.' Wullie said while he lifted the box up to head height for effect.

But it was the *way* he said it that put me on an extremely high state of alert. Forget the fact that he *knew* what my name was and that it wasn't the name he had just said out loud. It was the *way* he delivered the sentence. I, of course, couldn't rule out it just being my escalating paranoia but it really did seem like he was trying to tell me not to sign for what he had in his hands, without him actually *saying* so.

'Barry Green?' I asked cautiously while trying to buy myself a few seconds of thinking time. As part of this theatrical display - from the both of us - he looked down at the address label on the box to check before confirming that was, indeed, the name.

So I really was left with only two choices, there. Turn it away - and in doing so be left without a card allowing me to go and collect it from the sorting office with me formally denying that the name on the package matched who lived at the address - and say goodbye to our gear, officially. That or confirm that I *am* Mr Barry Green, accept the package and then take my chances with what then followed.

For what it was worth, paranoia or not, the general vibe I was picking up from Wullie was that it would be better if I stuck to my *real* identity of Paul Evans.

With the heaviest of heart and most sickening of feelings - knowing the gravity of what I was doing to us all by refusing the package - I reluctantly offered the postman some confirmation.

'Green? Nah, mate. Think you've got the wrong address. This is Evans. You sure it says number thirty five, aye?'

I asked, to make sure one more time. Since Wullie had - weirdly - began this exchange in a way that had made it look like he didn't know who I was, despite knowing me all my life. I fed off this by speaking to him like you would with a postie that you've never seen before in your life either.

'Aye, son. Thirty five.' He said after one more check, shrugging his shoulders as if it was just another part of his job, dealing with such postal errors.

'Sorry then, mate, but you'll just need to take it back to the sorting office again and return it. Nothing to do with me I'm afraid, like.'

Saying those final words to him were like a smashed pint tumbler to the throat, each and every word feeling like it was being plunged into my jugular again and again. The feeling of turning the Cocaine away - and the possible death sentence that it was going to give way to - leaving my legs almost buckling from under me as my grim future started to flash before my eyes.

'Ach, no problems, son. Happens more times than you'd believe. Sorry to bother you this morning.'

Wullie had barely got his sentence out when I heard the screaming and so close to where I stood I almost nutted the top of the doorway from the height I jumped out of my skin.

'GO GO GOOOOOOOOOOOOOOO'

All I heard before three plain clothed officers rushed my front door from either side. Them all seemingly stood there like statues - to either side of the front door - while Wullie and me had ourselves our brief chat. Our - in my case friendly - local postie being almost knocked to the ground in the rush that all of the filth were in to grab hold of me and storm their way into my house.

Chapter 8

Drummond

Where the fuck is he? I stressed out to myself. It was just touching half one in the afternoon and there had been no sign from Hummel. I'd missed a couple of calls from him when I'd been in the shower earlier on and by the time I was out and changed I couldn't get an answer from him when trying to call him back.

Despite the fact that my phone was now showing as having called him nineteen times - inside just under an hour and a half - I thought nothing of making it a nice round twenty only to get the same result, being put through to his voicemail.

I'd already been on to Hammy to see if there had been any contact from Hummel on his end but nada there, too. And anyway, Hummel would've called me before Hammy when it came to taking receivership of our gear.

Time is money, as they say but in our own case, time was worth even *more* than that to us.

Hammy - as usual - didn't seem to be too particularly worried about the fact that on the day our three boxes were arriving the one person out of the three of us due to *receive* it had gone missing.

'He's probably too busy on face time with his pretendy girlfriend and just blanking you, mate.'

He said casually over the phone. You could tell he wasn't long up.

'Why do I have to be the only fucking one out of us that ever seems to take things serious?' I shouted back at him, not in a position to see any kind of a funny side to things. Frustrated that I was the only one who appeared to be 'mildly' concerned over the fact that on the day we received so much product I'd received two missed calls in a row from Hummel and now - hours later - no one had heard from or could reach him.

'You know what the daft cunt is like. He's probably been looking for his phone for the past two hours and it's in his back pocket.' Hammy tried to calm me down by appealing to the very real facts that Hummel wasn't the sharpest tool in the box. He was just simply a tool.

Nothing could persuade me otherwise, though. There couldn't have been a coincidence that he would go missing on *that* particular morning, of all mornings.

Chapter 9

Hummel

'You know what I think, Bill? This clown sitting here thinks that you and me are a pair of simpletons.'

The copper in the suit delivered this little piece of thespian caper purely for my benefit.

'Now, now. That's not very charitable, is it?' The other one - also in a suit - replied to his colleague but while staring directly at me.

I honestly didn't know how much or how little I was in the shit at that point but until I was told either way I was left with no choice other than to just front things out. Say the bare fucking minimum and - if required - deny deny deny.

'Well, that's your words, to be fair, not mines.' I said back to him, not exactly going out my way to say that they *weren't* simpletons, mind.

'Buttoned up the back you must think we both are.' The original one - probably not much older than me and someone who must've been fast tracked into sitting in with suspected drug dealers like myself instead of doing his time in a uniform - continued. 'You obviously *must* do if you think that we're going to believe your excuse of 'someone must've got their addresses wrong' on the subject of the controlled delivery we carried out on your address this morning.'

'Was it my name on the package?' I asked while trying to display confidence mixed with arrogance, despite fucking bricking it, like I was.

'And you think that will be what gets you off the hook with this? That it wasn't your name on the package?' The second one butted in and laughed, his partner joining in.

This, I admit, was a bit unnerving because *that* had always been, I'd assumed, the get out of jail free card. How could someone be prosecuted for something like a delivery when it wasn't in their name *and* they were then seen to DECLINE the delivery *due* to it being the wrong name on the package? It had never seemed like anyone could get a conviction out of what you'd have naturally classed as mitigating.

The two detectives seemed to have a completely different idea to mines, however.

'No comment.' I said even though we weren't strictly being recorded. 'And anyway, where's my lawyer? Isn't you two speaking to me in here *without* him kind of like, illegal? I'm sure a couple of fine and upstanding officers of the law, like you pair, wouldn't dream of operating outside of the rules.' With this not exactly being all 'on the record' I was probably risking a dig from one or both of them for my sarcasm but that aside, I had a point about the lawyer.

'Your lawyer's on their way but we felt that it would be beneficial to you in terms of getting you on your way if we sat down with you as soon as possible, isn't that right, Crawford?' One of them patronised or, at least, tried to.

'Well I appreciate you both looking out for me, I really do, but I'm not saying a single thing until he arrives.' I told them straight and had fully intended for those words to be the last ones that I spoke to them. Bill, the older officer out of the two of them sat and sneered at me, almost with a face that suggested he couldn't believe that I was standing up to the two of them before sparking up a reek and getting to his feet and taking himself for a wee walk around the interview room.

'Maybe we don't need you to open your mouth at all, lawyer or not, smart arse.' The younger one smirked at me while reaching to his side and opening a drawer and pulling out an evidence bag. My iPhone X sitting inside it.

Considering the phone was locked and there was not a chance I was giving them the password to it - at least until advised so by a lawyer - I was hardly what you would call panicking at the sight of what I'd already seen taken from me when I'd arrived at the station and been processed in.

I didn't see any point in antagonising the pair of them any further so decided against telling him just how not arsed I was about him being in possession of my phone and waving the bag in front of me.

'One thing I just don't get, though.' I heard from behind me from the one walking around the room. 'You obviously knew that something was going down. You refused the package and - before we'd even arrived - had destroyed all your computers and hardware, yet not your phone?'

Fuck, that was *way* too much to explain to him, had I wanted to, which I didn't.

'No comment' all he got back in return.

'Yes, I'm sure you don't' The younger one sitting in front of me laughed while opening up the bag and taking my phone out. It all sort of happened quite quickly after that, mainly because I never thought coppers would be capable of the depths of the behaviour that the pair of them lowered themselves to.

I was too busy trying to work out why he had taken the phone out of the bag - and focussing on him - to sense that the other one had walked up behind me, reached his arms around from the back and grabbed me in an almost reverse bear hug of sorts.

Understandably, I thought that this meant the other one was going to give me a bit of a going over. Not that he looked capable, mind. Even while someone was having their hands metaphorically tied behind their back.

'Let's see where your *no comments* get you now, smart cunt.' He said, reaching over towards me while holding the screen of the phone closely towards my face.

Now I got what was going on. The cheeky bastards were trying to take advantage of the fact that they wouldn't *need* to obtain the password to my phone, just my face.

'Now you can officially start to struggle, if you like' I heard the voice say in my head because one cast iron nailed down shut guarantee was that if they were to get access to my phone then the whole thing was completely fucked. I struggled as much as I could while subdued in the way that I was. While the copper was holding my arms tightly into the side of my body that meant that my head was free to move up and down and side to side. Fucking lucky my head never fell off some of the gyrations I was putting it through to avoid being caught still for a second.

Realising it wasn't working, the one in front of me with my phone shouted for his colleague to change tact and to grab my head for a second and hold it still for him. Which he did, fairly successfully, despite my free arms now reaching behind me to thrash out at him.

'Perfect, keep him still.' The younger one said while trying to hold the phone adequately positioned enough to match up with my face. Then exploded in frustration when I usurped him by simply closing my eyes and opening my mouth wide to invalidate the Face ID facility. It had been one of my major moans about Apple and this whole Face ID tech that they'd been boasting about - that it didn't work when you had sunglasses on - but, fuck me, that 'flaw' didn't half save the day there in that interview room.

'Open your fucking eyes,' shouted the one with the phone - more in desperation than any real attempt to get me to do as told - while I continued to swivel my head around as much as I could.

If it hadn't been such a deadly serious moment for me personally I'd definitely have been pissing myself laughing due to how farcical it all was.

Fuck knows what the scene must've looked like to my lawyer when he walked into the room and found us all in this struggle. For the record, though. He couldn't have walked in a minute sooner. It really wasn't a good look for the Lothian and Borders detectives. To be caught in the act both questioning a suspect out-with the rules set out by law *and* illegally trying to obtain access to a suspect's property.

When the door to the interview room opened we all froze. The coppers *and* me.

'Am I disturbing you here, chaps? I can come back later if that suits?' Harper Finlayson - my go to lawyer and, on occasion, absolute hero - said sarcastically in his own cocky way of announcing to the detectives that he had now arrived.

The one behind me instantly let go of my head while the other - still sitting at the desk facing me - meekly put my iphone onto the table. They'd both been busted and - from their actions - fucking knew it. It was a beautiful thing to witness.

'Oh, Detective Inspector Billy Burchill. How good it is to see you again

'Harper.'

The copper - who had been on his feet - offered my lawyer a brief hello and nod back.

'And we haven't met before, Crawford Ardwick, I understand?' Harper set about taking control of the room, like he always did. Lothian and Borders' finest must've fucking hated the man which, obviously, meant that he was shit hot at his job.

'Pleased to meet you.' The young guy at the table replied back to my lawyer. You won't be thinking that in five to ten minutes time, I thought to myself, which wasn't too far off the mark, actually.

'So before my client and I have a chat, since you're both here, can you bring me up to speed with matters? On what grounds do you have my client on for you to have secured a section forty nine to gain access to their phone?'

I wished I'd had fucking *access* to my phone just so that I could've taken a photo of both their coupons at this question, such a picture they both were. The pair of them looking back at Harper with faces that looked like they'd been caught with their hands in the biscuit tin.

'Ok, judging by the blank looks I'm getting it's fair to assume that you *don't* have a section forty nine approved. Oh my that's a little naughty of you, isn't it? That and the fact that I arrived to find you questioning my client *without* myself being in attendance. Well you haven't exactly covered yourself in glory, here, have you. Even if my client *is* guilty - and from what notes I have so far it looks highly dubious that he is - good luck getting any charges to successfully stick, not when it appears that you're carrying out *more* illegal acts than the person you're trying to charge?'

I couldn't let it out but I was breathing a massive fucking sigh of relief inwards now that Harper was there and in charge of things. It certainly wasn't the two fucking bizzies running things, anyway.

'Now if you could please do the decent thing and allow me and my client some time alone, like we *should've* had before you started your tricks. And oh, before you go. You should know that me and Stewart Fredrickson play golf every Sunday morning at Muirfield and make no mistake he'll be hearing about the conduct of his detectives this morning when our next tee time comes around this weekend.'

I didn't know who Stewart Fredrickson was but from the look on their faces, they *did. A*nd it looked like the prospect of it had scared the living shite out of them. Almost as if Harper Finlayson *was* their gaffer they both filed out the room and left us to it.

'Fucking morons, they honestly make it too easy at times. Where's the challenge, I ask, Paul? He said this while surveying the paperwork that he had in front of him in relation to myself.

'Ok, *you* tell me what's going on. Better I get it from the horse's mouth and remember, Paul. I can't fully help you if you don't tell *me* the whole truth.'

There wasn't much to laugh about but I couldn't help have a little giggle at Harper taking me through his little spiel that he did the last time he'd come to my aid, and the time before that.

As always with him, I gave him full disclosure. That the Ching *had* been meant for me but that there was no proof, other than inside my phone. I explained that it was more a stroke of luck that Debbie had destroyed my laptop and computer as that would've been a treasure trove of evidence had it been something that they could've worked with. Their reaction - back at the house - when they found the destroyed laptop and desktop lying in the spare room was 'almost' worth getting into the shit with Debz in the first place to have her destroying my hardware.

Then again, all swings and roundabouts because Debz was more than likely going to move on to destroying my fucking *limbs* when she eventually saw the mess that the police had made of our house when she got home from work later on in the afternoon. Because if there was one thing I could've promised you, it was that I wasn't going to have it spick and fucking span by the time I - hopefully - got out and made an attempt at cleaning up after them.

You could only clean up so much, after all. Not much Mr Shine is going to be able to do about beds and sofas that have been slashed open with Stanley knives, to offer but one example of the carnage the bizzies had left behind.

Harper - as a lawyer - always did have a way with words that put you at ease. Wouldn't have been a stretch to see him representing murderers and him leaving them relatively chilled about matters even though they'd have known that they were facing a long time behind bars. Just the general tone and confidence, aura, actually, that the man had about him.

After listening to what I had to say, in addition to the legal speak / police shite that he had printed off in front of him he assured me that it was going to be fine and that they had nothing substantial to charge me with, other than the quarter of Kush that they'd found. Something he said they would make an absolute point of charging me with when they had to deal with the facts that they would get no further charges out of all of their day's efforts. A quarter of grass possession charge was something I could deal with, especially when matched up against a potential three *kilo* Ching importing / intent to supply charge.

He explained to me that it was only due to the weight involved that the bizzies had managed to get the warrant and that even then it was exceptional circumstances. And that the officers leading things would *have* to get something of substance to back up receiving such a warrant. Sixty pounds - as in currency paid for, not weight - worth of Cannabis Sativa is not something that would fall into that much required *substantial* category.

'We'll get the two of them back in here and get your interview over and done with and we should have you out of here within a couple of hours, ok?'

Don't get me wrong, *of course* I was happy to find my lawyer looking at things without any kind of concern or worry as far as yours truly. As far as he was looking at things, they *had* nothing which meant they would *get* nothing. It's just that by being released, and without charge, *that* did not mean an end to any of my problems. Or, technically mines, Drummond's and Hammy's.

On the contrary, like. Now the problems could *really* begin.

Chapter 10

Hammy

'GO ON YA LITTLE FUCKIN BEAUTY'

Old 'Reekie' Walker shouted, fist pumping high into the air and face an almost crimson shade to it from all the shouting he'd been doing from his chair as he watched 'Ringer of Spring' romp home ahead of the pack in the four forty five at Kempton.

'Did I not tell you, son? Eh? Eh?' He said after dialling down on the lack of composure and turned to me. He fucking *did* as well. Told me that he'd been watching the horse at other meets leading up to Kempton and the word was that its owners were ready to let it open itself up for that particular race.

Obviously, I just took this as fantasist jakey talk from someone that you can't even sit or stand close to on account of the foul stench that they are always in possession of. *Pre* race I'd have had to have had a fucking screw loose to have listened to the cunt. Watching my own horse - *this, that and the third* - come in a disappointing second last only serving to rub my nose in things watching old Walker doing a wee old man's jig up to the counter to collect his winnings. His antics making pretty much everyone inside the bookies that afternoon smile, apart from myself.

Hadn't come remotely close to a win that afternoon and if it hadn't been for fucking bad luck then I'd have had no luck at all. Mugs game, as they say but I generally only ever *feel* a mug on a day like that. The kind where it feels like you'd be as well taking the contents of your wallet and just finding the nearest drain and just shoving it down there and saving you the time.

You think I sit for hours on end inside a bookies alongside the clientele like old pishy smelling Walker because I enjoy the ambience of the place?

'AHHHHH SMELL THAT, HAMMY, SON? THE BEST SMELL YOU'LL EVER COME ACROSS, THE SMELL OF MONEY.'

He shouted across the shop at me while wafting his money underneath his nose. The fact that he only had three tenners in his hand meaning the thirty quid was doing some extremely heavy lifting when it came to an indicator of showing a display of wealth.

I suppose though, to someone like Reekie Walker, that kind of wedge *is* a windfall and sometimes I need to remember that kind of stuff.

'Aye, you enjoy it, pal.' I said graciously, semi pleased for the fact that *he* was so pleased. Even so, I couldn't resist with the follow up of 'Just thirty quid more for you to waste in here before you leave for the day, eh?'

Which, as wide as he maybe thought it was from me or if I was seen as a killjoy, I wasn't incorrect with that statement. Daft cunt had pissed it away over the next three races. Much like myself who had ended up on quite the remarkable streak of not even managing to pick a horse to even fucking place, all day. If you'd went into a bookies and placed a bet on *that scenario* happening the odds you'd have given would've been the like that you'd have been able to buy Edinburgh Castle if you'd wanted to. Which I wouldn't, like. Wouldn't fucking stay there if you paid me. Imagine all the tourists knocking on your door all times of day, eh? Fuck that, I'd be fucking scrapping with cunts all day everyday.

Like with lots in life, you really need to have the ability to know when to say when and gambling is no different, maybe even *more* applicable considering it's often your bank account - and its contents - that are at stake if you don't pull the trigger on your day and recognise that it just wasn't meant to be.

I wasn't quite there *yet* but was at the part of the afternoon where I was now 'thinking' about pulling the plug which equals not pulling the plug for at least another couple of - nothing more than - *Hail Mary* bets to try and reduce the deficit that you've been left with over the day.

I didn't even get to the point of wasting any more of my hard earned before Drummond came rushing into the place. Himself being averse to the ways of risking what is your money in the attempt at *increasing* it by taking some from *another* person. Clearly he was looking for me. I'd seen him before he saw me and the cunt was like the terminator, scanning a room for his target.

Once he saw me he was in no mood for warm salutations.

'Why the fuck aren't you answering your phone, you fucking bam?'

I had got so much into my losing streak that I hadn't looked at my phone in hours and - as always - it had been on silent. Who even has their phones *off* silent these days? The amount of different sounds for different notifications that you get across a day you'd go off your fucking nut having to listen to that shite. I know they say that you can tailor all of that stuff to meet your own individual needs but who the fuck do you think I am, like? Steve Jobs? I just need my phone to take and make phone calls, same with texts. Complete opposite of Drummond and Hummel with their insistence on always getting the latest one that comes out.

I mind when Hummel got the iphone with that Siri on it for the first time and he was trying to show it off to me and the fucking thing couldn't even understand what he was saying. Just told the cunt that aye I was impressed and to put the fucking thing back in his pocket again.

Same with his new one with the Face ID on it. Tried to show that off to me when we were sitting in a beer garden and it didn't work because he had his fucking shades on. Aye, very good, mate. Technology, eh?

I pulled my phone out of my pocket to see that I'd missed calls galore from Drummond.

'Aye,' he said with a disapproving look knowing that I was seeing evidence of why he was standing there with a right torn coupon on him.

'Listen, we need to fucking go, lad. We're in a *lot* of fucking trouble.' He urged me, not really bothering to stop and wait on my reaction, assuming that I was going to pick up on his urgency and follow suit.

Like I'd already told these other two, it was a shite situation we were in but there was no need to be getting heavy stressed over who we were owing the dough to. I know they were both a lot more freaked out about things than me - and by a country mile - but I was sticking to my position in that for all we knew we could've been dealing with some cunt that didn't have the power and or energy to even lay a glove on any of us.

That all to the side though for a moment. Drummond - on the whole - was a pretty chilled boy. Never got fazed by much and if there was one of us that you could have handed Paddy Power your money on keeping their cool when everyone around them were losing it, it would be Drummond.

So with that in mind, I didn't quite like the look of extreme panic that was written all over his face that he was staring back at me with inside the bookies that afternoon.

Fair play, once he *explained* what had all taken place over the day - while I had been relentlessly pishing my money up against a wall - I understood *why* my friend was struggling to maintain any modicum of calm or decorum.

'So what the fuck are we going to do, then?' I just cut to the chase having sat in Drummond's Golf passenger seat - while we sat in the car park in front of the bookies - and been told of Hummel's morning and afternoon and what it now, obviously, meant for the three of us. Ninety (nine fucking zero) thousand pounds of debt and with no drugs to sell to recoup and repay.

Obviously, if this was just some daft kids on the other end of the internet then the ninety could've been fucking ninety *hundred* thousand for all that it would've mattered. On the flip side of this though. If I was the one out the three of us who was wrong then while being in debt to some heavy people for over twenty k would've been quite concerning then *ninety* would've been, well I'm not even sure my vernacular is up to scratch enough to truly describe things, but it would've been *very* fucking dangerous.

'I'll think of something, I always do, don't I?' Drummond said looking across at me from the drivers seat but his face was hardly exuding confidence.

Don't get it twisted, we were *all* in the shit with this latest development but I couldn't help but spare a special thought for Hummel, even though it was the very *last* thing he deserved from a person, like myself, who had repressed a hell of a lot of urges to put the cunt on his arse over the previous few days.

What a few days for *him* though? Starting from his breadknife finding out about him and that girl online and up to now, back at a house that the police have turned over while having to deal with the head nipping he'll undoubtedly be getting from Debbie over the state of the place while *still* being nowhere near to be 'over' what had happened at the start of the week. And in between that he's got it on his head that he both lost us our money to pay the vendor and then doubled down on his fuckery by turning our three boxes *away*, when it was right there in front of him in a postie's hands. Not that the boy would be judged over that move, considering he had around twelve bizzies waiting to storm the place the moment the package was *in* his hands.

Nah, he did the right thing. Even if it *did* leave us in the worst kind of spot imaginable. As less flavour of the week the boy was with me, he was still a mate and neither Drummond or me would've wanted to see him banged up and serving the - not inconsiderate - years that three kilos of Cocaine would've brought him. Saying that, though. The head nipping that he was most likely taking - from Debz - right at that exact moment - as I sat there in Drummond's GTI - was probably of the scale that most likely was leaving him fucking *wishing* he'd been put away on remand to sunny Saughton.

'And what about our German connect, then?' The question had to be asked sooner or later while we sat there so I thought I may as well get it over with.

'What about them?' Drummond replied but just continuing to stare straight ahead out of the car and out onto the row of shops in front of us, like he was answering me but lost in another thought.

'Well, what they're making of the fact that they have sent us sixty thousand pound's worth of gear that we didn't even *receive*. Do they even *know* it's went tits up? Will they even *care?* I mean, like, I order a pair of trabs from Adidas and the postie doesn't fulfil his obligations and bring them to me? Well a scenario like that? Adidas either sort me out with a refund or send me a replacement pair of trainers. Do you think our supplier is going to be so keen to provide customer service in the same way with an online order gone wrong?'

Obviously I didn't actually need an answer to my very last question. No question about it, it would be shifted over to us.

Drummond just laughed all self depreciatingly.

'Oh aye, I'm sure they've got their pickers at the factory rushing around trying to make sure a replacement three boxes are shipped out to Hummel, pronto.'

He was evidently in agreement with myself that there would be no cavalry coming and that we'd be out on our own from here.

'When he got out and told me what had happened I told him to get in touch with the German to say, well, lie actually, that the delivery hadn't arrived yet. To say absolutely fuck all about what had *really* happened and to just more really send an *innocent* email simply letting them know it hadn't arrived yet. Maybe won't work, like but you'll never know if you don't at least have a go, eh?'

He left me thinking of that Wayne Gretzky quote where - and I'm paraphrasing the cunt here - he said about you having ride all chance of scoring a goal if you don't take a fucking shot in the first place.

'And no word back from him or the German yet?' Pretty much the only other thing that I could think of that was worth knowing at that point. I already knew enough and didn't exactly like much of it. Actually, *all* of it.

'Nah, not yet but that boy's got some major problems to deal with, like. Said that the bizzies turned the house over, went totally over the score in some ways, stuff they didn't need to do like emptying all the open food products out onto the floor, knocked a hole in one of the walls saying they suspected it had been hollowed out. That's only the wee portion that Hummel was able to tell me about. You know what Debbie's like at the best of times, eh? Throw in what happened to him at the start of the week and *now* he's got to deal with her coming home from work and finding her house looking like fucking Beirut?' I think right now, as in today, there's fuck all more any of us can do about things and we're just going to have to wait and see what correspondence comes back from Deutschland.'

Drummond had now seemed to have calmed down a bit from when he'd stormed into the bookies and looked like he was accepting things a bit more.

'Until I hear back from Hummel I'm just going to have to treat things as if we're due someone approximately ninety thousand pounds inside the next two weeks, have *no fucking gear* to sell to make any money to pay it back and that from this moment on I need to be looking at *alternative* ways of us bringing the coin in.'

When it was as stripped down as that and clear as day it really spelled out just how so very fucked things were.

'Ninety thousand, inside two weeks, with no product to sell to any cunt? The only 'alternative' *I* can think of is that the three of us pack our bags tonight and never look back again.'

Turning the ignition and sparking the car into action - and my cue to get back out so I could return to the bookies to lose a wee bit more money before calling it a day - he looked back at me without a hint of a smile, even one at his own cost and replied.

'I've had about fifty different ideas today when it comes to getting us out of this situation, all of them bad. *Yours* is the best one I've seen yet.'

Chapter 11

Detective Inspector Douglas McCadam

'Well you two made a complete James fucking Hunt out of things today then, aye you may well both stare at the floor.' I tore into Burchill and Ardwick, now fully abreast of how today's "meticulously" planned controlled delivery of a large amount of Cocaine in Pilton had gone. Even by my explosive standards, I was fuming with the pair of them, absolutely bloody livid.

All those resources used, the crimes that - no doubt - went unnoticed while we were dicking about wasting our time on something that (apparently) promised so much and provided us with nothing other than egg on our faces and threats of action brought from a nuisance like Harper Finlayson over what he claims he saw two of my detectives doing with a suspect.

There had been better days at the office and I wasn't for sparing the two members of the team who had been the driving force behind things from the moment H.M.R.C over at Edinburgh Airport had got in touch with us over a package that had been intercepted by them.

'But, gaffer? The intel was solid. Not only did we have a case of importation of controlled substances *and* to an address of someone already known to us as being involved in drugs in the city.' Young Ardwick tried to pipe up. The much more experienced and wily Bill Burchill - who knew better - stared at his partner with a look of contempt and shake of his head, which had been well earned.

'WELL IT COULDN'T HAVE BEEN *THAT* FUCKING SOLID IF THE SUSPECT WAS BACK OUT ON THE STREET WITHIN HOURS AND YOU TWO DAFT CUNTS FACING GROSS MISCONDUCT ACCUSATIONS OVER YOUR ACTIONS WHEN YOU *HAD* THEM IN CUSTODY.'

I rose to my feet and pounded my fist on my desk, accidentally knocking my mug of coffee over some paperwork. This enraging me even further with me booting the bin - sat at the side of my desk - and sending it flying across the room and just missing Ardwick as it crashed against the office door. Immediately I regretted my actions as while - as their boss - it was my right to lose the plot at my employees, when they'd earned such wrath, you can't take it too far otherwise you just look like a madman and, in general, make an absolute clown out of yourself.

'Misconduct?' Burchill asked. Notably only really taking a vested interest in things now that he was seeing that it was possibly going to impact on him personally.

'The pair of you with the boy's phone.' I replied without looking up while trying to mop up the mess that I'd just made over my desk.

'Oh, *that?*' Bill replied, almost sounding relieved.

'Bill? It's only ok to do that type of stuff WHEN THE BASTARD'S LAWYER ISN'T FUCKING WATCHING YOU.'

My moment of calm had been clearly just that. A moment.

Unavoidable, really, when you have a couple of inept reprobates - like Ardwick and Burchill - in front of you when you're already dealing with a serious case of red mist.

'I can only imagine the fucking mess you all made of the property as well and the potential claims that are going to be brought as a result. Fucking know you long enough Bill to know that when it looked like you weren't going to find what you were looking for you'd have started destroying the place and for *what*? A quarter of fucking Ganja? My son Kieran has probably got more sitting inside his grinder in his bedroom for fuck's sake.'

'With respect, gaffer we ...' Ardwick attempted to deflect but like fuck was I giving him the room to do so.

'Don't be surprised if you both don't end up with a suspension over this stuff with the phone, that lawyer's not the type to let things go. I've dealt with him enough over the years to know that he seems to take a bit of personal enjoyment in sticking the knife into us whenever the chance presents itself.'

I warned them but - in a man management way - decided to try and turn it into an advantage. Have the pair of them fearing for their jobs and they'd be sure to double down on their work and try and show me what they brought to the table inside our department.

The pair of them sat there in silence. Even Ardwick - and his inability of knowing when and where to shut the fuck up - remained silent.

'But you're not suspended *yet* and if - like you say - your intel is good in connection with Evans then if there's one thing that we all know sitting right here it's that by turning down a shipment of Cocaine of that size it's going to have started a ripple that will end in a tsunami. You two are detectives, go *detect*. Observe, spy, look, listen and see what you can come up with. A gross misconduct charge might not look so serious when you've managed to prove that it was in the line of dealing with one of the city's biggest Cocaine dealers.'

I sent the pair of them packing with - I'd hoped - a sense of purpose about them where they'd been given the carrot of putting right something that they had got so badly wrong.

Whatever the ins and outs were to the drugs - where they had came from, and sent by who, and the intended recipient that they were meant for - it was something that was now going to be impacting someone or even a group of people. A classic case of cause and effect, right there. By discovering the airmail package - and then informing Lothian and Borders - the combination of HMRC and Police Scotland had provided the 'cause.'

As sure as a Johnny Robertson goal in an Edinburgh Derby. The effect part - as the universe so dictates - would now soon follow.

Chapter 12

Hummel

Not my fucking problem, bro. I have PROOF from the carriers that your shipment both arrived in Scotland and that the delivery had been attempted this morning and that, and I quote the carrier here, 'recipient refused package.' Now I don't know what the hell went on this morning or why you refused to accept your delivery but like I said, that isn't my problem. I very graciously offered you a solution to the issue that you had. I cannot and neither should not have to help you any further. Now as previously agreed, you have two weeks, from today, to make payment. I will be in touch in a weeks time to see how things are coming along. And remember, you really do NOT want to let me down on this. Adios, amigo x : 4.47pm

After the day I'd had. If I'd been looking for any kind of sympathy then, evidently, I was looking in the wrong direction if I was searching for any from the man (group?) who had days before shipped me a hefty amount of Cocaine and was being told - well, lied to actually, - that it had not arrived yet.

Of course, it didn't exactly help matters that he was already in possession of the receipts that were confirming the arrival and "attempted" delivery to my house that day. Like any other delivery of gear from abroad from an online purchase. The day that it's due to arrive, you make sure that you're fucking there to receive it. Im-fucking-per-ative, like. Tell me anything else in the world that is more important that you need to organise that takes importance over being in place to take delivery of something - like a kilo of Ching - that you really *do not* need the postman having to take back to the sorting office for another twenty four hours. So the prospect of *three* kilos? Obviously I was going to be there for it and it certainly was not going to be a package that anyone at the address was going to be turning away when the knock from the postie came that morning.

It had only been the briefest of Telegram messages between each other and it wasn't difficult to spot that the 'dynamic' had changed between Arman88 and myself. Whilst fearing what the response was going to be - at the start of the week - when I'd had to fess up and admit that we didn't have the funds to square things up for the month - and being completely blown away by the proactive and helpful tact that I'd been greeted with - *this* was the exact response that I was now getting that I'd initially been expecting. It was just a few days later in coming around is all.

There was no further offers of help - and being honest, who would offer to give some cunt any *more* Ching when you'd already given them four kilos and not seen a single peso in return? - no suggestions that they would check with the carrier company for an update on the delivery, even if I knew that would've been a waste of their time in any case.

Arman88 *knew* before I'd even sent him that Telegram message that the delivery had been attempted. He answered back too quickly to me as we chatted for him to have manually checked the tracking. Replied to my 'it hasn't arrived yet' in real time with - paraphrasing the boy, here - a 'bullshit it hasn't, you just didn't fucking accept it when it got there' and called my bluff straight away.

Despite what Drummond had told me to say I'd never actually thought that it would've worked in any way but neither did I expect the vendor to be so on top of whatever deliveries he had going out to fuck knows where in the world each day that he would have known that this random Scottish buyer was talking complete pish to him which - when caught out - really is not a good look when it concerns someone that you are now in debt to ninety thousand pounds. Kind of blows whatever trust that you and the other may have had with each other and leaves you both in a bad place. Once again, not the kind of *place* that you want to find yourself in when you're in so much debt and to someone that - you would imagine - wont go through the standard legal channels when it comes to debt recovery.

I logged out of Telegram and attempted to get myself onto the dark web on my phone via that app that would've tested the patience of Ned Flanders when it came to *actually* getting yourself connected and then *staying* connected. After a bit of fucking about I managed to log in to the Feelgood forum.

I'm not exactly sure where the fuck I managed to find the chill from but once the dust settled that afternoon - well, *before* Debz arrived home from work and showed me that there had been various levels of anger that she'd been capable of showing that I'd never seen before *despite* being with her for so long and giving her 'plenty' of chances to show it - once I'd spoken to Drummond and given him the bad news, once I'd had a bit of a tidy up so that the place didn't look *completely* trashed for my other half walking through the door, once I'd communicated to our supplier that I effectively had not received the sixty grand's worth of product.

There really was no justification in it but once I'd done all of that and sat down with a much needed - and heavily loaded - spliff from the green that the bizzies had inexplicably missed when going through all of my clothes. A nice wee half q of Pineapple that had been tucked into my CP overshirt sleeve pocket that I'd last worn a few weeks before that, to be fair, I'd forgotten all about myself until I was physically being charged with possession of a quarter which had been sitting in my tub - hardly hidden - in the living room. It was only when I heard the amount of a 'quarter' mentioned that it led my mind into the fact that I'd been sure I'd had more than just that in the house. Finally remembering that I'd popped what was left into the side pocket of my overshirt when I was leaving Hammy's that night. Stroke of luck that they missed it, though. If you ever need a fucking joint then it's the moment you get back from the police station after they've raided your house. Facts.

Sitting there toking away on it while scrolling through the various threads on the forum I had an unexplainable feeling of chill and acceptance. There was *no fucking way …ON EARTH* that we were going to be able to pay back the money. Aye, we would be able to scrape together a wee bit from here and some from there, spot a wee hustle to capitalise on but that still wouldn't get us anywhere near to the outstanding figure, well not inside two weeks, anyway. There's some English Premier League players that don't even earn that type of wedge inside a fortnight so how the fuck were *we* meant to?

And *this* was why I found myself going straight for the forums on Feelgood. When you have accepted that you're not going to be able to pay back a debt to someone the best policy is to then do as much homework as you possibly can to finds out what kind of repercussions are going to follow as a result.

I'd already had a look previously - with regards to Arman88 - but it really had been just a case of dipping my toe in and having a cursory look and even when doing so it had been a case of looking at it from a completely different angle because *we* didn't and had never had any issues with the vendor so - as humans tend to do or quite possibly I'm just a selfish bastard - I'd looked at it in the 'not really my problem' kind of way before moving on and looking at something else online.

Now it *was* my problem, though. Which meant me reluctantly logging into the forum to have more of a thorough look at what the community had been saying about the vendor in recent times, even though word was that most of the negative comments about Arman88 were removed on a daily basis from any threads due to him having paid off the forum moderators. Some of the outspoken members of Feelgood and posters on the forum who spoke out against it would suddenly find themselves banned from the site. Like I said, it didn't affect me, so.

The comments that I *had* managed to have a look at - before being deleted - though, while not exactly as relevant at the time, were now feeling a *lot* more relevant.

The suspicions of which criminal gang 'Arman88' actually was and the power - as well as reach - that they really had behind the friendly chatty online persona that would answer each and every question that would fly into their inbox from all over the world each day and with a reply that made them feel relatable and almost - weirdly - as if they were your mate. That they were cool and friendly.

The quickly deleted comments accusing the vendor of some grim stuff when it came to how they dealt with customers when things turned bad.

The real problem about all of this is that it was all on the internet and - *especially* on an illegal online drugs marketplace on the TOR network - you never, ever knew if what you were reading was the truth.

Arman88 accused of chopping the hand off a buyer over a non arrival of a shipment, and the non payment as a result? That *could've* been a post from someone who had ordered something stupid like a gram of MDMA which didn't arrive, sending them online to spread lies online through spite.

That Arman88 was actually the Dutch police operating a honey trap? Quite possibly a grand plan to put buyers off from *another* Feelgood vendor so that the flow of business would be redirected towards them.

Arman88 had two bullets put in my best friend's head because he had only managed to pay three quarters of his debt? Possibly a troll who had bought a paltry amount of grass from the vendor and was pissed off that there was too many sticks inside it carrying the weight.

Arman88 had my sister raped because I didn't come up with the Ketamine batch on time that I had promised him? Fuck, that one was too gruesome for me to even attempt to make any excuse for on account of it taking a severely fucked up head to *make something* up like that.

Miraculously the app had kept me connected up to the half hour point, not that I'd found anything of note. Scrolling through - and reading - pages and pages of reviews and threads where I thought there would be relevance to Arman88, which - considering he sold pretty much *any* drug that you would realistically ever fucking need - was a *lot.*

It was almost hypnotising - as well as, considering my own predicament, nauseating - reading comment upon comment all singing the praises of the German vendor.

FAST DELIVERY + STEALTH DELIVERY = RAPID DELIVERY….. OF THAT SWEET DOPAMINE TO MY BRAIN!!! A+ ++ WILL BE BACK X

The enthusiastic comments from *Bexy78* who also appeared to have had their caps lock stuck as surely no one that happy about something could be so angry at the same time.

Arman's the fucking MAN. Why would I ever buy from anyone else when he has the dopest shit in town??? Until next time, bruh.

The endorsements of *Soopa_high_guy* who had he not been from America he really needed to have a word with himself about his vocabulary.

The BEST Cocaine on the dark web, surface web and even the other webs that I don't even know about yet.

Loopy_LouXxX

Received today and NOW I see why everyone talks about how stealthy the shipping is (taps side of nose) will update tonight after I've tried but the Mandy looks absolutely FILTHY ... just how I likes it!

Seshmonster842

Absolute FIYYYYYYYAAAAAAAAA. Bought an eight ball for the weekend for to share with mates. Six hours later we were all in agreement saying lets get ANOTHER eight ball!! I cannot say just how good this vendor's product is but the fact I've already reloaded with Arman88 should tell you all you need to know!

Not_A_Narc

It drained me to go through them all but I knew if I looked hard enough I'd find something, which I did. Even if the timing of it could have been a lot better. Reading through a thread that was discussing - but as the site rules dictated, wisely, not in any great detail - vendors and the quality of stealth that they used with regards to their shipments. How much effort did they put in to disguise what they were sending and what they did to hide the smell from within the package. Did they use Mylar sealed bags to get past customs? That kind of deal.

Tucked away inside this thread - which had only been started around twelve hours before from the OP - there was a lot of praise for Arman88 and how stealthy his shipments were and the high rate of deliveries that he could boast from feedback left on all his sales on the site. This wasn't even something that I would or *could* have debated on.

Earlier on in our business relationship he had sent me a batch of MDMA. Not a lot, just enough to sort out the young team who were going to that Patrick Topping gig at the Liquid Rooms. Think it was around twenty grams or something and had been an additional order to our regular monthly one that we always made. When I got the airmail package that day and opened it up I have to admit that the cunt had me proper baffled because inside the Jiffy bag was four fucking sticks of lipstick, and an *invoice* to go with stating that I had placed an order for four times 'Rossi Red.' It even thanking me for my business and that the company - which even had a cover name of 'Lovely Lips' - hoped to see me again soon.

I was fucking raging at first. Had never ordered any Mandy from him before but didn't expect to get bumped with four fucking lipsticks either? What the fuck was I meant to do with *them*?

Messaged him straight away asking him what the fuck he was playing it, kind of half hoping that he'd been just having a wee joke and that the *real* package was still on route.

'Ok, ok, ok what you need to do first of all is take a breath, calm yourself down, stop insulting me and go and pick up one of those lipsticks and snap them in half and maybe next time do not jump to conclusions, bro.'

The message I got back in return, leaving me fully chastised. And then when I snapped open one of the lipsticks and found five grams of MDMA carefully compressed inside the plastic casing, I was left feeling like a complete fanny. Have to say, though. I was in proper awe of the man from that day. To be able to disguise drugs so well that the person who is in possession of them doesn't even fucking *know* that they're in possession of them? Next level stealth stuff, like.

In response to all of these gushing and sycophantic type comments on the subject of the German vendor there was one reply from a member called *The_Grim_Pitta* who in all caps had replied with

ARMAN88 IS NOT YOUR FRIEND. PRIVATE MESSAGE ME TO KNOW MORE BEFORE THIS POST IS DELETED!!!

Obviously, in the kind of sit-u that I was in, this was an offer that I was left with not much choice other than to take them up on. Only this coincided *right* as Debbie arrived home from work to find the various 'alterations' that Police Scotland had made to her house, the ones that with the best will in the world I *couldn't* hide from her short of being given a couple of weeks apart from her, and Carol Smillie moving in with me for a bit.

Took fucking hours of her crying, shouting, moaning and talking before she calmed down although I'm pretty sure that was more down to a combination of working all day and then spending hours going radge at me and, eventually, tiring herself out rather than her anger subsiding.

Eventually I had managed to put a spin - that actually stuck - on things that seen us talking about how the place could've done with a bit of a spruce up anyway and with a likely settlement for the damage the police had caused we'd now have the opportunity to just go for it. *This* seemingly appealing to her and giving her something else to think about, decorations. Hey, she wasn't thinking about giving me grief, that's all that mattered, eh?

I waited until she'd went to bed for the night before getting myself back onto Feelgood. The app not really in the mood for playing ball with me and it taking a good hour plus of fucking around before I got onto TOR. With no idea who this member was or which part of the world they were even based I pulled up the thread I'd been through earlier - and had quickly bookmarked on my phone right about the time I heard Debz screaming

'OH MY GOD, PAUL. HAVE WE BEEN BURGLED?'

Finding the comment still there I wasted no time in clicking on the profile for The_Grim_Pitta and hitting the 'send message' button to.

I kept the message short but sweet.

Hi, seen your comment about Arman88. Need to know more. Hit me back please.

Wherever they were in the world they must've been operating under the same sleep patterns as my good self as I hadn't even chosen something to watch on Sky - just sitting flicking through each channel without really paying attention what was actually on screen - when I noticed that they had replied to my message.

What would you like to know?

Ok, I didn't know who this person was or if they could even be trusted but with them saying clearly in a comment about not trusting a vendor I thought that they might have been a bit more forthcoming *on* the subject when someone takes them up on their offer of info.

You said that he is not people's friend? How come?

His reply was a long one - and with how security conscious the private messaging service was on Feelgood it would disappear by the next day - which I screenshot for the benefit of replaying it back to Hammy and Drummond. It was horrifying reading.

They went on to tell me that Arman88 was not one person, or even just a small group of friends, not unlike the three of us in Edinburgh. Instead, it was a fake online profile for the *Hellbanianz* Albanian mafia branch that were based in Germany.

This was why the vendor seemed to have so much different drugs to offer, and in such massive quantities. It could only really have ever been through an organisation like Albanians, the scale that everything appeared to be on.

We exchanged messages back and forward - there on Feelgood - for around half an hour. The person wouldn't go into *why* they were blowing the whistle on Arman88 other than tell me that they were once in a position of knowing what was going on behind the computer and the Arman88 account.

The thing was, though. I knew for an absolute fact that a lot of what they were telling me was true. For example when they said about how while the Arman88 Feelgood account was marked as shipping from Germany the Albanians were also linked up to other families across Europe which would occasionally mean that when you placed your order to Germany you would *receive* your shipment from somewhere a lot closer to home than Berlin or Frankfurt. Something that had actually happened a few times where I'd placed my order one day and received it inside forty eight hours, without any foreign stamps of any kind.

Why are you so interested in Arman88 anyway?

The_Grim_Pitta asked as we were drawing to a close. Me now having completely been stripped of that whole 'acceptance' state of mind that I'd somehow managed to slip into earlier on that afternoon.

I'm due him / them a LOT of money

I replied, the words weighing on me far, far more than they'd had up to that moment when I'd had to think about it.

How much is a lot?

Four boxes 'a lot'

I messaged back, truly sickened by the level of debt things had spiralled to.

I'd been through a lot that day and you'd have forgiven me for thinking that the worst had passed with it almost midnight and - technically - a new day. I was wrong, though. Without a doubt that was being all gathered up and left waiting for fate to step in and me find The_Grim_Pitta that night where they would tell me just *exactly* who I, along with my two best mates, were into things with.

His reply back - and the last message that I would receive from him before he went dark again - enough for to kiss goodbye the chances of me seeing any sleep for the night.

Four boxes? Then please listen to me when I say that YOU SHOULD FUCKING PAY, and if you can't pay then I really do hope that you are good at hide and seek, my friend.

Chapter 13

Hammy

'Fuck, me! You would bring a tear to a fucking glass eye, you.' I laughed right in the cunt's face. You should've seen the state of it. Trying to slip into fucking tear jerk mode with me - of all people - explaining how the world had practically conspired against him which - in a knock on effect kind of way - had led to him not being in a position to pay me the one bag that he was due me and the business.

'But tell me one thing, Dynamo? Just what exactly does your gran going into hospital for her second hip replacement have to fucking do with why you don't have the money for me?'

I didn't want to appear the heartless cunt but the question was relevant, and needed asking.

Dynamo - one of the Muirhouse boys (named after an unfortunate attempt at cooking mini Kiev's when he was younger that went tragically wrong) that I had put to work punting our gear for us - was a complete mess, looked like the cunt had been up for days but I was guessing it was absolutely fuck all to do with his gran being in the hospital.

'Well, you ken how it is, Hammy, eh? Things take a back seat during times of strife, with the family, like. You ken what they say about blood and water, mate, eh? Some things have to come second during these unforeseen circumstances.'

'Are you trying to take the fucking pish out of me, Dynamo?' I asked in all seriousness. There wasn't any other explanation as far as I could see.

'No, no no, Hammy! Think I'd try something like that with you, mate? I'll have the money together in the next few days and get it to you. All cool and good, like, eh? You know me and my history with Davey McKenna, eh? Need to conduct my business like some crouching tiger hidden dragon style ninja, ken, mate?'

Now I wasn't about to tell this low level dealer about the current woes of his bosses and - in the general scheme of things - how this debt that I was chasing him for wasn't even what you could have called a drop in the ocean - when it came to the money we were due - but my attitude had been like those cunts from Tesco in that *every little* was going to help.

I had five others in the city (and two over the bridge in Fife) to chase up for the funds that were due to us - some, unfortunately for them, I was going to be asking for the money earlier than they'd have been anticipating but well, needs and must - and I wasn't going to be accepting *any* 'come back later' or 'give me a few days' nonsense from any of them.

And I *really* was not appreciating the fact that Dynamo - the biggest sniff head out of my crew and the one who was basically selling it just so he could get himself free gear - was sitting trying to blame his poor fucking gran on the reason he wasn't paying me when it was clearly fucking obvious that - instead of chasing up whatever money he had to come in - he'd had a couple of days of being 'on it' and was now sitting there at the other side of it with the absolute fear trying to get his head together. I can imagine that the very last thing that he'd have needed there and then would've been me nipping his head but well, that wasn't my problem. No room for sentiment in the drug game and *especially* when you're potentially scrapping for your life.

'So that's your final answer? That you don't have the grand for me?' I needed to get a move on as it was already going to be later on in the night by the time I'd chased down everyone and all the individual scenarios that were undoubtedly going to come along with them.

He stared down at his carpet, unable to look up at me.

'I'm sorry, Hammy. Totally am, like. Get it sorted ASAP for you though, eh? You ken you can trust me, mate. Haven't never paid you before, like.' He sat there shaking like a shitting dog, all nervy and shifty as fuck, like. He's normally a sound boy, Dynamo - bit of a radgey but still not even close to his big brother Boney who was otherwise being held at Her Majesties pleasure for manslaughter one night in The Gunner - but you know what Ching can do to someone when they don't know when to put the stuff away for the night?

Well fucking *obviously* I thought to that platitude, about never having not paid before. We wouldn't have been fucking standing there with each other if the cunt had bumped me in the past, above anything else.

'Fucking poor form, lad. Poor form indeed. All I ask is that you pay up on time, not hard for you to achieve and neither is it much for me to ask.' I started to lose my patience with him and it was coming across in my tone. I'd given him enough chances to come around and pay me but he just wasn't for taking any of them.

'And another fucking thing, as well. Since you let me in you haven't once asked me if I wanted something to drink. Some host you are, eh?'

'Fuck, I'm sorry, mate. I never thought, my head's all over the place with my ...'

'Aye, Dynamo, your gran, I know.' I butted in while he apologised to me for what seemed like the twenty second time in the short space of since I'd arrived.

'You wanting something, aye? To drink, like?' Dynamo said getting up to his feet.

'You know what, lad? Aye, make me a cup of tea will you?' I replied. The tea would probably only be reaching the cool enough and drinkable stage by the time I would be on my way. I never wanted a cup in the first place. It was the one thing that I knew would keep him in the kitchen for a couple of minutes.

Soon as I saw the back of him going through to the next room I sprung to my feet and - with one eye on business and one on the noises coming from the kitchen I had myself a wee snoop around Dynamo's living room. Checking in drawers and cupboards and in the - near fifty, I'm not fucking joking with you - pockets of his Superdry jacket. Nothing.

'YOU WANTING A PENGUIN AS WELL, HAMMY?'

He shouted through from the kitchen and getting a reply shouted back of the affirmative. Who's turning down a fucking Penguin? I thought to myself that I'd scran it when I was heading down the road to my next stop.

I heard the noise of the tea spoon hitting the inside of both cups and knew I was almost out of time. The only other thing that managed to enter my line of vision was a Bell's whisky porcelain style water jug. Like how I imagine was used in pubs years ago. It looked so out of place in amongst anything else in the living room but, to be honest, if it wasn't sitting inside some working men's club then it was always going to look out of place.

'AHHHH FUCK, MUST'VE EATEN THE PENGUIN'S. JAFFA CAKES ALRIGHT INSTEAD, AYE?'

An update on the biscuit situation was shouted through from the kitchen.

'AYE, EVEN BETTER, LAD. GOOD FOR YOU, AREN'T THEY? JAFFA CAKES, LIKE.'

I replied while crouching down and picking up the water jug to have a look inside it. I'd hit the fucking jackpot. Even from the quick thumb through of the notes that were sitting inside it that I'd managed to count through there was more than enough inside there to square me up. There was also half a dozen grams of our gear sitting in there although - with Dynamo on one - I wasn't sure if that was his Robin van Persie or if it was intended for sale.

Whilst I was happy that I'd now be spared a return trip or have Dynamo coming looking for me I was even further bammed up over him telling me that he had no money, when he clearly fucking *did*.

I placed the water jug back down where it had been sitting just in time for him to walk in with the cups of tea and a packet of Jaffa Cakes tucked under his arm.

I hadn't bothered even attempting to get myself back in the sitting position that Dynamo had last seen me in when leaving for the kitchen. Now that I knew that he had money I wasn't going to even bother playing this stupid game with him anymore.

'So, just one more time, Dynamo, because I'm a busy bastard today. You're absolutely *sure* that you don't have that bag of sand for me? Maybe lying down the back of the couch or something like that?'

'Fuck, wish I did, mate. Would save me a bit of stress, like.' The - confirmed - lying bastard said. Actually managing to look me in the eye while he even said it that time. The fucking nerve.

Because I was already on my feet and very visibly becoming animated, he wasn't ready for what followed. Walking - in no particular direction, back and forward, side to side - about the room I left Dynamo sitting there with a stunned reaction as I bent down to the side of the TV and picked up the Bell's jug and pulled out the wad of notes that was sitting inside it. A couple of grams of Ching coming out along with the notes before dropping to the ground.

'SO WHAT DO YOU FUCKING CALL THIS, YOU LYING WEE BASTARD?'

Acting on impulse is not always the advisable move for someone to make but it's all I'd ever known as a young adult and beyond. And *that* is why - with one hand grabbing tightly onto the bank notes - I took the water jug and threw it at him. Before he could even move it had cracked off his forehead and bounced back off, falling to the carpet without a single piece of it - so thick and heavy it was - breaking.

It was nothing more than an impulsive and angry reaction from me. I hadn't *intended* on hitting him on the forehead like that but fuck me, if I 'had' then I don't think I'd have been able to achieve a more perfect throw than what I'd just pulled off.

I'm not sure what he wanted to express first. The very real pain that taking a heavy water jug to the head brings or the pain that money can sometimes bring you.

'AHHH YA BASTARRRRD. Fucking hell, Hammy. That was fucking sore.' He screamed out. Bringing his hand up to his head and checking for any blood which - to be perfectly honest with you - I was astonished there hadn't been any.

'Aye well, you know all of that could've been easily avoided if you hadn't tried to lie to me.' I replied - unrepentant - waving the stack of notes in front of him.

'Please, Hammy. That's not 'your' money, mate? That's where Clair keeps our money for the month. Bills, rent and food and that, eh?'

I was listening to what he was saying, not that it pressed pause on me counting out the notes on the coffee table in front of me until I got myself to the magic number.

'Here's an idea, then.' I said as I was folding up the thousand pound and preparing to hide it away in my special compartment I had in my socks for 'collection day.' Whilst there wasn't many in my neck of the woods that I wouldn't have a square go with, you still can't be too careful, especially *our* neck of the woods.

'You're due me a bag of sand, correct?' I did not hang around for his answer which was not something that was up for any debate. 'So I've just made life a *lot* easier for you because now you don't have the hassle of having to pay me back as now you're only due *yourself* the money. Should make paying it back real nice and smooth, like.'

I laughed as I picked up the cup of tea to have a quick wee sip before leaving.

'Oooh, that's hot' I remarked automatically before quickly putting the cup back down again.

In no way in a position to do anything that was ever going to come remotely close to 'stopping me' from taking the money from him, he sat there felling all sorry for himself.

'You've ruined me, here, Hammy. Absolutely hung me out to dry.'

'Please,' I sneered back at the cunt, trying to now appear the victim.

'No, D, you fucking ruined *yourself* and once you start thinking clearly you'll know that and anyway, unless I'm missing something - and you were *also* lying about having collections to make and that you were going to pay me back in a couple of days - all you need to do is go outside your front door and start chasing the cunts that are due you money. What's your fucking problem, eh?'

I knew fine well what his problem was, and it wasn't that far removed from mines for the day. After being on a Ching bender for a couple of days the *last* thing in the world that he'd have wanted to have been doing would've been going out and trying to find the type of people that don't want to be found, those that owe you money.

Normally at time of collection I would then be talking of 're-ups' and when they would be taking place but with Dynamo being such a broken individual at that precise moment. Thousand pounds out of pocket and a golf ball sized lump that was already starting to make its presence felt on his forehead, he never stopped to ask. And I definitely never bothered to tell.

I left him sitting there along with my barely touched cup of tea as I got myself into gear for hunting down target number two. Jock Rafferty. Someone that had been due a couple of Gs for quite some time but me and Jock had been old pals since school and while I might not have been so quick to show as much patience with the Dynamo's of this world when it came to being paid back me and *Raffs* were all good. But all debts need paid at some point and - unfortunately - I'd now been put in the position where I was going to have to force the issue a bit. Wasn't exactly looking forward to it but this was the life that we'd all chosen and I couldn't remember any cunt ever telling me that it was going to be all sunshine and lollipops.

As I was leaving Dynamo's block - at Gunnet Court - and just as I was getting out the lifts at the bottom I bumped into a couple of plain clothed bizzies. About fucking shat myself when the lift doors opened and the pair of them were standing there facing me. Must've just caught me off guard for a second because it was definitely a bit of an overreaction on my part.

One of them - Burchill - I was no stranger to over the years. The other one was a lot nearer to my age and not a face I'd seen before. Could've been doing without seeing either of them but *especially* Burchill. First time I was ever charged by the police was through the bastard. Absolute fucking joke, sitting in a mates with a 'teenth' of Soap Bar. Fucking eight pound's worth of Hash and this fucking jobsworth - Burchill - made sure that I was charged over it, even though the actual reason for the drugs bust had been to take down a wee dealer that I just happened to be hanging out at when busted. Of course, things had progressed in a *big* fucking way since those days and - between Hummel, Drummond and myself - Burchill was someone that we always had to be wary of in the sense that we could never have ruled out that chance that he might eventually suss out what the three of us were up to.

Sometimes you'd bump into him and he'd drop a wee comment here and there that pure fucked with your mind and had you having para attacks to fuck thinking that the police *knew* about us.

You could never, ever rule that kind of shite out, obviously, but we - more or less - had things watertight. The only way that the cunts were ever going to catch us *with* any gear on us was at the point of delivery - ironically, not unlike recent times - because after that it was gone again, within hours.

My uncle Eck - bless his soul - used to say that 'money was just a sight.' For us? Replace Ching with money. We only ever had the gear on us for hours at the very most before it was released out into the wild to specific parts of Edinburgh and pretty much every single acre of the Kingdom of Fife that required a livener in whatever shape or form required.

'Ahhhh, Mr Hamilton. How the devil are you?' Burchill said, as the pair of them both stood back to let me out of the lift. The appearance of me now something that had made them think twice about even getting into the lift that they had apparently been waiting on.

'Alright, Bill.' I answered back - matter of fact, like - as I made to walk past the two of them.

'Not so fast, Jim lad. Where's the rush?' Burchill said in that sickeningly superior tone that he thought he could talk to people in on account of him being a bizzie.

'Of all the coincidences, we were just talking about you earlier on this morning, weren't we, Detective Ardwick?'

'We were, indeed, Detective Burchill.' The other cunt in the dark grey Next suit replied.

A pair of complete and utter fucking wankers, without question, the two of them. You'd have came to that conclusion *just* from the patter of calling themselves by their official title when talking to each other in that way that you could tell they actually thought was funny but - in reality - was really fucking dire stuff.

'Mon, you. We're wanting a word.' Burchill said, grabbing hold of my arm in the gentle but - also - spelling out to you that you're going fucking nowhere type of passive aggressive way cunts who think they've got something over you can - and will - do at times.

'Now whatever did I do to deserve such a pleasure?' I asked, choosing to meet *his* passive aggressiveness with a slice of my own. Aye, of course, I could've moaned about why were they grabbing me and that I hadn't done anything but where really would that have got me?

The three of us walked from the lifts and out from the block of flats and into the daylight where I was then asked to empty my pockets then given the laziest of searches before we then moved onto Burchill proceeding to - what is it the Italian Americans always say in the films? - *Bust my balls?*

Thank fuck for my chunky sock / collection day system, though. Fuck having to lie my way out of why I would have one whole bag of sand on my person when randomly stopped, cause you fucking *know* they'd have had something to say on that subject. Instead, all they found on me was one's vitals. Bank card, phone and keys. Fuck all else you *really* need in this world, if you ask me.

Once they were satisfied, if *that's* the word that you could've used, correctly, that I didn't have anything on me that they were going to be able to use *against* me - and the exact point where in Road Wars and such programmes the "suspect" gets to walk away - Burchill ushered me towards their drab charcoal grey basic of the fucking basic models of a Corsa - It's like Vauxhall makes a special edition of bland *just* for Edinburgh's C.I.D and Drug Squad officers and detectives - and got me in the back of it while the other two took their seats in the front and both turned around to face me.

'James, we're worried about your mate, Paul. Paul Evans.'

Burchill said. Fucking hell, even put some kind of pretendy concerned face to go with it. Pitiful stuff. Still, though. This wasn't the best of news to be sitting in the back of a bizzie's car being asked about one of my best mates who has - quite obviously non coincidentally - recently undergone some "police scrutiny" in recent times.

'I've been mates with him since before primary school and there's not been a day since where I've not worried about the daft bastard. Leave it to me, lads, I've been doing it for years and have it down to a fine art. Go catch some bad guys or something, or whatever it is that you get paid to do.'

I couldn't resist a *little* bit of sarcasm to rear its head. They'd practically fucking taunted me from the moment those lift doors opened and I'd turned the other cheek but - protected by that beautiful feeling that a copper has absolutely *fuck all* on you - I really couldn't help myself.

I tried to turn Burchill's question into something of a light comedy moment to mask the fact that I had two plain clothed asking me about my mate, and, of course, business partner, and about *his* business.

'I'm worried that the boy's maybe gotten himself involved in something that he can't get out of. What is it Bono said about being stuck in a moment he can't get out of? Something like that? We thought that, as one of his closest friends, you might be willing to look out for him by telling us anything that we maybe needed to know?'

I was actually astonished, amazed, flabbergasted, - whatever the superlative you would like to choose - but mostly insulted at the sheer level of the balls to the man for him to think that he could get me to sit there and talk about someone, as close to me as Hummel was, to someone like *them*.

But what *really* were the pair of them up to, though? Aye, it's easy to be paranoid when you're deeply woven into the fabric of the drug game but - when it comes to the police - I always assume cunts like that know more than they're letting on and that when they ask you a question, the chances are they already *know* the answer to it.

Technically I wasn't sure if any of it was even strictly legal or not, sharing information with a member of the public in connection with a potential criminal case. Not that rules ever seem matter to coppers like your Bill Burchills of this world, mind.

He had sat there and assumed - or simply didn't give a fuck - that Hummel had already told me about his recent visit by an all star (aye, right) team of Police Scotland.

It was a heavy few minutes sitting in the back of the Corsa, though. Had the feeling that part of the reason they'd grabbed me was simply to see what my reaction was towards certain questions or pieces of intel that they thought they were feeding me.

Was really just a case of winging things until I was released from out of the back. A very fine line it was to tread though in striking the balance of saying very little but not *too* little. Having to act like a bit of a cocky prick at times because if I'd been too silent then that - in itself - would possibly have been a red flag to them. Pressure, like.

The crux of it was the pair of them emphasising that just because they didn't press any charges on Hummel - over the Ching - that hadn't meant that they had given up on the assumption that the delivery *was* for him.

'Tell you what, Detective Ardwick. If I was responsible for that much money's worth of gear and it never arrived I'd be - quite rightfully - a touch concerned about my immediate future.'

Burchill went again with the weak patter.

'Oh, definitely Detective Burchill. Someone somewhere obviously is going to be missing out on their share of the cake and I'm sure they're going to be a little prickly about it. Wouldn't you, Mr Hamilton?'

'Wouldn't I what?' I asked, just really trying to avoid answering the question more than anything else.

'Wouldn't you be a little *irritated* if you were left whistling in the wind for your payment as part of a Cocaine shipment?

While there were moments where I literally felt that it was *essential* that I act the cunt with them. This was one of the moments where it all came naturally.

Looking at Burchill with a face that I'd intended to have come across as 'Is your pal for fucking real?'and I think I achieved judging by the small smile that appeared on his face at me.

'You're asking me a completely hypothetical question - not to mention also academic - and are asking me to give my opinion how I would behave if I was involved in the drugs game. Tell me, Detective Ardwick. If you were part of a lunar mission stuck in a capsule hurtling to earth and there were risk of you and your crew burning up on re entry what steps would you take to save you and your crew?'

While Burchill face palmed, his colleague was asking me what the fuck being an astronaut had anything to do with what he was saying.

'Well if we're just throwing out random situations to go with occupations that we don't actually have I thought I'd have a go at playing too.'

Just keep fucking deflecting and stalling, I told myself, hoping that they were going to have had enough and the younger detective was going to step back outside and let me out of the back, which wasn't much further after that.

'Ok, ok clearly we're not going to get anywhere here. We just thought that you'd want to be looking out for your mate, is all.' Burchill interrupted, trying some of that absolutely telegraphed reverse physiology shite.

'Look, what do you want me to say?' I asked with - for the first time of being back there - a fair bit of sincerity behind it. 'Someone clearly fucked up somewhere and sent those drugs to Hummel's address but then - after that - you pair have come up with a piece of fiction that sounds like it could've been a plot line in Miami Vice!'

'Detective, Ardwick, please can you let Mr Hamilton out of the back.' Burchill said - while still looking at me, - having taken a moment to digest what I'd said to them and choosing not to react or respond.

His face, though? When I was saying about Miami Vice and that? Sometimes you don't need a person to say a single word to know what they're thinking and what I was getting back from Bill Burchill was that either he knew that *I* was talking a lot of pish and lying for a mate and quite possibly myself, or even worse than that.

That he knew that he *wasn't*.

Chapter 14

Drummond

'You think I don't know what you're doing, you daft wee bastard, eh?' I was engaging in the absolute futile exercise of talking to a dog. And *especially* a wee fucking rocket like our Staffie, Bowie.

He just stood looking up at me, tail wagging excitedly which was all the proof you needed that dogs - apart from the obvious few words that they're hard wired to understand from the moment that they can walk - don't have a fucking clue what you're saying to them. Call them a dick - but in the correct tone of voice - and they'll never appear happier.

I was having a dig at him over stopping to sniff and inspect something or other *every couple of steps* on our way around the woods. And *despite* my moaning he's looking up at me as if I'd just finished off telling him that when we arrived back home Bren was going to have a sirloin steak sitting ready for his supper.

Not that he'd have understood me, anyway, obviously.

Since Holly had been born I'd placed a self imposed ban on smoking in the house - if I hadn't then Bren *would've* - so always combined Bowie's last walk of the night with my last *spliff* of the evening. It was kind of a win win for the both of us. Well, it was once those grassing bastards moved in next door and I soon found that they were the pathetic types that would call the police because they can smell their neighbour smoking grass. After that wee visit, Brenna got me told that I wasn't smoking it outside in the back garden from that night on. I think she had a wee bit of that post natal depression - after having Holly - because she was convinced that social services would come and take the baby off us because there had been examples of Cannabis use in the home. Tried to tell her that there's a *massive* drop off between cunts like me having a toke now and again and a fucking junkie when it comes to looking after your kid but she wasn't having any of it.

As a result, me and Bowie were good for each other. He got his walk and I got myself a nice final wee smoke to myself for the night.

We always had our regular route for our late night walk. Nice and simple and enough for him to sniff and pee until his heart was content - and me enough privacy to have a toke without anyone bothering me - squeezed into the kind of time frame that it would take the average person to casually smoke a joint.

That night, though I took him on a wee - not fucking wee at all - diversion as I'd seen Henry Will hanging about a wee bit down the road - saw him before he'd had a chance the clock me - and with him being one of the regulars that I supplied each month I really wasn't in the mood to have to talk shop with him, especially when the gear that he would've assumed was going to appear - like clockwork every month - was *most definitely* not going to be appearing. There would be a few that were going to be well put out when they learned that there was no Ching coming, no re-ups, nothing. I could care less about any of them but neither did that mean that they were going to be any less a pain in the derrière when reality started to bite.

I steered Bowie down the wee side pen that led into the woods, figuring that I would take him in a wee half circle and then out onto the main road and back home that way. Probably an easy extra half hour had been added to his walk and that's why I was getting so annoyed with his lollygagging and milking of things.

'You've already got a longer walk tonight, and you want to extend things further? Think I'm buttoned up the back, you.' I said pulling on his lead in an attempt to show who's boss but that's not an easy thing for an average sized adult male to do if a Staffie doesn't want to play ball. Fucking strength in their necks and heads, eh?

The woods was freakishly *active* when we walked around part of them and when I say active I mean that when walking out into that thick dark stretch of land, and at that time of night, you kind of have the idea that you're going to be the only one walking around there.

Well, you'd fucking *hope so*, anyway. Get it into your head that there's going to be cunts lurching around hiding behind trees and you'd never fucking go near the place!

Instead, we were only in there a few minutes - following the same trail that countless other dogs and their owners followed day in day out - before we came across a couple of teenagers that - were it not for the near on full moon - I probably would've walked past them and been none the wiser for it. The pair of them looked around thirteen or fourteen - didn't recognise any of them - and as far as any kind of boogeymen hiding waiting to pounce, then they weren't it.

'Gies a toke of your joint please, mister?'

One of them - with a keen sense of smell - shouted at me just as I passed. This slowing me and Bowie down as I turned to look at the pair of them while Bowie gave them one of his wee warning growls but I'm not sure if that was more to do with him just getting a fright when the wee cunt shouted out than anything else.

'Sorry, man. It's just for me and my dog.' I replied while taking a big extended toke. I blew the smoke out and carried on walking, feeling all chuffed with myself until I realised that it was probably one of the smartest and wittiest - considering the circumstances - things I'd ever said in my life and I'd said it to two wee cunts that probably weren't even *born* when that Kia Ora advert was on the telly, never mind remember it.

'Wanker' I heard the other one shout.

'Who needs hands when they've got your maw to do it for them?' I shouted back and immediately felt a wee bit embarrassed with myself that I'd lowered myself to even responding to a couple of wee fannies like that.

I kept walking, assuming that they wouldn't have been silly enough to want to make a mischief out of themselves by looking for any issues from the boy with the Staffie. And was right.

From then on it just seemed like it was one example after another of why I should've done anything *other* than went that route with Bowie. First of all I took my eye off the ball when he was standing having a good old sniff to himself and next thing the wee bastard is rolling around on his back, obviously picked up the smell of some fox shit. There's a *lot* I wont ever understand about dogs - and at times them licking their own balls is about the only thing I *do* get - but *especially* that fox stuff. The fuck anyone want's to smell like that?

I was still moaning away at him about how he was going to be fucking reeking until me or Bren - so me then - gave the little bastard a bath when - too concerned with lambasting a dog that cluelessly hadn't an idea what I was going on about - not looking where I was going my left foot managed to find its way under a massive tree root, tripping me up and sending me falling to the ground. Letting go the dog's lead and Bowie - not the most obedient of dogs at the best of times - taking the sudden opportunity presented his way to get some space between him and me.

'Don't you fucking do this, Bowie. Not fucking now.' I muttered to myself as I got myself up from off the ground again, already aware of the wet feeling on the knees of my jeans - and jacket arms and elbows - from where I'd hit the ground.

I'd heard the sound of him running - and the lead trailing after him - off to my right just about the same time as I was hitting the ground so thought the best idea would be to head off into the thicker woods and shout after him, like that ever seemed to help before whenever you were looking for the cunt, and that was generally in the daylight when you could have at least a chance of spotting him.

I shouted out after him which - alone in the dark - left me with a bit of an uneasy feeling that I couldn't really understand. Kind of like how by shouting out I was letting anyone who might be in the woods and in my vicinity know that I was there. Don't take it like I'm frightened of the dark and that, either. I don't know? Just the feeling of not knowing what was out there but me giving them notice that I *was*.

'COME ON, SON. I'VE GOT YOUR TREATS'

If it was a game of poker then I'd already showed my hand straight away by resorting to trying to coax him back by the sounds of his treat bag. With it being so quiet inside that patch whenever I stood still for a moment, I could hear him. Not that he was in any way into making an effort at returning back to me like what your stereotypical *man's best friend* would do.

Coincidentally I had on my Ma Strum 'Torch Jacket' which had come along with a wee flashlight as part of the coat and apart from the one time I'd taken it out to try - in my living room the day the jacket arrived - I had just treated it like the gimmick that I'd assumed it to be. If I want a torch I'll *buy* a fucking torch, same for a jacket, ken?

Despite it hardly being a beacon of light I figured that it would be a wee bit better than having nothing and that maybe even the light, in itself, would be enough of a distraction to have Bowie coming back in my direction.

Stopping again to listen, I did a three sixty turn while slowly trying to survey the small amount of distance that the torch would allow. He was near, and wasn't exactly being too discreet with the sounds he was making. Well, I *hoped* it was fucking him, anyway. To think of walking through those dark woods at night on your *own* and hearing noises like that then you'd definitely have a different spin on things.

Then I saw him and more importantly, he couldn't fucking see me. Looking in the complete opposite direction while he took a slash on a tree. Whether it was a *real* pee or one of his fugazi ones that he does just to keep out the house longer I couldn't have confirmed but it was enough to give me time to rush up and snatch hold of the lead while he was still on three legs.

Cue more - and at an elevated level - moaning towards Bowie and not one single fuck given by him. I'd come quite far into the woods to follow him and I wasn't sure if turning back the way was such a good idea but, also, In the darkness, until we emerged back out of this thick patch of woodland I wasn't sure *where* we'd end up if we kept going.

'Ah fuck it, lets just keep going' I said to Bowie figuring that eventually we'd hit some civilisation and get our bearings again after that. Fishing my hand into my pocket while praying that - to cap the night off - I hadn't done anything fucking stupid like drop my clipper when I'd tripped back on the public trail.

I hadn't and took enormous enjoyment in sparking up the half spliff that I still had on my person.

I thought that possibly my maps app would be able assist navigating me and the wee man out of the woods but we must've been deep as I was sitting with 'E' for my reception which pretty much meant - as far as being stuck in the woods and looking for any kind of assistance - that I was basically in possession of an iPod Touch.

Foiled with that we just kept walking while I hoped that Bowie and me weren't going to end up like Pauline Walnuts and Christopher Moltisanti in the Pine Barrens episode of The Sopranos. Hard times, that. Well, heavy. Bit of a difference though between woods in New Jersey - that are probably the size *of* a Scottish city - and a wee bit of woodland *inside* a Scottish city.

As we walked on, Bowie started to become a wee bit spooked by something but due to this being something that his supersonic dogtronic hearing was picking up, I couldn't tell what it was. Could've just been the sound of a mouse or something scurrying past us but it had got his attention whatever it was.

'What is it, pal? You hear something?' I asked him which got his tail wagging again while he tried to pull me in the direction that we had been going in anyway which was the most cooperative he'd been since we'd left the house, even if it was only unintentional.

As we continued I got the impression that the trees were becoming a wee bit thinner in the sense that you were able to see a wee bit further ahead than before. He was still straining at his lead and up ahead - which looked like it was still a wee bit in the distance - was the smallest of two red lights spaced perfectly apart, which I'd taken to be the rear end of a car.

'Good boy' I said, actually reaching down to give him a pat on his coat to let him know that he'd done good by finding what appeared to be civilisation. Even gave him one of his biscuits, so grateful I was to see something that suggested that we must've been near a road if we could see a car.

After that it was just a simple case of following the red lights. Is anything *ever* fucking simple, though?

As we got closer to the lights - and now able to see the dim white lighting that was positioned *above and centre* of the two red lights - I was able to confirm that it was indeed what I'd originally taken it to be.

By this point Bowie was like a fucking Bloodhound on the case, leading me towards the car, which appeared to be parked up in a wee bit of woodland clearing as there didn't seem to be much trees to speak of compared to the surrounding area.

It felt like the car was maybe only around a hundred and fifty yards - well, I'm guessing - or so away but still too far to tell what make or model it was. This further enhanced by the moon going behind a big dirty looking cloud which - in turn - reduced the vehicle back to being just blobs of light ahead.

Because of this - and with how dark everything was and, all focus was inevitably drawn towards the lights of the car - I didn't really know what was going on up ahead. And by the time I *did* it was well too late.

I'm not being funny, like. The whole thing fucking *scarred* me so much that - thinking back on it - my head is a bit fried when it comes to trying to recall it all, in the order that it went down. I kind of just get these powerful images and flashbacks on my experience that night and *none* that I could be doing with fucking having, let me tell you.

When we got close enough I was able to make out that it was one of those fancy Ford Focus ST's that was parked up. *Think* that's the correct model, anyway? The orange one, eh?

Straight away I connected things that *this* was that boring cunt from The Trap's - Leckie, the wank from the bank - car. On the rare occasion that the otherwise mono-subject boy spoke of something other than the bank it had been his car, private reg and all that shite, like any cunt even cared. You get a fucking private reg for less than a good jacket, so it's hardly something to be impressed about these days.

What the fuck was Leckie doing parked up in the middle of nowhere at - checking my phone - five to eleven at night?

The natural thought - and you could hardly have blamed me - was that the cunt was up to no good. No other reason than to find yourself there at that time of night. I was only there because of that reprobate of a dog of mines as well as - and I admit, which kick started the whole car crash of a dog walk - my unwillingness to hold a conversation in relation to the fact that we didn't have any gear to move to a dealer.

All of what happened next came out of pure instinct and - clearly - was not something that I left the house planning for on happening. Primarily things were led by the fact that I couldn't stand Grant Leckie. Neither did Hummel or Hammy and when it came to Hammy the fact that he hadn't glassed him at some point inside the four walls of The Trap was a minor miracle in itself.

Approaching the side of the car I fell into stealth mode, walking on all of the various stones, twigs and bits of gravel as if I was fucking levitating over it. Having already taken my phone out to check the time I took the thought that if Leckie was up to something he maybe didn't want any cunt to know about then it would've been fucking *gold* to catch him in the act, in a digital sense. Would probably give everyone a laugh in The Trap and - as an additional bonus - might've kept his mouth shut for a wee while so just as I was about to reach the driver side window, which was open, I shoved the video on and hit the red record button.

Complete darkness all around apart from the white glow from inside the Ford I pointed the phone towards the inside drivers side of the car - as I was reaching it - with one hand while keeping a hold of Bowie with the other. Once I was side by side with the car and able to actually see *into* it, though?

Well, as the now infamous fourteen second video showed. What I came face to face with was Leckie - eyes closed and head back against the ST Recaro seat headrest - sitting with a big smile on his face and saying

'Oh, that's fucking magic that is. Lick the shaft for me a bit.'

Camera then pans down from his face to someone giving him a blow job. Then you hear the bark from Bowie off camera which has the person immediately releasing Leckie's penis from their mouth and - startled by Bowie - instinctively look up - still got their hand around his dick, like - towards the driver side window - and me standing there with my fucking iPhone filming it.

And no judging here or fuck all but when I said 'person' I said that because it wasn't a fucking woman that was blowing him. No judging because people can do what they want with each other for all I care as long as everything's all cool with those involved and that. But Leckie was married to a girl - Janie Barker - who was in my Social Studies class at school. Actually fucking knocked me back in second year when I'd asked her out which made me laugh all the more when I'd heard who she'd ended up married to years later.

'Who the fuck are you?' The cunt says to me - with quite a bit of anger behind it - while Leckie's eyes looked like they were about to pop out his skull when he saw *who* was outside the car and had disturbed proceedings. From the light inside I was able to see his eyes almost explode first of all before the - up to that point very evident life that he'd had on his face - drain right from him. I was too shocked, myself, to have even been able to enjoy Leckie's reaction. He was evidently going to be scarred by this, but so was fucking I!

The fuck did I want to be watching two men in the woods having sex? Wouldn't have even have wanted to have watched a man and a fucking woman, either. Neither did Bowie who was now giving them both his trademark warning growl. He wasn't going to hang about and let any random cunt shout at his master, was he?

The last part of the video - and also involving stuff coming from off camera - basically had Leckie still sitting there with a broken appearance to him while the cunt in the passenger seat was trying to reach over to grab at me with one hand in an attempt at snatching the phone while - inexplicably - still holding onto Leckie's cock.

Just as he's doing this you then hear another *two* voices coming from off camera.

'What's the fucking score here, eh?'

And then almost joined on to that comment

'Aye, get a fucking move on. Standing here with my dick in my hand like, someone standing with their dick in their hand, sake, boys. I was told this was a good spot for action?!'

'IT'S THIS FUCKING BASTARD, HERE.'

The last thing you hear in the video.

The boy in the passengers seat reacting to the other voices and pointing from within the inside of the car in my direction while Bowie - spooked by the extra voices coming from the darkness - is going completely fucking crackers. It might have been the end of the video but it was just the *beginning* of the nightmare.

A mare for me, Bowie, Leckie but *mostly* the two fucking mincers that thought it would be a good idea to take it up with me and Bowie for ruining their wanks?

Can you believe that shite, eh?

'Haw you? What's your fucking problem, like?' The aggressive voice shouted out at me as the figure emerged from the other side of the car. He must've been there all along but we hadn't been able to see him because of how dark it was and - like I'd said, in a moths to a lightbulb kind of way - the lights of the car was the *only* thing of note out there. Then I clocked the other person - from the same side - appearing, shouting at me, and taking the direction of approaching from the back of the car, while his 'mate' was approaching from the front.

Are these pair of fucking bufties actually trying a pincer attack on me? *Mincer attack?* I thought to myself. Would've *laughed* to myself, actually, had it all not been on top in the way that it was. Not even ashamed to admit that I'd been a wee bit spooked myself by it all because if those two cunts had been standing there in the dark watching Leckie get a blow job then who was to say that there wasn't any other 'lurkers' out there?

Me and my trusted Staffie were really left with no other choice than to insert ourselves onto a level ten setting and just front up to the cunts, whatever followed next.

'Just where do you fucking get off on all of this? Just piss off and let us get on with things. We're not bothering you are we?' The one coming round from the bonnet side was shouting out at me and I'm not being funny here but even though it was dark he was still close enough for me to see that he literally still had his fucking knob hanging out of the front of his jeans while he shouted at me. I don't think there's anyone who could blame me for being a wee bit unnerved by this and taking my eye off the ball and due to this I completely forgot about the cunt coming round from the back of the car. Unfortunately - for him - he got himself too close, without my attention, and close enough to tap my shoulder while accusing *me* of being the *real* pervert because I'd been creeping around in the woods secretly filming people having sex.

Clearly not anticipating the hand on my shoulder I wheeled around and put my elbow right into his coupon. I actually didn't mean to do it and it had been the fright of feeling his hand unexpectedly on me - while dealing with other matters that were in front of me - that had caused a knee jerk reaction, of sorts. It didn't matter whether I had meant it or not but - and looking back on that night afterwards - considering all that was kicking off, it could have only ever looked intentional. Not saying I *wasn't* going to leather the cunt anyway, like but I still didn't mean to do it in the way that I actually done it.

It was that kind of a walk though, I suppose.

I've knocked this boy on his fucking arse, he's absolutely howling out in pain which I felt was a wee bit of over egging the pudding. When you're dealing with two people - and one on either side of you - you can only really look at the one thing at once though which meant that on seeing me send the boy to the deck with an elbow that Giorgio Chiellini would've given you a nod of approval and a flash of his trademark smile, this escalated things even further.

'RRRRRRIGHT, YOU BASTARD. I'M GOING TO FUCKING BURY YOU.'

The one with his cock out shouted and lunged for me. Still checking if the boy was going to get back up and react to me, I wasn't ready for the boy's lunge.

But Bowie *was.*

Meeting the boy's lunge at me with one of his own.

It was fucking chaos. The passenger seat boy has jumped out by this point - I assumed - to come and have a go as well but when he saw Bowie striking into action he thought better of it. The roar of the ST engine drowning out everything for a second as it started up. Leckie speeding off dangerously - in embarrassment - and not hanging around to see what the score was once the dust settled.

'AAAARRRRRGGGGGHHHAAA YA FUCKING BASTARD IT'S GOT MA FUCKING DICK AAAAAYAAAAHHH'

Thing was, he wasn't fucking lying either. I turned around and Bowie's got his head buried deep into the boy with each front leg placed high up on the thigh of each of the boy's legs.

He was trying to reach down and grab and punch Bowie to get him off but I reckon the pain was too much for him to be able to do *anything*. Or, any thing that would impact upon a Staffie when it has - quite literally - got the bit between its teeth.

All I could really do was pull at my dog to try and get him off the guy, but was that really the *best* idea to do either while Bowie had a grip on the boy's appendage?

'That was fucking out of order, I wasn't coming to fight you.' I heard from behind me while managing to squeeze in a quick glance over at the one who had been in the car and now left behind by Leckie who had definitely jumped out the car to start something but then - witnessing me and my dog in action - thought better off it.

'MA FUCKING PHONNNNE, BASTARD' He shouted after the the Focus which was now almost out of sight.

'Aye, you fucking stay over there, ya cunt.' I shouted at him aggressively, figuring it would be helpful if I'd had to deal with at least one less of them.

The boy who took the elbow? Well it clearly wasn't his fucking day - with one having been sparked out, one his blow job ruined and the other having his exposed tadger gnawed on by a defensive dog, was it *anyone's* day? - because when I pulled at Bowie to get him off the guy's cock I took a step back and - with my heel - slammed my trainer right into his face again. Him still on the ground from the elbow. I almost tripped over him, actually.

The sound of the boy's screams and Bowie's snarling and growling was the mix that would've provided a soundtrack to haunt you the rest of your days although, to be fair, there's about a hundred percent chance that it would've *also* been the kind of sound that would've been the stuff of *dreams* for a Rotterdam Gabber House producer.

It was fuck all compared to the shriek that followed next though, once I managed to free Bowie and put a bit of daylight between the two of them.

'AAAAAAAHHHHHHHHHYAAAAAAAAAAAA .... MA COCK, MA FUCKING COCKKKKK AWWWWW NAWWWWW .... FUCKKKKKKKKKK.'

He fell to the ground and rolled around screaming in a way that I doubt I'd ever heard an adult do in my entire life. And with good cause, too. His screams weren't without merit.

Bowie dropping part of the boy's knob at my feet - literally bouncing off one of my Forest Hills and onto the ground - and looking up at me as if that had been his *prime* objective when we'd set foot outside that night.

'What the fuck do you want me to do with it?' I thought looking back at him to the soundtrack of screams, moans and swearing all around us.

'Oh Christ, does anyone have a phone? That bastard's driven away with my phone in his car.' The one stood away from us was shouting. Felt a wee bit shit but there was no fucking way my phone was being used to call an ambulance and, *obviously*, not the police.

'You'll get the jail for this, by the way. You *do* realise that?' The one I'd elbowed and then accidentally kicked shouted up at me from the ground while - I think - the boy minus his knob had possibly passed out from the shock of things. He was definitely a lot quieter than the initial screaming that he'd - understandably - been doing.

This was serious stuff though and the boy was quite correct. It *was* something that you could see someone getting the jail for. Technically I wasn't the one who bit the boy's dick off but I was in charge of the dog, eh? Not much different when someone gets done for injuring someone due to dangerous driving and that.

But also, if something like this was all going to go down then fuck me, you'd have chosen for it to have happened in the darkness of the woods, and with complete strangers who weren't from the area and had - by the looks - travelled there because it was a 'known spot.'

Not known e-fucking-nough. I assure you.

'FUCKING FORGET THAT FOR A MOMENT. DO YOU HAVE A PHONE.'

The one from the car was now shouting at the pair of us. Finally getting one from the boy who was only now starting to get himself up and to his feet but making sure that he stood far enough back from me and Bowie. They both were. Having seen what my dog was capable of, I'd have done the same if I was a voyeur out in the woods watching men have sex and had just seen a Staffie rip the cock clean off someone else.

'Mon, Bowie. It's time we got moving again, don't you think, pal?' Despite everything, it was pretty funny to see him in a good mood with that happy wagging tail looking up at me expectedly waiting on us moving off again. Completely belying what he had just done moments before.

'You, you can't just walk off like that, as if nothing's happened.' Elbow guy said to me. What the fuck did he want me to do though, like? Help sew the boy's knob back on again?

Walking off was *exactly* what I was going to be doing, and at a brisk pace, as well. I was pretty shaken up by it all although not as much as the boy who was now definitely passed out while his cock lay a couple of metres away from him, but I wasn't as shaken up as to not be thinking straight. Thinking straight is what I *do*.

This - absolutely fucking mental - few minutes had all taken place in a dark woods with visibility at a low level so I was assuming that unless these cunts had been using night vision gear to watch the car sex with and I just hadn't noticed then good luck to any of them giving a description to the police of me because I'd have struggled to have done the same for them. I mean, I saw one of the boy's cocks closer than I did his face, to give you an idea of things.

'Your mate's cock's down there, by the way.' I said pointing down at the ground - and in my opinion - helpfully before me and Bowie hit the road while I heard the boy from the car screaming into the phone about an ambulance to the emergency services.

'Aye, just keep walking. You think you won't be found and charged for your HATE CRIMES. How hard you think it's going to be for the police to find you and that Staffie.' The boy that had taken my elbow - as well as boot - to the coupon screamed out after me as we departed the scene of the crime.

That making me laugh out loud as we walked.

Now I know he's *definitely* not from this part of the city, I thought to myself.

Chapter 15

Hummel

'So, in summary, we're fucked then?' Drummond said, cutting between all of the noise and hard luck stories that told of our collective attempts at finding a route out of this whole pickle we'd ended up in. Or as Hammy had alternatively put it, *I'd* put us in. I mean, the boy wasn't wrong, like.

'Aye, tell me something we didn't already know about a week ago?' Hammy said - reminding us that almost half of our time had now expired - although he really was making a tough job of looking like he was genuinely scared about things. This, probably because he wasn't. Even if he *should've* been.

The thing with Hammy, though? It wasn't like he didn't *have* any fucks to give, he did, like the rest of us all. It's just that it felt almost like he'd had *half* of his fucks brought out and executed in front of the *other* half, just to keep them in check.

While I was barely sleeping at nights - thank fuck for a wee Frankie Vallie in those times of need - Hammy looked like not one single thing had changed about him since we landed in trouble. Either that or he was just doing a better job at keeping a lid on things than either Drummond or myself were.

Pure heavy stress, like while he'd been more animated over Shrewsbury Town blowing his Saturday afternoon coupon by conceding a last minute equaliser - the day *after* my house had been raided, landing us in a world of shit.

Talking of sticking money away on something I'd have put a few quid away on Drummond coming up with *some* kind of a plan. Not to recoup the whole amount, like. Just enough - in the region of thousands - to buy us a wee bit of breathing space. Even a peace offering of sorts but then again, what the fuck did *I* know about any of that stuff? This was all new to us as things had been as smooth as a fucking Brazilian. Well, until they weren't.

Drummond was good with that stuff though. I'm not sure if the boy had ever got himself tested by those MENSA cunts to see what his IQ was but I'd have guessed that he'd score high. Actually, now that I think about it. If he'd ever had himself tested we'd all have heard about it, many times. Still doesn't mean to say that the boy didn't have a lot up top. Was invaluable at times when it came to taking a problem and turning it into a victory so to hear him say that he had fuck all in the way of ideas was a bit of a blow to the old morale.

We'd had almost a week to play with and when he was coming to us saying that he had fuck all then things were definitely looking on the bleak side.

'I've tried, lads. Been out hustling, meeting contacts and trying to make things happen but no cunt's biting. We picked a right good time to be on the hunt for other people's charity and you can rubber stamp that with a big fucking red CONFIRMED because I've spoken to *everyone.* You know when you've lost your keys in the house and you can't find them anywhere and you eventually reach the point where you start checking in parts of the house that you haven't fucking seen in years? *That's* where I'm at in my attempts at coming up with something, if you're looking for an analogy and for you Hammy, an analogy is a comparison between two things, normally for facilitation of an explanation or clarification.'

'Fuck you, fucking wide cunt.' Hammy's - on the face of things - aggressively worded reply not masking his smile back at Drummond.

Aye, it's good that with a countdown until fuck knows what - but it surely wasn't going to be nice - that we could still sit there and rip the pish out of each other like mates normally do when they're not under the threat of non payment of funds to a European drug importer.

'Seriously, though. That really *is* where I'm at. I'm checking in places that I shouldn't even be bothering but doing so because I haven't found my "keys" anywhere else.'

Sitting there and hearing about how far Drummond had went to try and get us somewhere I couldn't help but feel a bit guilty over the fact that I'd done barely fuck all in any attempts at recovering any money for the German, despite being the one who fucking *put* us in the position in the first place.

Fair enough, that wasn't really *my* area of expertise but it didn't mean to say that I didn't feel any less guilt about it.

'I've managed to get us around just over five bags, ken it's not close to it all but still.'

Hammy butted in but didn't get a reply as Drummond continued on his own path. The fact, though that we had Hammy sitting there telling us that he has five thousand pounds available to be used and neither of us even commented on it pretty much spelled out just how much debt we were truly in because - on another day - five bags would have been an absolute fortune.

'Know how fucking desperate I've landed this week, lads? I even made a trip out of Edinburgh to go and speak to Stetson at his garage over in the Kingdom that he has.'

'Fucking Stetson? Marky Letson? Cunt that used to own the car repair and MOT centre in Portie?'

Hammy asked, for clarification but already rubbing his face with his hand in a clear 'aye, we're fucked' visual display at the news *that's* how desperate we were.

'Aye, the very boy.' Drummond replied laughing at Hammy who clearly knew this guy as well. I didn't and had never heard Drummond mention him before.

'How the fuck does he have *another* garage? Is there not industry rules to stop cowboys like that from operating businesses?'

'Aye there probably is but I'm not sure they extend to stopping your breadknife from opening one up in *her* name.' Drummond tapped the side of his nose as if he was spilling some top secret inside info. Fucking insider trading and that.

'So why did he get his last garage closed down, like?' I asked Drummond, genuinely wondering what the score had been.

'Because he's a dodgy bastard, that's why!' Hammy decided to answer the question first.

'You know, Hamster? I'm not sure this boy is the first garage owner to be a dodgy bastard.' I answered back, almost sounding like I was defending this *Stetson* boy when the truth was I'd only just heard about him. 'Is it not normally assumed that if you're going to run a garage you're *meant* to have 'highly experienced at being a right shady cunt' at the top of your skill set?'

'Aye but there are levels to the game, Hummel, mate. And if we're talking consistency year in year out in fleecing both the customer - and insurance companies daft enough to put their client's cars in there - then this boy is like, a fucking Bayern Munich or something. Good place to go if you were looking for a no questions asked M.O.T, like but not so good if you're fucking Direct Line Insurance or someone and find your client's car's had lots of items charged to it that weren't even fucking damaged in their accident in the first place then aye, maybe not so good a garage.' It would've made for an interesting Trust Pilot review on the internet from Hummel, like.

'The fuck did you go and see him for, anyway?' Hammy asked.

'Well A. *Because we're fucking desperate* and B. Last time I knew him he always had bags of money kept in a safe and I mean B A G S. Think it was better for him that it *wasn't* sitting inside a bank, ken? So I figured maybe the same applied and that he would maybe be able to help out an old pal from the past. Figured that we'd throw him a bit of interest - since he's a businessman and that - and otherwise he wouldn't really miss it from his safe for a while. Obviously, the "while" that I was going to be telling him about was clearly pie in the fucking sky but what could *he* have done anything about it once he'd already handed the money over and we'd sent it to Germany?'

'And what did he say when you asked him?' I enquired although had already been given the 'spoiler' that it wasn't going to be anything positive.

'Could've been bollocks and just lip service from him but he said that he'd have genuinely helped me out but had just went away and sponsored a local junior team - proper vanity project stuff or if not definitely money laundering - for the season and didn't have anything close to an amount that was going to be of use to us. Fucking drove all that way but things like that have to go face to face, like. So aye, like I said. We're fucked. Have another week left but may as well have another fucking year - from where I'm standing - and *still* not pay ze German back.'

And I think that was pretty much the crux.

Hammy and me both let Drummond's words sink in for a second and when we were sitting there, waiting on one of the trio breaking the silence it was broken for us by the door to The Trap opening. Leckie - The banker - that rhymes with - came in along with that Aaron Walker, the boy that used to be a postie until he got busted that time dumping everyone's post in a skip and - instead - fucked off his round to go and play Fifa. It was even in the Evening Times and everything.

I can't really explain it too well but when they both walked past our table and up to the bar, Leckie and Drummond had what I can only really describe as a "moment." It was only really slight and if you'd been looking the other way you'd have missed it. Just something about the way that Leckie looked at our table and locked eyes with Drummond and the way my mate had quickly looked away again but kind of like he was edgy about even just being in the same room as the boy.

It passed and we continued talking, about the obvious. The *only* subject that we'd all spoken of for almost seven whole fucking days. I told the two of them that I was going to be receiving a "courtesy email" from Arman88 the next day and asked if they had any advice on how I should reply, if at all.

'Well you already know my opinion on things but you two cunts don't want to hear it so unless you plan on just ignoring the German and we then proceed right onto bumping him for the money there's no point in asking me for advice on which *tact* you might want to adopt.'

Hammy was out!

To be fair, I hadn't been asking *both* of them, even if it came out that way.

Now I'm not sure what kind of a lightbulb went off inside Drummond's head but all of a sudden - and pretty much the fucking *exact* opposite of how he'd been since he'd walked in the door of The Trap that afternoon - his face changed.

'Actually, I've just thought of something. Give me a few minutes, lads.'

He said before getting up and heading up to the bar.

Chapter 16

Drummond

'You'll not tell Janie about the other night, mate? She'd never let me see the kids again if she knew about, well, you know what I'm talking about, eh?'

For the *first* time in my life I was hearing this massive prick call me "mate." Funny the *timing* with it, though.

'Well I don't *want* to be telling her, Leckso. I hope you know that but me and her go back, maybe you don't know that, actually I'm pretty sure you won't, but anyway. I've known her for a while now. School days, eh?'

Now if I'd had one of those 'fact checkers' that CNN always has on Trump's case then their findings would have found that this was, of course, a lot of pish and that having been knocked back when I'd asked her out at high school I had retreated in embarrassment over it and - literally - never spoke to her again in my life. If she'd been able to even remember both my first and second name - all those years later - then I'd have been fucking flabbergasted.

Obviously, though. Admitting any of that would have relinquished a *lot* of the leverage that I held on the boy and when you're in the middle of shaking someone down, that would just be plain radge to cop to.

'You can see where it's a moral dilemma for me. Some spot you've put me in, lad.' I continued, turning the screw. *Righty Tighty,* I thought as I reeled the daft cunt in.

'On one hand I would *never* want to have anything to do with a family splitting up and a loving father, like yourself, being denied any rights to seeing their kids growing up, due to acrimony with the mum, you know what I'm saying? You really think that I want to have *that* on my conscience?'

I paused, just enough to give Leckie room to speak up, even though I already knew what I was going to go on to say, regardless.

'Well, aye, Drummond, that's exactly *it*. No one want's that on them, bairns growing up without their dad and the psychological impact it can have on some of them later in life. I can see why you wouldn't, mate.'

He was so thick - despite this apparent cushy as fuck job at the bank that paid for Focus ST's - he'd thought that here was me lining things up to give him an *out* when I was merely lubing the cunt up and getting him ready for entry. Metaphorically, like.

'BUT, Mr Leckie. There *is* an issue I have, morally like, in that me and Janie go back years and I'd have to get on with things knowing that I'd *not* said anything to her. You any idea what that kind of thing suggests, about one's loyalty? That they don't tell a friend something that a "friend" *would* tell them. Ken? Like what I saw the other night. That kind of thing could end up reflecting badly on myself. Now tell me, how that would be fair on me, eh? I was only taking the dug out for a walk And look at what I get roped into, fuck's sake.'

Emotionally I was pulling him all over the place but that was my exact *point*. I wanted him broken, a mess and full of nothing but complete and utter submission to what my plans were going to be, when I hit him with them. If he wasn't fully 'persuaded' by the end of our chat then it was going to all be for nothing.

And letting him know who was in charge from the first couple of minutes seemed like a good place to start.

'Awwww, Drummond. Dinnae, please. It .. it … it was the first time I'd even tried anything like that, swear down it was.' Leckie panicked at me flipping things back around to the subject of telling his wife what he'd been up to. Speaking to me but having to be also aware that no cunt else in the boozer could hear us.

I'd carefully managed things so that him and I could speak in relative privacy. This *wasn't* for the purposes of sparing the blushes of Leckie in any capacity. No, it was *purposely* because I couldn't risk anyone else in the pub finding out about what he'd been up to in the car park because, well, blackmail doesn't really work too well when the thing that the person has to lose - that you're holding over them - has already been lost.

I admit, I hadn't told any of the lads about what had happened out in the woods because it was such a fucking mental story to even sit and tell anyone and I hadn't got my head around things myself. Proper traumatising stuff, like. Plus, it had all went dangerously wrong and somewhere in Scotland - I presumed the East Coast - there was a man who was lying in a hospital bed with the best case being that he'd managed to have had his cock surgically sewn on (although the mess that Bowie had probably made of it with his fangs I'd have imagined it would've been a challenge and a half for the doctors) and the *worst* case being that the boy might not have *made* a hossie bed and bled out before any paramedics could reach him.

I'd had a wee look around the internet when I'd got home the night of the walk. Didn't exactly type in "what happens to men who have had their cocks bitten off by a dog" or nothing but had managed to find enough information to suggest that it was a dangerous area to be wounded (as all men would tend to assume) and that in some cases the amount of blood lost resulted in death.

I wasn't tripping over the potential for any knock on the door from the bizzies over it but had been scanning the news in case I could find anything as it would've been the exact type of news worthy story that you'd see put out for the public.

Once I'd had the brainwave to *utilise* Leckie to my advantage I was immediately glad that I'd decided to keep things to myself, instead of showing the boys the video as had been my intention when I'd hit the record button back there that night. All it would've taken would've been one comment from Hammy or Hummel when Leckie had walked into The Trap and the gig would've been fucked before I'd even *had* the idea.

Instead, however. Things were *exactly* where they were meant to be. I was convinced that I had Leckie right where I wanted him and it really was a case of *when* I wanted to reel him in and get it all over and done with.

'You, sat in your car, in the middle of nowhere while a guy gives you a gam, with men standing in the shadows watching you? Leckie, mate? You should be looking to keep me as one of your closest confidants and assets so don't try and take me for an absolute fucking muppet. Aye, first time you tried it, of course it was. Fuck's sake.'

I had leaned in closer to deliver this. The two of us face to face like those Smith and Jones boys that used to be on the telly.

'I'm just a bit confused, like. Curious is what it's technically classed.' Leckie admitted in a surprisingly - and unwanted - open and honest way.

'Woah woah, mate. I don't want to know about that stuff, eh? I'm not fucking Doctor Ruth, eh?'

I cut him stone dead right there. I was in the process of attempted extortion, not to talk about whether someone was gay, straight or bi fucking curious.

'And you know where curiosity got the cat, Leckie?'

He sat there in silence almost as if he'd been getting a lecturing from his gaffer or something, rather than a softly and carefully worded piece of advice. The coupon on him, I actually thought he was going to burst out crying there in front of me.

'Come on now, pal. It could've been *much* worse.' I tried to lift him up again, like a mate would do. Like this *pretend* mate *was* doing.

'Aye, right? How come.' He replied looking like the absolute essence of what someone who's feeling sorry for themselves would look like. Cheeky bastard, eh? Aye, fucking sorry he got *caught* more like.

'Well, imagine if it was some of the other cunts sat around us inside here?' I invited Leckie to have a look at the clientele that was sitting drinking alongside us.

'If it had been one of *them* the whole pub would know about it by now, never mind your Janie.'

The fact that it had been a few days and *no one* had said a thing to him - not even a single "cryptic" comment fired his way - clearly showed that I hadn't told anyone, yet.

It was time to turn the screw on him.

'Of course though, Leckso, that could all change with one slip of the tongue from me, or if my conscience gets the better of me and I tell your breadknife, couldn't it?' If my subtle - although in my opinion - but effective wording hadn't gotten through to him the tone that it delivered across to him *would've*.

Time for "mates" was now over and it was for the best - and to give Leckie a chance of making the correct decision - that he knew it.

'Awwww you wouldn't do that though, Drummond, eh?'

He pleaded with me, now apparently sussing that his actions - from out in the woods - were now in the process of being used against him.

'Well, that all depends, eh. Actually, all depends on *you*, Leckie which is not a bad position to be - all things considered - because who better to rely on, to save your own skin at a crucial point in life, like, than your own self. Tell you what, lad. If I'm ever in a similar situation - not fucking likely though, mind - I'd take that outcome, every time.'

'What do you mean, like?' He asked even if he really did not want to hear what was in my plans for his future.

'Well, I was thinking that if you were prepared to do me a wee favour then I would be prepared to forget about everything I saw the other night, and trust me, Leckie, it would be a fucking pleasure to.'

'It shall never be spoken of again, mate?' I assured him. Well, as much as you can *assure* someone when you've already insinuated to a person that you're about to blackmail them and just before you tell them *what* it is that you're using them for.

'YOU TWO LOVE BIRDS ALRIGHT OVER THERE?'

Hammy shouted over from the table to us while not having a remote clue over how much his words unsettled me, given what I knew that he did not.

'ANOTHER PINT, DRUMMOND, AYE?'

He followed with, already stood up to go to the bar for him and Hummel.

Without saying anything I just gave him a nod and a thumbs up, figuring that Leckie and me weren't going to be sitting together for much longer anyway. As far as my short term plans were concerned, they involved leaving him shell shocked and having one more pint with my mates before heading back to the house for my tea then do all the stuff with Holly before we put her to bed.

'W w what you talking, like? You wanting money off me or something?' He took a stab in the dark although maybe not so much a stab because doesn't it *always* come down to money? He was actually quite close, but *also* miles off to what he would've been thinking.

'That's *exactly* what I'm looking for, Leckie.' I affirmed giving him a mock smile and raise of the eyebrows in approval of him finally getting on board with what was going on.

He tried it, as well. Can you believe some cunts? Actually tried to shine the light back at me and make out that just because I'd sat there and pretended to be someone with a bit of empathy towards him - and that it was all just a show to build up to extorting him - that *I* was the one in the wrong?

'Are you really trying to get out a moral compass here, Leckso? I'll get my one out too if you like. Maybe I'll shout Hammy and Hummel over and they can all see our compasses, eh?'

This, enough to change his tune back.

'But I dinnae have any money, Drummond. Ken what it's like with a wife, kids, house and bills. You've just had a wee one yourself, you'll know what it's like, eh? Fuck, the repayments on my Focus alone ..'

It was pitiful for to see a man - like Leckie - try his psychological shite out on me. If he'd actually known me he wouldn't have even bothered trying having already known that I wrote the fucking *book* on all of that stuff.

'Oh aye, I concur, there.' I could hardly disagree with him. Having a bairn *is* fucking expensive no matter if you pick orders at Amazon, work in a bank or are a drug dealer. The price of everything is the same for us all, eh? Just that some can afford stuff a wee bit more than others and with how my "employment" situation was a little iffy I was going to have no choice other than to be lumped in along with the "the others."

'Here's the best part though, Leckso. You wouldn't have to hand over a single penny of your *own* money.'

I wanted to see what his reaction was going to be to this as - reading between the lines - I had felt that it was quite obvious what I was hinting towards, but wanted to see if he had picked up on this before I went all in and told him of what I needed -

demanded, actually - of him to stop his secret from being released.

I didn't particularly feel too good with myself sitting doing this with someone. Definitely not one of my more prouder moments I can assure you but when it is time to sink or swim you make your choice and you get on with it. If you fanny about and don't make a swift decision then you will - obviously - drown.

The *real* irony being that until Leckie had walked through the door of The Trap that afternoon I'd already pictured me, Hummel and Hammy all floating lifelessly at the bottom of an ocean. The three of us - with a week to go - weren't drowning. We were as good as already drowned.

Thank fuck for risky outdoor sex, eh?

'Oh, no. Surely you're not suggesting that ..'

Leckie asked with a frightened look on his face.

And oh, I certainly *was* suggesting what he was thinking. Now I'm not saying that this was all some grand perfectly laid out plan and was - in fact - a lightbulb moment where I'd had a spur of the moment idea that - even as I shared it with Leckie - I still hadn't fully worked out all the details yet and was quite literally - at times - making it up as I went along.

He sat there while I explained to him what it was that I needed him to do and how, if completed, it would be his safe passage out of this nightmare he was now a part of.

I didn't know if what I was suggesting was even *possible* but felt that I would've been able to detect whether it was or not purely by the response from a man who was fighting for his life. And that included any attempt from him to try and bullshit me. At the end of the day, I was the one who had bluffs that could all too easily have been called - if required - and it would've served the lad well to have remembered that.

Across this exchange. Leckie was told that if he wanted my silence on things he would have to transfer the sum of ninety thousand pounds to an account that, having just formed the idea, I was yet to decide on - before I quickly changed it to ninety five. Figuring that after what I'd witnessed the other night I deserved a wee bit of compo money - before close of business in one weeks time.

'I cannae do that, Drummond man, for fuck's sake. I'd get the bloody jail for that if I was caught.' I couldn't quite believe it but his eyes were even *wider* at this news than they'd been when being disturbed by a man walking his dog while he was getting a blow job in a public car park.

'Well don't be going getting yourself fucking caught then, eh?' I tapped the side of my head.

'You're the banker here out of the two of us, mate. You'll know what to do. Jesus, half of your fucking patter in here revolves around telling us what the wages are of any fitba player you see up there on the telly on Sky Sports. When you're getting paid millions a season do you honestly think that you're going to miss ninety bags of sand, all the money you've got flying in? Wages and sponsorship deals and that.'

It all sounded so simple, the way I was framing it.

'Drummond? Mate? I can't just be dipping into customers bank accounts and making withdrawals from them. There's an electronic trail, Barry and besides I'm *pretty sure* someone is going to miss that amount of money from their account, no matter how rich they are.'

'Well that's just going to be the chance that you're going to have to take, my friend. Be creative, like I said. You're the banker, here, figure it out.'

You could tell that he was considering it. Sitting there trying to work out the possibles and if - what I was asking - *was* possible. Then, just as I thought I had him, his tune changed.

'Actually, hang on a second here. You're asking me to commit theft of over *ninety thousand pounds* from my work. Serious stuff, Drummond. Jail time stuff. Now that I'm thinking a wee bit more clearly. This is just your word against mine here. I'm not stealing money from an employer over that. Don't get me wrong, like. I'd rather you *didn't* tell anyone but if you do then I'll just deny it.'

So sure of himself I almost pitied the boy for the hammer blow that was now going to come his way. I don't know what his recollections were from the other night but he was definitely forgetting one key element.

I pulled my phone out of my jeans and went straight for the camera roll on it. Having to scroll past a couple of pictures of Holly - and one of Bowie with an empty bag of roast beef Monster Munch stuck over his mouth and nose - I found the video that I hadn't come close to going to look at since I'd taken it.

I turned the sound all the way down and readied myself for pressing play before holding the phone screen up for him to look at.

'I've turned the sound off, for your discretion, like'

I pressed play.

Over the course of the short video he was left with a look on his face of a fitba player whose team had just scored a last minute winner, only to then *lose* an injury time goal with the very last kick of the ball.

'You were saying? Something about my word against yours, aye?'

'You absolute bastard.'

Fair play to Leckie, I'd have probably said the same had I been in his seat. Because of that, I let it fly. Choosing instead to hammer home my advantage.

'Ok, here's what's going to happen.'

I set out the ground rules and ones that were *non* negotiable. If he bit then all good and maybe I'd have found us a way of securing the funds when all hope had been lost. If he *didn't* then I - and the other two, still oblivious to my efforts - wouldn't have been in any worse off a position before me and Leckie had sat down at the table. If he'd knocked me back I wasn't even going to *do* anything with the video, probably. I was going to be having my own real issues to deal with to be worried about getting involved in revenge porn or whatever it's called.

'You're going to give me your number and I'm going to text you the financial details in a few days time or so. I don't care if it's all in one payment or a fucking hundred of them. I just need ninety five thousand to be in my specified account by next Friday close of business. You do as you're told and that video you just seen will be deleted from my camera roll. Fuck, I'll even *let* you delete it yourself from there.'

'And if I don't, or more specifically *can't*.' Leckie asked, wisely trying to find out the pitfalls that non completion of his mission would bring about. I could've just hit him with the old 'wouldn't you like to know' and let his mind run amok for a couple of days but I wanted him to *accurately* picture the scenario of what his life was going to be like if he didn't embezzle the required funds for me.

'Well by next weekend pretty much everyone that you know - and *thousands* of people that you don't - will all have seen that video. Facebook, Twitter, Insta. Fucking BEBO if it's still going? Obviously - and thinking of Janie, here - I'll do the decent thing and show her it first, so that she doesn't suffer the shame of having to be told by someone or simply coming across it on her time line. I'm not a monster, Leckie.'

'You utter bastard, Drummond. Karma will come for you hard on this.'

'Your number,' I ignored him.

He reluctantly gave it to me and was told that I'd text him soon - already thinking that for this kind of deal I would have been better off with a new burner, which I'd need to go out and get - but that him and I were going to be the best of buddies over the coming week and that we'd be in *lots* of contact with each other.

Standing up after that - and choosing to leave what was left of my pint and go straight to the fresh one waiting on me over at our table - I gave Leckie - who was just sitting there with his hands over his face - a wee squeeze on the shoulder and told him that 'it would be alright and not to stress' even though, admittedly, I'd given him *plenty* to be stressing out over.

With a mind that was racing at a hundred miles a second and quite literally getting myself by from moment to moment I now knew that *next up* it was going to be Hummel. It hadn't been mentioned by any of us but it was notable that while he had been the one who had left us in this mess he hadn't actually been seen to have been making any attempts at actually *rectifying* things, other than remind us that we needed to pay our dealer because of all the things he was learning about them. Hammy had been running around daft bringing in what was in the scheme of things to our debt, a pittance. I'd never rested for the best part of a week before finally running out of ideas. Hummel had done fuck all.

Now it was his turn to put in a shift.

If we were going to be able to set up a bank account using fake identification then it was going to require him - and his dark web contacts - for us to pull it off.

Sitting down beside the other two I couldn't help but look over at Leckie - still sitting on his own instead of rejoining his mate - and remark to myself just how wonderful - and confusing - life really can be.

And how - in a blink of an eye - someone's life can dramatically improve while another's can go in the opposite direction. Me and Leckie - sitting at separate tables as well as different ends of the spectrum of happiness - a classic real time example of this.

Chapter 17

Leckie

Awww WHIT? An absolute mess of the worst proportions, and worse still. One of my own making. Deep down I'd had a feeling that it - me and the Grindr meets - was going to get me into trouble, but that was one of the *turn ons* about it all, the *danger* of it. The thrill of being caught by a stranger. By fuck I wished I hadn't now though and had just stayed in the house and looked at Pornhub like any normal person. Deleted the app from my phone that same night when I got home but - by then - it was too late. It was a situation that couldn't just be deleted, like you *can* do with a smart phone application.

I was just a wee bit curious about that stuff, you know? Had only watched straight porn before, like. Then one day I'd ended up accidentally - no honestly - landed on a video of two men. That I never switched it off straight away and, instead, kept watching it, even got actually aroused by it. Well, that was a wee bit confusing to me but it led me down all kinds of rabbit holes after that while *exploring* things. Just started off by watching a few videos but that then led to exchanging messages back and forward with other bi curious men on specialist websites. All ending with me being told to get myself on Grindr. Which I did and I couldn't honestly believe the score on there.

From an adult teen I'd been used to the whole intricacies of trying to get off with someone - a girl - where you'd spunk almost your whole week's wages on buying drinks and that and even then you wouldn't have been guaranteed anything at the end of the night. Some you'd have to take out a good few times before getting any action off them where you'd have found yourself better off just paying for a prossie at the start and saving yourself money, while getting a ride off someone who actually *knows* what they're doing.

This being not how things went on the app. No joke, I'd only installed it - and set up an account, just out of interest more than anything else, like - around half an hour when I got the first notification, from a stranger, asking if I was free to meet. Fucking appeared on my phone right as I was sitting having supper with Janie watching Line of Duty. Was pure flapping when she asked who it had been. Lying, I told her that it was a goal notification from Live Score linked to a coupon that was already down from earlier on in the evening.

I ignored the first "invite" that night. And the next three that I received, the day after. And the four I had sent to me the day following *that*. Either people liked my picture and profile or they were just desperate for sex with another man and weren't too fussy about who they had it with. It really was like shooting fish in the proverbial.

The first time I *did* reply to a message? All a case of Pandora's box after that. The guy - messaging me - had asked if I'd had a free house, which for a man with a wife and two kids was rarely *ever* going to be a possibility. As a kind of neutral venue of sorts we'd, instead, agreed to meet at a local nature trail car park. Things kind of spiralled from there. I'd met four different men at that spot, the fifth - and last - being the guy that was with me when we were disturbed by Drummond and his dog.

What a fucking idiot I was for getting involved in *any* of it. While I - inwardly - was angry at the engineer of what was now being done to me - with the blackmail - that wasn't anywhere near as close as to how angry I was with *myself*. I don't know what I'd do if Janie was to ever turn the bairns against me and deny me visiting rights. My absolute world, them two, and I honestly couldn't tell you how I'd have been able to handle having them taken away from me. Because it goes without saying who would've *got* them. Not the father who would be leaving the kids in the house so he could go out and get his dick sucked by strangers in his car - as I'm pretty sure Janie would be framing it if I was to try to contest anything - that's for sure.

What a prick that Barry Drummond, though. One evil bastard to exploit me, *extort*, even, in the way that he was. Well sick and twisted. To hold my family hostage in the way that he was over me. Aye, extort, maybe that's the better word for what he was doing to me. Fucking asked for it though, didn't I? The thrill of being caught by a stranger. Well I *was* caught by one, only they weren't so 'strange' although how I wished that they'd been.

After a couple of days had passed though I thought I was in the clear. Was scared shitless at the prospect of the rumours surfacing around town and I thought that, if they were going to, then they'd have started pretty sharpish. Drummond maybe even telling people that very same night. Only takes a few seconds to tap out - and send - a text to your mate and then that's that. Cat well and truly out of the bag.

That this *hadn't* happened was, to me, a mark of Drummond - as a person - in that he hadn't just jumped in with two feet to ruin someone's life, even though he could've done. Obviously, I didn't know that he had *other* plans all along for me. The scheming dick. Never liked him, or the rest of his mates. Especially that Hammy who - for whatever reason - I'm pretty sure liked me even *less*.

That's the thing, though. Aye, I can call Drummond a bastard, a cunt, a wank *and* a dick, and I would not be wrong in any of that either but he was only being given free range to royally fuck with me *because* of my own actions and anyway, what good were blame games by then? The milk was well knocked over by that point and it was a case of did I want to mop it up - and hope that there wasn't too much of a stink once it had all dried out - or did I want to stand there looking at it crying.

It really was the stuff of being caught between the devil and the deep blue sea.

Did I want to commit theft and on a level that wouldn't just lose me the job - and the one that I'd put up with years worth of listening to whiny bastards calling up to complain about being given a bank charge because of *them* not being able to manage their finances like adults should be able to - but, going by similar cases across Scotland over recent years, something that would lose me my liberty along with the p forty five?

Of *course* I didn't want to, but neither did I want to lose Henry and Alice from my life. Janie? Well she came with the package, obviously, but I think that by me going out and meeting random strange men to have sex with them on a highly cavalier basis pretty much highlighted the "differences" that we were experiencing, relationship wise.

And there was my Hobson's choice, as I believe it's termed for when you're made out to have a choice but when you look closer, you actually don't.

While I had tried to tell Barry that I couldn't do what he was asking me to, he wasn't taking no for an answer. Told me that he'd be in touch soon with details he wanted the money moved to.

I didn't want to but had been left with no choice other than to try and work out *how* I'd carry it out. It hadn't been a lie from me when I'd told him that there would be an electronic trail left behind that would lead its way back to me. There's *always* a trail, always. Basically. You've got the scenario where everyone of us at the bank has our own login I.D. This then used as a way of tracking every single employee logged in during work, and what they're up to. This - in itself - isn't really an issue to staff because - other than for training purposes - the only reason the bosses are checking up on someone is as a *result* of some 'wrongdoing' reported by a customer on their account.

With it also being my opinion that with the amount of thousands Barry Drummond was looking for me to "obtain" for him it was the level of figure that someone generally would notice going missing from their account. Wouldn't *you* miss ninety five grand? Yet at the same time - and hypothetically speaking - making up *lots* of payments from accounts to make up to the ninety five k mark then that was even *more* riskier because it maximised the chances of someone noticing.

Rocks and hard places but then again, it was a fucking hard place that got me in the middle of a blackmail plot.

First of all, I couldn't perform any transfer - and by perform I obviously mean embezzle - from a terminal that was showing *my* login details as having facilitated the action because had I done so I'd have been as well just driving straight to the police station at the end of my shift and handed myself in on account of it not exactly being difficult for anyone to find the culprit, once the bank customer noticed that their money had gone missing and reported it. And they would notice.

That was only the *first* issue, not to use my own credentials when it came to carrying out the 'work.' The *main* issue was - once I was given use of a terminal with someone else's login - *how* I was going to attempt to get the money, and from who.

I wouldn't have much in the way of time to suss out either of those two questions - while not exactly lacking in any kind of motivation to do so being left having to fight for my kids - before Drummond would be back in touch with me with my next instructions.

Chapter 18

Hummel

'God speed, amigo. I don't think you need reminding just how much time is of the essence.' Drummond wished me as he handed over his dust covered and barely used Lenovo laptop to me. An absolute antiquated bucket of a machine but one that would be just enough to get me onto the dark web to arrange the documents for us.

He'd been cryptic - back in the pub - when asking me about how quickly I would be able to obtain fake I.D that would be classed as acceptable by a bank. Passport, driving license, utility bills etc. Mocking up a utility bill was something that even someone with a limited experience of photoshop could have easily done. Things like passports and driving licenses, however, were a different proposition and exactly *why* there were specialists in those particular fields.

Luckily, I knew where to find them. Actually *knew* a couple of boys down south who made them week in week out and I was now heading straight home to find out how quickly I was going to be able to get my hands on the goods. I'd already warned Drummond that something like this wasn't cheap and was going to cost even more if we wanted to be fast tracked to the top of the pile and receive a more urgent service from one of the vendors on Feelgood. Saying that we didn't have much of a choice and that we would just have to go three ways on whatever it was going to cost and, besides. Hammy had pulled in several thousand so we already had the capital ready to be used.

I'd built up quite a lot of contacts on the TOR network over the years on the various drug marketplaces and forums that I'd used. Hackers, phishers, drug dealers and those that offer more of a niche service such as weapons and fake documents.

You know how they say that you'll find anything you're looking for on the internet? Well that's simply not true - for the surface web - but it *is* for the *dark* web. I could literally go on there and arrange for a hitman to put a cap in your ass inside the space of half an hour if I so desired - or could afford because that shite isn't cheap on there - so to get hold of something like a fake passport or driving license? All just another day on the TOR network.

Didn't even bother speaking to Debz when I got home - things had continued to be frosty between us - and headed straight up to the spare room to get to work. You could tell that the laptop hadn't been used in a while just by the dust that was on it but this was confirmed when I tried to go online and was given the TOR update prompt, from *eight* updates ago. Advising that the laptop I was using had an older version installed and I would need to update before I would get into the network.

Once I'd got online I headed straight for the forum - and chat room - to see if there were any familiar faces who had either posted anything that day or if anyone useful I knew was kicking around in the chat. Bingo, I thought to myself when I saw *British_Bulldog66* with that wee green light beside his name to indicate that he was on. I always cringed when I saw the name because you could only have guessed what kind of a boy he was. I mean, I'd only ever spoken to him in the chat room or replying to comments on threads and that had always only been about 'business' so who knew what the guy's politics were but with a name like he'd chosen I'd have staked a lot of money on which way he'd have voted for Brexit. Actually, I'd stick a lot of *your* money on too. Don't worry, though. It would be quite safe, I'm highly confident in that.

I knew that he was one of the go to guys on there for fake docs and - in that moment - I could not have given a flying fuck if he dry humped the Union Jack every single night before going to sleep. He sold what we needed and - for the dark web, just as importantly - had a good reputation on the site with his customers.

Seeing that he was online I wasted no time in firing a quick direct message to him, asking if he was available to talk a little bit of business as I was looking for an urgent sale, thinking that by giving him a sniff of a willing customer he'd be straight back to me. He maybe only took five minutes tops before replying back asking what I was looking for.

I was as short as I was concise with him.

I need UK docs - something that will pass a back account check - and I need them FAST. Can you do?

He replied back to me in an instant confirming that he *could* do this for me, but with it being what he was classing as his "express option" it was going to cost me more than any standard order that would come into him. Something I'd already anticipated. If you receive an option to pay more to have something like a pair of trainers dispatched to you quicker then that was surely going to apply to goods found in the more darker areas of the internet.

Sensing the sale - and my impossible to hide desperation despite only typing words onto a screen - he advised that for what I was looking for I should go for the "platinum package" where I would receive a passport, driving license and various fake utility bills. This - including registered delivery - was clocking in at almost three thousand pounds.

Drummond, who had refused to go into any details over what he was going to do with a fake bank account - although there obviously wasn't a coincidence that this had all followed him having a chat with that Leckie who *worked* at a fucking bank - other than tell me and Hammy that he would fill us in on the details later on but that I had to get cracking and, as some kind of last throw of a dice, I was to use the funds that Hammy had pulled back in from the dealers that had eluded him up until then. An amount of money which, to be fair, wasn't anywhere near close towards paying our debt so it was probably the right thing to do with it by taking what little we had and trying to make something out of it.

What was it Tupac said again? Trying to make a dollar out of fifteen cents? Pretty much summed us three up. Always did have a way with words though, him.

With this being the Thursday night - and almost a week until our deadline - and in all probability *us* ourselves - expired he told me that as long as I supplied him with what he needed. Name, address and - of course - the all important passport photos by close of business the day after on the Friday then he would have everything created over the weekend ready to ship out on the Monday with me scheduled to receive the documents the next day. The rest - after that - would be down to Drummond from then on, whatever he was cooking up.

Just being on the dark web, while not having to try and access it via a shitty and unreliable iphone browser, was a joy but not without its bittersweet element to it. It had been the first time I'd been on there since Debz destroyed all of my hardware but by *being* on there it was now reminding me of all of what was now gone. The tendency had been to look right at the fact that we didn't have the ninety thousand to pay someone and, aye, we *should've* fucking looked at that matter first.

But there was even *bigger* pictures to the situation that affected me more than it did the other two which, I suppose, was only right, all things considered. Aye, by taking that hard drive for a wee swim Debz had "cut off" so much money from me it was fucking heartbreaking. Hell hath no fury like a woman scorned though, eh? Never more true than what she did that day, even if it had also cut her own nose off a wee bit. Well, I suppose that she would've been only cutting her nose off if she'd intended on staying with me. If not, then she'd have done a right number on me.

It wasn't *just* the money for the German - alongside the share of our profits from the business - that had been lost. I'd had years worth of fucking around on the TOR network and the contacts that I'd gathered for myself alongside some of the random people that I'd found myself talking to on forums and message boards. Bumped into a lot of interesting characters over those years, some, along the way, throwing a wee life hack your way here or there in the kind of way that you'd only ever get on the dark web.

What's the point in being a hacker if you can't boast about it to people, eh? As a result you'd get tossed something your way even if it was just a couple of hundred pound shoved onto your PayPal account from some online Robin Hood (definitely robbing, anyway) or something like that. It wasn't just illegal stuff, though. With the rise of Bitcoin - alongside popular sites like Silk Road - this, in turn, led to alternative crypto coins surfacing. Most were always going to be a waste of your money. Some not even costing as much as a penny which I know doesn't make sense in a monetary fashion but *does* when it comes to crypto currency.

At the same time, though. Everything's got to start somewhere, price wise. My first Bitcoin - in twenty twelve - had been the exact sum of two pounds and seventy three pence and by the time we reached twenty nineteen it was worth *thousands*. Something that had been reflected in my crypto currency portfolio which had been sitting at an astronomical - for someone like myself - amount up when matched up against my initial outlay. Like buying money, it really was.

With Bitcoin being the main player, that was where I'd focussed putting my money into over the years but at the same time - through all of my contacts on the onion router - I *had* dabbled in other forms of currency. Ethereum, Litecoin, Monero and countless small ones that I had bought large amounts of on account of them being worth practically nothing and had been given a small tip on them when they'd initially surfaced onto the market. I'd actually bought so many of those - as they were termed - shitcoins over the years that I was no longer fully aware of what I'd bought - and how much I'd bought of it - and what I hadn't.

While your portfolio was never sitting at the same amount from one minute to the other. The night before Debz destroyed the hard drive I had been in messing around and noticed that I had just - for the first time - passed the two hundred and fifty grand mark. There had been something special to me about reaching that landmark figure. Easily enough to get you a capable ten plus goals a season striker for the SPL. I'd actually spent a wee bit of the night thinking of which top division strikers I'd have been able to buy for that for that kind of fee.

Things were left between me and Bulldog66 with the agreement that the Bitcoin would be transferred the next day, followed by the passport pictures and name and address for the documents.

With my work done for the night I logged back off Feelgood and flipped the laptop down again and got straight on to Drummond.

'We good, aye?' He asked, as soon as he'd picked up, knowing that I had been heading straight home to get on with things.

'Golden, mate. As long as I have three thousand pounds, two passport photos and a name and address by close of business tomorrow, we all will be.' I responded, now back down stairs and - understandably - drawing a suspicious look from Debz on hearing me talking about passport photos.

'Cool, cool. Fuck all I can do about any of that just now but will get on it first thing tomorrow morning. If you're going to be in around lunch time I'll drop off the pictures to you. I'll transfer the money to you tonight so you can do your thing with it with your mixers and tumblers and all that stuff I don't even fucking understand.'

'What you got up your sleeve here, lad?

Before hanging up, I wanted to ask him again, so did.

'Look, Hummel. All will be revealed in a bit but for now it's better if you don't know anything about it but trust me. If I pull this off *all* our problems are over.'

Trust was the *one* thing that I had for the guy, and in abundance. I just didn't get the need for the secrecy about what he was up to. We were a team, a business, a friendship. The three of us. There was no "military clearance" and need to know stuff when it came to the three of us. We were drug dealers, not the fucking Pentagon.

And this was what made his behaviour stand out all the more, that he was - and out in the open about it - keeping something back and until he felt it was an appropriate time to share with the other two of us. But why, though?

Chapter 19

Hummel

Guten morgen, Herr Evans. You have seven days. Tick tock, tick tock

3FDfiu47xwsi7EddqpC2nvWoBNjyAc8 : 6.47am

I knew it was coming. He'd already told me as much the last time that we'd been in communication. That still did not soften the horrible gut wrenching feeling of opening my phone and reading the message from Arman88. A simple enough message for him - on the surface - offering a reminder that his debt was due to be paid in seven days time, and that he was leaving the bitcoin address he was requesting the funds paid into.

As short a message it was, though it was completely laced with undertones of threat to it. The suggestion being that when the clock ran out of time, so would we.

Or maybe that was just the paranoia starting to bed in for the week, with the countdown - as well as the *pressure* - well and truly now on?

Chapter 20

Hammy

'I heard that it had went for his jugular and that the lad's laying in the Western in a bad way, touch and go, they say.'

'Not what I was told. I got told in The Goth that it had bitten the boy's cock off.'

Harry and Bent Bobby Benson were sitting behind me talking about a news slot that had been on STV the night before appealing for the public's help over some "devil dog" attack in the city.

'Fucking Chinese whispers, that. Cunts actually trying to say that a dog managed to undo someone's belt, trousers and pull down their scants so that they can then bite his fucking knob off, aye? Some need to think about the shite that leaves their mouth before they fucking open them. Biting someone's cock off, aye right.'

Harry Low - who was the region's butcher for decades until reluctantly hanging up his cleaver for the last time. Trading it for holding a bookies pen or pint in his hand during each day - cut Bobby down in his - not so - prime.

'Well, that's all I'm saying that I heard, It was all over The Goth. Half the place was filled with men with their eyes watering at the thought of something like that happening to *them*.' Bent Bob countered not really interested in any arguing back and forth. by the sounds of him. Whatever the score had been - throat or crown jewels - I didn't envy *whoever* it was that had a staffie on its case. Drummond's Bowie? Beautiful dog and with such a pleasant and chilled nature to it but at the same time I wouldn't want to fall out with the wee man either, mind. Some men and beasts it's just better for all concerned if you keep them onside.

Clearly, whatever "incident" that had taken place *hadn't* been an example of keeping a potentially dangerous dog in the friend zone. I hadn't heard about it. Never watch the news if I can be completely honest. I know it makes you sound like a tin foil hat wearing nut job - which I assure you I am not - but what really is the point of watching the news on TV - or reading it online - when all you're going to get is the news that 'they've' decided to bring you, in the sense that it has to be from an angle that suits them and their organisation and politics? Once you suss that out for yourself as an adult it makes it much, much harder for these bastards to pull the wool over your eyes. Took me a while to get my head around that way of the world and how things run inside it, like.

Don't believe me? Then I've got two words for you. Boris fucking Johnson. Ok, that was three but do I look like I care? My point being that at any point, all the British newspapers might've felt the need to step in and state the fucking downright obvious by telling the public that our proposed Prime Minister was a liar, a racist and on top of that, a complete fucking clown of a man who couldn't run a bath never mind a country. That they didn't though and instead more or less *installed* him as Prime Minister tells you all you need to know about them and their convenient reporting of 'facts.' Case fucking closed. I'm not even into politics and only ever voted the once - just to see what it was like - but at the same time, when you've got your street smarts you don't *need* to know anything about politics to be able to tell when some cunt is taking the absolute fucking piss out of you. Like that fat marbles in his mouth imposter with the highly dubious hair at number ten, and his corrupt mates. Well, if it's actually possible for cunts like that to actually *have* mates, that is. Cant be easy forging long and everlasting relationships with people, like, when they don't trust a single fucking word that comes out of your mouth because they know that you're just like themselves. A heartless cunt who would sacrifice thousands of OAPs over a winter if it meant they could keep their cushy gravy train gig in London going for another term.

Genuinely - despite my lack of knowledge in how to actually run a country - reckon I'd make a better job of a Prime Minister than that posh cunt. Sure, I'd only turn up for work half the time, would leather fuck out of the French President if he got lippy during a state visit after we'd all had a few ales and would probably need the nuclear codes taken off me the week after Creamfields due to my comedown but even so, *still* reckon I'd do the business, like. The bar looks like it's never been so low so you'd have to give me more than an outside chance of managing that particular gig.

So by that reasoning, even if the media *had* reported that the Staffie had went for the boy's cock and bollocks, that would've *probably* meant that it had gone for his arse instead.

Sounded pretty fucking sore whichever way you looked at it. I'd been sitting in the bookies that late morning doing what I did *most* days. Taking what money I had and trying to turn it into *more* than what I had. An approach that was not always a successful one and is made even more difficult when you're sitting staring at your betting slip - trying to concentrate on the job at hand - while forced into thinking about angry dogs biting off boys' welts. If my imagination had been anywhere close to what it had *actually* looked like - presuming it wasn't a pandemic like speed urban myth travelling across Edinburgh - then, aye. Fuck that, for all concerned.

That type of shite was hardly going to assist me in picking any winners. Had to laugh at the irony in that around a few minutes later I saw that the two fifteen at Pontefract had a runner called *Problem Dog*. At nine to one odds. You'd have been mad *not* to stick a wee crafty five or ten on that, just on principle, like.

'I'm not giving a fucking Castlemaine Four X over what everyone in The Goth were saying, Bob. Think about it? A dog goes for you and bites your tackle off? You'd have to have had it out in the first place. That's all I'm saying.'

You know what? Fuck it, I thought to myself. These two old bastards clearly weren't going to give me a wee bit quiet time to concentrate, so I joined in.

'How do you know the boy *never*, Harry?'

That put a spanner in the works.

'Well, aye, aye I suppose you're right, son. Hell of a doing though for someone to be running around - exposed, so to speak - being attacked by dogs in the woods.' Harry replied but looking like he was trying to picture it all now that he'd just been provided with a different slant on things. If he was going to be coming up with anything in the ballpark - the fucking *sport* even, - of what I'd done in my own head then he'd been as well not bothering.

'You'd be surprised, some of the stuff that cunts get up to, Harry.' I egged him on, forgetting about my blank betting slip that sat on my wee table for a moment.

'Take Bobby sat next to you, there. In his spare time, when the boozers and bookies are shut and he's no choice but to sit in his house, he could be sitting on the internet pretending that he's an eighteen year old lad talking to girls and getting them to send pictures to him.'

'Aye, but I'm NOT, Hammy son.' Bobby, completely missing my point leapt to his defence. 'I don't even have a bloody computer.'

'AYE, THAT'S CAUSE THE C.I.D ALREADY TOOK IT AFF YOU, YA DIRTY CUNT.'

Tam Anderson - who was sitting playing one of the machines on the other side of the shop - shouted over which left everyone in stitches, apart from Bobby who was looking a wee bit wounded by the suggestion of him being some kind of a nonce which, fair's fair, anyone - who *isn't* one - should've reacted by.

'I'M NOT A FUCKING KIDDIE FIDDLER, *ALRIGHT?!*'

Poor Bobby lost the plot in an instant when it really didn't need losing. Talk about an escalation?

'Bobby, I'm, not saying that …' I tried to calm him down but it was too late for that. What was just a jokey wee comment to him was now resembling a car parked on a hill that hadn't had its handbrake put on and had now began to move off.

'OHHHHH, OHHHHH?' Brian - the shop manager for Paddy's - who had been watching on decided to chip in and keep things going. Had Bobby not bitten in the way that he had we'd have already been on to talking about something else, but he did and as a result some inside there just couldn't help it.

'Now you've been coming here long enough, Roberto pal. You know as well as I do there's a sign on the front door before you come in and what does it say? No under eighteens, no dogs, no smoking and no nonces. You better not be breaking the terms and conditions of gaining entry into my establishment, mind?' Brian said with a big smile while giving everyone a wink to spell out that he was only joking. I think Bobby was too much into his own fume by that point to notice.

'Fuck the lot of yous, I'll take my money elsewhere from now on, Brian. Plenty other bookies that will gladly take my money.' He said as he started to put his coat on before grabbing his walking stick and - well, I can hardly say *marched* - hobbled his way across the floor to the front door and left despite the cries from some for him to come back and that they'd only been messing around with him. The other half were just laughing, me included.

'I'll tell you what?' I shouted out to whoever had been watching or partaking. 'I was only joking about the old cunt on his computer noncing but with a reaction like what we've just been treated to? Not so sure now, eh?'

The scene properly energised my morning, having been sitting their slightly ropey after a couple of days of being on it with Drummond and Hummel. After the previous week I don't think anyone could have begrudged us a wee bit time - ok, two full and consecutive days - to let our hair down after the most stressful week we'd ever had to face since forming our *Onion Ring* as the three of us had termed it due to the fact we were getting our drugs through - what Hummel had called - the 'onion router.'

We'd started around lunch time in The Trap before heading into the town. Next thing you know it's Saturday night and we're sitting in a taxi on the way through to Glasgow to The Subbie to see Eats Everything on his U.K tour. That finished around five in the morning and we were then off to an - ill advised - afters that was being held in a flat in Easterhouse by a boy that Drummond had got talking to in the smoking section at some point across the night. It wasn't a pretty sight - the state of the three of us - when we left that high rise flat at around three in the afternoon, jumping into yet another exorbitantly priced ride but - to avoid us in having to sit in a train carriage alongside other people - one that was worth every single penny. Stupidly - instead of just going home and praying for a *comedown sleep* to take us through until Monday - we went straight to The Trap. Drinking pints and making the occasional trip to the bathrooms for a pick me up while we sat and watched the Sunday fitba on Sky. All going slowly more and more demented as the day passed.

I should've been still in my bed - if my plans had worked out - but had been woken by a fucking seagull outside my window. Fuck knows what had happened for it to get itself so worked up but it was enough to pull me out of what had to have been a deep sleep because I'd banged a couple of blues into me before going to bed. Normally you could've had the fucking Foo Fighters playing in your bedroom and you'd sleep on blissfully unaware so it kind of said all that needed to be said for the volume of the seagull. Those bastards really do need to fucking grow up but I definitely wouldn't be holding my breath on it ever happening in my lifetime.

'Tell you what, Brian? I'm not sure how you're going to get over this blow to the business. You'd be as well just putting the shutters down now, mate.' I shouted across towards him at the counter in what was a rare show of camaraderie between me and the shop manager.

'Those fifty pence accumulators that old Harry sticks away are bound to mount up, like.' I laughed at the drama of him - fucking high roller that he was - making some point in taking his gambling money elsewhere. What Harry generally gambles with across a session you wouldn't even get through the fucking door of Starbucks with in your pocket.

'Aye, Hammy. That's the dream over and done with, pal. Just when I was about to get myself a boat as well.' Brian joined in. For a manager of a business he definitely wasn't looking too concerned over a punter saying they would take their money to another establishment, other than theirs.

Commotion now passed I turned my attention back to which horses I was going to be backing for the day. There were a few that I had already known in advance would've been running and that their previous couple of run outs had been specifically to get them up to fitness for today's meets so - naturally - they were the top of my list of 'lump ons.' Twenty each way on both *Luggy's Socks* and *Steak and Cheese* - who were running at Pontefract and Leapardstown - and another twenty each way on the double coming in.

These two being my great hopes for the day while I dabbled with some other punts and tips that caught my eye. Nothing major, like. Just a wee fiver each way on one, sometimes even less. Just to give me an interest in between the races that *really* mattered.

Luggy's Socks, the earlier one out of the two absolutely romped home - and at a tidy twelve to one price - at such a canter it could've finished the final furlong in its slippers while puffing away on a pipe.

'Decent wee start to the day, eh?' I chirped to Brian while he was taking my slip from me and swapping me two hundred and sixty quid for.

'That's the first of a double, mind, so you might see me back up here again.' I reminded the shop manager.

'Oh aye? I'll look forward to that, Jim.' Brian - someone who had a history with me - said sarcastically.

With there being about half an hour between any races that I had any kind of a vested interest in, I fucked off to Baynes to get myself something to eat. Normally - after a couple of days right on it - I had what was best described as an uncomfortable relationship with food. So to find myself actually *hungry* round about early afternoon on a Monday? Well it was a gift horse that I wasn't having a peek into its mouth.

Scranned a couple of sausage rolls - while keeping one eye out for any seagulls who I was sure had managed to suss out what a fucking Baynes bag looked like by that point of their evolution - on the way back to the bookies before heading back in for the best part of the afternoon.

Obviously, I hadn't just discovered the joy - and most definitely the pain - of gambling inside the space of a week and more days than not you'd have found me in there at some point but since Hummel's bust I'd found the place to be almost a safe haven where you were protected from the shite that was going on in the real world. Hummel and Drummond didn't gamble which automatically meant I'd have been free from the pair of them. Safe and sound sitting there in Paddy's. Aye, of course, they were mates and I loved them and would do anything for the cunts but this whole caper with the German dealer had been dominating everything that we did or said. That's what was so good about the weekend. That we'd managed - at least for a wee while - to forget what was going on in our lives. Well, until the Mandy started to wear off, at least.

No doubt, though. With it being Monday and five days left of our deadline. Things would be back to *that* subject again. I'm not saying that I was *completely* chilled about the whole sit-u because if *I* was wrong and Hummel was right and we were going to have a mob of UK based Albanians on our case then aye, what *was* there to be chilled about, there? I was chilled, though in the sense that there was absolutely ride all that I could do about it until it all came so - as a result - I didn't see the point in it leaving me a nervous wreck and being the only topic that lived and breathed.

Obviously, though. By trying *not* to think about matters, I only ended up thinking about them.

Steak and Cheese, to my absolute exuberance managed to squeeze home in first place by a nose, giving me another single and the much more lucrative double that was linked to my earlier horse. An absolutely magnificent day at the office where my "take home" pay had ended at more than what the average person would earn in a week at *their* office.

Sometimes when you're on a streak like that you can't help but ride it. Obviously, that's *what* the bookies want you to do, so you can hand them your winnings back but with how the day had gone up to then - and the feeling that I'd been left with as a result - but with all the horses that I'd liked having now run I decided to stick a bet on something else - while the luck was still with me - and then cut and run for the day.

Looking back at it I'm still not sure why I even put it on because it was the *exact* kind of bet that I'd have laughed at others sticking away, and so would the bookie taking your betting slip when they looked at it. I just kind of got carried away once I'd started. Swept away, like.

With a combination of a couple of the day's newspapers sat in front of me, an internet search engine on my phone and my own general sporting knowledge - which, being the kind of gambler I was it was my *business* to possess a high standard of that - to call on I stuck that wee green pen in my hand and set to work to see if I could piggy back onto that wave of good luck over the day for one last time.

Away from the horses I took a look at what other events were going on around the world. I noticed that Nadal was playing at Flushing Meadows in about an hour's time. Absolute beast of a player, no doubting that *but* I'd watched his first match of the tournament and he looked fucked. Was hobbling about the court. Legs all strapped up to fuck and generally - by the end of a long and draining five set match - breathing out his arse by the end against the Croatian boy he was playing.

The Spaniard was obviously not fit for the tournament but not willing to admit defeat and had still entered anyway which was a complete 'Nadal' thing to do such was the fight that the boy had in him. Didn't take fucking Sue Barker to tell you that he wasn't going to be making it far this year in New York, though.

When I noticed that he was up against that mouthy - but, on his day, talented - Australian who had breezed through *his* first round match three sets to love, and this up against the six hour epic match that a clearly unfit Nadal had been through, I had a feeling that a wee upset was on the cards so decided to go for Jozinovic - who was out at twelve to one - to win in five sets, figuring that while I fancied him for an upset you'd have had to have been supremely on your day to have seen Nadal off without him winning at least a set over the piece.

The odds then increasing to a further eighteen to one. A decent wee bet and something that I could've stuck on and then went home and put my feet up with a couple of beers while cheering on the Aussie.

Of course, though. I didn't stop there. My train of thought taking me to the plans that I'd *already* thought I'd made with myself for how I was going to spend the night, watching Liverpool play Manchester City on the Monday Night Football. This putting doubles in my head although being brutally honest with myself I didn't have a clue who were the likely winners. Definitely one of those matches where you know that *either* team could win and that to risk any outlay on a match like that then you better be prepared to lose your money at the end of it. Whilst I'd been confident that Nadal would be bumped out of the American Open I had *no* confidence on what to call for the winners of the match at Anfield. I *did* have a lot more confidence though when it came to the more inner workings of *how* the game would be played.

Selecting Man City's Fernandinho to be carded at any time during the ninety minutes for the most generous odds of five to one. It wasn't like I watched City a lot but it had seemed that any time I did he was always getting a card shown to him. Good player but also a bit of a shithouse and when you're looking to bet on a player to be given a card during a game of fitba, *always* bet on the shithouse.

A decent wee double for the evening that - if successful enough - carried the promise of making a great day an epic one with it.

Only I never stopped there.

Why not combine it with one final bet to round things up? Three's the magic number after all. I started to think of what I could include for a third selection that could have been considered as sure fire as you could possibly consider as sure fire. Looking over things I noticed that there were a few Argentinian matches being played during the night. No stranger to them and the madness that they would often bring I found that around three in the morning Newell's Old Boys were playing Córdoba, - according to the handy Soccerbase stats that I'd quickly found - two teams that over the season had averaged three bookings a match. Throw in the riot that both sides had partaken in earlier on in the season in Cordoba when four players were sent off and the fans had came onto the pitch to batter fuck out of the Newell's players, it was sure to be a bit of a hot affair. This telling in my selection I wrote down that said that I needed either six yellow cards in the match or a few reds thrown in to decrease the need for yellows. As long as the referee clamped down on things early doors with a wee yellow to get things started then the bet would've been safe as houses.

It was probably through this sense of confidence - the kind that you can only really have after you've been winning all day - that instead of heading over to Brian and putting it on and getting myself gone for the day, I pushed things even further.

While I was looking through any other potential picks. Niko, a Serbian boy who had moved to the area few years ago - and actually quite sound - had come in and was talking to me and asking about what I was putting on. When I'd told him that I'd landed up on sticking a wee acca away he grabbed my arm and whispered.

'Tomorrow afternoon. Red Star play Partizan, basketball league. Red Star will crush them, put *all of your money* on it, to win by over twenty points.'

'You're not just saying this because you're a Red Star fan though? I can't be losing my money just because you're too proud to say that your rivals have a decent chance to win, eh?' I said in a passive joke kind of way.

'No no no, Hammy. Partizan are resting half of their side because they have a big European Cup match coming up against Madrid. They won't risk their best players against Red Star so are playing most of their reserve team. You *can't* lose, friend. It is causing lots of arguments back home because they have effectively handed Red Star the points. Of course, there are not so many people here in UK who know of this, more importantly, not the bookmakers, eh?'

He winked while tapping the side of his nose.

What can I say? He tugged at the correct heart string of mine. How could I *possibly* have resisted getting one over the bookies with a cheeky wee bet that involved knowing more about the situation than they did? The answer being, of course, that I couldn't.

Niko was correct. The bookies had Partizan Belgrade installed as favourites which showed that they'd had no knowledge of the Serbs playing a fringe side. Because of this I was able to get thirty three to one on Red Star winning the match by twenty points.

Some call it an addiction, others a sickness. Whatever you call it I was Exhibit A of what a gambler was sat there. I'd started off wanting to place one last bet just for a bit of interest when I got home and was watching TV and my bet now involved events from New York to Liverpool and then to Rosario and back across to Europe and Serbia.

Fuck it. In for a penny - although when I eventually *placed* the bet it was for a lot higher stakes than that - in for *thousands* of pounds. You know you're placing some kind of an elaborate bet when you find yourself stopping midway through writing it down to go outside for a smoke.

I can't explain the feeling that day - and why I went back in there and continued adding even *more* layers to the accumulator - I'd had. I'd gambled for enough years to have seen it all but for whatever strange reason I just felt supremely confident about things.

Going back in I immediately added Serena Williams to dispense of the rookie German who was playing in her first major - inside three sets - roughly at the same time the Serbians were playing basketball the next day. Aye, wasn't the best of odds the bookies were offering but then again, it was Serena Williams against an unknown. The price was fair enough for what I was looking for and beside, once you get started on an acca, you'd be staggered at how that shite begins to mount up.

By the time I had walked up to the counter - and almost given Brian an aneurism upon seeing the madness that was printed out on it - I had selected the combination of ten different bets out as an accumulator.

Once I had broken through into the next day with it - and the Serbian basketball tip I'd been given - my (usual general rule) resistance towards placing combined bets over different days went right out the window in the most far fetched of bets I'd ever put on in my life. The actual type that I'd have pitied someone else if I'd seen them sticking on.

Monday afternoon - I was placing the coupon - and the last bet on my coupon was scheduled for *Friday morning?!* The - to the untrained eye - most random of bets looking for over four and a half goals out of the match between Slavia Prague under nineteens and their counterparts from Sigma Olomouc. It was a sad indictment that I even *knew* what a goal haven the Czech Republic youth league was but well, it was what it was and I knew what I knew. To go looking for five goals out of a fitba match may have seemed a bit radge to even begin with but I knew what I was doing. That last match as - obscure as it may have been - was almost the biggest certainty *on* the accumulator and due to that I didn't mind extending the long running bet into a fifth and final day. When you get to a fourth day of an accumulator what's one extra day?

'Ok then, Brian. Here's ma betting slip. Take a good look at it and memorise that amount since you're going to be coughing it up my way on Friday lunchtime. It works out at ninety two thousand and seven hundred British pounds. Might get yourself a wee tip out of it, likes, eh?

Brian tried - but failed - to hide his amusement at this.

'I'll make sure I have the funds ready for collection for you, pal.' He mocked as I folded the slip up repeatedly and stuck it in my wee pocket in my jeans to keep it safe.

I'd got so much into entering the bet into the machine and seeing the potential wins out of them that it had taken Brian's reaction - on seeing it - to remind me just what a fucking ask it was going to be for it to come off.

It pretty much summed up life in general though that I was walking out a bookies having just placed a ten bet multi sport accumulator and was thinking to myself that despite the laughter behind my back - as I exited - from the wide bastard of a shop manager, that I had more chance of the bet coming off than myself, Drummond and Hummel had of paying the German back by Friday.

Chapter 21

Drummond

I felt my phone briefly buzz inside my pocket just after I'd dropped Holly off at 'Little Angels' and was walking through the reception and on my way back out to the car.

'Boat's in, mucker. Swing by to collect.'

It was only eight forty one in the morning but the postie had already been to Hummel's with our *before nine am* delivery. Can't say fairer than that. Buy illegal documents, ask for a rapid service and there it was. Signed sealed delivered and ours.

I was going to be a busy boy that day so went straight from Little Angels to Hummel's gaff to collect the passport - and supporting documents - and get on with things.

Fucking glad at least *someone* had a business head on and was ready for grafting, the first thought when Hummel opened the door. Hair all over the place, parental discretion is advised t shirt, Hibs away shorts from about ten seasons ago. Cup of tea in his hand and a pre rolled joint tucked between his ear.

'Coming in for a cuppa and a smoke, lad?' He invited me over the threshold. Refusing his offer, I told him that I was reserving the right to both until *after* I'd taken care of business. I'm sure I saw Samuel L Jackson say in a film once that weed robs you off your ambition and *that's* why he didn't toke until later in the day. The boy maybe had something in that, like.

Chances were I'd have already taken care of most of the vitals needing dealt with that day and Hummel would *still* be sitting around in those Hibs shorts with a joint in his hand.

I'm not ashamed to admit that - once I collected the fake documents from him - I started to get a wee bit nervous. Actually, my arse was proper flapping. Fuck your 'wee bit nervous' for a game of soldiers.

I'd thought the plan was sound, completely solid, like. Now though, it was time to try and put it into action. Like those cunts that build the planes. Aye, easy enough talking about what you're going to build, maybe even draw some fancy pictures to go with to show people but sooner or later that baby is going to have to go up into the air and *that's* when you're going to see if you were right, or wrong.

Maybe wasn't building a passenger jet but *was* about to go walk into a bank and commit some premeditated fraud. And genuinely didn't know if it was going to work or not. I'd checked online and had confirmed to me what documents I'd need to walk into a branch and open up an account. With all documents in place, *technically* it would've been a case of child's play and you'd have walked out of there with an account opened for you. Of course, things like your debit card would be sent out to you at a later date, but we weren't going to be needing things like that. Just the "loan" of a bank account for a few days and long enough to receive a transfer - or transfers - in and for to withdraw back out again. *If* things were to go our way, by Friday evening none of us would ever have to look at it again. Only temporary, a disposable bank account, if you will.

I'd been cagey with the lads - in relation to the wider plan - as I literally couldn't have trusted either of them not to say something about Leckie to anyone. I'd just felt that the stakes were too high for anything to go wrong. I hadn't yet been able to tell them about what had happened with me and Bowie either, even though it *was* a subject that I'd heard a few people now mentioning. Was even on the fucking tea time news and everything.

I thought - even as a bit of ribbing - someone might've made the connection that it took place in a part of Edinburgh that I didn't exactly stay a million miles from - and owned a Staffie - but no one had, and I was glad for it, not knowing what kind of a reaction I might've had for anyone who brought it up.

All I'd told Hummel was that with him being our so called whizz kid on the keyboard, that he needed to obtain some top level fake documents - enough for to open a bank account - and then for him to work out a way that we could get money *from* that account and to then disappear into the crypto world in an untraceable fashion before we settled up with the German.

Hummel telling me that this would all be a piece of piss to take care of but that the fake docs would cost us thousands. Sometimes you really just have to speculate to accumulate though, don't you?

Took me a while to go *into* the TSB branch, though. Sat there in the car just looking at that fake passport and thinking of all the planning that had gone into it and questioning if it looked *real* enough to pass any bank worker's eagle eye. Worrying if the banking system had measures in place just waiting to pounce on someone trying to open up a bogus account in the way that I was. Aye, I had utility bills made out for the address that I'd given to Hummel to pass onto the counterfeiter. An address that some baffled resident was - in three to five days time - going to be receiving bank letters - and debit card - confirming the opening of an account, and for a person, that they knew absolutely ride all about.

By the time whoever lived in 37a Marchfield Drive had began receiving the TSB correspondence - addressed to Martin Wilson - we'd have finished off with what needed to be done and already *be* at the sunset sitting having a well earned beer, never mind appearing to be riding off *into* it.

The passport looked - and felt - bang on. Had you not already known that it was a fake then there was no way that you'd have picked up on that. Same with the drivers license, the utility bills - one from N-Power and another from British Telecom - looked just like any other bill that you would dread coming through the door seeking payment.

Covering my arse as much as I could. I had went to the trouble of buying a pair of glasses with plain glass lenses figuring that the difference between someone wearing specks and not was always a big one. Same with the hat. Generally wouldn't be seen with a baseball cap on but for the purposes of knowing that there would be cameras inside the branch - and that when the crime was eventually exposed they'd be going back to that day's camera tapes, I wore one. Even went out and bought new clothes just to wear for that trip to the bank before throwing away the same day later on.

Maybe I was getting a wee bit too much into things with the glasses and that - even went to Primark to get my gear which was a shop that I'd never been into in my life and figured some of the stuff inside there would be perfect in a 'you'd never see Drummond wearing stuff like that' kind of way. *That* was just it, though. At least for the next half hour or so I *wasn't* Barry Drummond, I was Martin Wilson. To help me get through what was coming next I felt that I had to truly *believe* that I was him, in his glasses, blue cords, Chicago White Sox hoody and snide white leather "Gucci" trainers.

Come on, man. Sooner you get this account open the sooner this wank at the bank can get the money for you, I coached myself enough to get out of the car and take the few steps through the car park which was pretty much deserted for that time of the morning.

The girl - Sarah - couldn't have been more nice or of assistance. To recognise this, I was more than happy to accept her offer of upgrading my account to one where I would have to pay a monthly fee but *for* this I would receive all kinds of perks a month like free phone insurance, fifty free songs from Amazon music a month, along with a few other perks that I hadn't even been listening to her bang on about. I knew how sales people work though. Just the fact that she was going to be getting another 'sale' added to her quota would've been dominating things and - who knew? - possibly helped her miss anything thing that might've looked a bit 'off' with my application.

The only real nervy part out of the whole process was when she had reached the end of the application and had entered it all into her computer. *This* was the first point where I had even considered things like a credit history for a person. Fuck, if the bank was to check something like that then the gig was fucking blown straight away and if I was lucky I'd have been able to get out the place before they locked the doors on me.

With it being an account that offered no credit facilities and was fully dependent on having payments paid into it through the account holder then I can see why it wouldn't been an issue that they'd feel was ever worth checking.

'Ohhhh, k, Mr Wilson. We are good to go.' The girl who looked to be maybe mid twenties tops but was already showing the title of manager on her name badge said to me with a smile as she collected all of the details that had been printed off for me and put them all into an A4 sized TSB envelope.

'All your information is contained in here, sort code, account number and so on. With regards to the free phone insurance you will find a phone number to call and register your phone. It will only take you a few minutes to do so. Do you have any other questions about your account, sir?'

She said wrapping things up.

'So that's the account now open? It can now receive payments and make withdrawals?' I asked although was pretty sure she'd already said as much. I just wanted to ensure that this had all went as easily as it had appeared to. With paranoia ripping right through me there was an element of me feeling that aye it had all gone so smoothly because it had all been a ruse to keep me sitting there while the bizzies got their arses over to the branch to pick me up.

None such a thing happened, however.

'Yes, that's you now set up. If you receive any transfers and wish to withdraw any funds *before* you receive your Visa debit card - which will be arriving in up to five working days - then all you need to do is come into branch with proof of ID and you will be able to withdraw from your account that way. We also have a phone and internet banking service which you have been set up for today also. Your login details are contained in your welcome pack although - for example with your internet banking - you can easily change your passwords to something more preferable once you have logged in for the first time.'

Music to my ears. An absolute *symphony* to hear that - once the money was in - we'd be able to move it out of the account in a relatively anonymous way.

'Perfect, Sarah. Can I just say that you have made opening an account such an effortless joy. I thought I would be here half a day filling in all kinds of documents and reading small print. I'm impressed!'

Seizing on this she told me that putting the customer first was what they did but if I would like to leave some online feedback in relation to my experience she would happily write down a link for me to use which I agreed to even though it was all just lip service. While Hummel might've been the internet boffin out of us all I wasn't so daft enough not to know about IP addresses and how leaving feedback from my computer in relation to the fake bank account I'd just opened probably wasn't an idea that would need pursuing any further.

Still, fuck me. It *worked*.

A lot more steps to go though before any kind of daylight would have been able to be spotted by any of us. And, of course, there was Leckie's part that had to be played. I'd had no contact with him since we'd sat down in The Trap and - for want of a better terminology - I'd blackmailed the cunt. Had thought about him over the weekend though, even finding the time to consider how his Saturday night was going while me and the boys were out our tits on a wee bit of the dirty girl at Eats Everything at The Sub Club. Fair to say I'd left him in a bit of a tailspin that Thursday night when he was given that ultimatum. Can't help but feel it might've hampered his weekend, somewhat, though.

I knew there was a low probability of him answering - with it being business hours - but wanted him to at least *see* that I'd been in touch looking for him so gave his mobile a call. Not even ringing before pushing me through to his voicemail.

'Emmmm hello, I'm not sure if I'm through to the correct department but I was looking to speak to someone about a deposit into my account. If you would like to give me a call back on this number I would be glad to provide you with the sort code and account number for you to assist. Thank you.'

I left the professional voice message for him. Aye, professionally sarcastic, like. I took a thought to send him a follow up text with the sort code and account number inside of it but thought better of it. There was going to come a time - I was sure - where Leckie was going to be huckled for stealing the money for me and - because of this assumption - from the very moment that I'd formed the plan I'd known that *any* incriminating stuff would have to stay in a verbal sense between the pair of us, burner phone or not. And of course, it went without saying that I'd be going through his phone before him and me came to a parting of ways again.

Couldn't have him showing the police any text messages sent from me with the fraudulent bank account in them or anything like that, eh? Do it correctly and there would be *no* actual proof for him to show anyone such as bosses or the police, when they came calling.

Instead, I sent a "mates" text saying that if he was in The Trap that evening I'd see him for a pint as had felt that was also acceptable for a form of contact between each other. I just wanted him to receive the sort code and account number to allow him to get on with things.

Didn't have a clue *if* he'd been able to come up with any kind of a plan or not but when I spoke to him later on he would be reminded that his deadline was five o clock on the Friday. A minute past and the video was going out on all socials.

This came via him calling me at lunch time a few hours after my voicemail had been left on his phone. I liked that. Showed the boy was keen. Had half expected that I'd be blanked at least until after he was done for the day but by calling me back within hours - and when he most likely should've been relaxing and having lunch before going back at it for the afternoon - it showed me that he was anxious to get this all done as much as I was.

Something I pounced upon by telling him in the phone call we had that 'the sooner all of this was taken care of the sooner it would all be over.'

'Aye, aye I can only agree with you, there. But it's not as easy as just going and doing it. Needs to be executed in the correct way.' He replied which I took as meaning that I shouldn't have gone looking for it arriving in the account the next day on the Wednesday.

'Well you know the score, Leckso pal, eh? Five bells on Friday, mind?'

Ideally I didn't want to be playing such a cunt like that, leaning on someone and turning the screw but for the purposes of the play that I'd decided to pick, I'd been left with no real alternative. You don't get someone to steal thousands of pounds like that for you by being *nice* to them.

'Aye, I know, I know.' He said, letting his frustration get the better of him.

'Come on now, *mate*. That kind of tone's not going to help matters, eh? I don't know, like? If it was *you* who had a video, like what I have, to use against me I'd be of a mind to be a bit more respectful.'

That shut him up.

'Just keep thinking of those two beautiful kids that you've got and all of the happy memories that are just waiting there to be made with them both. Birthdays, circuses, zoos, soft play areas, feeding the ducks at the park. Possibilities are endless, *if* you do as told. Just imagine the weight that's going to be lifted from your shoulders by the end of the week, eh?'

By this point I knew that the man would've despised me to an insane level. He had to, I'd have been the exact same. That was cool, he was someone whose respect or admiration was something that I didn't need or ask for. I just wanted the copious amounts of money that he had access to.

I left him with the sort code and account number that had been created earlier that day with his assurances that he was working on things while - not for the first time across the phone call - I reminded him of the perils of him failing.

I was done after that for the day and felt like I'd more than earned the right to head out to The Trap for a couple of pints. I'd done enough for one shift. Had committed fraud by opening a bank account with fake identification and then doubled down on that by then moving onto blackmailing a bank employee.

If I'd got this all correct and we *actually* landed up with the money and then moved it onto the German / Albanians (?) and dug us out of that Grand Canyon of a hole then fuck me, what a plan it would've been.

Had I fucked up with something along the line in the planning of fraud and blackmailing of someone in a financial organisation, though? Then it was *definitely* something that you would be going to jail over, no question about it.

Chapter 22

Hammy

Ahhhhh that beautiful - but very, very novel - feeling of waking up, checking the internet and finding out that the coupon that you stuck on the day before - and which has had events taking place during the night while you slept - was still *alive* and kicking.

Fuck all to get carried away with when you've only got three up out of a possible ten and the next seven still to follow but hey, you've got to start somewhere and if anything, it was three more bets up than I had when I'd walked out of Paddy's with Brian the manager pissing himself at the 'waste of time' he'd just put through his system.

I'd been absolutely bang on with the tennis. Went all the way to five sets but Nadal - fresh off the back of a *previous* five set match simply didn't have enough in the tank for the Australian who it had looked like had won the mind games before actually winning the match itself. Shouting across the net to Nadal about him being an old man and not being able to hack it anymore, getting a warning from the referee which barely even registered with the outspoken antipodean with the tag of the bad boy of the sport. Nadal hadn't liked the trolling, mind. Looked well rattled by it which - for the purposes of the accumulator - was most welcome.

What *wasn't* welcomed though was Pep Guardiola not selecting my guy Fernandinho for his starting eleven at Anfield.

'I'm trying to make some fucking money here, Pep, you slick bastard.' I found myself shouting at the TV while the interviewer from Sky Sports quizzed Guardiola - stood there in a majestic black cashmere Stone Island jumper - over why the Brazilian was only on the bench. The reason being that he'd suffered from a recurrence of a calf injury he'd had a few months before and as a cautionary measure was being put on the bench.

Fortunately Jordan Henderson went straight through Fabian Delph inside the first twenty minutes that led to an enforced early substitution which saw my boy sent on to the pitch. Made me sweat though. Wasn't until around ten minutes to go before he finally *did* get a yellow card. Fucking good one, too. One of those take it for the team where you already know you're getting a yellow before you even commit the foul.

'Cheers you magnificent shithouse, you.' I toasted him as he gave a bashful thumbs up to Michael Oliver who was stood there brandishing the card.

Would've been a nice wee double to have cashed in on, the tennis and the yellow card but obviously that was all out of my hands. I'd went super radge on my selections and there was none of that fancy cash out stuff to play around with either.

The cash out system - I'd felt when seeing it introduced - was something that had been devised by one sick bastard of a person, a seriously twisted individual that wants to play around with your emotions. Gambling fucks with your head at the best of times so adding that cash out function just wasn't for me. As a result though, my coupon really was in the laps of the gods. I'd went to bed knowing that the Argentinian match was on during the night and that I'd know one way or the other how things stood, when I got up the next morning.

Newell's and Cordoba not letting me down in a three one win for the home side but the away team beating them on red cards. With two for Cordoba and one for Newell's Old Boys - alongside all the yellows - meant that if I'd had the balls to do so I could've added a lot more points onto the bet and still comfortably achieved it.

Still, three out of three and we go again.

As for that day? We had Niko's Red Star and Partizan basketball match and round about the same time, Serena Williams in the U.S Open.

There was a third bet taking place over the day - I was sure - but with all that I'd placed on, all the way up to ten, I couldn't remember *what* it was. Going over the slip - while having a cup of tea and getting some breakfast into me - I found that there *was* a third bet, after the earlier two. Valur reserves versus Keflavik reserves. A quick look at recent results for both teams had showed me that Valur weren't exactly shy when it came to hitting the onion bag. Most weeks they'd been taking four, five and six off the teams they were playing against. Keflavik being rooted to the bottom and looking like they'd been sat there since day one of the season.

I'd taken Valur to win the match with Keflavik getting a two goal start. *That* wasn't anything to be concerned about at that time of the day, though.

Maybe start worrying about if a group of Icelandic players who you wouldn't recognise if they came to help you move house wins their game when we get to that part of the day *if* we get to that part of the bet and it's not already rolled up into a ball and lying in a Paddy Power wastepaper bin, I thought to myself.

What can I say, though? Niko was as good as his word - with the basketball tip - and was even inside the bookies for during the last period of the match, so confident he must've been at getting paid. Showed me a bit of it live on his phone. It was *too* fucking radge. Could've only been one or two o clock in Serbia (what am I some world time speaking clock or something?) but the arena was filled. Proper ultras and that, too. Flares being lobbed, cunts bouncing all around the place singing. It looked class.

So did the final result of **Red Star Belgrade 125 - Partizan Belgrade 92.**

As for Serena Williams? Well she was just Serena Williams. Dealt with the poor girl in the kind of way that someone does when they've got a tennis match to win but are also concerned about the chips that they have frying away in their chip pan back home in the kitchen.

If the Icelanders did the business for me then we we'd be on six out of six with four left.

Noticing that he'd been looking over my way when celebrating Williams snatching her first out of her three match points on offer I shouted over to Brian.

'Still laughing, mate, aye?'

'Oh aye, brought a few spare pairs of underwear with me today.' He responded with but I *knew* that *he* knew.

Fuck knows where it even came from but my brain made a connection with the situation to the theme song from that Smokey and the Bandit film. Jumping on this - and to wind Brian up a wee bit - I started singing some of it - and its, to me, topical lyrics - to him as I left the shop to go and meet the other two over at The Trap.

'East bound and down, loaded up and truckin we gonna do what Brian says can't be done. We've got a long way to go and a short time to get there I'm east bound just watch ol Bandit run.'

Choosing to ignore Brian's 'Aye, you're a bandit, right enough' which followed my wee outburst of song. I left to meet up with Hummel and Drummond to see what was good in the world although, going by our recent track record, you'd have been forgiven for just going ahead and assuming that it would have really more been a case of finding out what was *bad*.

Chapter 23

Hummel

'Nah, man. Naples - for the whole week, like - when Maradona won them their first Scudetto. That looked full on insanity. Imagine waiting all your life to see something, and, in particular, a specific thing that you'd lived your whole life being told by the rest of the country that you would *never* experience? No wonder they fucking partied for a week.' Hammy said while looking like his mind was already *in* nineteen eighty seven Naples.

We'd been sitting there talking about the mother of all parties we were going to have once the pressures and stresses of our recent times had finally passed.

It was true, though. Once we - *if* we - got that whole monkey off our backs then we were going to be in one monumental mess but one that was going to be a *lot* more enjoyable than the one we'd been in leading up to that.

Plans were being hatched but - the superstitious side to me - I was hoping that it wasn't going to be a case of plans being made and leading to a chicken and hatch scenario.

Hammy was talking about Amsterdam for three days which, aye, sounded well rare but considering how Debz and I had been - relationship wise - over recent times Amsterdam was never going to fucking fly with her. To be fair, I don't think Hammy was thinking of my domestic situation when suggesting it. Neither was Drummond when he said 'fuck that, we do it in style. Vegas for a couple of days. What do you say? Get weed there just as easy as you do in Amsterdam, like.'

Hammy, going by his reaction wasn't opposed to this. Neither was I, if my other half was cool with me going, which I'm pretty sure she *wouldn't* have been. If I'd asked her *before* she'd found me talking to that Irma girl then she'd have literally packed my case for me, kissed me on the cheek and wished me a great trip. All of that goodwill that I'd held with my partner - and of that I had *loads* - expired the morning she opened up the MacBook and saw what was on the screen.

She definitely wasn't stopping me from going completely AWOL inside my *own* country though and well, if you've went completely off the grid for a couple of days then truth is you could almost *be* away in another country, for anyone knows, if you catch my drift, eh?

That right off the bat Amsterdam and Las Vegas had been suggested though showed what kind of level of celebrations the three of us had in mind.

This was what had led to us then talking about some of the greatest parties that there had ever been and if, given the chance, which ones would we have wanted to have been a part of and to experience.

And Hammy sitting wistfully talking about a party in a city that he'd never been to, involving a fitba team that he didn't fucking support. It *was* a good shout, though. You have all your organised week - or more - long parties like Rio Carnival and Burning Man that - as long as they are - have been planned and prepared to last as long as that.

Napoli winning the Scudetto (and the first league title in their history) produced an unplanned and very much spontaneous outpouring of celebration throughout the city - and so explosive - that its citizens just didn't know when to drink the last drink and dance the last dance.

It must have been the most beautiful carnage to witness, and play a part in. But me and Drummond had stiff competition for it as the party of all parties.

Drummond's - well, *one* of his suggestions - to counter this being a decent one too.

'Cali, the day that Escobar was killed and the news started to break, lads. It's said that *no cunt* paid for a drink that night and that the whole city partied, courtesy of the Cali Cartel. Any alcohol or Ching you wanted it was on the *gentlemen of Cali*. Proper ding dong the witch is dead stuff, like. Obviously they didn't party anywhere near as long as Naples but had a good couple of day's crack at things. I'm not sure I could handle a week long party, anyway. I'd be risking losing my mind by the forth day, as has already been made evident on our trips to Creamfields before and the state of me by the Sunday night.'

'To be fair, you've got a point. I don't even want to think about the state of you with another three days added to the nick of you down there by the time we reach the Sunday. Your own fault, though, lad. Moderation never really was your thing which doesn't even make sense considering *you're* the most logical one out of the three of us.'

I cringed thinking back to Drummond - two years before - on our last trip down to Daresbury Farm. Inside the Paradise tent repeatedly asking me if I'd seen his feet and saying that he'd possibly left them back at the main stage when we'd been to see Annie Mac. Went on for a good few hours about his feet until I had the brainwave of asking him if he could feel them, which he said he could not. I then deliberately *stood* on each of them and asked if he could feel anything now.

The case of the missing feet, solved. What an absolute mess for someone to get themselves in, though. And it wasn't exactly a one off for him and our four day benders down there.

'Hey, the boy just loves his drugs, eh? He's not alone, there.'

Hammy laughed at me trying to find logic where there maybe wasn't any to be found.

People loved taking drugs and getting as much off it as they could. Drummond was no different to *thousands* of others inside all of those tents at that festival.

I'd initially been about to plump for Colombia myself and the night where Colombia beat Argentina five nil in Buenos Aires because you just *know* how fucking mental that night would've been in a city like Bogota or Medellin. I remember reading that something like fifteen people *died* in the celebrations because of cunts firing their guns up into the air. Bullets have got to come down again at some point though, eh? Even so, looked a top night and one of those results that might never come around for your fitba team again so you fucking cherish every second of it when it comes along.

Didn't want to pick another Colombian example though - following Drummond's own one - so, instead, went for the day Thatcher died. We were all a touch too young to really celebrate it in the way that those Scots older than us did but going by the way everyone was getting fired into the drink that night you could tell that it was a bit of a momentous occasion. Obviously, you then go on to find out just how much a boot that she really was and - now in possession of that knowledge - if given the chance to, that night's party would've meant a lot more than it really did to the three of us.

A wee (fucking HUGE) shout out to the days May twenty first and twenty second, twenty sixteen and the day that me and Hammy saw our team win the Scottish Cup for the first time in our puffs. In terms of fitba celebration? The fucking *ultimate*. That was something that Hammy and me were in complete agreement over. Being a fan of the side that played in the Gorgie part of the city, Drummond was not in so much agreement over. Instead, trying to condescend the pair of us. Saying how it had been cute that we'd been given the chance to celebrate a Scottish Cup win before adding that for most other teams it's not something to celebrate a whole weekend over. His insinuation being that *his* side was a big one - and ours not - being there for all to see even if he was working his ticket, there. Jambos, eh? What can you do?

Debbie went *so* fucking radge at me when I came home on that May Monday lunchtime - still absolutely pished - having last seen her when I left for our supporters bus at eight in the morning on the Saturday.

Completely immune to any abuse or criticism due to the state I was in I thought that your team winning the first Scottish Cup in your lifetime would be something that your better half would completely understand and give you a pass over, but she wasn't seeing things the same way that morning.

I'm giving it the '*But, babe? We beat Rangers and won the Scottish Cup?* While she's bawling back at me about not giving a fuck and how she'd thought I was dead because I hadn't been answering my phone. The same one that I'd lost somewhere after Sir David Gray had scored the winner and before we arrived back at the boozer after the match. Aye, that phone.

The only part from yesteryear that we were all able to agree on that - if given the chance - we'd go to in an absolute heartbeat was one of the earlier Scottish raves, Technodrome. It was held on some shooting ground and apparently everyone into raving at the time from around Britain went to it. The older cunts - who weren't even raving anymore - still spoke about it decades later. As if it was some kind of "Raver's Woodstock" or some kind of similar deal. We all agreed that it would've been sound to drop one of those mythical White Doves and go to, just so we could answer everyone back when it came to being told that *things weren't as good now as they were back in the day.*

In amongst our planning of parties that we would never, ever get the fucking chance to go to we also managed to find time to talk about the ever present elephant that wasn't a case of being in a room but piggy backing onto us wherever we *went.*

Drummond, deciding to share some more with us than he'd previously been, up to that point.

'Look, boys. As you both know, absolutely fuck all in this life is guaranteed so, as a consequence, I can't sit here and offer *you* any, but.'

Talk about places to choose to pause in the middle of what you're saying? Hammy and I sat there hanging on his every word and he fucking "buts" us.

'Well fucking spit it out then, Drummer Boy. You're not announcing the winner on fucking X Factor here, mate.'

Hammy - in his own eloquent way - tried to move our friend along. I didn't want to build my hopes up on what came from Drummond next but - given that we had absolutely fuck all else - his tone and cadence was something that *offered* hope. Either that or I was just desperately looking to hear things that I *wanted* to hear.

He looked around us to check no one was listening before continuing on.

'Well, 'but,' I think I *might* have secured us an out.'

He went on to tell us that he had taken the passport and paperwork that I'd given him in the morning and opened up a bank account that morning and that by Friday he was expecting the full amount that we were due Arman88 to have been deposited into this account. Once the money was in then things were over to me after that as we needed to get the money back *out* of the TSB account and converted into Bitcoin but in a way that couldn't be traced back to myself, which in itself wouldn't have been difficult and, in fact, would've more been a case of which way to even *choose* to do it.

My initial thought had been - as a form of plausible deniability - to call upon a hacker friend to simply just lift the money from this newly created bank account, convert it to Bitcoin and then transfer it back to a wallet I'd have created for the transaction but really? When you're talking about ninety thousand pounds, are *any* hackers really friends? There were plenty of other ways, however.

The hard part, for me - undoubtedly - would still be the receiving of the money, however the fuck Drummond was even attempting that. Because he still wouldn't spill with that part, yet.

'But *where* the FUCK are you getting us the money from, and how? We all fucking know that you don't just stumble across ninety bags when you're out walking your dog or putting the bins out.' Hammy asked.

I'll admit. I wanted to know too, or did I? That amount of money could not have been acquired without some form of risk being attached to it, and maybe I didn't really want to know if that then impacted me directly. I honestly did not need any more to weigh me down than I had already. The combination of problems with Debz and then that running directly into the destroyed hardware and the lost Ching. I think I'd had enough, don't you?

I trusted Drummond, though. Knew that he wouldn't be stupid enough to have done something like taken a loan off some dangerous fucker closer to home than any German dark web vendor, and making life even *more* uncomfortable for us.

'Look, boys? You've both known me since we were at primary school so you already *know* how loyal I am and how you can trust me?'

Hammy and me looked at each other and nodded in agreement. Drummond, a boy - if on your side, obviously - had always been a word is bond kind of boy.

'So, you just need to do what you've always done and trust me here. It's been a mad as fuck week plus for us all but I'd be astonished if either of you would be able to top some of what's been going on my side. Whatever happens, we get to Friday and you'll get all the details, whether we get the money or we don't. Until then there's not much more either of you two can really do but mind now, Hummel. You *need* to be ready to rock on Friday, once those funds hit the account. We're only going to be getting one shot at this and, miraculously we've even managed to get ourselves one in the first place.'

'So I've got the next few days off then, aye?' Hammy said, almost like he was a wee bit jealous that I had a major role still to play but it appeared that he *didn't*. Drummond corrected him on that, though.

'Mate? If it hadn't been for you chasing down the money that had still been outstanding to us we wouldn't have had the scratch for the passport and the supporting documents. It's *you* who set it all in motion, mucker. If we pull this off it, while - and without being big headed here and completely sucking my own dick - the majority of it will come down to me and the moves I've been making, it will have been started off by you and *finished* by Hummel, here. A proper team effort from The Onion Ring boys, as always. Greater than the sum of our parts, us. '

Hammy - in that 'not arsed' way of his - took the compliment that was handed to him and done absolutely nothing with it. Him not being the type to be sucked in by a bit of praise even though, from what I could see, Drummond had been straight with him.

Hope though, eh? That's all man needs at times, just a wee bit of that good stuff. I'd seen absolutely nothing near resembling anything in the way of positivity for around ten days in a row and that shite can get to you in the end. Day after day. For the first time I actually felt *something* that I could liken to 'hope.'

At least from Tuesday night up until Friday I would be able to lift my head, keep hold of that morsel of faith - tight - and add some prayers in for good measure that whatever the fuck Drummond had in the works was going to go the way that we all wanted it to.

Needed it to.

Chapter 24

Hammy

'ARNASONNNNNN YA FUCKING WEE BEAUTY YOU, YAAAASSSSSS.'

No one, and I repeat, *no one* should have been so delighted at a goal being scored in an Icelandic reserve league match. Not the manager, not the player, not his proud parents. Not even the fans of Valur Reykjavik who - and lets face it, this stands for most of us and our fitba teams - probably either didn't even know the match was being played themselves or couldn't have cared less what the result was. I honestly couldn't tell you where Hibs reserves ever were in their respective league at any given moment and that doesn't make me any less a fan of Hibernian Football Club.

I'll tell you, though. Fuck all leaves you feeling as helpless as shoving money on a sporting event that is so obscure that you're reduced to looking at a poorly designed primitive simulation - of what's going on hundreds of miles away - on your phone screen. No live footage, fuck all in the way of commentary. Why would they even? I was probably the only cunt in the whole of the British Isles who even *acknowledged* it. And that simulation was already proved by me - the year before - to be a complete fabrication towards what's *actually* going on out on the pitch. To be fair to the betting app, it's about as accurate as half of the match newspaper and website reports you read on a match that you watched yourself.

Doesn't help your nerves, though. When you've got thousands riding on the match and you're looking at the screen telling you that the team you're wanting to score are on a 'dangerous attack' while you know that the chances are that the ball is out for a throw in to the other team, up the opposite end of the park.

Whatever happened over in the Icelandic capital I needed the home team to win, and with the away side being handed a two goal start. Bit of a stretch to look for that ahead of a ball even being kicked but I'm a numbers man - like that American boy that used to be on Dragons Den, you know? Wasn't really interested in the sales pitch from cunts and just wanted to see their figures and *that* was what led him to a decision - and it was the, speaking like a businessman myself here, bottom lines of Valur and Keflavic reserves that led me to *my* selection.

I thought I'd fucked it with my choice, though. After having a few ales with the boys I'd headed back over to the turf accountants for a couple of hours. Stick a few horses on to pass the rest of the afternoon. When I was sitting around inside there - for the first half, at least - I was only occasionally checking what the score was between the two Icelandic sides.

Used to have that goal notifications option set on my phone but had switched it off after one embarrassing moment when I was visiting my dad - who was on death's door with pneumonia - at the hossie one Sunday afternoon and had stuck a wee accumulator on before leaving the house. Fucking hell? Me, my mum and my wee brother - Aiden - were all sitting silently and sombre around dad, who was passed out asleep but looking well ill. Three of us all - at once - fucking shat ourselves when that loud crowd cheer came from my phone to indicate that PSV Eindhoven had scored against Breda. Thing is, I'm not a dafty. I'd stuck my phone *on* silent before heading into the hospital ward so there was no reason for it to be doing any of that nonsense, not that mum was for hearing it. Had a right fucking beamer, though. Fumbling and grabbing at my phone -

while not just *my* family watched on - to stop it from doing it again the next time a team on my coupon scored.

Fucking lucky it never woke my dad up, it was that loud. Proper scarred me, that, so the notifications were taken off sharpish and never put back on again.

I was slightly concerned to find that the half time score was nil nil between the two teams. Not too cool when you need *any* team to score three goals inside forty five minutes, while keeping the back door closed at the same time. This was the Icelandic reserve league though and - throwing all the usual logic associated with fitba to the side - and I'd seen five and six goals being scored in one half before so for that reason I wasn't ready for ripping up my coupon just yet.

Valur just needs to come out all guns firing in the first five minutes, pinch a goal and things will be back on track, I thought to myself while waiting on the second half starting. And that's - more or less - *exactly* what happened. The first time I went into the app to check if the second half had kicked off it was already showing as one nil to Valur. The time of the goal down as forty six minutes and so fresh that it had not had a chance to name the scorer yet, not that I really cared for such minor details. The goal was enough, thank you very much.

Keeping emotions in check, I allowed myself a wee silent downwards punch into the air, Robbie Neilson style. Brian - who was out from behind the counter and sorting out some of the midweek fitba specials - noticed this. I couldn't help but clock by this point that the longer my coupon had dragged out the less cocky he was acting. It was a beautiful thing to see, a bookie who is a wee bit worried but pretending that he isn't. Almost wasn't bothered about the bet coming in or not if it had ensured that I could've got an extra couple of day's mileage out of it, and given Brian a few sleepless nights along the way.

227

'Sweating like a fucking Yewtree P.O.I, you, eh?'

I laughed over to him but he claimed not to know what I was getting at. They added a second goal on around the hour mark which - as far as me and my knowledge of Icelandic reserve fitba went - pretty much confirmed that I'd - and Valur - be on easy street. Just a formality from then on in. Would've been sound if some cunt had been arsed having a word with Keflavic though and filled them in on what was going on because a couple of minutes later they scored to make it two one which, of course, now meant that I was now back to needing a couple of goals to be scored. Didn't really plan on *Keflavic* scoring, admittedly. For me it had only really been about how many goals *Valur* would score over the match.

Hope is everything to a gambler and as those minutes ticked down - I'd more or less stopped everything there in the shop to just sit and watch the "coverage" on my screen - on the clock I could feel it being sucked out of me. Suddenly, that "there's ages yet" feeling had now turned to "if they don't score soon then there's not going to be any time *left* for another." Any person who has ever put a bet on a game of fitba will know that feeling. Time is a cruel mistress they say and you can't really argue with that statement when you're watching a timer count down and a potential large windfall ebbing away from you with no further change in the scoreline.

Then the goal icon flashed up on screen - after what had appeared as being stuck on 'dangerous attack' for a few minutes - for Valur. When the goal info was added it showed that it had been a penalty which only validated what I'd felt about the coverage they gave you as no penalty had been mentioned at any point. Well I was hardly going to complain about *how* they'd scored, was I? This must've been around the seventy fifth minute mark so it came at a good time.

How your mind can go from one extreme to the other, eh? Apart from the - obvious - feature of winning money I think that's the reason a lot gamble as well. They're addicted to the dizzy highs and the sickening lows that it can all bring. Before they'd made it three one I was sitting there doubting that they would even score one. Only when they *do* I'm sat there thinking , fifteen minutes plus injury time? They could probably score another two or three between now and then. I only needed one.

Entering injury time - and the score still three one to the home side - it must've been written all over my face - that losers look - as suddenly *now* Brian was up for talking.

'You alright over there? You look like you've had a bit of bad news, mate?' He shouted over, now back behind the counter alongside his assistant, Janice.

Completely rubbering him, I chose to stay focussed on the phone screen. Only takes a second to score a goal, eh? You *also* know that you're struggling a bit when you *start* saying things like that too! With it being three minutes into injury time - and the actual betting on the match now suspended - I'd been waiting on the confirmation that the game was over. Coupon down into the bargain but, hey? It wouldn't have been the first coupon of mines to end up a burst one and sure as fuck wouldn't be the last one either.

Only we got to six minutes, and the game appeared to be still going on. Maybe they'd lost one of the match balls into the North Atlantic or something and took too long getting a replacement. I pictured the scene.

Really didn't have any kind of a scoob what was happening by the time that it got to eight minutes of injury time, and the game still being played? For all of the eight minutes it had - pretty much - been one way traffic. Alternating between attack, dangerous attack and shot. By the third minute of injury time I'd already begun to look at the game as a loss and was comfortable with it. Would've been some win - had the coupon come up - but when you go to ten selections on a betting slip - combined - then you've already crossed over from 'in with a good chance' to *no* fucking chance.

That's what made the goal so special when it flashed up.

Ninth minute of fucking injury time. Absolute scenes, well in the bookies, anyway. Can't really speak about the reaction - over in Reykjavik - to a goal that had come so late in a reserve team match, whose winner had already been established between the two sides, that I could hardly have imagined a Marco Tardelli running about the pitch in tears following it.

The whole shop stopped what they were doing to look over at me celebrating. Once I'd calmed down and composed myself a bit I was a wee bit embarrassed over the overreaction and one that had led half the shop to believe that they were watching a man celebrating a massive win, not someone approximately *halfway* towards the prize.

'All that jumping around, and you haven't even fucking *won?'* Ralphie Patterson - still in his construction site gear and apparently in the bookies straight from work - said shaking his head at my theatrics. My reaction was more because I thought I'd lost than *because* the team had scored, as such.

'Baby steps, Ralphonso pal. Baby steps.' I winked back at him, as I worked on getting my breath back. It had been fuck all other than a stupid bet while I was high on winning and had those endorphins flowing through me. The kind of emotions that leads to silly decisions, like fifty quid on an un-winnable bet. The logical in me wouldn't have even went near a bet like that but just saying I had then it would've just been a wee 'fun' bet of a fiver or a tenner. Fifty was just mug behaviour but - as things stood - it had been the stupidity in me that was now making things *very* interesting. There was still a long way to go yet but there was no denying it. That late, late goal in Iceland had definitely put a different spin on things. Bets can - and will - fail in a moment and there were plenty of them left before Friday morning and the last of the selections.

Like any fitba player who's shoved in front of the cameras after the game coming out with all of the standard cliches like being over the moon or sick as a parrot. You could only win what was in front of you and - for the second day running - that's exactly what I *did*.

And god bless you to Serena Williams, Red Star Belgrade men's basketball team and Valur Reykjavik reserves. Individually - as well as collectively - they all helped keep the dream alive for one more day, at least.

Knowing that you really could not ride your luck any further than getting a ninety *ninth* minute winner in a fitba match I took that as my line to leave for the day.

I'd be back the next day, as always. Wild horses wouldn't keep me from there.

'You working Friday, Brian?' I asked just as I was getting myself together to leave.

'Aye, I've got a long day Friday. How come, like?' He replied while combining this with serving one of the shop jakeys.

'Just asking so I can remind you to make sure you've got my money ready for collection Friday lunch time, eh?' I teased him although with six bets scored off from the list it wasn't as fanciful a statement to have been shouting about than it would've been a day or two before.

The irony was definitely not lost on me later on at night when I was lying in bed and couldn't get to sleep, while I was thinking about the bet. Earlier on in the day I'd been laughing at Brian while enjoying the prospect of giving him a few sleepless nights over the thought of paying out on my coupon. That Icelandic boy's goal changed things, though. Took me right over some kind of invisible line and to a place where - despite the permutations, still - I couldn't help but feel that I actually *had* an outside chance of pulling it off.

Three very winnable races at Newbury in the afternoon and then what? Win *them* and it was all down to one single under nineteen fitba match in Prague.

It looked like it was going to be an interesting next couple of days for the lads, one way or the other. This beautiful blonde - I assumed - Icelandic bastard - Mr Arnason, who I'd have been surprised if I was to ever hear of again in my life - had went and added an extra layer of intrigue to things.

I tried to put it to the back of my mind and get some kip but did so safe in the knowledge that if things went my way the next day - and, by the end of it, I was left waiting on that one youth team match in Prague being played on Friday morning - then in twenty four hours time it would've been a waste of one's time if I was to find myself back in bed same time, same place looking for anything resembling sleep.

Chapter 25

Hummel

'Right, you get one more chance, Paul. And that's one *more* than you should be fucking getting.'

Debz said to me with that same hard faced exterior that she'd had as set to default for over a week - by then - when it came to interacting with her other - but definitely not *better* half. Despite the face she was holding while laying out how things were going to be from now on, you can't fake what's going on when it comes to the eyes. Window into the soul, them.

I could tell just how *much* I'd hurt her and that made me feel like the absolute worst person on planet earth. Seeing into those eyes and knowing that I was the one responsible for taking the sparkle out of them.

She'd already been getting weighed down with work and all the shifts that they kept giving her to the point she barely knew if she was going to be days, nights or back shift from one week to the next. A few of her colleagues had been caught stealing and dismissed on the spot but until more staff were brought in she - along with a few others - was having to take one for the team.

That kind of stuff isn't exactly conducive for a happy work life balance at the best of the times.

Throw in finding your partner sexting with some younger - and in Debbie's mind - better looking girl … And a drug squad unit from Police Scotland raiding her place of abode and tearing it to to pieces in a way that you wouldn't have expected squatters to have done while enjoying a stay there. She'd been through such a shitty time of things, of late. And it was something that - now able to see clearly with a few days to play with before D Day on the Friday - I had recognised in all ways and knew that, if I wanted to save myself from losing her, then I was going to have to do something.

Didn't want to be left with that 'what might've been' feeling once things were officially too late and she'd already gone. I'm probably not the first man to take his other half for granted. Men are fucking morons and cannot stop themselves from reverting to type, take it from me, I know.

That Laurie Foster - who drinks in The Trap and goes out with Lizzie Diamond although you should use that term a bit loosely - is a classic example. Half the cunts around here, more than half probably, would chop off their left bollock just to be with Lizzie. She's not just pleasing on the eye but has a really good funny and warm personality. So what does Laurie do? Spends half his time shagging anything with a fucking pulse, and then brags about it in the pub. He's obviously not a special case, either.

If anything, Laurie could've been the ideal barometer for me to aim towards being at the complete fucking other end of. Make myself out to be an absolute shagger as well with that kind of talk. Like it would be an absolute 'choice' of mines to make to not cheat on Debz again in the future. Hardly Mr Slick with the ladies, me. Never was or claimed to be.

All those nights out - before me and Debz got together - where I'd have went all night without even getting a sniff at successfully buying a member of the opposite sex a drink. Not even one of those skanks that have no interest in riding you at the end of the night but will happily take a free drink or two while you're still waiting on the penny to drop that you're getting nowhere with the person.

While I was the most likely to be going home on my own at the end of the night - and Hammy in a police van after leathering someone - it was Drummond that had been the one to have stuck your money on getting off with someone. He had the looks, good clothes and the patter to go with it all. They were like putty in his hands. Finding out you're going to be a dad fairly changes all of that stuff though, eh?

It had been Drummond - without even knowing it - who had given me the breathing space to take a few days out from what had been going on and concentrate on me and Debbie. By telling me that I would next be required to do my portion when Friday rolled around and the payment had to be made it allowed me to stop thinking about it all twenty fucking four seven and look outwards at everything else.

Because make no mistake. You ever cheat on your wife or girlfriend and are going to get caught? Make sure you do it in a timely manner that does not involve it happening inside the same week as your house is raided for drugs while - alongside this - you find yourself in debt to ninety fucking thousand pounds to some German - possibly Albanian mafia - drug dealer. If and when your other half rumbles you. You *need* to be prepared to dedicate *every single fucking minute* towards fixing things.

Something that is difficult to do when you're sitting in a police interview room or trying to work out a way to see you pay back thousands of pounds that you have no idea where it's even meant to come from.

All self inflicted, I know, but my head was completely bursting with it all. Actually thought I'd spied a couple of grey hairs when I was shaving the other morning but - even if it was, which it wasn't and had just been a trick of the light - as harrowing as recent times had been I'm not that sure grey hairs can be summoned as quickly as that. Would've been appropriate, though. Felt like I'd aged *years* inside those ten days.

Hearing Drummond tell me - on Tuesday - that we pretty much had to just sit and wait until Friday coming around it had given me the space to breath, take a step back and try to - belatedly - fix things with Debz. Once we got talking, it soon turned into the equivalent of one of those summits that world leaders sit down and have a blether at and once they start you can't shut them up after that.

The morning had began with Debbie opening the door to a massive bouquet of flowers that I'd paid for the day before in the town. I've never been a flowers kind of guy. Had always found it to be counter productive because basically any man I knew that ever bought flowers - for anything out-with the standard occasions - for their wife or girlfriend immediately found themselves getting accused of doing something that they hadn't even done. Sounds too much like hard work for trying to do something nice for someone, like?

The window for *buying* her some had well passed by then but well, having all your money destroyed - and landing you in the shite with drug importers - and then to follow that being busted by the drug squad? It's that kind of stuff that can hamper with things like buying flowers and trying to talk your way out of trouble with the love of your life.

I'd never want her to hear it repeated but from the moment that she destroyed that precious hard drive, our relationship was no longer sitting at the top of my priorities. Horrible thing to say - I know - but what good is being in a relationship with someone when your name is in the process of being put on a kill list? With the greatest of respect to Debz, her and me could wait. Didn't make for a happy fucking home though, for that week plus, mind.

It had been a lot like that Resident Evil game I used to play on the PlayStation One. Like how you had to walk about the house with the zombies inside it? Not saying my girlfriend was a zombie but there were a lot of similarities between me and that game as in you were walking about a house absolutely hoping and praying that you weren't going to come across any zombies in any room or down the hall. For me, I just wanted to avoid Debbie.

Not that by doing this it would fix anything, obviously. Fuck all gets fixed without talking. Sometimes, though. You maybe need a bit of *action* to kick start the talking. I'd felt this would come through the gesture of a bunch of flowers with a wee personalised card. Had to throw the girl in the flower shop a fiver to herself to get her to write down the message I wanted delivered along with the flowers.

'He may be the world's biggest fanny but he's YOUR fanny and he just wants to say how sorry he is xx'

She'd tried to tell me that she couldn't write anything like that down on a card because of its profanity and how it broke their terms and conditions.

Had to talk her round and get her to admit that 'fanny' was hardly the most foul language that she'd hear in a day around our part of the city which she kind of didn't have a chance to oppose but *still* said that - what I was asking for - was still in the grey area.

A wee blue spot slid over the counter her way and suddenly her moral stance about what and what wasn't acceptable for to be written down on a piece of card wasn't so rock solid.

I knew Debz was off for the next couple of days and - with how things had been between us - I wasn't exactly relishing the prospect of the two of us being stuck in the house with each other. At best I could've seen us arguing for the two days and at the worst I could've seen her packing her bags, or mines for me.

With a few days before I had to seriously think about that one subject which had done fuck all other than dominate things - morning noon and night - I took this as my time to try and bring about a better state of affairs between the two of us.

In a moment of inspiration on my way back from the pub in the afternoon I'd had the idea that I have some flowers sent to arrive early the next morning. Try and set the tone of things between Debbie and me for the day ahead.

Fuck me, it worked, too.

I was in the middle of washing the dishes left over from breakfast when the doorbell went. I could hear her excitement and animated chat with whoever it was at the door, although I'd obviously had a decent idea *who* it was.

She came through to the kitchen straight away holding them in her arms with the first smile that I'd seen on her face since *it* had happened.

'You're right, you *are* the world's biggest fanny, but thank you *so much* for these.'

It was all a bit shameful - from me - but I literally had been living on my wits for almost a fortnight and even after putting her last - in the first place - I'd *continued* to put her last, right when she *needed* to be feeling like she was coming home in first position, and by a distance.

That she hadn't really felt that from me, at all. No reassurance of how much her worth was, how attractive to me her looks were. That she was someone's number one and a person worth fighting for. She'd received absolutely *none* of this from me.

A bouquet of flowers wouldn't rectify everything and just wipe the slate clean, but it would be a place to start.

Following the flowers being delivered - us both stood there in the kitchen - there was hugs, tears, shouting and swearing (the last two left to the, emotionally, all over the place other half of mines) but overall, there was talking. Lots and lots of talking, and in a way that neither of us had *ever* found ourselves communicating with one another. The levels of maturity, something I didn't even know I was capable of but managed to find from deep within.

Debz had admitted to having felt unattractive for ages and was standing there blaming herself for it all happening. Got her reassured straight away that it was all down to me if there was any blame to be laid out, which of course there *was*. Lesser men would've pounced on that 'out' and ran with it but fairs fair. I'm not a fucking sociopath, like.

As part of the chat, I had to come clean over some of what I'd been keeping from her regarding the visit from the drug squad the week before. Aye, obviously she knew where my contribution for the money coming into the house was coming from but her rule - from the start - had been that none of the stuff would ever be inside our house for any sustained period of time. What she *didn't* know however was that at the time of us standing there talking in the kitchen I - personally - was responsible for thirty thousand pounds of debt that needed clearing inside the next few days.

'B b but it's cool, babe. Drummond's handling things.' I'd said while she was expressing the fears that she had over what might end up happening to me, and possibly her. Having already said that she'd heard me talking about fake passports on the phone and asking me if we were all getting out of our depth with all of it.

While it was the precise time for the truth to be spoken, as we got things out in the open. It wasn't the time for *all* truths. Fuck, go ahead and say exactly how it was and it would've probably undone all the good work that had been carried out across the morning and rendered the flowers a complete waste of my fucking dough at the same time.

Was I going to tell her that it appeared that had we not made the payment on the Friday then - most likely - a select team of Albanians would be pressed into action to track us down and execute us all? Was I fuck! At least until Friday, anyway, there really no point in giving her *that* truth. If it was *still* a problem by Friday night *then* she'd have been the first to know.

Even though she'd said her piece to me. Told me just how much I'd hurt and disrespected her and how she had thought long and hard about just walking. Telling me that when a person does a thing to their partner - like what I'd done - how it changed everything and affected the trust in the relationship. I wasn't fucking daft enough to take that as being the *last* time that she was ever going to bring it up again. God no. That shit would be banked and kept in reserve for those moments where she might've needed it.

That was cool with me. It was as close to "forgiveness" as I was ever going to be getting from her and far, far closer to the kind that I ever *thought* I'd get.

She was going to give me another chance, that's all I had asked for and would now be down to me to make sure that I snatched it.

I barely recognised the feeling - such the opposite direction I'd been situated in - but that morning I felt some much required positivity surface. The feeling that, you know what? Shit was all going to work itself out and it was going to be nothing other than a couple of bad weeks. We all have them, woman twelve times a year, minimum.

With me and Debz - and the bridge between each other - in a much better state of repair. It properly put a brighter spin on the day with a fresh new attitude and one that I could actually face the day with and lift my head up a wee bit while facing it.

Fuck it, eh? Drummond - and the secretive moves that he was making - was going to do the business for us all too. All that nonsense about Albanian killers just waiting in the wings to be deployed? The stress that I'd put myself through over everything that I'd caused? A waste of time and effort that I'd probably shaved a wee bit off from my life by playing on a loop in my head.

Having a wee cuddle in the kitchen with Debz as we were wrapping up our piece of morning soul searching I just *knew* brighter days were coming. I'd obviously just needed something to kick start that frame of mind.

As we were still holding on to each other - bodies pressed tightly against the other - my phone that was sitting in my front pocket buzzed for a moment through a text or other notification, giving us a both a fright which broke the two of us apart again.

Looking at her with a smile - and getting one back that had felt like the first time I'd seen her smile in so long, in that way - I fished the phone out to see who or what was looking for my attention.

And well, mission accomplished, I guess. My attention as certified as being 'got.'

Not wanting to potentially undo all of the good work that had just been carried out there in the kitchen I pulled the phone out and saw that it was a Telegram from Arman88 and on seeing who it was I made - I'd hoped - a noncommittal face which would've looked like it had been just a stupid notification - the type we get hundreds of times a day - that hadn't been worth taking my phone out of my pocket. Putting the phone back again and choosing instead to see what he / they were saying in an environment when my girlfriend wasn't in the same room and given access to any reaction I might've had upon opening up said message.

When her mum called - around ten minutes later - while we were still standing in there chatting about much less heavy topics such as the saving of our relationship, that's when I took my chance to see what was waiting for me in the message.

Excusing myself while Debz hadn't even noticed, so deep in conversation, I headed through to the living room, pulling my phone out as I went. Going straight to Telegram and opening up the message. It was short, in no way of fucking sweet and *very* hard hitting.

'48 hours. Tick Tock.'

None of this exactly required. I *knew* which day of the week it was, and what and how important two days from then *was*.

That wasn't his main reason for the Telegram that had been sent, though. *Attached* to the short message was three pictures. The first image of the end of my road, with someone's arm creeping into view *specifically* so that you could see their watch, to go along with this whole tick tock thing that he had going on. The other two pictures similar to the first one I looked at, only for Hammy and Drummond's addresses.

Pfffft that 'positivity' stuff that I was talking about?

Overrated anyway, eh?

Chapter 26

Drummond

I could hear it in the boy's voice. The fear and the indecision that was radiating from him. And it worried me, big time. I could only do so much when it came to the blackmail and the threats that I was making, should Leckie not carry out his part of the *bargain* that we'd struck exactly a week ago. Maybe *that* had been the problem, though? Maybe he'd been given too *much* time to sit and think about everything. Sometimes it's for the better just to act straight away on something, even if it's a case of being *forced* into it.

As far as I was concerned, by the time I spoke to him on the Thursday night - in what was intended by me as nothing other than a wee last minute pep talk that you'd find a manager giving his team before they went out and crossed the white line for the ninety minutes - he would've had all his shit together and the next day was going to be nothing other than a formality. I'd spoken - or texted - Leckie pretty much every single day since I'd enlisted him in my whole plot to get the money for the German. This final call - before he went to work the next morning - really was just a motivational 'don't fuck it up' courtesy call and nothing more but with how it had gone it had left me more nervous about things going to plan than I had been at any other point. Which wasn't exactly too cool when the countdown was very much now on.

If he let me down there wasn't any plan b to deploy, which was fine because we wouldn't have had any fucking time to put it into action anyway.

I'm about the furthest thing from a control freak. Couldn't give a fuck why, how and or what people do but when it involves my immediate future then aye, admittedly I might tend to become a wee bit more hands on and involved. Because of that I wanted to know what and how Leckie was intending on doing to ensure that there was going to be ninety five thousand pounds sitting in my sock account by the end of the banking day. Wanted to see if there were any glaring issues that I was going to hear that may have presented a problem. Obviously, he was the banker out of the two of us but sometimes you can get value from a second opinion that comes from a fresh pair of eyes.

Plus, Leckie had slowly regressed across those seven days into an absolute wreck of a man. Fuck knows what he must've been like at work or at home with the family over more extended periods of the day because what I was seeing in front of me or hearing over the phone did not seem like a man who could ever have claimed to have had 'everything together.'

Aye, made me feel like a piece of shit to see - and know - that I was the cause of it and - having still to find how it was all going to play itself out - no doubt it was something that I was going to have to live with while telling myself that at the end of the day if it was either Leckie. A cunt I barely knew and who I had zero loyalty towards, or myself and the two boys in my life that I'd have done anything for? Then obviously, it was a choice made that would be taken a million times out of a million if ever presented my way again in the future.

'He'll get a custodial, when it all eventually gets uncovered. How am I meant to do something like that knowing that someone who is completely innocent gets fingered for it? I'm not sure I can handle something like that on my conscience, Drummond mate.'

He whined to me while explaining that he had got the login details of one of his colleagues which would allow him to transfer money, without Leckie being down as the staff member who facilitated the transfer. I didn't want the ins and outs of this but had actually thought it a good idea. Commit a crime while it gets made out as if it was someone *else* who had carried it out. Classic stuff.

'Look, Leckie. Who's your loyalty with here? Some random cunt that you have to work with five days a week that you never had a fucking choice in working with anyway … or … your two kids who *need* their dad at such key young years of their lives. And anyway, cunts that aren't guilty go to jail all the time. You not watched that *In the name of the Father* with Daniel Day-Lewis, no? Proper barry film, like.'

He'd tried to counter this by saying that the boy he was going to set up *also* had kids so what I was saying also applied to the patsy. This, as you can imagine, wasn't met with whatever kinds of understanding that Leckie thought this may have received.

'I'm not giving a fuck if he has more kids than Mick Jagger, pal. Just get it done or else you're going to be in for an interesting night this time tomorrow.'

I really don't know what kind of a fanny he took me for - which wasn't exactly wise, given what I had on him - but he tried to say that ethically it wasn't something that he felt that he could do to someone else which - more than anything else - just wound me up the wrong way.

'So let me get this straight, here? Your *ethics* would see you protect someone that you work with from losing their job and *maybe* picking up a wee spell inside but will happily take a backseat while you get your cock sucked in a public car park by some man while your wife and kids are back in the house? Aye, right proper man of principle, you. Well if *that's* where your priorities lie at least by tomorrow night you won't have to scurry about in the woods in secret from everyone anymore. I'm sure the weight off your shoulders, of you coming out will be an enormous lift, eh? If you change your mind though I'll be expecting a non incriminating text message - or phone call - from you before five bells to confirm that we're all good. All in your hands though, mate. You can either have a really good day tomorrow or you can have the worst one of your fucking life and the *best* part is that it's *you* who gets to pick which one.'

I left it at that. Ending the call feeling I'd said just enough and had hit all the sweet spots required. I'd still been left sitting at a well below hundred percent confidence that he was going to do it though which didn't exactly make for a chilled and relaxing Thursday night although, in all fairness, *nothing* was going to be chilled and relaxed until I saw that money sitting inside the newly created bank account the next day.

I wasn't a gambling man - that was more Hammy's forte - but basing things purely on what I was detecting from Leckie's tone of voice - I'd have been inclined to place things, on him succeeding, at about evens when - up to that phone call - I'd had things sitting at odds on. Maybe that was just the pre match nerves that were kicking in though, I tried to reason with myself. I'd been quietly confident that what I'd came up with was just the correct level of crazy to actually work.

Now that it was time for it to be actually put into practice though, it just felt, crazy.

I went on to spend the rest of the night - while sitting playing happy families with Bren and Holly - working myself up by convincing myself that this wet wipe that I'd brought into the fold was going to either bottle it or completely fuck things up and bring the whole gig crashing down with him.

Looking at the smile on Bren's face as she bounced Holly up and down on her lap while singing *Teddy bears picnic* - and Holly's giggles to this - it provided me with a bit of a brutal reminder that while I had placed the whole 'family' issue right onto Leckie, as his *motivation* to fall into line and do as told.

What I'd neglected to mention to him, however was that if he *didn't* fall into line then it was going to potentially be *my* family that was going to be on the line.

And - if the case - then I was going to have a *lot* more problems to think about than just visitation rights.

Chapter 27

Hammy

'Hummel? Can I ask a question? No matter how blunt it may be?'

I asked him after - just previously - almost choking on a bite of my Bayne's Steak Bridie on hearing what he'd just told me. While I was sitting combining eating some lunch and watching a race from Chepstow my best mate was telling me - from the safe and convenient distance of a phone call - that he had knocked a bottle of Bucky over one of my Adidas Stockholms. Two thousand and eight reissue, like.

'Well you're going to fucking ask it anyway, eh?'

He answered, already trying to go on the defensive.

'WHY IS IT THAT OVER THE PAST COUPLE OF WEEKS YOU'VE TURNED INTO THE ABSOLUTE FUCKING WORST CUNT EVER?!' PROPER FUCKING LIABILITY, LIKE.

'Hey you, less of that.' The girl - who must've been filling in for someone as I hadn't ever seen her in there before - shouted over to me from behind the counter. Fair enough, it *wasn't* acceptable customer conduct for a patron of a turf accountants and not something that you'd have found me normally displaying but - if any cunt is feeling charitable here - I *had* just been told that my grail-esque trabs had just been ruined by tonic wine. You'd *expect* a reaction for something on that scale.

'I never fucking meant to, Hammy. Fuck's sake, man.'

Aye, because someone stating the blatant fucking obvious at a stressful time like that is *always* going to help matters?

'Hummel? Of fucking course you didn't *mean* to do it, why would you? You're my fucking mate, eh? Hardly like you're going to do it on purpose, is it? Doesn't fucking change the fact that you *did* it, though?'

'Well I'm sorry, anyway. I know how hard it was for you to get them in the first place. Typical though, eh? I try to do *you* a favour and it fucking backfires and now here we are.'

I could see what he was doing and if he tried to go that way any further then he was going to be getting closed down. He was hinting at the fact that my trainers were only *in* his house because I'd worn them down to his one night we were all sitting having a few beers and playing FIFA. Only, when it was time to leave and he opened his front door to see me out we found that it was absolute fucking cats and dogs outside.

Even in that wee ten minute walk from his to mines those soft suede blue and yellow trainers would've been ruined so he volunteered to let me wear one of his *leather* pairs - a battered old pair of Grand Slams that he didn't wear anymore - to walk home in. Even with him being one size below me I was glad for his offer and had squeezed myself into them and hobbled home.

'Yes, Hummel and I was very fucking thankful for it. Your kind gesture was the difference between my Stockies being completely ruined or not. That all kind of becomes irrelevant though when you save them from rain damage only to get FUCKING BUCKFAST over them. You not think that one kind of defeats the purpose of the other, no?'

'I WON'T WARN YOU AGAIN, YOU.'

The girl raised her voice the second time around which was met with a hand gesture from me that - if she'd read it correctly - was simply appealing for a couple of more minutes of calling out my mate for the stupid fucking fanny that he was and then I'd be done.

I looked around to see if anyone was paying any specific attention to me - other when I was raising my voice - but everyone inside the shop all appeared to be deep into their own things. I continued.

'You know what, Hummel? You've really fucked me and Drummond the past couple of weeks. Fuck knows what you've landed us in, or not but we're all about to find out. You not been thinking about just how much more of a hard ride I could've been giving you on it all?'

He seemed to stop to think about this before answering.

'Not really thought about it, Hammy, like. You any idea what my head's been like the past couple of weeks? Hasn't been easy being me, like. The stuff with Debbie and then everything that has spiralled since then.'

I'm never going to be someone that would ever be short listed as a candidate for becoming a life coach but one piece of advice that I could give someone for free - that I think would serve them well in life - would be that they should not go fishing for sympathy from someone *directly* after telling them that you've just fucked their trainers that had last been released eleven years before.

'AND. WHOSE. FAULT. IS. THAT?'

I said, irritated by him as much as the news of my Stockholms.

The correct answer - as to why I hadn't been giving him some serious grief over what he'd done by losing us our money and then, with a knock on effect, putting us into a hefty amount of debt - had been that, while pissed off at him over my share of the money that had been lost, I had still been a bit sceptical over *who* it was that we were due the money to.

Drawing daggers from the girl I decided to do the smart thing and continue the phone call outside the front door to the bookies.

'Right then, what's done is done but now you're going to do something about it, one way or another.'

I said to him in a raised voice only this time around it was through the need for him to hear me over the passing traffic than it was through any aggression. I'd had my count to ten - and failed - moment and now it was time to be proactive. Aye, he'd fucked up - again - and, like anyone else, the onus was on him to do something about it.

'What do you mean, like?'

I'd actually been in a decent enough mood that day but it was feeling like he had called me with the specific intention of sucking the life out of any of that vibe. Telling me about the Stockholms was the starting of a fire but everything that seemed to come out of his mouth after that was like the equivalent of someone pouring a wee bit more petrol onto it.

'By that I mean you fucking well make up for what you did. This isn't fucking difficult, pal.'

I think *that* was what was winding me up the most, that he'd called me to tell me what he'd done but hadn't offered up any ideas of what he was going to do about it. As if a sorry was all that needed said to wipe the slate clean, while my trainers were left anything fucking but. I know all of our heads were a bit scrambled by that point - and who knows? maybe *I* was the one in the wrong for being so worried about a pair of trainers that by the end of the weekend I might never see again never mind *wear* - but this was just basic stuff. You break it you bought it kind of ethics, eh?

'What you're going to do, mate is you're going to take that pair of trainers and jump on a train to Dundee and ...'

'DUNDEE?' He butted in but was spoken right over.

'You're going to go straight to Dundee Sole in the city centre and give them to Kris and tell him that I - the boy who brought him the 450s - sent you.'

'Hammy, mate? You *do* realise that we are a potential twenty four hours away from having all kinds of bad bastards on our case, families too, maybe. And you're asking me to go all the way to fucking Dundee to get a pair of *trainers* repaired? A proper international incident we're all involved in here and you're more worried about a pair of Adidas?'

Fuck knows where he found the balls from but aye he got them from somewhere. Picked them at the entirely *wrong* time, mind but that probably summed up the daft cunt. The smartest *and* dumbest person you could ever wish to meet. Stick technology in front of him and he comes alive but just don't ever go looking for any common sense out of the cunt.

'Well either that or you buy me a new pair and if so then good luck finding a pair and then when - and *if* - you do, coming up with the money to *pay* for them. Need I remind you that it's *because* of you that the three of us barely have a fucking pot to piss in. The way things are going I might have to fucking *sell* the Stockholms and thanks to you I now can't even do that.'

'Is there not anywhere in Edinburgh I can take them to, no?'

Hummel asked, apparently now accepting things, having been reminded just how guilty he was in all of this. Possibly having no choice but to come to terms that - while things would never come to violence - I was going to be a complete dick with him on the subject of the trainers and that regardless of what a shit show his life presently was he was going to need to drop it all and go take care of this *latest* issue.

'Yes there is and no you're not fucking taking them there.'

I shut down any attempt at Hummel asking for something more convenient. Fuck him and his convenience. Next time screw the fucking cap back onto your bottle of tonic wine, radgey.

Since fucking up my original pair of ZX 450s the season before outside Easter Road at the Celtic match - when I'd agonisingly stepped in a huge steaming pile of police horse shite when not looking where I was going - and getting put in touch with this lad - fucking wizard more like - from the City of Discovery, and the repair job he'd done on them that had them back to me almost as if they'd come out the box. Reflectors were still scratched but the boy wasn't fucking *god* was he? Since then, why the fuck was I going to risk my pride and joy with anyone else?

If that meant an over hundred mile commute for Hummel then that really was none of my business.

He wasn't chuffed - telling me all of the shite that had been going on that week and how the last thing he needed was an out of town trip - but well, that made two of us.

Away from the whole sorry business with the Bucky and the Stockies, though? An absolute fucking dream of a day at Newbury. When I woke it was unavoidable really, thinking about the accumulator. The second my lids raised it was the first thing that popped in and way sooner than the kind of trivial shite like it being the day before our deadline with the German expired. What had started - at the beginning of the week - as a mug punter adrenaline filled bet put on by someone who was experiencing the giddy thrill of a winning streak was now, by the Thursday, something that was now feeling all too real. As each selection was ticked off as the week went on I was feeling less and less the mug, while - in turn - increased the sweat that I was getting on with regards to the gravity of what it would mean for it to be a winner.

That's the very *last* place you want to be, when putting a bet on. In a position where you 'need' it to win rather than are - like your average punter - *hoping* for a winner.

I'd have been happy enough to have stuck it on and maybe have had a couple of winners at the start. Get that nice wee burst of endorphins like - for example - when I didn't think Fernandinho would even get onto the pitch never mind get his yellow card. Had I got up on the Tuesday morning to find that the Argentinian match had burst the accumulator then aye, nothing ventured nothing gained and it would've just been another bet that you'd have thrown onto the 'lost' pile, with the next one waiting to be shoved on top of it.

To get down to just four though? I'm not sure if - by then - it even was *possible* to think of anything else. It really was too large a sum of cash for it *not* to fuck with your head. Checking my betting slip - again - and seeing that the first of my three races wasn't until twenty past two I knew it was going to be a long morning.

Time waits for no man though, eh even if - on occasion - it feels like it's a pair of concrete slippers dragging you down in a day. About fucking wore the carpet all the way through to the floorboards from pacing back and forward across my living room floor - that Thursday morning - while chain smoking some strong Gorilla. Obviously not strong enough to put me on my arse for a few hours and chill me the fuck out, mind.

Right then, if we've got any heartbreak coming then lets just get it fucking over with, I thought to myself - hours later - while sitting and watching the horses lining up for the twenty past two race at Newbury. My eyes scanning for the decked out orange with black diamond Colm Flaherty - the wee Irishman who had been hotly tipped by a lot of respected and informed pundits for winning all *five* of his races that day - who was riding his first of the afternoon on *Bad boy for Life.*

Well if there was going to be any heartbreak that day it wasn't coming through that beautiful grey specimen of a horse that romped home the three and a half lengths leaving *Protect the Statue* staring at hoofs in front of it.

If there had been a brown paper bag lying around there inside the bookies I'd have been grabbing and using it as if I was Roni fucking Size. The hyperventilating was well real, like. And I think I spoke for Brian the manager of Patrick Power as much as I did myself. That 'banter' from earlier on in the week between him and me now completely banished. My bet was too high stakes now for jokes. I was now officially too nervous about it and didn't want to risk hexing anything by then while Brian was now - whether he wanted to acknowledge it publicly or not - in a position where he was going to have to admit that this far fetched bet placed at the start of the week (and the same bet that he had laughed his punter out of the shop over) was now in with a *very* good chance of coming up.

Aye, it wasn't *his* money that he'd have to be paying out so what was the problem, eh? While true, I was sure that shop managers would've all been measured on what they brought in, and what was paid out. A bet in a small Scottish branch that netted the customer over a ninety grand's winnings would've been the type that would make Brian famous with his bosses, and not in the way that he'd probably have liked either.

The thing is, it was more than just that - business - between Brian and me. It was 'personal' too. Maybe around six years or so before - and well before he ended up working in the bookies - he'd been a bit mouthy with me in a city centre club when he'd had a bit much to drink. We were in the same year at school so knew who each other were but that was about it.

Cunt bumped into me when he was blootered and knocked my pint all over the front of me, and then blamed *me* for it? You know how it is, eh? There's ways to diffuse a situation, like when you knock some cunt's pint over them due to your inability to even stand properly. Aye, you apologise and offer to to buy that person another of whatever it was they were drinking and hope that nothing more comes of it but prepare yourself for the possibility that it might well do.

Him? Nah, fucking staggers and falls right into me. Pint goes all over my shirt and I'm left with this fucking reprobate with his arms kind of around my waist to stop him from falling to the floor. When he gets himself back properly to his feet that's when he starts shouting at me about not looking where I was going, called me a prick as well.

Well I gave him a *reason* to think of me as one, once he'd sobered up the next morning and looked in the mirror. Look, maybe I went over the score a bit, breaking his nose and knocking his eye so far back into its socket it's a wonder he wasn't able to spit it out of his mouth. Didn't have to happen though, mind. All the cunt needed to do was show a wee bit of remorse for what he'd done and it would've played out differently.

He was initially going to press charges until one day he decided to withdraw his statement. Saying that he had been heavily drunk that night and how he couldn't make a clear ID of his attacker without there being an element of doubt about it.

As you can well imagine, the boy must've been thrilled to get himself a job at the bookies - years later - and find out that *I* was one of the shop's regular customers, eh?

While I was grown up enough to be able to recognise that this had all happened years before and it was just another night out and something that probably happens *every* weekend to some poor cunt who can't handle their drink and be prepared to let bygones be bygones, Brian was a wee bit more resistant to this. Actually tried to get me fucking banned from the shop, which, obviously, didn't help those initial customer and shop staff relations in those early days.

Stupid cunt found out that technically he couldn't ban me if I hadn't actually *done* anything to earn a ban and - through my own experience - considering some of the abuse that I'd seen some sore punters dish out at the poor girls working the counters at the various betting chains across the UK it appeared that you'd have to be some cunt like fucking Pol Pot to get yourself a ban from your average bookmakers. Brian was stuck.

Through time - and while very much in possession of the facts that he didn't want to ever get into anything with me, knowing how it would turn out - he eventually developed a bit of a thicker skin and found himself in a position where he could dispense the insults inside his shop as much as he took them.

He obviously despised me, though. Something I could hardly have blamed him for, given his reason. Still, it always gave winning an extra edge to it, if Brian was the one that had to hand over my takings. That door swung both ways though, mind.

And *that* was what added the delicious sub plot to this whole mega-acca situation. Did I want to lose the bet? Of course I didn't but that shite was an every day occurrence and wouldn't have normally put me up or down. The thought of winning that money *from* Brian was almost as good as the money itself. Once again, though. He'd have been thinking the exact same thing.

If the bet was to go the distance there was a good chance that things were going to be emotional inside the shop, whatever the eventual outcome.

Things got a whole lot more emotional when - after the most tense steward's enquiry of my gambling life - Flaherty got his second winner of the day. I'll be honest, I thought Dens Park Fox had beaten Hit the Mattress (Flaherty's) by a nose but after what felt like a *year's* wait on the verdict the result fell in my favour. I was overcome with a strange feeling that stopped me from running around the shop Careca style like an aeroplane. I *wanted* to. If I'd acted on my urges they'd have been able to hear me back in Flaherty's birthplace of County Wicklow. Something was stopping me though.

Things felt *so* close now that I didn't know 'how' to act. The excitement bubbling up inside was engaged in a battle of wills against the side of me who wanted to prepare myself for the inevitable boot in the fucking balls that was in the post and something that would completely invalidate the whole need for getting excited about in the first place. You could call it pessimism but I'd have called it a case of not my first rodeo.

It's funny how that worm turns, though. With one horse race left at Newbury and an obscure youth football match in Prague the next morning left to go. *Then* I was fucking wishing I'd done the bet online and had been given a cash out option! What must the pot have been worth - by then - that I'd have been getting dangled in front of me from the bookies who were bricking it in case the bet went all the way and were taken for even more? Sixty, seventy grand even? *Enough* to have me thinking that maybe I shouldn't be pushing my luck and, instead, hitting that cash out button pronto and before Flaherty got on his last ride of the day and anything happened to take that amount offered to you and turned into a big fat zero.

Too late for that stuff now though I had no choice but to think as I watched the list of horses scrolling up the screen. The scarily named *Nowhere to Run* sitting as second favourite with the much decreased odds of three to one compared to my tens that I had been given at the start of the week.

Would just be peak me though for such an outlandish bet to go all the way only for to end through a horse called 'Nowhere to Run' I said to a few of the old boys sitting around who had their own interest in the race all be it the chance to bag themselves under a tenner as opposed to me looking to get myself one step closer to the biggest win of my life. All relative, I suppose.

By this point everyone - all the regulars - all knew about my bet that had been gathering pace across the week. I hadn't shut up about it for one thing and it really had taken me up to the Thursday before taking on the ability to stay silent on it due to eventually starting to brick it that I might actually *win* the fucking thing. I'd made too much of a noise about it previously though for anyone else to forget so from the moment I'd came into the shop that Thursday it had been a topic of interest.

'Haw Brian? How you feeling now, pal? Are you scared, mate? You look scared.' Joe "The Pole" Leishman who had no skin in the game and really just liked winding people up in general shouted over to Brian who was trying to put on a wee front as if he wasn't up nor down about the prospects of my bet, but we both knew that wasn't the truth of the matter.

'He's fucking shiteing it, look at his face.' One of Joe's drinking buddies - Pat Walker - chipped in with the two of them laughing away.

If my horse turned out to *know* where to run to, and was faster than its opponents. Then I'd *maybe* allow myself a wee chuckle but even then the chances were that, instead, I'd have just set my face to stunned and carried that on for the rest of the night all the way onto the next morning right up until I knew which way the wind was starting to blow between Slavia and Sigma under nineteens over in the Czech Republic.

I don't even know where I went off to - during the race - but had some, I don't know? Like an out of body experience but not exactly like that. Kind of like my mind body and soul took itself off to a safe space for the length of the race to stop all of my vitals from shutting down. I can't explain it, it was something that you really more *felt*.

One moment I remember barely even being able to hold the bookies pen in my hand - so sweaty it was - while I felt like my temperature started to go right up. Was maybe all in the mind but it literally felt like my hair had become drenched in just the one wave of heat that rushed up and over me. I watched the race but kind of stared *through* the telly to the point that I could no longer focus on what was *on* the screen. It was the roar from everyone around me and the feeling of hands grabbing and pulling at me that somehow brought me back into the room, in the real sense again.

Should there have been any doubts over what had taken place on the screen of the Samsung HD telly attached to the wall, it was now there fixed there for my convenience while the commentator spraffed on about what an amazing race it had been and how it had been anyone's to win up to the final furlong.

1.   **Nowhere to Run**
2.   Have a nice Trip
3.   Fun time Frankie

Cunts around me were all slapping me on the back and congratulating me. What the fuck were they congratulating me for? The job wasn't done, yet.

One. Small. Step

Like that spaceman boy said.

Fuck knows what I looked like - exterior wise - but I tried to keep a lid on things and play it cool. No point making an arse of myself today when it might make me look an even *bigger* one tomorrow. The kind of advice that should be found inside a fortune cookie at a Chinese restaurant.

In my mind - anyway - I *was* cool. Gambling done for the day I'd seen all I needed to. After taking everyone's congratulations and without bothering getting into why they shouldn't have - they meant well at the end of the day - I got up and left. Making sure to look over Brian's way and give him the slightest of winks before telling him that I'd see him the next morning.

When I hit the street the instinct - from after Flaherty's first race - to do that Careca celebration returned to me but I stopped myself otherwise I'd have fucking aeroplaned all the way down the road.

Just wait until tomorrow, Hammy lad. I said to myself out loud as I started walking while fixing out some tunes to listen to and getting my fags out to spark up what was one of the sweetest tasting cigarettes I'd ever lummed in my life.

Those young Slavia and Sigma lads give you five goals tomorrow and you can put out the last call for boarding, close the gate, have the air stewards do that in flight safety thing they do and *prepare for fucking take off!*

Chapter 28

Detective Bill Burchill

'It's clear that there's a connection, Bill. It's just the working out a way to link everything together and in a way that will get us convictions.'

Ardwick said, stating the bloody obvious - as he tended to do - but I'd been asked, well, *told* more like, by the gaffers from up above that I was to take the young one under my wing - a very much wet behind the ears newbie protected by way of being related to the assistant to the Chief of the whole of the country - and show him the ropes. Fuck did he wear me out, though.

Don't get me wrong or nothing. You're *looking* for keenness and enthusiasm from someone starting out in a career otherwise the signs aren't looking good from the very start. It's just that the constant barrage of questions and opinions from him really did tire you out. Sometimes you just had to throw a ball for him to run after and bring back to you like you would with an overexcitable Golden Retriever.

I'd treated the investigation into Evans - and his close knit group of friends Drummond and Hamilton - such as that. A worn and well chewed tennis ball for Ardwick to run and chase after and keep him occupied.

Obviously the bust on Evans's house didn't exactly go to plan and it was only *because* of that which led to us now having to try and wipe up our own mess by squeezing some form of victory out of things. Whatever it might have been, or wherever it came from.

It hadn't been the stab in the dark - the bust on Evan's house that day - that it might've appeared to have been. Evans, Hamilton and Drummond had already earned a place on our radar *before* HMRC alerted us to the package containing three kilos of Cocaine that had entered Scotland via airmail and with Paul Evans's address marked on it.

Nobody can ever *really* keep things secret, as much as how 'watertight' you might think you have things.

They hadn't been blatant about things - and more importantly not be seen to rub things in our noses - but we had began to hear whispers that the three of them were involved in the drug game, maybe two or three months before that package was intercepted at Edinburgh Airport.

All it takes is to arrest the correct person who will do anything and name anyone if it saves their own skin and you're on the board. Don't give me that honour amongst thieves pish. It simply doesn't exist. More singers than bloody T in the Park - in an interview room - once we begin turning the screw on suspects and persons of interest.

The thing is, just because some scumbag - who if they were to tell you that the sky was blue you'd still look up to check - sits there and names names. That still doesn't give you the right to just steam in there and act on their word. Doesn't work like that and neither it should when approximately three quarter of the things said to a police officer or detective are generally not the truth to begin with.

Still, once a name - or names - is brought up then they'll need looked into. Never goes well for someone in the force who gets handed a piece of intel that they don't act on only for it to later reappear and bite them on the behind, and there's been *many* examples of that.

We'd taken a look into things but hadn't been able to come up with anything that was even close to concrete enough for us to proceed any further. No links to them and any of the bigger players in the city that would've been worth us exploring. Barely any charges between the three of them and were it not for James Hamilton out of the three then they'd have hardly had any. And even at that, none of Hamilton's offences were ever *major* drug related, always violent.

All we could really find was two or three - consistent - stories that the three of them were supplying dealers in the immediate area while also stretching across the bridge and into Fife. These had all come from 'off the record' chats with informants but the fact that this intel had come from people who had no direct relationship with each other showed us that there *was* something.

None of the three had a job but appeared to be doing ok for themselves. I'd attended a training morning - more out of interest and because I had a few spare hours waiting on a prisoner being transferred - that was being held by our football hooligan unit and a section of it involved the clothes that they wore and for how it made spotting the hooligans a little easier while they were in amongst wider crowds. This part of the lecture focussing on the brand names and what their distinctive labels looked like.

It was because of this that I knew for a certainty that Barry Drummond - who was constantly decked out with either a black lens on his arm or that Stone Island compass - appeared to be doing ok for himself despite not appearing to have a job. Evans? Well once again for someone 'unemployed' he had been someone with some amount of cutting edge technology inside his house for someone who was on benefits. His telly on the living room wall was about the size of one of the Odeon screens at Kinnaird Park. That, amongst all of the other expensive gadgets that were sitting inside the place when we raided it. I don't know how he knew to destroy all of his PCs and laptops though, but he knew somehow. *That* in itself was highly suspicious but I'm afraid you can't get a conviction out of suspecting someone, sadly.

The third - James Hamilton - was not a stranger to me, and the force, by any stretch of the imagination. Right nasty piece of work if you catch him in the wrong mood, and many had. From the intel we'd collected on him he was hardly someone who existed by living in the shadows. If you ever wanted to find him it could generally be achieved by checking one of three places. Paddy Power bookmakers, The Trap Door public house, or his *own* house.

None of them had jobs but with Drummond looking like a fashion victim, errm I mean model. Evans with a home entertainment system that would rival a cinema chain and Hamilton - who it was mentioned was not a small time gambler - being able to subsidise a life of gambling, I wasn't stupid either.

Money doesn't just grow on trees which you give a shake any time you're a wee bit light.

Everything had made sense, that they'd have been involved in *something*. Evidence though, eh? It can be a bit of a bitch, that whole side of the job. They had that whole side of things well wrapped up in that *Minority Report*, didn't they? How beautiful would *that* be? Hardly any actual detective work. Just rocking up in the Corsa and knocking on someone's door and lifting them because they're *about* to commit a crime. A man can dream.

They'd been officially marked as POI's months before but the combination of higher case priorities, low manpower and the three of them never coming close to slipping up between them had meant that nothing had ever really been done over it. We didn't even know the quantities that they were responsible for distributing across the city and Fife and - for all we knew - it might've been a case of over committing on something only to find out that the juice wasn't worth the squeeze. We can't stop it all, don't claim that we *will* so don't even attempt to. All we can really do is as much as the hours and resources we're given in a day.

Sometimes though, someone will vie for your attention and literally *beg* for you to put them at the top of your 'to do' list. Evans did that the day that we were told over sixty thousand pounds worth of product was sitting in a package marked for his address.

That though created the biggest conundrum of all. How are you supposed to catch a drug dealer, when they don't have any drugs? This something you are almost certain is the case because you have just watched him - from a car parked down the street - *refuse* to accept his delivery of product?

We based things on that while Evans had not accepted the delivery this would then have - in turn - created a knock on effect of which no one would have been able to predict and, instead, would just have to monitor things to see what followed.

Knowing that movement of any sort was going to be made in the immediate aftermath of the bust on Evans's house we arranged to have a small undercover team watch the movements of the three of them. Hardly round the clock watch - they weren't *that* high value - or anything but a case of keeping an eye on them that hadn't been there previously. Hamilton and Evans had been a waste of time as you could've employed a bloody *webcam* to be fixed on Paddy Power bookies

- for Hamilton's coming and goings - and another one on Evan's front door, due to 'Hummel' barely leaving the place other than to meet up with the other two in the pub. Barry Drummond, on the other hand, was a different kettle of fish to the others. While his two mates were almost predictable in their behaviour - after two or three days of observing them - Drummond was not so much.

Apart from the frequent meet ups with the others at their regular boozer, his movements were barely ever the same. In the short period that we'd had him under watch he had seemed to be almost constantly on the move. Travelling to houses and areas of business for short periods of time before jumping back into his car and off in another direction. None of this, obviously, illegal but neither was it what you'd have classed as 'everyday behaviour' either, for someone unemployed. At times, also, the lad was seen to be visibly upset and frustrated upon leaving some of the places he'd been visiting. Booting over a row of blue recycling bins sitting on Pennywell Road when he'd left a house on one particular occasion that we'd been sitting watching from a distance.

That was why we took the punt that early Friday morning when we were sitting outside of Greggs having a couple of breakfast rolls in the car when we seen the man himself walking in and - minutes later - emerging back onto the street, already tucking into a roll of his own as he walked back to his car.

'Get the engine started.' I urged young Ardwick to get us into position.

He looked at me with the suggestion that he still hadn't finished his breakfast.

'Oh I'm sorry, should I run over to Barry Drummond and ask him if he could hang on for a few minutes until me and my partner have finished our breakfast before he pulls away for us to covertly follow him?'

He saw the point though my sarcasm. Turning the ignition and the engine sparking into life. Looking behind and out of the car I could just about make out the angle of Drummond now sitting in the drivers seat of his car while he continued eating before throwing the empty brown bag out of the window and driving off, with us tailing behind.

If he was only heading back home then it would hardly have been a major inconvenience to us had that been the case. What *would've* been an inconvenience however would've been if he'd been going somewhere that we'd have *wanted* to have known about, but had chosen, instead, to sit and eat bacon rolls in the car.

After a few minutes of being a a couple cars behind him it was clear that he wasn't heading home and, instead, looked like he was heading out and away from the town. About fifteen minutes later we crept into the sprawling car park - at the call centre for the bank - and parked up alongside a few other cars that had all driven in at the same time which helped Ardwick and me blend in just perfectly.

'Why's he coming to the call centre of a bank, and at *this* time of the morning?' Ardwick said rhetorically or I'd taken it as much because he had to have known that I didn't know the bloody answer.

'Well, Crawford. That's what you're about to find out for us.'

He just looked at me with that dumb face.

'Well? Get out the car and do a bit of snooping. Drummond doesn't know who you are but I've worked around here long enough for him to *definitely* recognise me. Follow him, keep close but not too close. Close enough to hear if he's speaking to anyone.' I ushered him out of the car, telling him that with all the staff flooding out of their cars and all going in the same direction towards the main entrance of the building he had the ideal cover for being in the immediate area and wouldn't stick out in anyway. If *anything*, with his age and choice of suit. He looked more of a banker than he did a member of C.I.D.

He got out of the car and joined the throng of staff all either getting out of their cars or already on their way towards the front door of the huge building at the start of another day. I'd noticed that Drummond had got out of his car up ahead too. Him being the only person really sticking out due to his clothing up against everyone else's smart business casual attire while he was just *casual.*

Him - as well as Ardwick - eventually disappeared from view, obscured by more staff who were closer to me while still sat there in the car.

I could've been nothing but sometimes you can get a feel for when something is a little irregular and someone like him - who was on our radar - spotted out and about that early in the morning while not having a job to go to. Making journeys out to financial institutions was just that, irregular.

Maybe he was going for a job? Not when you look like you've got a fight planned with Aberdeen Soccer Casuals you wouldn't. Could've been all innocent and a waste of a good Greggs breakfast. There was no point speculating on any of it.

I sat and had a cigarette while listening to the breakfast show on the local station. Couldn't bloody stand that DJ and his -

obvious - put on cheesy radio voice but well, the *name that tune* pot was now up to six and a half thousand pounds and I'd been trying to call in from the point I first heard it - back when it was sitting at five hundred pounds - but up to that point I'd had no luck in getting through. It was seriously doing my head in that I knew the answer, but couldn't get through to give it. How the hell did the listeners across Edinburgh and Fife *not* know that it was Hey Bulldog by The Beatles anyway? *That* was as concerning as not being able to get someone to answer my call each morning when I tried.

As always, there was no joy when trying to call into Forth One. Felt like I'd been engaged more than that bloody Darren Day - the actor - the amount of times I'd tried.

'And we go again tomorrow with name that tune. Surely *someone* out there must know which song it is and wants this money. I have it here and am just *waiting* to give it to you. Listen in again tomorrow.'

The DJ taunted me from through the Corsa speakers while playing that little stab of piano one more time for the listeners before moving onto some traffic news.

Cursing my luck - like I'd done the day before and would surely be doing the day after - I noticed Ardwick making his way quickly back to the car. Serious look on his face and just stopping short of actually running towards the car.

'Something's going down today, Bill.'

He announced with a fair bit of pride behind it and feeling well chuffed for himself that he'd done some form of police work that had potentially produced a result of sorts.

He then went on to explain to me that Drummond had been standing around outside the main entrance - having a smoke like some of the bank's staff, squeezing in a last puff before getting started for the day - so Ardwick had done the same.

I was actually a wee bit proud of Crawford when he'd told me that he'd actually asked Drummond for a light. In doing so then ensuring that him being stood around would not have been viewed by Drummond as anything worth noting.

Ardwick told me that as he'd been stood smoking his cigarette Drummond had grabbed one of the bank employees on their way in and pulled them to the side of the entrance where they had a bit of an animated conversation.

My young assistant showing me a photo that he'd discreetly snapped with his phone that showed a clear angle of the employee's frightened face.

'So what was it that they were talking about?' I asked, listening to Ardwick but other than speculation I wasn't hearing anything with much meat on the bone.

Crawford went on to explain that it wouldn't have been possible to hear everything without getting too close to the two of them but from what he *had* heard and mixing this with the body language that was on show from both of them it appeared that Drummond was potentially exploiting the bank employee and pushing them into doing something.

'When the member of staff was grabbed by Drummond *that* was the loudest part of the conversation, when he - surprised - shouted 'what are you doing here?' And was told by Drummond that after last night's phone call he wasn't sure that the employee was going to go ahead with the plan and that he'd felt that he needed to pop over and see him - before he started for the day - to make sure that he finished the job for him.'

'*What* job, though?' I wondered out loud.

Ardwick couldn't say as either it had been said too low for him to hear or had been spoken about *without* being spoken about. From the description of events it sounded like Drummond was very much in charge of things. Ardwick saying that Drummond had demanded to see the employee's phone before having a look through it and pressing it back into the man's chest in a threatening manner while saying that he'd specifically told him to delete all messages from him.

'He's shaking him down for something. It was obvious from the passive aggressive way that they parted ways with the tone of how he wished the guy a good day at work while remembering him of how he hoped hat he would have an even *better* night. The guy looked shit scared by the end of the conversation and he hadn't exactly looked relaxed even at the mere prospect of finding Drummond stood there outside his work.'

'Now why oh why would someone, who is linked to a gang now out of pocket for product that must be worth easily seventy grand, want to shake someone down, who works for a *bank?*'

I said sarcastically to Ardwick and regretted it straight after because he really had done a good piece of police work to gather the intel we now had.

Maturely seeing past my sarcasm, Crawford's mind went straight to what I was more than hinting at. His face lighting right up once the penny dropped.

'Come on, Detective Ardwick. I think we need to go pay bank security a visit.' I confirmed as I flicked away my half smoked cigarette out of the window - across the roofs of two adjacent cars before it dropped out of sight - and got out of the car, followed by my young assistant, and headed across the busy car park towards the call centre.

Chapter 29

Detective Bill Burchill

'If you'd like to follow me this way we can sit down and discuss the matter.' *Stewart Parker*, 'head of security' said to Ardwick and me after coming down to meet the pair of us at reception. This coming after I'd flashed my badge to the receptionist - a woman with a smile that could've grown tomatoes, so bright it was - who was sitting behind the desk that morning and had asked her to call whoever was responsible for security within the building.

He led us up a flight of stairs - making small talk about how they weren't used to police visits - before taking us left and down a corridor and stopping to open the door to a meeting room to let us in.

'Can I get you both a drink before we get started?' He asked, slightly harassed and - like most people at the very start of their morning - probably not in an ideal position to have to deal with visits from the police. 'I could do with one myself. Me and my wife have just had another baby so it'll probably take me until lunch time to wake up if I don't.' He added. The bags under his eyes testament to the broken nightly sleep that the poor guy was going through. Thank god that I won't be seeing those days ever again. If I don't get my eight hours it knocks me all out of whack, which pretty much means that anyone who has to be *around* me is going to be feeling a bit out of sorts themselves.

We both nodded our heads to him and - once he'd showed us to our seats at the long meeting table and sat down himself - he lifted the phone that was in front of him. Pressing a single button before asking whoever it was on the other end of the line to bring three cups of coffee along with some milk and sugar, as well as a selection of fruit.

'Ok, then, now that's all been taken care of, how can I help you? You mentioned something to Ellie at reception about a matter of security?'

He asked, appearing like he could finally settle himself now that we were all sat down.

'Yes, we did.' I confirmed.

'Well then, you're speaking to the right guy. What's the problem?' He said - and for the first time since I'd set eyes on him - *sounding* like he was the 'right guy.'

'It appears that one of your employees, here at the call centre, may be, how should I put this? Compromised.' I replied while looking across the table at Crawford and motioning him to get out his phone and pull up the picture of the worker who had been seen talking with Barry Drummond.

'*Compromised?*' He asked before his brain quickly caught up with him. 'Oh, 'compromised?' When he had realised what I had hinted at his face was one of distinct recognition.

'Ok, what information do you have on them?' He asked.

'Well, we have this for starters.' Ardwick said while sliding his phone across in Parker's direction.

The security guy, picking up the phone for a closer inspection, sat studying the image.

'Nope, don't recognise him but someone *will*. If it's ok with you if you can email it to me I can have the photo distributed to managerial level across all of our services here in the call centre.'

He passed the phone back to my colleague who was already on the case asking for Parker's email address to forward the photo on to.

'Good, thanks. I should have an answer for you before you leave. Now what is it that they've done?' He asked while sitting with his inbox open on his phone waiting on Ardwick's email arriving into his inbox.

'It's not really a case of what they've done but what it is that they're *going* to do.' I answered back, cryptically. Mostly because I didn't have a straight answer for him.

Ardwick went on to explain that in the process of following a suspect it had brought us to the front door of the call centre and - with what was overheard during the conversation - it had appeared that this unknown employee was potentially being coerced into doing something, in his capacity of a bank employee. Obviously, this was going to be money related.

But the one thing that *wasn't* obvious was which method of stealing they were intending on deploying.

Parker told us that - all under the one large room - the call centre had its general banking floors in addition to the more specific high level banking services, loans departments, insurance and credit cards. There was billions of pounds to steal and almost the same amount of potential ways to bloody *steal* it, according to this security manager.

'First of all, we just need an ID on him and then from there we can bring him in and question him. Thank you for letting us know. I'm sure that you've got better things to do than be worrying about bank employees with their hands in the till?'

Normally, when someone is trying to steer the police away from helping them I always tended to assume that there was an ulterior motive for that but I didn't get that off Parker. Instead I took it as a genuine offer from someone who was not in any way fazed by what we had just told him.

'Now lets not go too …'

'Maybe this wouldn't be the correct move to make'

Ardwick and me both replied at the same time. Both sprung into immediate action by the thought of this 'helpful' security boss actually doing more harm than good.

'Look, Stewart. We believe that your employee is actually a victim in all of this. We don't have the specifics and even if we did we might not have been legally permitted to give you them anyway but it is of our opinion that, now that you've been alerted to things, you can possibly just *monitor* the employee's movements, without actually making them aware that you're doing so. There's a bigger picture here at play and we believe that it may be linked to a local drugs ring.'

I tried to make him see things from our point of view and that while he saw the chance to take someone out of the game as soon as identified. Why we thought that it would be more advantageous if they were kept on the field of play.

'But, you're suggesting that? We just let him carry out what his intentions are? Which I *assume* to be - in one way or another - stealing funds. You can't seriously ask me to sit back and watch an employee, for example, stealing money from out of a customers' bank account?'

He was amazed by our hinting that this had been what we were looking for.

'Yes, Stewart but *obviously* we all know in advance of this so any funds stolen will not have been taken without it being monitored.' Ardwick tried to persuade him that letting this slide wasn't as monstrous a move as Parker had reacted to it as.

'Detective Ardwick, with the greatest of respect. When a customer trusts us with their money they trust *us*. Where does that trust go when they notice that some of their money has been removed without their authorisation, by a bank *employee?* What would you say if it was *your* money that went missing?'

I wasn't going to sit there and admit it but Parker had a point. Plus it was funny watching someone put Ardwick straight.

'But anyone, found with funds removed, would receive them back again.' My young colleague wasn't for listening to the guy.

'Once again, with respect. That really is not the point. Trust cannot be bought by refunding money to someone that already *had* the money. What we'd 'need' to do on the most basic of levels would be to reimburse a customer for their trouble so, in that respect, if we were to willingly sit back and *allow* an employee to commit fraud or theft it would - in turn - impact the bank in not just customer trust and reputation but also *financially.* I'm sorry but it's completely out of the question.'

He wasn't having any of it. Once again, not because I believed that he wanted to impede things for us. Simply because he knew what *his* job was and as much as he would've wanted to help us, he wasn't going to cut his own arm off while doing it.

I'll be honest, this - dealing with bankers and financial institutions - wasn't a part of the job that I'd had much in the way of experience of but I could already tell that Parker knew where he stood legally so there was no point in us pushing things further and it souring things.

'You've just had *another* kid, Stewart? Does that suggest that you've already got some?' Ardwick wasn't done. I'd always had the impression that a lot of what he did was for my benefit, knowing that I'd have to give evaluations to top brass on him every now and again. This didn't feel any different to that but I was happy to let him carry on and see where he went with this. Was intrigued, actually.

'Ermm, this is our third, and last hopefully!' He appeared thrown by Ardwick's question.

'I'm sure you'd agree that one of the biggest dangers of your kids growing up is drugs. We're the people that's out there trying to *stop* them. This is your chance to help us do something about it, Stewart. If Bill and me are correct with our assumption - and I'm sure Bill won't mind me divulging some delicate information that otherwise we wouldn't be telling you here - we believe that your employee is being pressurised to carry out 'something' during working hours to benefit a local drug dealer that we are monitoring. *This* could be a chance to put someone like that away and make it one less dealer on the streets.'

It was a passionate speech from the young one and I was begrudgingly proud of him. He'd showed an ability to think outside the box which was an absolute fucking *necessity* if he wanted to make it at that level.

'I hear you, I really do.' Parker pleaded with my colleague ' but if I sign off on this I'll be the one who gets the sack and, I'm sure you'll agree, that while I would like to help my future grown up kids from the perils of drugs I need to help the *present* kids by possessing the ability to do things like feed and clothe them. Things like that, which this job provides.'

No father could argue with that, even a copper that desperately needs a result. Ardwick wasn't a father, though.

'No one would have to know though, Stewart, would they?'

This was the point that the bank security guy's patience with Crawford possibly ran out. Looking at me as if for me to step in and start to help him before looking back at Ardwick.

'No one would have to know? What about the *customer* when they notice that their funds are missing?'

I'd been of a mind to step in and back up Parker and put an end to proceedings because there hadn't been anything he'd said that had given me any cause to disagree with. It wasn't the result that I was looking for - because it was clear as crystal that Drummond was up to something - but well, hey ho, even when you're the police there's that stuff you can't get past. It wouldn't have been the first time red tape or bureaucracy would get in the way of our work and I'm not even sure it could've been classed as that? Just the basic principle of how you don't fuck with other people's money. Treat others as you wish to be treated yourself, aye? Numero fucking uno, there, is not to touch their doe rae me.

On the other hand, though. We'd made the effort to be *in* the call centre so we may as well squeeze as much time as we had inside there in a productive way. Plus, that coffee was *very* special. I made a note to ask him where they got it from but only *after* we'd conducted business otherwise he'd have been given the impression that he was dealing with people that were less than professionals.

'That's *exactly* my point, Stewart.' Ardwick's overuse of Parker's christian name was in danger of becoming patronising. 'You guy's are going to be all over him like N'Golo Kante on a football pitch and the moment that he carries out any wrongdoing you can immediately reverse the transaction *but* the crime will have been committed *along* with the direct link to the third party account that we need for the intended conviction of our suspect. You're literally going to be doing the same thing as we need you to be doing anyway, we just need you to do it for a few seconds more and let it take place and that's the key part of it. Because you'll be watching it take place in real time you'll know exactly when to have the transaction reversed with zero impact on anyone impacted by his crime.'

Parker - when explaining to us how him and his team would be taking care of this - revealed that the key to this would be to have one of the team 'mirror' the employee's movements down to every key stroke, once they had logged into their own personal banking system account. Ardwick pouncing on this and trying to turn it into an advantage and try to give the banker a reason for not being able to say no.

'There are too many variables. Depending on the customer's preferences they may already have selected the facility to be called or sent a text informing them of a major purchase or transaction on their account. Our own fraud team may pick it up for a random spot check if it shows up on the system. That's *two* to speak of.'

But still Ardwick wasn't done. I truly felt that morning that the young man came of age, sitting in that cold meeting room.

'And, Stewart. If only we knew someone who worked within the bank that had the ability to *de*select that option - temporarily - from customers' accounts and also someone with a direct line to the fraud department to give them a heads up that any transaction linked to a certain employee's login details is *not* flagged up today?'

'Trust me, play this the correct way with us and your bosses will be receiving a letter of commendation from our department, with heavy vibes of 'look after this guy or we might just pinch him for ourselves. You *any* idea just how significant a letter from high up in the police force can be for someone already working in the security sector? A form of thanks and recognition, like *that?* Priceless, Stewart. Antiques Roadshow.'

The young man's spiel was impressive. So impressive in fact that it had been enough to make the - it would probably be a bit unkind to describe him as a jobsworth - man from the bank think twice.

He sat there looking at us both for a moment while turning things over in his mind.

'And you'd do that, for me? Write a letter stating how I had been key in your investigation to catching someone such as as wanted drug dealer?'

And there we had it. Mr Ethical and all of his noble reasons for why he couldn't have *possibly* allowed an illegal transfer of funds was just like anyone else. There's 'always' a weak spot. His being a case of self interest and - for his gaffers at the bank attention - self promotion.

'I'll give you my card, Stewart.' I joined in for the first time in a while. Sensing indecision in the security manager and pouncing on the show of weakness by helping take the decision out of his hands without it coming across as too blatantly forceful on my part.

'The moment that you have any news for us - once your employee makes their move - call me and we'll be right over to arrest and interview them.

While not displaying any visual confidence over what the way forward his Friday was now going to entail, he didn't resist me in any way either. Instead, nodding his head with a tinge of reluctance that was being outweighed by his own sense of self ambition.

'It's going to be fine, Stewart. Bet you didn't know that you were going to end up employee of the month when you got up this morning with eyes like a half shut knife and were so tired that you probably couldn't have rattled out your ABC.' I gaslit him while he was still in that vulnerable and suggestive state.

'Ok, you'll be the first to know once anything happens.' He nodded his head as he tucked my card into the chest pocket of his white shirt. As he did so, the phone in front of him burst into action with a futuristic style ring - as opposed to the old school ones we had in our antiquated office that was a world away from this place with its cutting edge technologies like white boards and projectors - which he wasted no time in answering, after quickly asking if we would both excuse him while he took it.

While engaged in his conversation Ardwick and me exchanged a brief look of hope and expectation between each other. Me adding a small wink and nod of approval in the direction of my colleague in acknowledgement of his performance which had been the difference between us walking out of there empty handed and us looking forward to a day of catching Barry Drummond - on extortion for a kick off - and then seeing which dominoes might begin to fall from that moment onwards.

Our 'moment' was sharply broken by the sound of Parker putting the phone down back into its cradle before following things up by asking.

'Does the name Grant Leckie mean anything to either of you?'

Chapter 30

Leckie

Friday's, eh? Best day of the week? Well there are Fridays and then there are "Fridays." *That* final day of the working week, for a classic example? Well forgive me if I didn't go buying a four pack of Crunchies on my way in to work that morning. That horrible sickening feeling that I woke with. One that I wouldn't have wished on my own worst enemy. That whole feeling of dread and impending doom where you *know* that you're going to be in for a bad day and possibly your worst *ever*, even.

Maybe if I just don't get up out of bed and skip going in today it'll all work itself out, I tried to convince myself. Aye, and maybe by tonight the whole of Edinburgh wont have watched a video of me getting my cock sucked in my car from, well, I didn't even *know* his name. Not that this was really important. What *was* important was for that video to be ending up in Barry Drummond's deleted folder on his phone.

In truth, the chances of things just "working themselves out" or Drummond not releasing that video online - should I not have followed his orders - were about as slim as each other which, obviously, meant, in a more accurate way of putting it, no chance, at all.

I kissed Janie and the kids goodbye as I was on the way out. Normally I'd have sat and had a spot of breakfast with them before leaving but with the way my stomach had been churning, food was the last thing that I felt I'd needed.

If ever I'd needed an extra reminder of motivation, it was seeing the two kids sat there at the breakfast table that morning. Alice with a face covered in jam from her toast while wee Henry had knocked his cup over and was taking much enjoyment out of spreading as much of the spilled milk across the table with his hand as he could. The pair of them a mess but could not have been more happy and beautiful, right there.

Janie mentioned about me picking up some Chinese on the way home from work at night for tea. Family tradition dictating that we always got a takeaway on a Friday. How on earth she could be standing there in the kitchen thinking about - and *deciding* on - what were going to be eating as far away as tea time was anyone's guess.

I agreed that I'd call her after work to decide on what we were getting but while doing so was - inside - questioning on whether I'd be eating my tea there inside the family home or some low quality microwave meal from a police cell.

By that Friday - having had a week to deal with the situation that I'd been left in - I'd already decided on which policy I was going to adopt to secure the funds for Drummond. Not that I was feeling proud about it, mind. One of my team, an employee called Alex Sandler who I'd habitually had to get on to over his cavalier attitude towards security. I'm not even sure how he'd managed to bag himself a position in the department. Was forever failing his half yearly money laundering tests, marked down on his call monitoring for not asking the correct, or enough, security questions with clients and - crucially for me - someone who did not possess the ability to remember what their *login details* were.

He'd even received a written warning from our gaffer over the amount of times he had forgotten them and had to have them reset by our IT department. Aye, I know it might only take fifteen to twenty minutes for it to be taken care of but those fifteen to twenty minutes all rack up, in a productivity sense.

After that written warning - clearly not willing to trust his own self to do better - he had elected to write down his login reference number along with password and then *sellotape* the piece of paper underneath his desk. He didn't think anyone knew of this only - the day that he did it - I had been over at the photocopier and in what could only have been the most perfect of timing I had bent down to fill it with paper and when I'd stood up to press the print button I saw Alex crouching down underneath his desk taping something to it.

I kept myself out of view until he was back from underneath the desk and sitting down at it and working again before I returned to my own workstation across the aisle from him. Waited until the end of the day and everyone had gone home, me with my coat on as well ready to go, before taking the opportunity to have a little look underneath his desk.

Employee login - ASandler3187

Password - password12345!

The moron - and with a password like that I literally mean in *every* sense of the word - had only written down the keys to his system and taped it under his desk so that he would never forget them. Smart enough thinking, were it not for the fact that such information could help gain someone *else* entry into what was access to untapped riches. Which would normally be safe enough, as long as your colleague has not been plunged into the most twisted of blackmail plots and *needs* access to thousands of pounds.

Despite how cavalier he approached the job he definitely didn't deserve to be pulled into something as heavy as all of this but then again, maybe he *did*? Teach him a lesson once and for all that access to a banking system that can link you up to millions of peoples of bank accounts filled with *billions* of pounds of money was something that should've been treated with respect rather than just forgetting your login details for Ebay when you try to sign in? Aye, that's some good justification for stealing near on a hundred thousand pounds while pinning the blame on someone else, I thought to myself while I made my way through the rush hour commute that always seemed to be at its heaviest right at the same time as when I was going to work each morning.

That was one of the worst parts of it all, the fact it was premeditated. I'm driving to work already *knowing* that I'm going to be carrying it out. Would walk into the office and look Alex straight in the eye and wish him a good morning while knowing that I was about to steal all that money, in his name.

When I pulled up into the car park, which was a lot more full than usual and proving my own point that I'd made to myself - on the road - over how late those four-way temporary traffic lights were going to make me arrive. Even though part of me wanted the lights to never change to green and just leave me sitting there all day.

Even though I was a little late. When I pulled into the space, instead of just jumping right out the car as normal, I just kind of sat there for a few minutes in silence, staring ahead at the main entrance to the call centre and thinking about what I was about to do. I pulled out my phone for a second just to have a quick look at my favourite picture of me and the kids, the one from the previous Christmas with the three of us sitting by the tree and the floor completely covered in torn wrapping paper and various Christmas presents.

Get the job done and you'll see *this* Christmas with them too. That thought, enough to pull me out of the car and on my way in, joining the crowd of others all heading towards the main doors. Because of how many people were all rushing - trying to make it to their desks and logged in before their official start times - I didn't see him and it was only when I felt the hand grabbing my arm and pulling me back from continuing any further that I even registered his presence at all.

Can you believe that Drummond had actually got up as early as that just so he could be there waiting on me going into work, just to give me one final reminder about what would happen if I didn't transfer him that money?

YES, BARRY, AFTER A WEEK'S WORTH OF GOING OUT OF MY MIND THROUGH WORRY, I GET IT!

God, how I felt like screaming out at him but creating a scene outside my work on the day I was about to commit theft probably was not a good idea. Or shouting out at someone who has some serious dirt on you, full stop.

I'd already felt sick to the stomach. The sight and sound of Barry Drummond near enough put me over the finishing line. He'd told me that the chat we'd had the night before had left him less than confident that I was going to keep up my part of the bargain and felt that he should pay me a wee visit at work to remind me of the implications of non compliance. Sick fuck even pretended like he was going to grab a random passer by - going into reception - and show them his phone, and the video that was in it.

Talking of phones. He physically grabbed mines from off me. Snatched it right out my hand and went straight into my messages. What a liberty? He didn't look chuffed when he saw that all of our conversation - since the week before - was still there on my phone. Said to me that because I *hadn't* deleted our messages as I went, this had shown how slack I was and completely validated his concern and early morning appearance at the call centre.

He offered me a chilling passive aggressive 'have a good day' with the sociopathic undertones of the hint of me having a *better* evening before walking away and leaving me to show my pass to reception before hitting the stairs and taking myself up to our department floor.

Due to those temporary traffic lights I was the last of the team in by the looks. Everyone already sat there with headsets on ready for the green light, *apart* from Sandler.

Shit.

Because no Sandler equalled no *plan*. Doesn't take someone of eight years experience in the banking sector to tell you that an employee can't physically make a transfer - from one customer account to another - if they're not physically *at work*.

A cold sweat came over me when I saw that empty desk as I turned the corner. I said my mornings to everyone and left things just long enough for it to not be conspicuous for me to ask if Alex was ok before experiencing the massive wave of relief to hear that he was going to be in an hour late due to a dental appointment he'd had scheduled.

My plan had been to log in with his details during lunch and when he was away from the office floor - due to the staggered scheduling of lunches and breaks we were never all off at the same time - but that, obviously, could not have flown had he been marked down by management as 'absent.'

God was it a long morning leading up to lunch. Drummond filling *his* morning by sending me a text every now and then asking if I'd done it yet. Each text appearing more desperate as he lurched from asking for updates to issuing threats. It's mad what the paranoia does to you, though. That morning? I genuinely felt that Harrison - my gaffer - *knew* what I was up to. He'd called me into his office regarding a report that he'd asked me to run for him the day before which I had still to give to him but it was in his office - while we spoke - that I picked up a bit of a vibe from him. Not something that you can put your finger on but just the way that I felt he'd looked at me. It's easy to feel that way though when you know what you're about to do. Guilt is some heavy emotion, well heavy. Does all kinds of things to the point of driving you up the wall with insanity.

The way he'd asked me if 'everything was alright?' with me and the family, that kind of stuff. Reece Harrison *never* asked questions like that to the team. Harrison only gave a fuck about Harrison and I was sure that had I decided to play devil's advocate and ask him, perhaps, to name my wife or kids he'd have been left with nowhere to go.

I took his - strange - question though and replied to it with the usual platitudes that a man with wife and kids would reply with that ensures that no more needs expanded on.

Telling him that all three were making my hair grow more grey by the day but that I'd throw myself in front of a bus in a heartbeat to save. Which was a not bad analogy for what I was going to do from the more relative 'safety' of an office floor.

In preparation I had engineered the situation a few nights before at the end of the shift where I was the last one to leave the office. On the way out making the smallest of detours past Sandler's desk and - faking having to bend down to tie my shoe lace - snapped a couple of pictures of his login details under his desk so that I could memorise it as I was going to have to be in and out of his system as quickly as possible. Due to security reasons we would always have to update our password every so often and straight away had noticed that what I was looking at was a completely different piece of paper taped to the desk from before. The idiot simply changing the '**12345**' in his password to '**23456**'

Memorising the details was not the hardest task I'd ever had to take on.

My plan had been that - knowing that his bank of four desks all went for lunch at once - when he'd disappeared I was going to quickly log him back in, perform the transfer and then lock his screen but *not* log him back out again. By doing so it would have looked - to security - that he had logged out for lunch and came back to his terminal early and logged back on. With how "vigilant" he was with his system I was pretty sure that when he unlocked his computer he wouldn't have even *noticed* that he was still logged into the banking side of things.

I'd already decided on the target and I mean singular. I'd thought about spreading the payments to Drummond from across several accounts but by doing this it would've meant me having to spend a lot longer sitting at Sandler's desk and terminal, which simply could not happen. Apart from that which was on the no fly list there was also the 'small' matter of multiple transfers opening things up to much increased chances of someone noticing their missing money and inevitably reporting it.

Pick the *correct* target however and possibly even Alex doesn't land up in trouble with his bosses and law enforcement, never mind myself.

I'd had a week to do my homework and pick one and - out of all options of the rich and famous who banked with us - I'd felt that I'd given things a more than outside chance of succeeding and when you're talking removing the best part of a hundred grand from someone's bank account and hope that they don't notice then "more than an outside chance" is as good as it's going to be getting.

Mario Buzzini, the Italian international centre forward who had signed for Man United from AC Milan in the summer - and someone who had been on the front pages as much as he'd been on the back - had been one of the more high profile accounts that we'd been given to handle. You could only have imagined how buzzing the big bosses were to be getting to look after someone with the amount of funds that he had. The papers had said that due to him going to Old Trafford on a Bosman they'd given him a straight up twenty five million pounds signing on fee, with them saving five or six *times* that on a transfer fee. You can only imagine the wealth that a top drawer and potential world player of the year would pull in. Monthly wages, bonuses, sponsorship deals. Staggering for some of them.

Buzzini, though? He was someone who - if the tabloids were to be believed - was intent on spending his money as soon as he got it. The story of how he'd bought six Ferrari's of the same model *just* so that no one else in Britain would have the same one as him, already committed to English footballing folklore. Some serious commitment towards attaining individuality but no way to ensure you hang on to the majority of your rainy day money either.

He was generous, too. Always donating thousands to good causes by turning up unannounced with a sports bag full of readies. Never not decked out in the most expensive of labels even if they did make him look a complete fool at times. The man exhumed money and extravagance.

While I obviously knew nothing about him, other than the newspaper and internet reports. If anyone looked like they might not clock ninety five thousand pounds going missing from their bank account, it could well have been Mario Buzzini. Someone, still relatively just a kid, who was more rich than his tiny mind could handle. It was the smart move, to go for someone like that. Most kids don't even know *what's* in their bank accounts and it only becomes an issue if they try to spend money, and find none there. When you're a world famous international striker with the whole world at your feet and millions of pounds in the bank you're hardly likely to be seeing the 'insufficient funds' message on the screen of an ATM anytime. Having decided that I was going to use his account to siphon the money from I'd taken a look at it a few days before so that I could note down - and memorise - his account number and sort code.

For my own sanity I just wanted it to reach the first block of lunch breaks - and to see Sandler and his wee team get up and leave - but yet at the same time I didn't want to be seeing Alex leave his desk because I knew that it would represent my now or never moment. And it *had* to be 'now.'

Half twelve eventually coming after what I can only describe as a "coma morning" where I did my job but it had been done in some kind of a trance where I'd barely have been able to have told you three things that I'd done over the first half of the day.

That sickening feeling returned when I saw Alex - along with Kate, Jenny and Sean - standing up and grabbing their things to go to lunch. Then Harrison - the only boss on the floor at the time - followed suit a minute later, leaving us all to sit and fend for ourselves taking calls, which had been literally non stop since I'd logged in that morning.

This had to be it. Things were so busy it was the ideal time for me to quickly slip over to the bank of desks and do the transaction. I'd performed some training style dummy runs while sitting at my own desk for the previous two days - once I'd decided upon my plan - and figured that I'd have been able to pull it off within the space of two minutes, shorter than the average call time - three minutes and twenty seven seconds by the latest group of stats that had been sent out to the team - of a customer contacting us.

Taking one last look around the office - to establish who and where everyone on the floor were - and finding that the conditions were as perfect as they were ever going to be. I took off my headset, put it down on the table next to my keyboard and with my heart feeling like it was going to beat its way right out of my chest. I took myself over to Sandler's terminal.

Chapter 31

Hummel

Despite it being *the* day, and the one that we'd all been dreading rolling around. There I'd been, up at the crack to get myself ready and on a fucking train to Dundee and for what? To drop off a pair of *training shoes*.

It was nice to see that in what was potentially the very end of times that Hammy had his priorities right. While I'm worried about being able to live through the whole of the day that radge cunt is losing his hair over a Buckfast stain on one of his Stockholms.

The boy - Kris - over in Dundee was actually pretty sound, like. Offered me a cup of tea while I took the time to tell him about what a fanny I was in spilling Bucky over one of my more volatile mates trabs and, unfortunately for me, one who had a bit of an Adidas addiction and did not see the trainers that I had ruined as *just another pair* of trainers.

With a promise that if I left them with him at the shop he would get around to repairing them and getting the stain gone - and in the process saving me from some major fucking earache from the big hamster - the two of us bumped fists - gave that cool wee bastard of a Jack Russell - Alfie - with a bandana round it's neck a pat on the head - and I was off back on the short walk back to Dundee train station to get myself home to the capital city again. Job done.

Or at least *one* of my jobs that had been on my list for the day, anyway. The *much more* important one was still to come although if you'd asked Hammy he'd maybe have had a different opinion on that, though.

Speaking of the big abrasive bastard. I was just getting off the bus - up from the city centre after jumping off the train back from Jute City - when I saw him running out of the bookies. Jumping higher in the air than Mike Jordan before taking off running around - with arms out like he was a fucking plane or something - like a mad cunt shouting and cheering. Stopping to grab a frightened old lady and hugging her within an inch of taking her last breath. Traffic had to stop for him - due to the running all over the road - with a few car horn peeps following as a result.

'YA FUCKING BEAUTTTTTTTTTEEEEEEEEEE!! SLAVIIIIIAAAA UNDER NINETEENS AH FUCKING *LOVE* YOUS YA WEE CUNTS.'

He screamed into her face. Whoever it was that had been sounding their horns, without question, wasting their time. The man was clearly living in his own moment and one separate to the rest of his surroundings. Even when I'd crossed the road and had got close enough to speak to him - grabbing his shoulder to make him aware of my presence - and he turned around to look at me, it was like he was off somewhere. The look in his eyes? Almost felt that despite looking at his oldest and best mate he - in that moment - didn't recognise him.

'Get a winner, aye?' I asked, completely stating the obvious.

'Fucking *winner?* Hummel? I've just won NINETY TWO THOUSAND, SEVEN HUNDRED AND FORTY FIVE FUCKING POUNDS AND TWENTY SIX PENCE. FUCKING *WHIT?!*

If every single living being who had found themselves out there on the street at that moment hadn't already been standing looking at him, the figure he'd just shouted out would've caught their attention.

My first instinct was to tell him to stop talking pish but no one makes such an intentional arse of themselves - as Hammy was that lunch time - on a busy public street just because they feel like it. Nah, the hamster was quite obviously acting out of pure instinct, unadulterated joy.

Once his words had properly sunk in, I started jumping up and down and screaming along with him, like you'd do with a mate when they'd just had some amazing news like that.

'WOOOOOOOOOO YAAAAA FUUUUCKKKKKAAAAA'

He screamed with fists clenched looking up at the air like he'd just clinched the championship winning point on centre court, leaving me to look at the reactions of people looking in our direction.

'Big winner.' I said pointing to an oblivious Hammy who still had his eyes closed with fuck knows what going through his head.

'Thought for a minute that you'd maybe read my text I'd sent you from Dundee saying that the boy was going to fix your Stockholms, eh?' I joked with him but should've kept things a bit more simple to bridge the gap between where me - and the rest of the world - and wherever the fuck Hammy was.

'Eh?' He asked, genuinely confused by what I'd said when it should've been one of the more obvious things to him.

'Your trainers, mate. Kris, the boy at Dundee Sole said that he'd get them sorted.' I said, as a reminder.

'Oh, *that?* Ah who the fuck cares about a wee bit of spilt Buckfast, eh?'

Now he says it? *After* I'd already been up and made the trip there and back to drop the fucking things *off?* And now he's saying not to worry about it. Funny how winning almost a hundred grand can change one's opinion about an eighty pound pair of training shoes.

'I can always get myself another pair, eh?'

Seriously, though. I was well made up for him and couldn't ever remember ever seeing him so ecstatic about anything in his life. No example of getting his hole, no injury time derby match winner, no examples I could come close to equating with what had him losing his mind that day, in the way that he was.

I handed him an L and B and sparked up one myself, figuring he'd probably *need* one after what was more than likely the biggest orgasm of his life.

'So how the fuck have you managed to bag that sum of money?' I asked him, still trying to process it all. My heart beating fast enough for it to have been *me* that had won the money.

'I'd say about the perfect mix of good luck and stupidity.' He said in all seriousness as he sucked hard on the Lambert and Butler before puffing out the smoke again up and into the busy Friday lunchtime street.

'Been a woolly mammoth of a coupon, like. I've had it on the go since Monday. Needed Slavia Prague and Sigma Olomouc -

under nineteens, like - for over four and a half goals in their league match. Fifth goal just went in. Four one to Slavia, fucking radge league. Soon as I saw that 'goal' icon going up on the app I just took off. I'll be honest, kind of know now how it must feel to score a big goal in a World Cup or Champions League or something. You want to see the fucking scenes inside there, as well.' He motioned back towards Paddy Power and who was sitting inside the place.

'Well, I guess it's time to go collect your money then, eh?' I said, more as a figure of speech than anything else because first up I'd have been surprised if they'd have just had that amount lying around in their safe on a single day and secondly, I had no fucking concept just what that amount of money would even *look* like.

I assumed it wouldn't fit neatly into the average set of pockets that man has combined over a pair of jeans and jacket.

His face lit up at the thought of it.

'Oh I'm going to fucking *enjoy* this, Hummel lad. Brian's on today. You'll need to take a video of me going up with my coupon, just so that you can capture *his* one when he has to serve me.' He laughed at the idea of capturing the real time disgust on the face of the man - the same face who Hammy'd once rearranged for him years before - who was going to rubber stamp the fortune that my mate - and *his* nemesis - had just officially won.

And then it hit me. Fuck, that *relief.* I mean, it wasn't even my place to say it and say it I one hundred percent was *not* going to be but Hammy had won over ninety grand, and we needed ninety by the end of the day. I felt a proper right cunt by even thinking of it in that way. It wasn't *my* money to think that way about for one thing. Plus with it being me the sole reason *why* we needed the ninety grand in the first place I wasn't exactly feeling too proud of myself when I was already - mentally - spending Hammy's biggest win of his life and the kind of win that once you experience you should just quit gambling because you'll *never* win that amount again.

I tried to put myself in the position of him. Winning as much as that, and then just handing the vast majority of it right over to someone, hours later? Hard times, that. Well harsh, like. How to kill someone's fucking buzz one o one.

Hammy had already been - what had appeared - less stressed than the thought of an Albanian kill squad coming looking for him should've affected him. Even when I sent him the picture of his road that the German had sent to me he'd replied back that 'any cunt could've mocked that picture up.'

If I'd had access to the madness that was going on inside of his head - following the confirmation that he'd got the required amount of goals in that last match - I'd have walked straight into the bookies and stuck everything I owned on Hammy using that money to pay off our debt as being the *furthest* fucking thing from his mind.

The reality of things were much different, though.

'If' I'd mentioned to him - what was in *my* head - he'd have told me to take myself to fuck, moaned about why *he* would have to give up all of his money for something that I'd caused and not thrown in any contribution myself. And would keep doing it until the very last minute before, being a mate and not wanting to consign us to whatever fates awaited the three of us, would cough it up to pay Arman88.

While details of what Drummond had been scheming on had remained thin, *this* was what could only have been described as tangible thickness.

While I had called Hammy pretty much every name under - and a few over - the sun earlier on in the morning when having to surface at that unsociable hour to get myself to Dundee I could have given him a big sloppy kiss - with tongues - there in front of the whole street, and happily taken the broken jaw that would've accompanied such an action.

Fucking hell, through the most unforeseen of ways, the Onion Ring boys were saved.

'Right, lets go get that paper, eh?' He said, flicking away his still lit cigarette which just missed a wee black Scottie dog - out being walked and stood having a pee against a lamppost - by inches, which showed that my friend still didn't quite have things together yet but having never won anything close to that amount of money before in my life I couldn't have blamed or judged him for any odd behaviour on his part.

'Get your phone out, mind. I want this momentous occasion captured.' He said to me before we made to go in. Actually getting me to press record on him walking the few steps up to the front door of the shop and then him going in. Me following behind in a kind of fly on the wall Scorsese type of camera action, or that's what I told myself at the time, anyway.

When he appeared inside the bookies he was greeted like some local boy done good. Olympic gold winner or a returning war hero, not some cunt who had managed to select enough winning bets in a row on the one piece of paper. I took it to be some kind of gamblers camaraderie that you only felt if you were one of their community. They were well happy to see Hammy though and it looked the same back in return. Almost saw a different side to the boy, the way he was with all of those old jakeballs. I'd say that he appeared more friendly with them than he'd *ever* expressed with Drummond and me but the boy had just won the biggest amount of money that he'd ever see at the one time in his life. He was - naturally - happy.

'Thought you'd forgotten to run off without your winnings son?' One old boy dressed in a dated looking suit matched with a pair of Hi Tec trainers on his feet which looked an absolutely wild look but he was just about pulling it off. The old boy had winked at Hammy.

'You'll be buying the beers tonight in The Trap, I assume?' Davey Fortune - one of the pub's biggest pissheads - chipped in, sniffing out an opportunity to bank himself a few free pints later on that night in the pub, no doubt.

'Really pleased for you, young man. Always good to see the bookies take a good spanking. ' An old man in a tartan flat cap and chunky beige seventies style cardigan - the kind that looks like it has conkers for buttons - said, slapping Hammy on the back as he headed past the group on his way to the counter. Me recording every step.

'HEY HEYYYYY' He shouted with a big smile - kind of like Krusty the Clown - 'Brian, my man! Did I not tell you that I'd be back on the Friday for my money? Seem to remember someone laughing me out the shop when I'd stuck the bet on? Mind of that, Brian? No?'

Hammy was clearly enjoying this moment on a level that a normal 'winner' of a bet simply could not understand.

'Well they're not fucking laughing now, eh?'

Meanwhile, the manager standing behind the counter stood there - arms folded - visibly unimpressed with the show that Hammy was putting on for the whole shop.

'Read it and fucking weep, ya cunt' Hammy announced jovially following fishing out the betting slip - from his tiny jeans pocket - that looked like it had been folded so many times it now resembled a cube rather than a piece of paper. Unfolding it, he shoved it under the perspex barrier towards the manager, looking around at me and the camera making sure that it caught his smile *exactly* as he slid the betting slip over the counter.

'Ok, sir, let me just check that for you, I won't be a minute.' Brian said, noticing me filming and deciding to play up for the camera.

'Oh, take your time, my good man.' Hammy met patter with similar patter. While waiting on Brian doing whatever it is that a bookie does while they process a winning bet I kept recording while Hammy took some more congratulations from some of the punters. Turning again to the camera to say that we were soon off for the biggest piss up we'd ever had in our lives, on him.

'A meal, as well, like.'

He clarified before turning back to face the perspex screen again.

As long as you're still left with ninety thousand pounds in your pocket for our German mate you can have Gordon fucking Ramsay shoved into a cab to Muirhouse to cook for us, I thought to myself - and once again felt an absolute prick for thinking - while he waited on his money, or however form of payment it was going to be made to him.

I'd thought it a sign from god, as in the fact that we'd been in need of an astronomical sum of money and on the *same day* that it needed paid, one of us just happened to come into a near identical amount. Tell me that shite wasn't meant to be? Aye while Hammy could - and definitely *would* - moan about having his winnings taken off him there was some subscribers that would say that had I not fucked up in the first place then he wouldn't have *won* his bet as a result. Like how one thing has to happen for another to take place. Pure butterfly effect stuff, you know?

'Ah but here's the thing, sir.' Brian said while looking over the betting slip and whatever it was showing on his monitor.

'This isn't a winning bet, I'm afraid.'

I don't think anyone was prepared for that. Definitely not James Hamilton. It was all captured there on the video. He was looking directly at it smiling and giving a big thumbs up with a little piece of commentary saying how that in a few seconds time he was about to become more than ninety two thousand pounds richer. I'd caught the sudden change on his face perfectly even though all of me had wished that there hadn't been anything *to* capture.

'Aye, good one, Brian but you can't escape the inescapable my friend. Get that fucking safe cracked open, ya cunt.'

Hammy said after a worrying second before he took Brian's joke and ran with it.

Only, Brian *wasn't* joking.

'I'm serious, Hammy. Your bet isn't a winner.' He stood there with a straight face holding out the betting slip, making sure that he turned to give the camera a wee glance while he delivered the killer line. Depending on how the rest of the day was going to play out, the term "killer" might well have went on to be appropriate.

'Fuck off, Brian. Stop pissing about, eh.'

You could hear it in Hammy's voice - the concern - despite him putting the front on that this was all nothing more than some good light hearted jokes between betting shop manager and customer.

'See, look here.' The manager said as he calmly slid the betting slip back towards Hammy then pointing at something on the slip.

Hammy went in closer towards the perspex to meet Brian and the slip. Myself and the iphone continuing to zoom in on things but - turning around for a moment - I wasn't the only one taking a keen interest. It had seemed like all betting had been suspended for a moment - there wasn't even a race going on at the time - just so that everyone could look on and watch the outcome of this exchange between Hammy and Brian. The tension in the room could've been sliced through with an aeroplane plastic knife.

'Look fucking where?' Hammy's tone had now changed, along with his mood as he began to sense that possibly all was not well and in order.

'Well, see where you've got Slavia Prague versus Sigma I don't know how to pronounce that second name but you know who I mean.'

Brian attempted to explain but had a panicking Hammy interrupt before all had been explained to him.

'Aye, and I put that for fucking over four and a half goals. Check the score if you like but I've just seen the score confirmed, on your own betting app. Cough up ya cunt. No one likes a sore loser, *especially* a fucking bookie.' Hammy said still with a defensive tone to him but not without a wee bit of confidence behind it. After all, he'd seen the score from Prague, confirmed on Paddy Power's own smart phone app.

'Yes, Hammy but that was the *under 19's* match, mate.' Brian said as casual as you like which I suppose is an easy thing to do when it's not you that's losing out on that amount of money.

'Aye, and what about it? Why the fuck do you think I've been jumping about like a mad cunt for? I fucking *know* what teams were playing. I'm the one that put the fucking bet on ya daft cunt.'

I'd seen and heard this tone of voice - and the descent of his patience - before from Hammy and it generally never ended well. If Brian *was* fucking about then he was in danger of taking things too far. Actually, he'd already went past that point.

'In that case then, James. If you'd intended on putting on *that* particular bet then you should have selected the *under 19* match. Slavia and Sigma - in the sense of your accumulator, and what you selected on the machine back on Monday - don't play until seven forty five, tonight.

When he said it, it was only there for a fraction of a second but you could see the smile of satisfaction all over him as he delivered the bad news. No joking, man. If someone had broken your nose in a nightclub assault and years later you got the chance to break that same person's dreams. Well, you'd have jumped at the chance, wouldn't you? As did Brian from Paddys.

His words left me stunned, gutted and heartbroken.

Hammy? They left him angry, very fucking angry.

I don't know if it was just the blow of realising what he'd done, or if it was seeing that smirk on Brian's face but whatever the reason, he lost it, big fucking time.

'Ya fucking baaaaaassssstaaaaarrrrrd' Hammy exploded. Grabbing indiscriminately out for anything that he could lift - which was a wee stool - and threw it at the perspex. Barely making a scratch on the screen before picking it up again and repeatedly ramming the legs into the screen which - fortunately for Brian - was separating customer from staff.

The celebratory vibe, there inside the shop, turned ugly, quickly. As soon as - not just Hammy - the punters inside began to suss out that there was a twist in this massive winning bet. They all went for Brian, verbally.

'Well ootay order, Brian son. You'll get a reputation with that kind of caper.' The boy in the tartan flat cap shouted with a disapproving look on his face.

'Pay the fucking boy, ya tight bastard. It's not as if it's your money or anything, is it?' This stranger to the side with smoker's dirty blonde slick back hair dressed in an even dirtier well used leather jacket joined in.

'Ya fucking snake, cheating the laddie out of his payday. Snide behaviour, that.' A shout came from behind me which would've suited the narrative that is normally pushed out when a bookie doesn't want to pay out, but if what I was seeing was true, there was no one *else's* fault here other than Hammy himself. Fucking schoolboy error of the highest order because he'd been looking for minimum five goals in his game. Something you'd only do if you were sure that the game would be a high scoring affair. Could you ever really put *any* money on, with a high amount of confidence, on any top league match having five goals in it? You wouldn't be going sticking it on a multi sport accumulator anyway, if you had any sense.

Clearly Hammy had *meant* the bet to be placed on the kids match but he hadn't selected it, specifically? I really needed us - sorry, Hammy - to get the money but the bookies were never going to just accept that all encompassing "Slavia v Sigma," not when there were more than one match that day played under the names of those two teams.

'YA FUCKING CHEATING BASTARD. THINK WHAT I DID TO YOU AT THE LIQUID ROOMS WAS FUCKING BAD? THAT WAS JUST A FUCKING *APPETISER,* YA FUCKING WANK'

Hammy had thrown the stool across the floor of the shop and was now full scale punching at Brian at the glass while having no way, realistically, of ever laying a glove on him. Which the shop manager knew fine well.

Which was exactly why he stood there with a big smile on his face while Hammy went fucking radge at him.

'Cheer up, Hammy. Maybe you'll get your over four and a half goals tonight, eh?' Brian's words - deliberately measured - enraging Hammy even more.

As he stood there raging, trying to lift a table - even though it was clearly fixed to the floor - to throw at the counter I felt that I should now probably stop recording and get him out of the shop, before the police arrived and lifted him.

Chapter 32

Drummond

Where the fuck is this scratch? I asked myself while staring at the phone screen and seeing - for what felt like the hundredth time that day - an outstanding balance sitting at £10, the token amount that I had deposited, more for appearances than anything else, on the day that I'd opened the bank account up.

All other plans for that Friday morning had been ditched for the mindlessly boring and monotonous activity of opening up a banking app to check a balance only to log out, and then repeat the process five minutes later again, and again. This combined with 'motivational' texts being fired randomly at Leckie across the morning.

The fucking poker face that I'd had to pull that morning with Bren and Holly where I'd had to hide the all too real worry that I had *for* them, if the day didn't go how it had been planned. If I'd let the thoughts that I'd had about 'them' - since we'd landed in the shit - and what potentially might happen to the two of them get the better of me I'd have went off my nut well before "due date."

Fuck the money that had been lost through Hummel doing Hummel stuff. That could be rebuilt if we could get ourselves back in the game again. It was the thought of a single hair on either my girlfriend or daughter's heads being touched that had been the driving force and my own source of inspiration for me to find a way out of it.

The absolute fear that ran through me at the thought of some fucking filthy Albanian cunt going even fifty foot near to either of them was what kept me going when I'd already taken it that we'd run out of options short of pulling off a fucking bank or a bookies job which simply wasn't who we were. We were 'accidental' drug dealers and - while the courts would have a rare old time arguing about the technicalities - barely even what you would class as 'criminals.'

I cringed at the thought of taking Hummel on a bank or bookies job. He'd probably use mine and Hammy's names inside the first few seconds of us being in there, take his balaclava off to scratch his face because it was "itchy" and, for good measure, drop his driver's license out of his pocket when he was running out the door. The fucking Keystone Cops would've had a better chance of getting away with a robbery than us three.

I'd found an 'alternative' way to rob a bank. More than one way to skin a cat, like. That all depended though on Leckie complying. I'd depended on the fear of what I'd do to him - with the material that I had - pushing him through whatever obstacles or moral dilemmas that he might've had in doing the job for me. Self preservation can be a powerful thing and *the* thing that can push all sense and logic out of the window for a person. Exactly like I'd hoped would be the case with him.

Fuck, did I feel helpless though. Placing my - as well as Bren and that beautiful wee girl's - entire future in the hands of a fucking wet wipe like Grant Leckie. No wonder - by Friday - I'd been left a nervous and paranoid filled wreck. Couldn't *be* around the two of them that day as Bren - out of *anyone* in the world - would've picked up on it, and then the questions would've started.

Up until that point she hadn't known a single thing in terms of our problems that me and the lads had been experiencing although - whether it was through a team of bad bastard Albanians coming and kicking our doors down or me having to admit that I didn't have the money to pay our bills for the month - I was running out of time when it came to keeping her out of the loop.

The fact that Hummel had cunts - who were due the dough to - sending DMs with pictures of our streets and front doors was evidence that the walls were starting to close in. If the Friday didn't go how it was meant to - in terms of what I'd cooked up with my man from the bank - then like it or not, Bren was going to be finding out.

That picture business had got to me. I mean, I'd - despite all of the grim variables - pretty much remained cool through it all when lesser men would've wilted under the pressure. Seeing that picture changed the complexion for me. Hammy dismissed it saying that it wasn't exactly difficult to mock up a photo like that but I'd done a wee bit more investigating and found that the Google Maps images of my street didn't match up to the photo that Hummel had sent me. Google hadn't updated their images for our street in years, something that you could tell by a few of the cars that were parked the day that their car came down taking a three hundred and sixty degree capture of our street.

The picture that "Arman88" had sent to Hummel - of my street, anyway - was a more recent picture. Just a couple of minor differences that you wouldn't have picked up on if you weren't specifically looking or lived there yourself. Number twenty seven had a different colour of door in one picture to the other. And the one that Arman88 had sent to Hummel was showing the more *updated* mahogany - with three small glass panels - door that they'd had fitted.

I know none of that confirmed anything other than that "someone" had been travelling around taking pictures of our streets. The hand in the picture, though? Well, it looked pretty *handy*. Almost double the size of mines as well as that thick arm that you could see running off the side of the picture. Didn't look a wee kid that had taken the picture. Don't get me wrong, I'd have *loved* the reality of it to be more aligned with what Hammy had been saying, but it didn't look that way. It was obvious - with the subtle but effective - the kind of intimidation tactics that they were engaging in that we were in with some serious people here. It would've actually been of benefit - to not just Hammy but the group as a whole - if he was to pull his head out of the fucking sand on that score.

I'd already planned to head out early and catch Leckie going in to work - more for my peace of mind knowing that I'd done all I could going into that last work day of the week - but once I'd done that - which was around ten to nine or so - I just stayed out. Had grabbed some of my gear before leaving the house and planned for being out for most of the day, or at least until better news arrived and I could go back and consciously face my family without the need to suppress the rising fears that harm was going to be coming to not just me but the pair of them.

I'd had to put on one serious amount of fronting since it all turned to shit when it came to Bren. Woman's intuition and all of that stuff, eh? You think life was hard enough being responsible for a third of a ninety grand debt to possible Albanian mafia bods? Fucking multiply that by *ten* times if my other half had got wind of all that had been going on.

Sometimes it's better if a person *doesn't* know and I sincerely mean that not in a keeping something back because you're being shifty kind of way. What good would it have done Bren to have known? In all honesty, as long as the pair of us have been with each other I wouldn't have been surprised if she'd taken Holly and fucked off to her mums, if she'd known the reality of things. Part of me had thought about *suggesting* that her and the bairn go somewhere else for a couple of weeks but obviously I couldn't have done so without telling her *why*.

Because it really went without saying that if that ninety grand wasn't handed over, we would *have* to expect a reaction. Every action as they say, eh? Doesn't take a genius though to tell you that no cunt walks away from being paid an amount of money like that *without* a response.

I know a boy who was due a *tenner* from someone, didn't get it back and had felt that it was too small an amount to make an issue of. That though, did not stop him from having a fucking wank into the boy's Chicken Chow Mein - when he found himself with a telephone order for the guy who hadn't paid him back the tenner - before getting it packaged up and given to the delivery driver. My point being that this happened *months* after the tenner had ever been thought about being paid back, but the boy - outstanding the money - was still sore over it.

And that was a ten pound note.

You'd pull the fucking head right off it before you'd revenge wanked your way towards getting back at someone due you a debt that was nine thousand *times* that amount.

I don't know why I was even bothering to continually check the bank account balance on the app because it had already been taken as read that the very moment that transaction had been carried out I'd have been expecting a text from Leckie to confirm it, and help secure his freedom. I'd assumed that the self preservation that had him doing such a thing as committing theft would be the same that would want me to know he'd done it as soon as possible.

To get a away from things - after swinging by the call centre to lean on Leckie - I'd jumped in the Golf and taken a drive down to Portie. Following breakfast I parked up by the beach to knock up a wee joint for myself. Sighing when I'd noticed that in my rush I'd grabbed my "evening" weed instead of the day time smoke I would normally use in the am and early pm. Sativa in the earlier part of the day - if at all - and Indica in the evening. Only I'd grabbed the fucking Gelato in my rush to get out of the house and be at the call centre before Leckie.

Despite how stressful things undoubtedly were I had to laugh at me moaning to myself because I'd picked up the strong Indica. Oh the pain of it, only having a strain that cunts would kill for a quarter of to smoke that morning. I thought back to when we were all fourteen at school, having a wee toke at dinner time away from the school and then going back to class completely baked. None of that "choices" stuff back then. You just took what was there to smoke and you'd be happy with it. The fact that I could plan out a day and in which way I'd smoke - throughout it - only showed just how far things had come on.

Pure spoiled our last trip to Amsterdam that me and Hammy went on when - in our first coffee shop - we found out that it had *less* choice than we would've had back in the capital. That's progression, though. Can't stop progress and you definitely can't have it both ways either. Can't have all that choice of grass in Edinburgh and then hope to be blown away by the selection that you get offered in the Dam, eh?

As I held the *Elements* skin up for to run my tongue all the way along its gummed edge I stared out the windscreen at the sea and visualised me throwing this burner phone into it the moment that I knew the money was in. I'd made sure to cover all steps as best as I could and - as far as I knew - the only iffy part might be when a potential police investigation led to the bank account that the money had been moved to, and how and where it had been opened. I'd anticipated that and that was why I'd worn the baseball cap and glasses. Even wore clothes that you just wouldn't have seen me in that were the exact opposite of a brand like your Stoneys or CP's of this world.

I'd went radge at Leckie when I'd checked his phone and saw that he'd had every single message still there in our conversation thread, even though I'd specifically told him to delete as he went. With it being a burner phone I'd used it probably didn't matter anyway but sometimes you really should adopt the better to be safe than sorry way of thinking.

No doubt - if and when he got caught and shat the bed from the police - he would probably try and bring me into things but good luck with that when there's no proof and it's just his word against mines.

There wasn't even a choice of what you'd rather face. A mob of vengeance filled Albanian gangsters with your name on a list or a wee fanny like Grant Leckie grassing you up to the police with some unsubstantiated allegations?

We would, of course, deal with all of that down the line, as and when. For now, I just needed him to take step numero uno on matters.

I checked the app - once again - to find the same amount sitting in the account since checking ten minutes before. I remembered that old saying about a watched clock never moving as I grabbed my phone, lighter and joint and left the car for a walk along the beach, hoping that by the time I got back to the car things would've changed and I would've lost a burner phone that the River Forth would've now gained.

As I walked along the near deserted beach - save for a couple of dog walkers and joggers - while very quickly feeling the effects of the high THC count of the Gelato I floated off, thinking about the others, and how they, themselves were facing the day. No doubt Hammy would've been in the bookies pissing away what money he had left from his own reserves that he'd had kicking about from before Hummel's bird decided to 'drown' the majority of the money that we had to our names. Hammy had clearly been either not paying attention throughout all of this or actually didn't *give* a fuck because - apart from going out and seeking any funds that were still outstanding and by doing so being the difference between us obtaining the fake ID and us not - he did not appear like he'd been going through any stresses throughout it all. He'd kept expressing his theory that - who we were in debt to - was probably just a couple of German kids hiding behind a computer that would do absolute fucking Scottish Fitba Association about our non payment and that let's just say they *were* to come to Scotland looking for their money?

Hammy's opinion was that they would get a complete chasing from the MCF boys in the area before they even *got* a chance to receive a leathering from Hammy himself.

As for Hummel? Once it was all over and done with him and I were sitting down for a serious chat. Now - while we were still going through it all - wasn't the time but he had completely fucked us - and in so many fucking positions as *deeply* as possible - to the point that he had lost us all our money, the funds that we had worked so hard for and risked so much over and, crucially, what we all needed to live, and in doing so had placed a potentially dangerous target on our backs. And for what? A fucking webcam wank? Fuck me, he never was the smartest out of the three of us but still.

I hadn't had the chance to *truly* express to Hummel just how fucked off I was with him over it all. I'd *wanted* to but at the time it had been a choice of letting myself go or save Hummel from Hammy killing him on the spot. Someone had to be the the voice of reason in the middle of Hummel telling us that he'd put us in the shite and if it hadn't been me then I reckon that Hammy and me would've both been sitting in a cell in Sunny Saughton on remand over a murder charge.

If we could just get past today - and give Hummel a chance to at least semi redeem things by getting the money moved and over to our dealer - then we'd be sitting down to talk, and I'm not sure that I could guarantee that things would *stay* at just words, mind.

Above all else, though. It was Leckie I was thinking of most of all, and why the money hadn't yet appeared.

I tried to put myself in his position. Waking up that morning knowing what he had to do or else what the consequences were going to be. Didn't much like the thought of it, being honest. Didn't much care for the idea of being gunned down in the street by a South Eastern European gangster either though, mind.

What he was doing right there and then - at work - and what was going through his frazzled head?

Was he going to bottle it?

Had he already *tried*, and failed?

Was he *going* to do it and was just waiting on the right moment?

An alternative flex; Had he decided to pre-empt - and completely fuck right up in the process - my blackmail plot by coming out to everyone at work as gay? Not likely, that one, I told myself.

For all I knew, though he could well have been in the middle of facilitating the transfer *right* as I walked along the sand because - like for the three of us - his time was running out.

Chapter 33

Leckie

It was as if I was operating under some kind of autopilot state of mind, with how fast and diligently - considering the circumstances - I swooped into his chair and, without even a pause to think, entered his login details without any incorrect password or name warning flagging up on screen. It was smooth, it needed to be.

I almost *wished* that I hadn't been working to a timescale because on opening up his system - and seeing exactly where things were before he locked his screen for lunch - I was looking at an email that he had been in the middle of constructing. Before quickly minimising the page I'd been able to see the name of who he was sending it to. Babs McClure, who had been through more of the guys - in not just banking but the credit card department before she'd got her move upstairs to specialist accounts - than that bad virus a couple of years ago that had left the place with a skeleton staff for the best part of a week, and the slightest of glimpses of the nature of the email.

It wasn't *work* related although definitely appeared that Alex was putting *in* some work. Before minimising - and in the way that your mind does its own thing at times and helps you along - I'd managed to pluck out the sentence 'once you try me you'll never sleep with another man in this building' and the main take away being that Sandler hadn't *already* slept with her which almost put him in the minority amongst his fellow men at the call centre. Me included though, mind. The fact that

Sandler was married himself with a kid momentarily made me feel a touch better about what I was doing to him. I was doing what I was doing to *save* my family while he was in the process of trying to cheat on his wife.

Getting rid of the screen I looked down towards the taskbar to pull up our system that gained us entry into customer accounts. It could only have been a minute by that point but fuck did it feel like hours. I didn't dare stop to look around. It was literally the equivalent of someone trying to run out the prison. You *know* that there's guards up high in towers and that if they just so happen to be looking in the same direction as the way you're running then it's all over for you. But also, *this* is your only way *of* escaping. Ride or die.

This was *my* prison escape. To just get the head down and run - type - as fast as I could and hope that by the time I stopped running - logging out of Sandler's system and getting myself back the fuck into my own chair - no 'guards' would have looked in my direction and put a metaphorical couple of rounds into my back.

Feeling like there were fifty pairs of eyes boring into the back of me I quickly opened the system up and made the necessary amount of key strokes to bring up the search bar so that I could find the account I was looking for. Fortunately this wasn't a time consuming "Smith" search and there wasn't any surprise to find that we only had one match for a Mr Mario Buzzini. Frankly, I'd have been astonished - and pissed off - had I found more than that.

I'd taken the liberty of snooping around his account - earlier in the week - and had the pleasure of sitting and reading through the lists and lists of transactions that had been made through his account. It had been mind boggling to see an example of how the other half lives but someone who looked a fun person and wasn't shy about spending money in the pursuit of a good time.

Most of us - when looking at our bank account - will never see a transaction that lists any particular purchase sitting at the hundreds of thousands of pounds point.

He had three, in the last ten days worth of transactions. One to BMW Motor Company to the tune of a hundred and twenty k, another car purchase with Porsche for around two hundred and seventy thousand and one non automobile splurge with Cartier which wasn't that far off the Porsche one.

You sometimes see examples of kids that - overnight - are turned into multi millionaires just because they have a bit of promise of being one of the best to kick a fitba. A lot of them aren't ready for that amount of wealth and Buzzini looked like he was one of them and intent on spending as much as he could upon receiving it. Couldn't blame the man one bit. You're only here once and what good are all those millions at the end. Good on him. It was *why* I picked him. Think a Lineker or a Shearer would miss ninety five grand from their bank accounts? Too fucking right they would. I at least had a *chance* with the Italian.

Just bringing up the account and seeing it there in front of me - and knowing what I was about to do - brought on some involuntary shaking in my hands as I moved the mouse before progressing to arranging the transfer. Knowing that this really was going to be nothing more than a one time deal and that I wouldn't get another chance to attempt it for the day I'd taken no chances - even though one of my strengths was my sharp memory - and written Drummond's sock account details down on the inside of my left hand so that it would shave off a few seconds of time spent sat there. When every second really can count then you don't be fucking around with what precious time you have.

I could barely read my own writing - the scribbles on my palm - for the amount of shaking that I was doing as I held it open to type out the numbers written down. The shakes weren't the only part. I could feel my heartbeat increasing to the point where you could hear it as much as feel it.

Not for the first time since Drummond had began to - and let's call it what it was - blackmail me I felt that horrible panicking feeling where it felt like my temperature was rising while - even though sitting on my arse - experiencing some dizziness. Out of natural instinct I brought my hand up to wipe my drenched hair that was stuck to my forehead and move it to the side in a small flick. Stupid idea because my hands had already been clammy through the pressure that I was feeling - big time - and then what had I went and done? Taken that clammy hand and then wiped it against an even more moist and burning surface of my forehead.

When I brought my hand down to try and regain my composure to move forward with the transfer to Drummond I found that I'd managed to slightly smear some of the numbers that I'd written down. Only slightly but enough to ensure that I now no longer knew one hundred percent what the sort code and account number was. I was 'sure' the the eight looked a little suspect and was probably a smeared three.

This I did not bloody need.

I had the account and sort code written down in my notebook - that was lying on my desk - but I didn't have the time for running back and getting it. I had no choice but to press on.

Arranging the transfer for the sum of the ninety five thousand to the account number that was written down on my hand and then bypassing all the banking advisory checks that were popping up on screen asking the standard questions such as had the customer answered the necessary additional security checks due to the level of the amount being transferred.

With this being the kind of transfer that you couldn't get wrong I'd been left with no choice but to hold my horses for a moment and make ultra sure all details were correct before hitting the confirm button.

It taking me to hit the confirm option to find out that the bank account number I'd typed in was not a match for a TSB account in the name of Martin Wilson.

Seeing that incorrect information tab popping up on screen - as opposed to "transfer complete" - instantly raised my temperature further.

'FUCK' I screamed out inwardly to myself as I tried to stop myself from crumbling under the pressure of it all.

Ok, maybe that *was* a three after all then? I'd tried to reason with myself and keep things cool. No way was I pulling it off if I didn't retain some form of cool. The doubts inside me were saying that none of this was to do with the smeared details on my hand and that I'd maybe written the incorrect one down on my hand to begin with but I knew that - as much pressure I'd been feeling put under - I had double, triple and quadruple checked the details. If they were wrong then they were wrong because Drummond had supplied me with the incorrect details. I risked a quick - guilty as fuck, how could you *not* when sitting at unauthorised at a colleagues desk when working for a financial institution? - look around to survey the lay of the land.

The place just looked like any other minute of any day. Either rows of staff all chatting away and staring intently into their screens and barely daring to look away for fear of their call time stats racking up if they've not dealt with the customer enquiry in a timely manner, or the opposite of that. Banks of desks sitting empty due to lunch time.

I turned back around and attempted my second go at inputting the bank account. Simply changing the eight that I'd type to a three while knowing that I didn't have anywhere more to go if it was wrong a second time. Maybe, just maybe that other smeared seven *might* be a one, I thought to myself but if we were getting into that area then I would have been officially down to guesswork.

I didn't have time to really sit and hover the mouse over the "confirm transaction" tab like someone wondering whether they really can justify buying that extra jacket when they already have twenty four in their cupboard, but took a few seconds, regardless. Just staring at it knowing that if I did not see the 'transaction successful' message then I was going to be having a *very* bad Friday night. Very bad *life*, in fact.

It was the kids - popping into my mind - that brought me out of my moment's pause and back to the real world. The one where I needed to get the job in hand done, rather than sitting there baiting myself up to any colleagues or bosses.

I literally had the small arrow icon hovering over the confirm tab and my right index finger in the process of going on to click the mouse when I bloody shat myself at the voice from behind me.

'Emmmmmm excuse me, what do you think you're doing, mate?'

I'm sure that every single part of me left the seat for a second before my arse fell back down onto it again.

I already *knew* the voice.

I wheeled around to find Sandler - along with Jenny Nicholson - standing over my shoulder and - I'd been left with no real choice other than to assume - had been given an eagle eye view of what I was doing, from his workstation.

It's hard to defend one's self, when you already know how guilty you are. I couldn't see my face but bloody hell did it feel hot. Something I'd assumed would have been visible *externally*.

'Alex, I, I, I I was just ....'

'You were just performing a transfer from a colleague's terminal. I'll fill that sentence in for you, shall I?'

Jenny said - and without taking any mind to watch the levels that she spoke in - like the right stuck up bitch that she'd practically created her own brand of in the office. If you were in her clique then you were all good but she could be a right cow if you weren't. There was too much needing done and said and nowhere near enough time to do and say it all in.

First thing I should've done - even though in such an un-winnable position as I was in, it would have also left me looking guilty - would've been to hit that red and black x in the corner of the screen of the transaction. I didn't though and by the time that Jenny had looked past me and in further detail of what was on the screen - while I tried to explain to Alex that my terminal had gone down and I'd been asked to jump onto another one short term - and in doing so confirming that I was working on there *as* Alex and not my own login details. There was no 'explaining' things after that point.

Within five minutes, security had come for me. Asking for me to hand over my lanyard with my ID card that was attached to it, and led me to one of the meeting rooms that normally lay empty for the majority of a working week.

Within the hour two detectives from C.I.D had arrived. What a bloody mess, eh?

Naturally I was going to be sacked. That went without saying. The bank had a zero tolerance policy when it came to any staff putting their hands in the till. Unfortunately when the bank *caught* you in the act, losing your job wasn't the only bad part of your day because police would then be brought in. The grassing bastards. The bosses, not the police.

I'd only heard second hand info about what happened when you were caught stealing but none of it matched my own scenario sitting there in the meeting room. First of all - and it was maybe just the paranoia that I'd been dealing with all day - it had felt eerily like the bank security weren't surprised in what I had done. Maybe that was because it was all in a days work for them, I tried to reason.

I was sitting talking to the two security officers that had come and collected me at my desk when their gaffer - Parker - had come in. Not even bothering to look at me while beginning shouting at the pair of them.

'I thought you were fucking monitoring it? That was your exact words an hour ago when I phoned you up for an update?'

The boss laid into one guy in particular, out of the two of them.

What did that mean, though? Monitoring what?

'I'm sorry, boss but I can only do so much when I'm watching things from a completely separate area of the building?' He risked further ire from his gaffer with a hint of sarcasm in his reply.

'The minute that he changed desks he then .....'

'Oh just shut up, the pair of you.'

Parker spat in disgust before then looking at me for the first time and no doubt getting a look of complete confusion back in return.

'Those two detectives from this morning are going to be a pain in the neck when they find out.' The boss added.

Why all the cryptic shite, though? I expected to be held there and told that the police were on their way to collect me and that my employment had been terminated. But there felt more to this?

Finally finding out *what* when the two C.I.D detectives arrived. Burchill and Ardwick.

'You had one job? Fuck's sake, mate?' Burchill said to *Parker?*

Now the gaffer of security was getting a bollocking from C.I.D. What the hell was going on here? For the most part - up until that point - my actual presence inside the room had almost been of irrelevance as everyone had been too intent on giving each other grief, that I was left relatively unscathed, which felt strange, obviously.

'It was out of our hands, in the end. He used an attempted method of money transfer in a way that we couldn't have anticipated,' Parker replied defensively with his hands up in the air as if Burchill had pulled a gun on him.

'Well it's all fucked now. Should've never left the work of police with someone of lesser talents, no disrespect meant.' The older detective replied before his partner grabbed his arm to calm him down.

'It's fine, it's fine. Let's see what we can salvage out of things with Mr Leckie here, shall we?' Detective Ardwick said as he - and everyone else in the room - turned to look in my direction and switched the focus onto me for the first time.

I honestly had no idea what was going on, at all. It seemed like they were all in on something and filling me in on it had seemed unnecessary to them.

The younger detective asked Parker if they needed anything further from me before they took me in for questioning. The security boss of my - now - ex employers confirming to Ardwick that they had retrieved everything they needed from me that would stop me from getting through the front door again - once I'd left for the last time - and that they were free to escort me from the building.

A walk of shame and a half, I can tell you. Handcuffed and led out of a busy call centre by two detectives. Funny how at times like that staff - for a moment at least - stop worrying about their bloody call time stats? I just stared at the ground and tried to blank out all of the comments, gasps and whispers that I heard as I embarrassingly passed each bank of desks.

Despite it edging me closer to being shoved into the back of a C.I.D car, I was glad to get out of the place and away from all of those eyes watching me leave the building for the last time.

I'd never been in trouble with the police before. No arrests, charges, cautions, questioning, or convictions. The *exact* type of person that the police would be able to run rings around. Luckily for me I was into my crime programmes. Line of Duty, Frost and Silent Witness, all that stuff. Lapped it right up and it's just as well I did because it came in handy for having to go to the station and be interviewed by the two of them.

They gave it all the "help us to help you, Grant" patter. Telling me that they already knew that I wasn't the type to attempt to commit a crime and that their intelligence had already suggested to them that I had been coerced into carrying out the theft.

That panicking me quite a bit because it proved that they knew what Drummond was up to with me but how because it certainly hadn't come from me and my panic lay in the fact that where do you think Drummond would have thought the police had *found out* from? With what he had on his phone - and regardless of what trouble I was undoubtedly in - I could not afford to piss him off. He was already going to be a major problem when he found out that the money transfer wasn't going to be happening for him and I prayed that the only thing that would save me from him maliciously posting the video of me hours later that night would be that I had *attempted* to do it for him. And that I'd been caught and charged by police but that I had not said a single word to them about *him,* and the part that he had played in it.

The two of them tried various approaches with me, to get me to talk - and expand - further than the repeated admission from me that I had been caught bang to rights in attempting to transfer the money. Fortunately I hadn't been able to press the transfer button before being rumbled and because of that there was no actual link to the bank account that I'd *wanted* the funds to go to - and in the sense that the recorded keystrokes of me getting the account wrong initially only helped there - so when it came to that question of where I was attempting to send the funds to I was able to bat that question away with a no comment and leave it to the imagination that it would have been an account belonging to me that I'd have been attempting a transfer to, like most embezzlers.

In private, my lawyer had advised that with me being a first time offender and that I appeared to have information that the C.I.D were looking for he was of the opinion that if I was to help them with their enquiry. The detectives - and their influence - could be the difference between a judge sending me to prison or not. My lawyer also, however and to be fair to him was not in the position of having a video of him receiving head from a stranger in a car being put onto social media depending on which next steps he took.

The two detectives got quite annoyed with me in the end. I don't know? It was almost like they *expected* me to play ball and when it dawned on them that I wouldn't they started to change their behaviour with me.

The old one saying to me from one side that he would personally make sure that the judge at my trial would be marked down for giving me the largest sentence he possibly could. Adding that being in the masons was a wonderful thing and always helped smooth the wheels of justice. He's saying that while the younger one is trying to mess with my mind by telling me that I was under suspicion of working with a known drug dealer and how did he think this story - or fabrication to give it its correct title - was going to look in court, or the newspapers, which he was of the opinion would be all over a story like that.

'I can see it now in the Evening Times - as well as nationwide -
Bank worker caught stealing a hundred thousand from English
Premier League player to fund drug business'

Ard*prick* sat there and said as he almost pictured the front page
headline.

'*Sensational*' His partner chipped in.

'I think my client has made his position quite clear by this point
Detective Ardwick' my lawyer stepped in.

'Oh fucking shut it, no one asked you.' The annoyed and
irritable older detective unloaded at him.

'Fortunately, Detective Burchill, your opinion on that is not
relevant. Now what *is* relevant is that you charge my client or
not and then we can get his release processed. Now my client
and I have sat here and listened to your attempt at what I can
only liken as buying a raffle ticket to try and win something but
it clearly hasn't worked so let's stop wasting everyone's time
here, shall we? Mr Hamilton, up until today, has had a clean
record and you're sat here trying to accuse him of being mixed
up in illegal drugs? You really should listen to the pair of you.'

I'd been left impressed by the cool and composed attitude to
him inside that room - when the conduct of the detectives could
hardly have been described as similar - and knew exactly when
to say when and call time on them. And the way that he *did* was
chef's kiss material.

I was charged with theft, bailed and released within the hour
and back out on the street by tea time where I had the
unenviable task - or *series* of tasks - of not just telling my wife
that I'd both been charged by the police which would
potentially see me going to jail but along with it had lost my job

- and as our main bread winner for the family - but on *top* of that. I was going to have to tell Barry Drummond that I'd failed and that he wasn't going to be receiving the money he'd spent a whole week shaking me down for.

And what he was then going to do, once I told him that?

Chapter 34

Hammy

'Mon, mate. You need to get out of here. That woman behind the counter has called the bizzies, Hammy.' I could just about make out Hummel's words filtering their way through the thick and heavy red mist that had come down inside the bookies that lunch time, while I took the legs of that wee stool and repeatedly rammed them into the perspex. It didn't even matter that I knew there was no way I'd be able to pierce the transparent shield which had been built to withstand a whole lot more than a chair leg - so aye, a wafer light metal tube - shoved at it. It just made me feel better to do so and anyway? The shit eating grin that Brian was standing there - from his safe haven - looking at me with was hardly the kind that would have me peacefully putting the chair down and just admitting to everyone, as well as myself, that it simply hadn't been my day.

'YOU'RE FUCKING LOVING THIS YOU, EH? ABSOLUTE FUCKING PIECE OF SHIT WANKER'

I screamed at the manager. Him smiling with wide eyes while nodding his head up and down repeatedly. This only enraging me further.

'Come on, man. The cunt's not worth it, mate.' Hummel tugged at me again only this time with a bit more force. A few other voices from some of the punters joined him in trying to diffuse things a little.

'Still got the match tonight, mind. Keep the head son.' I heard from someone else. Honestly felt like turning my wrath on whoever the fuck it was because to say something like that was as much of a wind up to me as Brian Mathieson shop manager of Paddy Power turf accountant was with his conduct. Aye, never say never and all of that but don't try to tell me that my bet - looking for five goals or more - which involves a professional fitba match being played in a country's premier division is a bet that's in with a good chance.

I could tell that the gadgey was only trying to inject a wee bit of positivity to things but honestly? When I've just found out that the ninety two grand - plus change - that I'd won turned out *not* to be so, I'm not the person that you should try and give a bit of lip service to.

I didn't need any platitudes from anyone. Knew what a proper James Hunt I'd made of things. A bet like that will come up once in your life, if you're lucky, as well as fucking stupid enough to put one on in the *first* place.

All I needed to do was have the simple words 'Under 19s' onto the slip beside those two teams names. I didn't though and as a result the bookies were *never* going to pay out. Not on a 'Aye but I was betting on *that* match' situation. Fuck, that's a bookie's *dream* scenario when someone rocks up to collect almost a hundred grand from them. Like an insurance company when it comes to finding an excuse not to pay out, them.

You can imagine how I felt, knowing that it was *me* who'd given them their out. And I couldn't even admit it there that day, not after going as far as I did. It was a stressful time and all kinds of emotions surfaced, although mainly violent and abusive ones. Once I'd went down that road my pride couldn't let me do a complete one eighty and then announce that aye, it was actually my fault.

It was too late for that and - in my mind at least - it would've been even *more* embarrassing than any embarrassment I might've made of myself with my reaction to being told it was a non winner. And besides, to admit that I was wrong would be to confess to anyone there in the shop that I James Hamilton had been fucking stupid enough to fill out a bet incorrectly and at the *worst* possible time, and lose himself over ninety grand in the process.

Cunts standing in the boozer talking about me later that night while wincing at the thought of such a kick in the balls of the level that I'd received. No doubt getting their phone out to check what the score was in Prague between Slavia and Sigma and seeing that it's nowhere near to over four and a half goals while all laughing at me.

Fucking felt like the world's biggest fanny. Actually, the world's biggest *loser*. That's exactly what I *was*.

Had never come close to that sinking feeling. The one where you're convinced that someone has completely scooped out all of your insides. I could've been sick, *if* I'd felt like there was anything inside of me.

Such a feeling of crushing defeat, the likes that I never even knew existed until that day. Because the thing was. I hadn't mentioned it to the other two - had been so wrapped up in my own life that we hadn't seen much of each other since that messy trip to Glasgow the weekend before - but I'd quietly settled on the reality that there was going to be a heavy chance that the majority of my winnings was going to be needed to pay off our debt to the German, Albanians or whoever the fuck it was that we were *actually* due the dough to.

It hadn't even been anything worth considering - up until I was sat in my house on the Thursday night and one game away from winning - so had not been anything I'd mentioned to the lads but I would have had to have been a complete cunt, and in no way a mate of either Hummel or Drummond, if I was to have won practically the same amount that were were due what either was or was not a highly dangerous group of people. I know - back at the start of the whole nightmare - I'd been of the opinion that we should just bump the payment and how it was probably just a couple of kids who were good with the internet that had been supplying us and not exactly the kind of characters that were ever going to be in with a chance of harming any of us but well, that was when I saw no way of us being able to *pay* it back. When that's your reality then you just have to cut your cloth accordingly, eh?

Having the money to pay back though, that changes things. Always pay your fucking debts, one of the things my dad told me when I left school and entered the outside world. That was one of the pieces of advice that he gave me that was actually of worth and maintained the respect you'd get from your fellow man.

Some of his other nuggets of advice didn't stand me in as good stead that he maybe thought they would though, like. Such as always to make sure I got the first dig in with someone. The amount of fights - that probably weren't even going to *be* a fight - that I'd had in my life that had probably came *through* that first dig. Cheers, pops.

Paying what you're due someone is just what you do, if you've got anything about you as a person, as well as the *money* to pay back of course, obviously.

Aye, Drummond had told us that he had a plan in the works but neither was he willing to say that it was one hundred percent guaranteed to come off, and unless he had kept me out the loop - which I know the boy wouldn't do - then as far as I knew he'd *still* not received the money into this phantom bank account that he'd had set up with the fake docs.

Obviously, the ultimate happy medium would have been for Drummond to get us the money he was in the process of hustling up *and* for my bet to come up. Proper chicken dinner stuff, that. Realistically, though. On the Thursday night I was - as the one who was the gambler out of us all - putting our odds of both happening at quite high. Maybe say what you'd get for St Mirren away to Parkhead. Easily fourteens and upwards.

It was one beauty of a safety blanket to have though, providing I got those five goals required that morning in Prague. Drummond got us the money then him and Hummel could have looked forward to an all expenses paid trip to any destination in the world for the three of us to go on. He *didn't* get us it. Then, as hard as it would've been to have handed the money over - having only just won it - we, at least, had a solid plan b to move on to.

But now it was all completely FUCKED and all through the most idiotic of mistakes from me.

I'm going to be so fucking pissed off at myself if I end up tied to a chair in a disused warehouse surrounded by gangsters and all because I couldn't remember to write *under fucking nineteens* onto a bit of paper, the thought rushed through me - and out of nowhere - as Hummel helped me put the chair down in the same kind of way that you see the police handle someone with a gun in their hand on the times where they think they can resolve things without having one of their snipers putting a couple of bullets into the person from a safe distance.

'And needless to say, you're barred from the shop.'

Brian shouted, finally being allowed the chance to say the words that he must've dreamed about saying to me for years. That he chose to say that - and in doing so state the fucking obvious - at the exact moment I'd appeared to have calmed down and was putting down my weapon only served to show that the boy was fucking at it when it came to trying to keep the kettle boiling. Like, he should've been trying to ensure that I wasn't behaving like I was inside his shop but, instead, was doing all he could to keep me in the red zone.

Thank fuck for Hummel. It's funny how that stuff all works its way out, eh? Had he not spilled his bottle of Buckie over my Stockholm's then he wouldn't have had to go to Dundee that morning and if he hadn't have been to Dundee then he wouldn't have been getting off the bus - from the city centre - right at that moment I came flying out the bookies celebrating the fifth under nineteens goal going in during the second half of the Czech game. The lord and his mysterious ways, eh?

Well whether it was the lord's work or not Hummel was a man precisely in the right place at the right time.

'Me and you aren't fucking done, by the way. Unless you plan to live behind that perspex all of your life.' I dealt Brian a wee warning as Hummel was leading me out of the place. *That* wiped that fucking nauseating and self satisfying smile from the prick's coupon right enough though, mind.

If Hummel hadn't been there I'm not quite sure *when* I'd have stopped, probably would've been still there going radge when the coppers arrived so at least Hummel had managed to keep things to a minimum. I sure as fuck wasn't the first person who had reacted adversely to a bet not going their way. The fact that there even *was* perspex told its own story.

I'd seen a punter three or four weeks before *spit* on the barrier between customer and bookie staff. If someone wants to tell me that ramming a stool into the perspex is worse than someone spitting then they know where to find me, eh? I was obviously going to get done for it once the bizzies caught up with me. I'm sure Brian would've wasted no time in showing the video of events when they'd asked what had happened. Aye it was all something that I could've done without having to face but as far as the day went, there was still bigger fish to fry.

I'd deal with the police as and when regarding the bookies incident but - considering I hadn't *actually* leathered anyone - I wasn't exactly shiteing myself at whatever charge - or charges - I was going to land up with as a result.

Once we'd got ourselves out onto the street and making a hasty retreat and directly away from Paddy's I was able to see just how gutted Hummel was for me. Proper mate stuff, like. You'd have thought it was *him* that had lost the ninety two thousand, seven hundred and forty five pounds and twenty six pence.

He looked as deflated as I did about things.

'I'm not saying that the coupon isn't technically kaput like but ...'

I stopped him before he even said another word.

'But it's kaput.' I said, bringing a bit of closure to what he was attempting to try and open with. Aye, I'd hang on to the betting slip just in case, obviously, but already had given up its chances of going anywhere further.

'My mind can't even deal with the ups and downs of what has just happened back there. That feeling when you'd told me that you'd won and now what we're left with.' He continued, as we walked directionless, as long as the direction was in the opposite one of the bookie shop.

His fucking mind? Jesus? He should've tried living inside *my* one over the five days of the accumulator building and building.

'I don't even know if I'm happy or sad that the blame lies with me? Like, would it be better to have someone to blame in this or is it better to not have to use that energy? All I know is for a brief moment I thought I was ninety two grand richer and have since found that it's not good for your mental health to have your mind and your emotions pulled off in completely opposite directions in such a short space of time. Like taking a couple of lines of Ching and then following that up by taking a jelly. You're not meant to go through such shit inside the same moment. There's a very definite line that you sit on either side of when you win or you lose. You're literally a winner or a loser. You can't be both and as such you don't ever experience the feeling of *being* both. I did.'

'Aye, it all depends which angle you want to approach things from, I suppose?' Hummel reasoned with me while having his attention diverted by the vibrating in his pocket from his phone. Pulling it out and having a look at the number and - not recognising the number calling - deciding not to bother taking the call.

'Probably some cunt asking about the car accident that I haven't had or something.' He said, making the classic assumption that when it's a number you don't recognise coming up on your phone then - generally - it's definitely no cunt worth talking to.

'Well, the fact that you don't have a car might've been a bit of a dead give away, eh?' I said laughing back at him, surprised I even had any humour in me at that moment.

He went to reply but the vibrating started again in his pocket. The first time it had went off I had semi hoped that it would've been Drummond calling Hummel with some kind of status report over how things were going and had been left disappointed when seeing Hummel's response to the caller ID on his screen. For what it was worth, the second time his pocket buzzed I *still* walked along hoping that it was going to be Drummond.

'These cunts, again?' He said before declining it.

He didn't even get a chance to put his phone away before they called for a third time.

'Actually, know what? Fuck this.' Hummel said, apparently antagonised by this person calling three times in a row. 'Take a fucking hint, eh?' He quickly said before hitting the green button and raising the phone up to his ear and mouth.

'HELLO' He shouted angrily into the handset. Not exactly Dom Jolly levels but wasn't that far away either, to be fair to my man Hummel.

I watched his face as we walked along the street, and how over a matter of seconds it changed from hostile to friendly with the caller.

It went along - in the sense of watching a conversation take place from the one perspective - the lines of.

'Yes, it is.'

Whatever was said next to him must've got his attention because the hostility went right out the window and he was acting nice as pie with the caller. Proper friendly, like. And the more that he gave them a chance to speak, the more excited he appeared to grow.

'My favourite sports team, aye? Well that would be the world famous Hibernian Football Club, Edinburgh's premier football team.'

He said to the caller with a smile beginning to set on his face, while reaching out with his free arm and putting it around my neck tightly as we carried on walking down the road.

Chapter 35

Hummel

Was literally dealing with all the ups and downs and the messy fallout of Hammy's win slash wasn't a win at the bookies when she called me.

Fuck knows how the big hamster was feeling inside because - and within the short space of around five minutes or so - I felt like I'd been picked up by Hammy in a Joe Maxi on his way to heaven only for us to arrive there and us get a knock back from the bouncers, leading to the driver re-routing things and taking us down south to *hell*.

My heart had only just managed to start to find something in the region of a normal heartbeat pattern again only for that phone call to send it to the fucking moon once more. Proper rubbered it the first time it popped up, like. Some o eight hundred random number that you just know is going to give you a sore head if you answer it. Nine out of ten times it's an ambulance chaser of some shape or form that normally leaves you in a worse mood for answering the phone to them. Tell you one person I *would* like to have a wee spraff with though, mind. Whatever cunt it is that keeps giving *out* my fucking phone number!

When I'd felt the phone buzzing in my pocket - that very first time - I'd prayed that it was going to be Drummond who had - up to that stage of the day - been worryingly conspicuous by his absence in terms of any form of contact. That he had went dark on us did not exactly enhance any feelings that one might have had over him saving the day with his need to know basis - apparently - scheme that he said would, if successful, secure us the funds required.

Thank fuck she phoned me back, that third time, though. If the first call I'd looked at before putting the phone back in my pocket and let ring out, the second I'd been as blunt as to actually press the decline on it. Looking at Hammy while showing him them calling me again with a 'these cunts, eh?' face. That really should have been that and it was only *because* this number had brazenly called me back for a third time - in quick succession - that I only answered so I could tell whoever it was on the other end of the line to fuck right off and stop calling me. I was in a bad enough mood for to have had things escalated further by some jobsworth who could've been in Birmingham, Bangalore or anywhere in between.

The first words I opened with genuinely were going to be profanity filled. Glad I never now, mind. Something told me - just as I was about to speak - that whoever it was on the other end of the line had not been handed any inside info that would've allowed them to know in advance of calling that they were catching me at a bad time. Actually, a fucking horrendous time.

I'd just watched the payment for Arman88 - whether Hammy really appreciated this in that moment or not - slip from our hands. It was literally there, and then it wasn't.

Not the time for someone sitting with a headset strapped to them in a busy noisy call centre to be trying their luck with you. Not the time, at all. I'd intended on giving the caller a harsh lesson in this along with setting them straight on their unwillingness to take no for an answer.

Things didn't quite work out that way though.

I'd thought my opener of a 'HELLO' - which I'd felt was something similar from what you'd get if you were to wake some poor bastard up who's on nightshift - would've let the caller know what the Hampden was.

If thinking that this unfriendly answering of the call of mines would have already put the caller on the back foot and already now regretting phoning this particular number three times in a row instead of just moving onto whatever poor sapp they had on their pages and pages of names and numbers for the day ahead, then I'd have been wrong.

Poor sapp? I couldn't have been *further* from the truth.

'Good afternoon, is it possible to speak to Mr Paul Evans?' She answered in such a pleasant and vibrant way it had made me question if she had even *heard* my attempt at hostility because of the passing cars or that maybe she'd heard the cars and taken this as *why* I was shouting at her on answering.

I confirmed - to her - that I indeed was the man that she was looking for, while questioning if by doing so was actually a good idea because all it was now going to do would be provide her with additional questions.

Upon confirming I was Paul Evans, and she told me which company she - Rebecca - was calling from, I soon found that I would've been *more* than happy to assist and accommodate with her enquiry.

When she sat there and told me that she was calling from *EZ-Coin* I was all of a sudden a lot more open, honest and receptive to the conversation.

'Good afternoon, Mr Evans. My name is Rebecca and I'm calling from EZ-Coin with regards to an auto set up transfer of crypto currency into GBP pounds that you have scheduled for your account.'

I - at that moment - had no fucking idea *which* auto set up transfer that she spoke of, but the fact that she was calling in the first place? *That* was most definitely a *good* thing.

I knew about the auto transfer function on EZ-Coin and I had used it quite a lot, for my "shitcoin" purchases which - with names like that - would suggest that they were crypto coins that while you could own they were - on the face of it - a complete waste of time and not worth the money that you've spent on them. I'd always looked on them as something similar to those penny shares that the Wolf of Wall Street was selling people near the start of the film but the only difference was you didn't have some gift of the gab salesman pushing you to buy shitcoins. You had enthusiastic nerds that you would sometimes bump into on the dark web shouting about this new coin that they had learned of and how - long term - they believed it would surpass the price of Bitcoin. All pipe dreams, as well as all talk.

That didn't mean to say that I didn't buy any myself. Some that I'd done research on and wanted to take a punt on while others I'd actually bought as favours or a show of support to someone I knew on the dark web. It would only be fifty to a hundred pounds I'd spend. Just enough to provide a screenshot to show them that you'd backed their earlier venture while knowing that I would eventually need a favour back from them as part of my e-commerce role with our small business venture that we had been - until recently - successfully operating.

I'm not sure that Hammy or Drummond had ever really appreciated all of the work that I was doing online, especially in those early days where I was making connections for supplies while fighting the everlasting fight of finding the Feds busting the site you were using and then - in the *exact* way that everyone predicted it would be following take downs by the Federales - finding the next hot site that everyone - vendors and customers - had moved onto and moving our business supply chain onto the new home, until the next time it happened again.

I'd kept things basic for the two others. All they knew - and cared about - was Bitcoin so why complicate things by bringing them into all of the multitude of other side purchases that I was making with my own money. I easily had twenty to thirty shitcoins and - even when I had access to my portfolio - it was quite a drain on checking them, so barely did. What point in doing so when the majority of them don't even move in price while the other ones might fluctuate by one or two pence in a day, either up or down.

I'd never spent much *on* them so there was never the fear of investing in something and losing it. What I paid on any shitcoins singular purchase over the years I'd been on the dark web was less than what you'd have found Hammy sticking on a horse or - for a topical example - that mad as fuck acca. To be fair, the pair of us would've had almost the same amount of chance of getting anything for our money with the different purchases of ours.

The reason that she got my attention straight away, turning my mood with things, was by saying the magic words to me about the auto transfer set up.

Basically this was a function that I used on EZ and *only* for the shitcoins that I owned. The reason for this being that with how much that I'd purchased over the years - more than I could've even been fully able to rattle off to you, so many there were - I literally didn't have the time, interest and motivation on checking something like - to give an example - a coin that you only bought because someone promised you an invite to a private growers club in return for showing them a bit of support with the coin they were trying to gain traction on.

The auto transfer was a facility that you could set the parameters of how seriously, and when, one of these "shitcoins" should be looked upon. The example of how I used this being that I had set auto transfer set ups to kick in if any of these crypto coins prompted a profit percentage based trigger point klaxon of sorts. This, in turn, would set up an automatic sale of the coin to the market and replacing your crypto with the proceeds the sale brought in.

Which meant that her calling me - for whatever coin I had that had "mooned"and what price I'd paid for them and how much I owned - was for a *good* reason. An ambulance chaser, this wasn't.

'So if I can just take you through some security questions Mr Evans and then we can discuss your transfer, ok?' She asked. I was happy to accept.

Favourite sports team? That was dealt with ease, even if I over embellished things with my answer. She giggled anyway so it was all good.

Then I had to give the name of my first school. It was all the standard questions that I had set back when creating my EZ-Coin account up for a day like today, if it was to ever come around and rear its head.

'Ok great, thank you,' she said in that pleasant tone of hers that I'd taken to from the very off. Well, from the point she said she was from EZ and wanted to talk to me about a potential transfer of money. Money that I'd had - otherwise - no chance of accessing it without my hard drive that had my portfolio on it. Fuck, I'd tried until I was ready to throw my phone against the wall calling EZ-Coin to explain what had happened but advised that I was effectively locked out, without my hardware. *This* was a different scenario, though. This was a scenario where I had requested something to happen *before* I was effectively locked out of my money.

Probably was going to be two or three thousand pounds - at best - because some of these fucking shit coins were costing me mad amounts like zero point zero zero zero zero four seven pence which blew my mind at first because I didn't even know currency could be like that. Either you've got a penny or you've not. Don't be bothering me with your three quarters of a penny, mate, eh?

Still, given what had happened the past five minutes back at Paddy Power. Any good news, you'd have taken.

'You have an auto transfer set up for RAJ - previously pre-set by you on your account - for all of your holdings to be sold upon reaching your chosen designated trigger point. Yesterday that price range was hit and stayed inside it for the regulatory length of time so to complete the final step - as bound by financial regulations - we need to inform you and confirm the transfer - verbally - before we go ahead and process the sale of your crypto currency.'

Trying to think on my feet I couldn't place it, as in where and when I'd bought it. Just another tiny purchase that I'd made that got lost in the cracks amongst all the other ones that were deemed not to be bread and butter like Bitcoin and Ethereum. As I played it out in my mind while she waited on me speaking I could not rule out that I'd bought it *purely* on the strength of me thinking it was radge that there was a crypto coin *called* raj. The last time I'd put a bet on at the bookies had been because I'd seen a team were about to play and their name was *Shan*

United and - thinking it was a brilliant name for a team and figuring they wouldn't be as shan as their actual team name - so I had form for making splurges due to catchy names. Unsurprisingly, they turned out to be an aptly named fitba side.

Whether I remembered it or not, EZ and their systems *did*.

'So then Mr Evans with RAJ Coin holding its market position by this morning we are bound to advise you of the transfer which is now waiting to be made. I do apologise as you should have received a call straight earlier but - as you'll be fully aware I'm sure - there has been a lot of movement in the markets the past few days and we have been *extremely* busy.'

Me? Fully aware? Was she sure? From the moment that Debz sunk that fucking hard drive I had kind of developed a lack of interest in the crypto market after that point. Be as well taking all of your possessions and having them put in a shop window for you to see, only the shop's closed and you know that you're never, ever getting your shit back.

'Of course, you'll be happy that I've called you a little later on in the day, what with the price rise as the morning has went on. That tweet last night from Evan Hust really sent things skyward.'

While Hammy walked along in silence but noticing the rising smile that was forming on my coupon you could see him asking - without asking - *who* was on the phone.

Rebecca, who had continued to completely not patronise me in any way and pretty much take it that I - as the crypto owner - would have already been in on what she was talking about spoke in assumptions that I knew her references which were really only part of the small talk as she was on the phone to me to confirm the transfer.

'With how the price of RAJ has been building up of the past year.'

Something I had absolutely no idea of because I had just tucked it away with the auto set up function for a day that wasn't going to fucking come around anyway.

'And then with a few celebrities beginning to mention it on social media it's kind of taken off. Then, like I said, Hust's tweet last night. One simple tweet saying the word *RAJ Coin* going out to his army of millions of followers and well, here we are with me calling you. Now, Mr Evans there are two reasons that I have to call you over this price shift in your crypto currency, apart from the actual price movement itself, of course which triggered this whole transfer. One is simply because it falls over the amount of money that we're legally obliged to inform a customer of before transfer.'

'And the other?'

I urged her because by this point I just wanted to find out how much I was ready to pocket. Who knows? It could maybe be enough for us to make a "peace offering" to Arman88 over while telling him all of what we'd went through to try and *get* the money together for him. God bless Evan Hust, though. Some Uber rich Silicone Valley tech wizard playboy who seemed to think that he was some kind of Tony Stark character but was also someone who - for whatever the reason - had gained quite a massive social media following and - as such - had the power to make or break *any* product that he so desired. By merely giving RAJ a mention - according to Rebecca - it had sent the price haywire with all of his devoted followers all rushing to buy it.

'Well, Mr Evans, the other reason for the call is that to remind you that your crypto currency can go down as well as up and to state that once you have sold your coins you will no longer be able to claim any further price increase of them.'

She couldn't have said to me outright which one I should do - buy or sell - as that decision has to come from the customer in a financial environment but reading between the lines, and her tone of voice. She was telling me *not* to sell. Which was really sound of her. Trying to ensure that I would go on to make a wee bit more on them in the long run.

Obviously, though. She wasn't in on my financial situation and how critical it really was. And anyway, with no hard drive I wouldn't have *had* the chance to sell at a later date. Whatever she had in mind for transferring over I was having it, no matter if it jumped in price by another pound or two or whatever, fucking twenty pounds. For that stuff to happen *after* the Friday meant that the amount of money from then on was irrelevant anyway.

'No, I think - given the price shift of late - I feel that now may be a good time to sell.' I replied, doing a decent job of coming across as someone with a scoobie of what was actually going on. The crux of it though? I was literally telling her I was wanting to sell a coin that I couldn't remember purchasing, how many I'd bought, what price they were, *why* I'd bought them and the most relevant at that moment in time, what they were now *worth*.

'Ok then. Your original purchase was at a price of point zero zero zero zero seven five pence - per token - and for a *total* sum of ten thousand RAJ tokens.'

This sounded about right for those random shitcoins purchases that I'd made over the years. They were practically worthless - in price - so to just "dip your toe in" and buy ten or twenty would have been the ultimate in wasting your time. These things were hardly going to make you your fortune and they *definitely* weren't if you only held a few of them. Because of how cheap they were - in reality to something like a Bitcoin - you were always able to get five to ten thousand of the things for - at times - well under a hundred pounds.

'And at todays current price - that we will commit the sale to go through at within the duration of this call - sitting at Eleven pounds and sixty seven pence. Times your ten thousand shares...'

My maths were complete shit and at the moment, my mind in general too so hadn't been able to calculate what amount she was about to come out with but the excitement that instantly rose - the minute she told me the current market price which had completely blown my mind because I'd expected possibly one or two pounds which for a shitcoin was an astronomical figure - was telling me to prepare for something a wee bit more than the two or three thousand I thought I might be getting at the start of the call.

'Which brings things to a total of one hundred and sixteen thousand, seven hundred pounds. Minus our conversion fee this will bring the sum slightly lower to one hundred and fifteen thousand, nine hundred and twenty five pounds.'

My head went after those words came out of her mouth and missed the follow up question from her, this being 'would you like me to go ahead with the transfer to your registered banking account ending in 3462?'

Instead - upon hearing the figure - and once my mind had managed to engage with my mouth all I'd been able to say to her was a *FUCK ... OFF!*

Hammy,'s face dropped for a moment as he watched me on what could only have appeared as a cordial conversation between the two people involved only to have me telling them to fuck off.

But I wasn't telling her to *fuck off* fuck off. Not that she knew this immediately.

'So you don't want me to go ahead with it? You know? There were many other options open to you that you could've chosen to answer my question without being so abusive about it.' She replied a wee bit hurt sounding. This facilitating me having to rush to correct and assure her that what I had said had been nothing other than a *positive* figure of speech - when using those two words - reserved specifically for times of amazement, like there and then.

Once she'd had this explained we were back on track and with my confirmation that she had the correct bank account that she was about to begin the process of transferring to my account, warning me that the payment would need to go through various standard checks before being released and that I should expect it to appear in my account inside the next two to three hours.

Expressing my undying love for Rebecca while wishing her a good weekend before ending the call I turned to Hammy who had now stopped walking completely and was standing with an inquisitive - but also bemused - look on his coupon.

'Hamster, you are not going to *fucking believe* what that phone call was just about.'

Chapter 36

Drummond

I only received two phone calls that afternoon and had they not arrived in the order that they had then who knows what I'd have done as a result. It had been a pretty tense day and that can bring out all kinds of strange acts or behaviour in a person when the chips are down. Something that I excelled at, normally. But this was in no way any kind of a 'normal' day with the stakes way too high to remain fully rational. Not when you were dealing with the possibility that by the evening you, your girlfriend and kid were potentially going to be officially marked as *at risk*. Luckily for Grant Leckie, his call came second out of the two. Had he been the first - and before Hummel - then I may well have done things that I wouldn't have been too proud of along with actions that I would not have been able to undo, once done.

I'd found myself in the middle of a leisurely trance like drive because I sure as fuck didn't know how I'd managed to get to where I was, when the phone went. Doing that thing people do when they're expecting an important phone call and the phone goes off. I'd been left disappointed when it had been my usual day to day phone that had started ringing, instead of the burner. Had been in danger of burning a hole *in* my burner phone if I'd sat staring at it any longer when I was parked down at Portie.

Thought it would've been a good idea to just go for a drive somewhere as they say that helps clear the head. Didn't clear the head though as all I'd thought about had been the obvious.

Thought about it so hard, in fact, that I had managed to get myself out by Bilston near Ikea, with not much recollection of how I'd managed to get there.

Instead of Leckie calling, it was Hummel. No doubt - by this point of the day - getting itchy about if things were progressing or if they weren't. I couldn't have blamed the boy for possibly being a wee bit on the nervous side with things moving into the afternoon by then. Couldn't be bothered with telling him that there was no news yet but also knew the cunt would keep calling me back anyway so I answered it straight away.

'Ahoy hoy,' He said upon hearing me pick up and - give the boy his dues - he wasn't sounding like someone in the position that he - we - was in that Friday.

'Alright, lad.' I replied.

'Any joy yet?' He came straight out with it. Fair enough, like. I had never taken it as if he'd been calling just to check how my health was.

'Nah, afraid not. Still time though, eh The day is yet young?' I said coming across more hopeful than confident. Which was pretty much just about the order with things.

'Awww shit, gen like, mate, aye? Such a shame, such a damn shame,' He said, but his tone didn't really back it up.

I then heard what I thought was someone starting to snigger and giggle in the background.

What the fuck was Hummel's game? That daft bastard put us *in* the shit, then grabbed our heads and firmly shoved them even further down into it. And with hours to spare - and no fucking word from this Leckie prick - Hummel's standing - in what was possibly The Trap - fucking about having a laugh.

'Who's there with you?' I asked, now thinking I was maybe on loudspeaker and hadn't been able to tell due to being in the car and out on the busy bypass.

'Just the hamster, mate. We're in The Trap.'

Aye, nice one, eh? I'm up with the fucking seagulls and out the door to do one final twist of the knife into my blackmail mark and then doing anything but sitting around my other half and kid because I can't even consciously look at them in the face without thinking of the fact that I've potentially put them both in danger. While these other two are sitting in *the fucking pub?*

I was actually in the process of attempting to choose my next words carefully - while in no way going to miss my target with any less effect - when Hummel followed up with.

'Listen, man. Obviously I still don't have a fucking clue what it is that you're trying to arrange for today, or how possible it even is was or is *ever* going to be between now and our deadline but fuck that for now. Get yourself down here soon as, I've got major news - good news - but not going to go into it here on the phone. All I'm saying is. Problem solved, lad. We fucking did it.'

Right as I was in the process of excitedly trying to ask further details the connection dropped a little, leading to him only hearing portions of what I'd said and the same back when he'd tried to reply. Then it dropped altogether.

I didn't bother calling him back and trusted in him in that he would not have said something like this if there hadn't been *big* news. Maybe Arman88 had been lifted in Germany and

Hummel had just found out that morning on the dark web? Hammy'd found out that he'd had an auntie who had recently died and left him all of her will? Just a couple of random possibilities that had sprang to my ever hopeful mind once the call was over.

It's hard to describe the feeling that one minute phone call left me with. Because I'm an analyst type - and didn't know the finer details of what had been taking place that morning - I couldn't allow myself the complete release of relief. Not until I knew for myself but Hummel - who had been more or less a wreck for the previous couple of weeks - and his own tone - and return of the spirit that he'd been missing - spoke volumes about how the situation had evidently improved in my absence.

And once I arrived to meet the pair of them and found out the Hampden. Fuck me, had the situation improved.

I wouldn't have believed Hummel's story had he not pulled up his bank account on his phone and showed me the recent deposit that it had received, of over a hundred fucking thousand pounds! The fact that Hammy had won - and lost - around ninety bags inside the same half an hour was almost a footnote of sorts, when it definitely shouldn't have been.

Man wins then loses then wrecks bookies is something that would generally take more of a higher billing. We were *all* happy for it not to be.

'Didn't I fucking tell you one of those shit coins was going to go to the moon at some point, eh?'

Hummel sat there saying while basking in the glory of having unexpectedly coming through for us. He actually *hadn't* because if he'd told me that I could've bought a currency - that

I couldn't even fucking see - for under a hundred pounds and I'd have been able to turn it into a hundred *thousand* then of course I'd have done it too. There was no need to correct him, not then, not that night.

'So what *was* your plan? Now that close of business has come and gone, like? You said you'd tell us one way or another, eh?' Hammy asked me. To be honest, once I'd got to The Trap and saw the smiles on Hummel and Hammy I knew that it was fixed and - along with that - I instantly forgot all about fucking Leckie. And don't get me wrong, should the boy have ended coming through for me you can be sure that I wasn't going to be telling him *'sorry to put you through all the trouble but it's cool, don't need the money now'* and would be getting that money straight out of the account and hoped that the police wouldn't find me but with it being past five now and - I'd assumed he'd finished work by then - and after one final check of the banking app and finding that same sum of money that had been in there all day, I gave up on Leckie.

He definitely hadn't give up on *me* though. Called my burner about tea time. With the time that it was I had half hoped that he was calling to say he'd worked a wee bit late but that the transfer had now been sent over. Instead, when I answered I was connected to a crying and sniffling Leckie telling me that he'd just been released from the police station after being arrested while trying to perform the transfer at work, earlier in the afternoon.

'Ah tried, Drummond. You can't say that I never, eh? I'm now missing a job, have a theft criminal charge hanging over me and now am probably going to lose Janie and the kids now anyway. I'm ruined. I tried, I really did surely you can see? Don't release that video, I'm begging you, please.' He whined down the phone to me.

Like I said, I'm not sure I'd have appreciated that call, had it came before Hummel's or worse still, that *was* the only call I'd get on the whole subject. Luckily for Leckie, it came at time where I was now settled. Knew we had the money safe and sound and at the end of the day. I wasn't an extortionist. Ok, well, on this one occasion I suppose I *was* but it was nothing personal against Leckie at any point. I just needed him for the money. Once I didn't need the money anymore, then I didn't need *him*.

I wasn't vindictive or malicious as a person. I'd got what I'd wanted as a result - even if it had come from a completely different direction to where I'd been looking - so why need to cause any additional problems for the boy? By the sounds of things I was kind of (?!) responsible for him losing his job and being charged with police. Fuck having Janie leaving him or not being placed at my door though. That would be her decision when she found out. Fuck all to do with me, that. You can only blame someone so far with things, eh?

He'd told me that the two C.I.D guys had mentioned my name during his arrest - which I have to admit worried me as well us fucked with my head how *they* knew when I hadn't even told my fucking best pals - but that he hadn't brought me into it and as far as it had gone it was being viewed as employee theft. There was no link to the fake account I'd had opened so as far as I knew, there was nothing that could connect me to things.

I decided that - due to my name being brought up and him now being charged - I would hold on to the video for now - as insurance - but as long as he didn't do anything stupid then his secret would be safe with me, and possibly - *definitely* - Hammy and Hummel.

'Look don't worry about it, Leckie. You tried your best and the fact that you got yourself caught, arrested and charged as well as losing your job at least counts for something even if it didn't result in money appearing into account. You're safe, pal. I won't be putting the video on any socials or showing it to anyone. Obviously, you'll understand if I hang onto it, at least until you go to court, eh?'

I said it without *having* to say it.

I made a throat slit gesture to the others while still on the call to indicate that my plans for the other scheme had fallen by the wayside. The two of them both kind of accepting this news in a what can you do kind of way and not really appearing up nor down about it.

Apart from the majority of profits that we'd lost in that hard drive - which given time we could return to again - we had just needed to gather the funds due to the German and have enough spare money to get us back in the game once more, preferably with someone *other* than Arman88. My feelings had been that when he'd started sending pictures of our homes, that had crossed a line when it came to a 'healthy business relationship' between seller and customer. And also, after all that we'd been through I'm not sure a 'credit agreement' with a drug dealer was the way to go moving forward. One thing for sure. A week or so ago if we'd been given the chance of sitting in The Trap on the Friday tea time and us already having secured the funds and us finding out that our *other* plan had failed then we'd have fucking *mugged* you for that scenario, never mind wait to be offered it.

'Aye, fair enough.' He sighed, sounding utterly broken down and defeated by his day and even if he wasn't in agreement with my statement he sounded like he didn't have anything other than grudging acceptance in him.

'If I was going to say anything about you I'd have said it there in that interview room this afternoon. You're safe, I won't say a word.'

'Then neither will I, Leckso. Neither will I, my friend. For what it's worth. I'm sorry the way it worked out for you. It wasn't personal, just business.'

'Aye, thanks, Drummond.' He said like the absolute cuck that he was. He literally had *nothing* to thank me for and everything to hate me over. Yet the end of our phone call - and our whirlwind week of being in close contact - ends with him thanking *me?*

It's a mad, mad world but I'm extremely proud to contribute my share to it.

I knew she'd go absolutely fucking postal but I called Bren and told her that I was ditching the car and staying out with Hammy and Hummel. This was an exceptional circumstance and *well worth* taking the metaphorical bullet of my other half being in a stinker of a mood with me the whole weekend over.

With the monkey gone from our backs we got ourselves deservedly - and suitably - drunk over a night where nothing or no one was going to touch us or the mood we were in.

Not even the gut wrenching injury time penalty miss by that fucking stupid Slavia Prague player - we'd all crowded around Hammy's small phone screen eagerly watching - with them and Sigma Olomouc drawing two apiece at the time impacted us too badly on a day that - over the piece - we'd collectively had more ups and downs than if the three of us had put on our Patagonia and went Munro bagging.

Chapter 37

Hummel

@EvanHust Yoou literally saved my life today, ladd. I promice that I will never, everrr6rr

3.33am - 07/09/2019

@EvanHust call you a cunt again. You're actually a pretty 'sound cunt" like tbh..;

3.37am - 07/09/2019

@EvanHust Respuct ma man and fuck the haterzzzzx

Hummmel x

3.42am - 07/09/2019

The combined series of tweets - in full - that I'd tapped out and pressed send on when I'd - eventually - got myself back from Hammy's after we'd all ended up there after The Trap had closed its doors for another night. It was as sincere a tweet as it was stupid. But it really *did* need said. As much as I'd thought the boy was an attention seeking fanny, he literally *had* saved my life. And because of this I felt it important - at that exact time of morning - to tell the man before I brought the curtain down on what was always going to be a monumental day. It was definitely fucking *mental* anyway. That part we had completely nailed down shut and stuck with Gorilla Glue for good measure.

I only remembered about it when I finally surfaced the next day and found my phone on less than ten percent battery but filled with a screen of rows of notifications, all leading back to my middle of the night badly spelled - and obviously MWI led - tweet. Hust - ever the unpredictable maverick with a devilish streak and an ability to laugh at himself - had seen the funny side - one that hadn't *actually* existed - of the tweet and decided to like *and* retweet the first two to his millions of followers.

I suppose I deserved it, I thought to myself as I cringed at the thought of all of my mentions where it was almost a guarantee that everyone who'd replied would have completely got the wrong end of the stick and been giving me unnecessary grief. You know what the Americans are like with the c word as well, eh? All of the fanboys all rushing to defend their hero alone - and within seconds of them seeing the tweet appear on their timeline - would've meant that I'd have been better taking a few weeks away from the app altogether.

Anyway, I meant well, likes, eh? Someone saves your life the least you can do is thank the fucker, in my honest opinion.

Fuck was my head feeling it on opening my eyes, though. I guess if we'd managed to get ourselves out of that massive fucking hole that I'd dug us into then you really *would have* expected some appropriate form of a 'response' from the three of us. And we did not disappoint.

It was one of those hangovers where you can barely remember the day - and night - before and what had taken place until you slowly begin to piece things together with a little flash of something here and there which will lead you to as much of the whole puzzle as your mind and memory will allow.

In the complete wrong order I had memory flashes of the video that Drummond had shown us - and one that I could've lived my entire life without ever seeing, even if it *was* tremendously funny - which then merged into earlier in the day and Hammy trying to break the perspex inside the bookies with a chair then onto what had to have been near the end and me making an absolute cunt out of things trying to get in the house without making a sound by knocking the mirror off the wall in the hall - seven years and all that - before being transported back to the pub and Hammy shaking that champagne bottle around like an F1 driver as he stood up on our table spraying every one inside The Trap, and there not being too many in the room that much chuffed about it.

I think an accurate assessment of the evening would've been that we - to every living being inside the boozer - had been a trio of intolerable as well as insufferable - but extremely happy - arseholes who were so high on life that they were bombproof to any other's comments or criticism sharing the same establishment. What a night though and one for the ages. What I could remember about it, obviously.

That Drummond story? About when he was walking Bowie in the woods? I'll admit, I couldn't remember too much about it as I lay there in bed trying to come to but *could* remember just how crying on the floor Hammy and me were left as Drummond told us it.

Above all else, it felt good to be around the two of them and *not* have the feeling that either - or both at once - wanted to give me a piece of abuse or possibly even further than that. Relations had definitely been strained between us because of matters but that's what money can do to people I suppose, even mates. It hadn't been just the financial aspect either though and when I stopped to think about it. The potential of how much danger I had maybe put them and their families in as well as my own far outweighed the money issues that I'd brought on us.

I'd have probably been just as pissed off at either Drummond or Hammy if *I'd* been in their position so there was no judging here. Fuck did it feel immensely amazing, though. Spiritual even, to see karma in action and in such a pivotal way. Because that's the thing. I'm not a bad cunt and I know that a bad cunt would probably say that too but I'm a decent boy. I'd fucked up with what I'd done with Debz, which had caused the whole situation to spiral out of control and that was probably karma in action. I disrespected my bird and well, look what happened. But, I'd done enough good things in my life to surely have had some goodwill karma kicking around in the reserves just waiting to be used. Fuck me, what a time for it to have been deployed, though. Too fucking radge, amigo. Too fucking radge.

I'd been left with the feeling though that there had been a correction of sorts. Almost a reset. I'd ever so slightly fortunately managed to pay off the debt and *still* have enough left over to pay for a kilo of Ching up front and get us all right back on that horse again. I took down our business and I would be the one who would initiate its resurgence after a brief two wee hiatus. That felt about right. What *also* felt right was that my two mates would be paid back every single penny that they lost out of things. It hadn't been spoken about, that topic. We were too busy trying to swim rather than sink and elements of what had went wrong weren't even discussed while we all attempted to start doggy paddling but it wouldn't have needed a word in my ear from Drummond, Hammy or both. Wasn't their fault - literally *any* of it - and I would make sure that they would be paid back every single penny that they'd (I'd) lost.

With the memories still hazy I checked through my phone which I'd long since found to be an excellent piece of kit to help you establish some of the things that had gone on the night before. Text messages sent, pictures taken, which calls were made and at what time.

Seeing the text message from the Royal Bank of Scotland - around nine in the evening after us sitting for hours toasting our great escape while none of us had remembered to actually *pay* the fucking money to Arman88. He'd told me five of clock but I was chill about it being four hours later. - asking me to call their anti fraud number. This jogging my memory over the transfer of ninety thousand from my bank account - on route to being converted into Bitcoin - that was flagged up by the anti fraud team (due to its unusually large amount) who would want to ask me a series of questions before they'd be satisfied that the transfer was a legit one. The one call I'd now began to remember was a complete farce due to the combination of how MWI I was and the volume of the pub on a Friday night. I kept getting the security questions wrong but was managing to get away with it by claiming that I hadn't heard their questions correctly due to the noise around me.

Eventually we got there though and somehow from that point I had managed to keep a degree of professionalism - even if it was for only five minutes - to then get the ninety bags worth of Bitcoin transferred over to the wallet address that Arman88 had provided me with on Telegram earlier in the week.

With the memories of the car crash of the bank call - and just for my piece of mind - I felt that I better check my app to make sure everything *had* all went smoothly as I'd remembered it. And there it was. Twenty six thousand and seven hundred pounds difference still remaining in my account, and the ninety thousand pound transfer showing on screen as my latest account transaction.

When I was in the middle of just staring there at that figure of funds sitting inside my account the level that I'd never been able to come anywhere close to calling my own in my whole life. Aye, I'd seen that amount when transferring funds to Arman88 many times before but that wasn't *my* money.

But neither was *this*, I had no choice but to look on it. I - through my own shitey behaviour - obliterated all the money that Hammy and Drummond had. So it was no question that those thousands were going straight back into the business again as some new and much needed start up capital. We were good at what we did and had been making good money from it. Why let a wee bad spell spoil what was otherwise a good thing, eh?

While I was still in the app a Telegram notification from Arman88 popped up on my screen, having seemingly battled its way for attention over the constant stream of Twitter notifications that had incessantly been flashing up since I'd picked up the phone. Intrigued to see what he was saying while having a mini panic attack that I'd sent his funds to the wrong address and here he was wondering where his money was? Bricking it, I opened up the message.

Brooooo? You fucking PAID? Every single cent. I'm impressed. : 10.37am

The choice of words from him? He didn't expect the money. It was only words on a screen but I took it as him being genuinely surprised - and delighted, of course - that the outcome had ended up being different to what had been expected.

I almost replied back something along the lines of that he had seemed almost disappointed for that to be the case, the weight of owing money to him now released and me not left with the need to be a good little doggy to whatever he'd chosen to say. For diplomacy reasons however I typed out a reply of.

Never in doubt, Herr 88 : 10.38am

He'd already showed me - over the previous couple of weeks - that he was someone who'd access to info - about me and my mates - that I'd otherwise have taken for granted that he'd have had *no way* of knowing, and I *still* had been left with no clue over how he'd managed to come up with all of our names. It was practically one of the main *reasons* for the dark web, anonymity. Something that he'd been able to work his way around. With that, I no longer even assumed what he knew or didn't know about me or my mates. So when I said 'never in doubt' I had no idea how much he'd known - or not - just how *much* doubt there actually had been. The polar opposite of *never in doubt.*

That morning, though? I didn't really care what he maybe did or didn't know anymore. When your debt is clear from someone - such as an Arman88 - then things like that don't seem to matter so much.

Truth? I doubted you, a lot. Today was not going to be a good day for you, bro. Or your friends. I'm happy this is not reality and trust me, so will you be. : 10.40am

Pressure or not. Reading that particular message sent an uncomfortable shiver right up my spine as I contemplated a few of the possibilities and permutations that this could have meant, had things worked out differently.

While I wasn't exactly in a position to recall with eidetic memory much of what had went on the night before - while I sat having a bit of 'chit chat' with the German dealer - one thing that I knew for an absolute certainty was that we had all been in agreement that things had 'soured' between us and whoever the fuck Arman88 was. It's a little difficult to go into business with someone - in good faith - when you already know that they had been putting in some arrangements to do you and your loved ones some serious harm. Takes the edge off things wee bit, eh?

We were going to have to re-strategise and streamline our operation, anyway. From over the past couple of weeks one thing that had sprung up was that our names had appeared to have already been on the radar of the bizzies so as much as we were ready to get right back on things and get that 'open for business' sign flipped back around we were going to have to do a bit of rethinking. Deliveries to *mines* were definitely fucking off the menu, that much was obvious and it didn't take the fact that Debz would leave me in a fucking heartbeat if we saw a repeat performance of the day the last dark web delivery had arrived for me to know that.

Broooo? You still there? : 10.46am

Arman88 asked following the non reply back from me after I'd got myself lost down a series of tunnels thinking about how badly this Saturday *could* have went on to become.

Yeah, had to take a call : 10.47am

I lied as there was no point in replying back to him about his hypotheticals. There *was* a tiny part of me who had wanted to ask him what - just out of interest - he had decided on doing with us had we not paid the debt but - whoever he / they / fucking them - this was a serious person that I was dealing with and it would've been an insult to their intelligence to think that they would write something like that out in a message. Even his intimidatory Telegrams that he'd sent to me did not *technically* contain any actual threats. He'd known that they'd have been implied, regardless. So why say it yourself and risk potentially incriminating yourself at some point in the future? Proper gangster stuff, eh? Never actually *say* what they want done but yet have an ability to get it done anyway.

I decided to leave that side of things and just be glad that I - and the other two - didn't have to find out.

So we all good then, yeah? : 10.48am

I asked, even though I pretty much knew to be the case. I just wanted to wrap things up with the boy. There was no need for any chit chat. Like the last telly I bought? Didn't have fucking Curry's texting me later on that night for a blether or fuck all, eh?

In the hood, brooo : 10.49am

So, are we going back to your usual shipment for next time? : 10.49am

That had been the reason for the Telegram? Not because I'd paid and he'd wanted to congratulate me. It took him to actually come out with it and because I was so hungover I couldn't see it before then. Had thought that one of the dark web's biggest drug dealer had nothing else to do on a Saturday morning than text back and forward with me!

We're taking a step back to recalibrate. So no shipment please. : 10.50am

I thought I may as well tell him things straight, without telling him any *further* straighter than that but being the smart guy that I'd imagined him to be he saw straight through it.

No shipment? Or no shipment from ME? : 10.51am

That he had actually said that straight away showed that he probably already knew the answer. I saw no point in lying. Telling him that - given how relations had went of late - that we wanted to look elsewhere. Reminding him that people don't take too well to threats to them or their families.

'Where did I threaten any of your friends or family?' He had asked, trying to be cute but making his point at the same time, because he hadn't, and I'm telling him over Telegram that he *had* been.

It wasn't just that part though. I'd told him that through being in debt to him for such an amount of money as I was I'd looked him up on the dark web to see just who I'd been fucking with.

And what did you find? : 10.59am

That your group is Albanian. No offence but that comes with a reputation too : 10.59am

He just replied back with about twelve crying laughing emojis before following up with.

If you looked even further you'd have also found that I was Hezbollah, selling narcotics to fund their struggles against oppression. Maybe speak to someone else and you'd have heard that I was the Calabrese Ndrangheta, someone else, Jalisco New Generation from Mexico branching out into Europe with a new strategy. They cannot all be correct but they can all be INcorrect. : 11.04am

It took him a few minutes to type out to me. With the volume of gear that the guy shifted on Feelgood alone he could've cared less for whether he'd have sold an extra kilo a month to that guy over in Scotland but I guess that I'd poked him with a stick sharp enough for him to bite.

By the end of our wee chat he'd reminded me over how charitable he had been the previous couple of weeks. How he had given us a second chance when I'd had to tell him that we'd lost our Bitcoin. How he'd kept his part of the bargain and *had* sent the three kilos to Scotland, only for me to refuse the package at my door. Whether he was Albanian mafia or not he had taken exception to me painting him as some boogie man when all he'd done was give me chances to get out of it. He actually had a point as well.

In this game, does it ever really matter WHO it is that you have to pay, as long as you pay them? : 11.06am

Wise words from an - undoubtedly - wise man and who could argue with that? As long as you paid what you were due there would be *no* problem, whoever it was that you were in business with.

It wasn't as if he was going to fucking dig me one over the phone - when I confirmed that we were stepping away - but I'd been concerned how he might take it, after all of his persuasion tactics hadn't worked. In reality though he was cool as. Like I said, I'm sure that missing out selling a kilo of Cocaine to us in Edinburgh each month was hardly going to force him into having to tighten his purse strings. Choosing to sign off with.

Ok bro, I have stuff to do. If things don't work out with your new connect then my door is always open although you will have to pay a "penalty tax" on your orders if you want to come back. I'm sure you'll understand? Loyalty brings rewards. Enjoy your Saturday, friend. You have no idea just how close you came to NOT enjoying it! C ya x : 11.08am

You can keep that fucking door ajar all you like, mate. I won't be setting foot inside, I thought as I exited the app.

We'd be cool. Mistakes had been made - and learned from - and while we'd been given a proper fright and an insight into how things can potentially go at that level when they don't go right. We were still standing and without a single hair harmed on any of our heads, eh? Over the weekend I would go on to do a bit of digging in the forums, send out a few DMs here and there and by the Sunday night I'd have found us someone reliable and vouched for that could claim the spot as our new distro and have us back in business by the middle of the next week.

Echoing my guy Carl Johnson from GTA at the beginning of San Andreas, as I thought about us now and how we were effectively back to square one.

It really all did feel a case of *ahhh shit here we go again.*

Chapter 38

*Article taken from www.narconews.com; First published 27/11/2019

Berlin Police In Largest Ever Dark-Web Narcotics Bust.

Berlin police force just seized under a ton of drugs from an online drug seller, and it's a group of kids.

Matthew Prentice - 27.11.2019

In a dramatic dawn operation yesterday morning Berlin Police conducted a series of narcotic related busts across three city centre locations, seizing over 900 pounds of illegal narcotics and arresting three teenage high school friends. In a show of the flourishing online illegal drugs market, an amount - while substantial - that experts predict will barely even impact the markets that are found on the "other internet," the **Dark-Web.**

Last night at an animated press conference at its Platz der Luftbruke headquarters in the city. Berlin Police announced that they had conducted a cross city operation, raiding three locations - two houses and a storage unit facility - and arresting three people who it is believed form the Dark-Web gang known to its customers as "Arman88."

The first raid of the morning was carried out on the home of a nineteen year old Berlin born citizen accused of leading the drug ring from his city centre flat. While this was being carried out similar raids were following across the city leading to the arrest of an eighteen year old in his Holiday Inn hotel room and a third teenager - nineteen years - who was arrested at the *Steck es hier rein* storage unit facility in the Stralaeur Allee area of the city, along with the haul of drugs.

Manuel Littbarski - Chief of the Berlin Police anti narcotics taskforce.

'Today we seized a sum of illegal narcotics totalling over nine hundred pounds from a city centre storage unit facility. This included Cocaine, Amphetamines, Methamphetamines, Heroin, Marijuana, MDMA and LSD as well as various prescription pills. We have also arrested and charged three individuals who we believe are connected to and - as a group - have been operating on the Dark-Web drugs marketplace Doctor Feelgood under the name "Arman88" for over a year. Doctor Feelgood, we believe to be the most active Dark-Web narcotics marketplace at present and one that has been the home of various major players in the Berlin narcotics scene and underworld. Today's bust has removed approximately five million euro's worth of narcotics from the internet and ultimately, the streets of Europe.'

When handed over to questions from journalists. Littbarski - while hesitant to reveal any names or certain details related to the investigation citing it as *ongoing* - revealed that all three arrested were - quite remarkably - under the age of twenty and were connected to each other through the unnamed High School that - until 2017 - they had all attended.

News of the busts sent the Dr Feelgood forum into overdrive with panicking customers - from all over Europe - of *Arman88* voicing concerns over whether *they* might now be a target of law enforcement as a result of what hardware had potentially been seized.

"There were always rumours that Arman88 kept a spreadsheet of his customers. I guess we about to find out."

A user called Bwad_Bwoy84 posted, following the breaking news.

"PEOPLE! CLEAN YO SHIT BEFORE IT'S TOO LATE. DON'T GO THINKING THAT L.E ARE ONLY WORRIED ABOUT BIG BUYERS!!"

Proppa_G - another member of Feelgood, warned other users of the site.

While an undoubted major coup for the Berlin Police force with the seizure of such a haul of drugs - in addition to putting the Arman88 group out of action - it is, however, only a small dent in the burgeoning online illegal drugs marketplace which began to boom following the creation of Silk Road in 2011.

Dr Feelgood - where Berlin police believe the group sold the majority of their drugs from - twenty four hours after the bust - and with all of Arman88's listings taken down - alone and at time of writing has almost 40,000 listings whilst a cursory look through the site shows hundreds of "vendors" ready to ship out the same range of narcotics that the Arman88 group supplied to its customer base.

Internet blog *Deep Dark Web* a website that specifically monitors the illegal drugs trade posted last night that the operation had been the biggest in Dark-Web history and had taken down one of the biggest players although also adding that - with the "whack-a-mole" way the illegal drugs marketplaces operate - someone else would merely come along and replace Arman88.

'Rumours persisted inside the Dark-Web community over the past year of just 'who' Arman88 had actually been with - due to the volume of narcotics that they were shipping across Europe - accusations ranging from Italian, Turkish, Russian and Albanian mafia to terrorist organisations such as ISIS and Hezbollah all the

way to Mexican cartels supplying Europe through a more streamlined way that removed the need for any European based middlemen. And after all of this, it appears that they were just a group of kids? The Dark-Web never, ever fails to surprise.'

With details sure to emerge over the coming days it is a story that has captured the imagination of millions with many asking just how a group of teenagers could have managed to pull such a large scaled operation off.

Without raining on the parades of the German anti drugs task force this is *all* that it will be. A story that captures the imagination. As for the Dark-Web and its illegal drugs and goods marketplaces. Regardless of the powerful aesthetics of the Berlin Police photo op showing their officers beside the large haul of drugs in the storage unit.

Go log into T.O.R right now and search for one of the numerous drugs marketplaces and you will find that it is still very much a case of *open for business.*

Also by Johnny Proctor

The Zico trilogy

Ninety

A great portrait of a seminal time for youth culture in the U.K. A nostalgic must read for those who experienced it and an exciting and intriguing read for those that didn't' Dean Cavanagh - Award winning screenwriter.

Meet Zico. 16 years old in 1990 Scotland. Still at school and preparing himself for entering the big bad world while already finding himself on the wrong side of the tracks. A teenager who, despite his young years, is already no stranger to the bad in life. A member of the notorious Dundee Utility Crew who wreak havoc across the country every Saturday on match day.

Then along comes a girl, Acid House and Ecstasy gatecrashing into his life showing him that there other paths that can be chosen. When you're on a pre set course of self destruction however. Sometimes changing direction isn't so easy. Ninety is a tale of what can happen when a teenager grows up faster than they should ever have to while finding themselves pulled into a dangerous turn of events that threatens their very own existence.

Set against the backdrop of a pivotal and defining period of time for the British working class youth when terrace culture and Acid House collided. Infectiously changing lives and attitudes along the way.

Ninety Six

Ninety Six - The second instalment of the Zico trilogy.

Six years on and following events from 'Ninety' ... When Stevie "Zico" Duncan bags a residency at one of Ibiza's most legendary clubs, marking the rising star that he is becoming in the House Music scene. Life could not appear more perfect. Zico and perfect, however, have rarely ever went together.

Set during the summer of Euro 96. Three months on an island of sun, sea and sand as well as the Ibiza nightlife and everything that comes with it. What could possibly go wrong? It's coming home but will Zico?

Noughty

Bringing a close to the most crucial and important decade of all.

Noughty - The third book from Johnny Proctor. Following the events of the infamous summer of Ninety Six in Ibiza. Three years on the effects are still being felt inside the world of Stevie 'Zico' Duncan and those closest to him. Now having relocated to Amsterdam it's all change for the soccer casual turned house deejay however, as Zico soon begins to find. The more that things change the more they seem to stay the same. Noughty signals the end of the 90's trilogy of books which celebrated the decade that changed the face, and attitudes, of UK youth culture and beyond.

Muirhouse

Living in the 'Naughty North' of Edinburgh, for some, can be difficult. For the Carson family, however? Life's never dull.

You'll give them that.

'Muirhouse' by Johnny Proctor is a story of the fortunes of Joe 'Strings' Carson.

Midfield general for infamous amateur football team 'Muirhouse Violet' on a Sunday and petty criminal every other day of the week. Above all, though. Strings is a family man and, like any self respecting husband and father, will do whatever it takes to protect his household.

A commitment and loyalty that he's about to find being put to the ultimate test.

Available through DM to help support the independents.

El Corazon Valiente; The ballad of Peter Duncan

El Corazon Valiente ; The ballad of Peter Duncan. A Zico trilogy origins story.Picking up where Noughty left off. El Corazon Valiente offers a look at how life is for Peter Duncan following events in Amsterdam, 2000. Finally find out how Stevie Duncan's father - through his own charm, ruthlessness and sense of self preservation - went from small Scottish town chancer to a vital component of a well known Colombian cartel. And how it all came crashing down around him.

Available via DM at : Twitter @johnnyroc73 and Instagram @johnnyproctor90

Also available through Apple Books, Kindle, Amazon, Waterstones and other book shops.

Printed in Great Britain
by Amazon